Detour

A

Beautiful Biker

Romance

Book One

by

DD Prince

Copyright: DD Prince http://ddprince.com. 2016.

This book is fictional and the product of the author's imagination. Any resemblance to persons alive or dead is unintentional. Copyrights are the property of their respective owners.

Thank you for respecting the author's work and copyright.

Obtaining this book through legal channels allows authors like me to continue to bring you stories because I can keep my power on, food in the pantry, and the creative juices flowing.

Thank you very much for reading my work!

NOTICE:

This book is not intended for those under the age of 18. It contains strong language, violence, and explicit sexual content. If you do not enjoy such books, this might not be the book for you.

Potential Triggers: Assault

1

He was far too beautiful to be a biker.
        Seriously.

I was in complete awe. And I hadn't even seen him straight-on yet. I was staring. No, not just staring. I was analyzing everything about him that was visible to me.

I was standing in a gas station and convenience store line-up, behind him, and my eyes were hard at work, roving over every visible inch of the back of him as well as his profile.

In profile, I could see that he had the longest eyelashes I'd ever seen on a man. Eyes light golden brown, with swirly bits of darker brown and amber, like a tiger's.

Stubble. Not a 5 o'clock shadow, maybe a 23 o'clock shadow of stubble that made my thighs quiver and tingle at the imaginings of that sandpapery feeling those whiskers would evoke on my bare skin.

Yowza.

And he had thick and dark nearly black hair that'd touch and curl around his defined collar bone if it weren't tamed in a loose ponytail at the nape of his neck. His hair had a loose curl to it, not unlike my own curls, though mine were a golden blonde. His sunglasses were propped up on his head. They looked like they were expensive ones.

He was wearing a black leather jacket and black leather motorcycle boots. Both looked expensive but well-worn in with plenty of heavy silver zippers. He had on motorcycle gloves and he wore faded jeans that looked like they were so soft, so over washed that they were one or perhaps two washes away from disintegrating. And they fit. They fit like … wow. Not skin tight but they showed he had an ass you could bounce a quarter off of.

His thighs were muscular-looking. The smell of him? Oh God, it was heady. He smelled like leather and wind just standing behind him so I couldn't imagine how good that would smell if I buried my nose behind his ear. His left ear had a tiny pewter hoop. Sexy. And he had a tiny pewter barbell in his left eyebrow. That was somehow sexy, too.

I hadn't even seen him face-on but I wanted to climb him like a tree. I'd never had this strong of a physical reaction to a man before. Never ever.

He shifted and I could no longer stare at his profile but I kept on staring at the back of him. He was tall. I could curl up on his back and just sleep between those shoulder blades. His back was broad. He had big shoulders. I could tell that he held bulk underneath that thick leather jacket. Not fat. Muscle. Serious muscle. Not steroid-user level but definitely...this guy worked out. I wondered if he had a defined six pack. I'd bet the pink fuzzy dice hanging in my shit box of a car that he did.

He took his gloves off and stuffed them halfway into his back pocket. He then reached into his other back pocket for his wallet, which was attached with one of those thick silver chains that linked to his belt loop.

Of course it was a biker wallet. Everything about him screamed biker.

Except how beautiful he was.

I'm not bigoted against bikers or anything, I've been around a lot of them, it's just that I've never ever EVER seen one who looked this good. We were in a medium-sized town in South Dakota and it was a place that saw a lot of bikers, bikers who lived here and those who passed through. Either this biker was passing through or he was new to this neighborhood. I'd have noticed him. Girls would be talking about him. For SURE. I spent lots of time doing community service type stuff so I knew a lot of people.

The glimpse of his ungloved hand turned me on. He had a gorgeous hand. How silly was it to think his hand was sexy? But it was. Strong. Clean. Heavy silver rings on both third fingers. Married? It didn't look like a wedding ring. The silver ring on the right hand was a silver eagle set in black onyx. The one on his ring finger was a skull ring with amber gems in the eye holes.

My uncle is a biker and Dad has plenty of biker friends who'd come over and jam and / or party with him in our garage, known as Dad's man cave. Most of the bikers I'd been around had long grey or greying beards or some of them had goatees or varying facial hair styles that more often than not were long enough to touch giant beer bellies or were at least reaching in that direction.

Most of Dad's biker buddies smelled like garages and usually a mix of tobacco and beer. And weed (but that might've just been due to the ever-burning cannabis potpourri in Dad's garage).

Some of his buddies had younger sons that were bikers, too, but they all looked like they were aiming to be younger versions of their fathers. I hadn't met a hot one yet. Not this hot, at least. There were a few that I'd seen around town that were okay-looking, maybe bikers just hadn't been my 'type'. My best friend thought my cousin, a biker in training (but a douchebag one) was hot. Maybe I hadn't looked real closely before. But this guy?

Okay, so this guy might wind up like the others in twenty years, because it seemed to be a biker rule, or something, that you had to work on building up a belly and letting your facial hair go wild, but this guy just looked like he hadn't had time to shave in a few days; he was just beyond stubble. And it looked good on him, amazing, actually. He looked real, bona fide. Not a biker wannabe. A little older than me, not much, most likely in his late 20's.

Something about his face (what I could see of it), his jaw line, the look in his determined and slightly impatient eye said authentic, not wannabe anything. He wasn't wearing the clothes he was wearing to *look* like a biker, to look like a bad ass. He looked like he was wearing clothes that were divinely created for his body and his body alone. And he looked *seriously* bad ass. He wasn't standing there, puffing his chest out, trying to look tough. He just had an aura of badass genuine biker. Tingles trilled up my spine.

What made me the expert? I'm not an expert at all. I'm just an observer of people. I know bikers, yeah, some of them. Dad wasn't a biker, he was a part-time musician, part-time cab driver but he had an eclectic mix of buddies and I'd grown up around people in the motorcycle culture. Dad was often partying with bikers in their clubhouse or in one of the biker bars in town and again, they were frequently at Dad's man cave buying weed or sitting around smoking it.

Because my Dad's band *The Dubes* played locally in bars he hung around a lot of people in the music and motorcycle culture. People liked him so it was almost as if people hung around him, rather than him being a real hang-around. Dad's buddies liked to drink, smoke dope, many were aging hippies or bikers, and so forth. Dad sang and played guitar and was really good at it. Rarely did a day pass without one or more of my dad's buddies hanging out in his man cave for at least a while. But none of the bikers I'd met, nor their biker-in-training sons, in my twenty-three years had affected me like *this*.

Beautiful Biker, as he would henceforth be known, pulled a few bills out of his wallet and then stuffed the wallet back into his pocket. This action told me he was anxious to move things along so he could pay and get out of here. I would normally be anxious, too, considering how long we'd already been standing here, except that it'd mean the time of staring at the fine specimen in front of me would come to an end. And if he was just passing through, I'd never see him again.

We were in line in a gas station slash convenience store. I was on my way home from my job at the cab office taking orders. The Shitbox (my 1974 snot green Impala) was thirsty. It was always thirsty. The Shitbox was a gas pig.

Dad called it a beauty, a classic. He'd proudly given it to me for my sixteenth birthday and had spent the upcoming five years tinkering with it, taking his time fixing it up "just right" for me.

When I suggested he paint it another color in front of a few of his buddies they'd looked at me like I had two heads. I didn't like The Shitbox. It was too big, too much on gas, and it drew attention all the time because it was in such good shape so I was always being asked about it like I was some muscle car aficionado.

I'd wanted a cute little VW bug. Or maybe a Mini Cooper. But I got this boat of a car, this old guy magnet, instead.

I would've saved up for my own wheels but Dad presented me with this clunk of junk like it was the keys to the kingdom of Car Nirvana. So I smiled and kept my disdain for my car to myself and then I waited for about five years while he tinkered away when the mood struck him until he got it road-worthy. For the past few years I'd driven it, I'd called it a myriad of horrible names. Shitbox, Snotbox, Geezer Magnet, Gas Hussy, the list went on…

I hefted my purse up higher on my shoulder again. It was beginning to start killing me. It kept sliding off and this was due to the Ziploc baggie of rolled up coins that had to weigh at least as much as a bag of potatoes in it and so my shoulder was beginning to ache fiercely.

I needed to hit the bank in the morning and deposit the seventy-seven dollars in rolled quarters and dimes plus one roll of nickels so that we'd make rent.

Clearly, my parents weren't financially comfortable, not even close; my parents were constantly straddling the poverty line but things weren't always *this* tight. Dad had bought a boat as an impulse buy. It was a shitty boat that needed a lot of work to be water-worthy and it'd drained their account. It would also likely sit where it was in the yard for the next three to four years before he got inspired enough to do anything with it.

So, in typical Dad fashion, he drained their account to buy it. But then he'd gotten the flu and hadn't yet made up the money with cab shifts. I'd just finished paying for repairs on The Shitbox that were above Dad's skill level, or at least above Dad's attention level (he had zero sense of urgency with repairs, any repairs -—household or vehicular), so my minimal reserves had been drained dry, too.

Mom and I had even raided the Rummoli money jar, which was like sacrilege in my house because once a month there was a big Rummoli tournament with a good chunk of the large Forker (our last name) circle of friends and we'd have to replenish it by then.

But my Dad couldn't say anything. He was still in the dog house, or should I say *boathouse*, because he'd bought that boat.

Mom's version of the dog house was a cake walk. She was really laid back and gentle and sweet with a 'pick your battles' mindset. She shook it off with him all the time with a shrug. And sometimes it drove me crazy. She didn't battle with dad too much and I'd always suspected that her being as laid back as she was was the reason my dad was who he was; I was convinced of it.

My father smoked too much, spent too much, didn't get things done nearly fast enough, and regularly drained their precariously low savings account (and their checking accounts, as well) on "deals" (term used loosely) he'd found. He wasn't real motivated in general. But he was a nice guy and everyone liked him.

This time, as we'd scoured underneath the sofa cushions for change, she'd been more annoyed with him than usual after one of these stunts and in a rare hissy fit she'd sworn to me that she was confiscating Dad's credit and debit cards and putting him on a strict cash budget. She'd lectured him while we were rolling the change, telling him he'd have to find a way to fund the boat because no money from any of their existing earning methods would go toward it.

The problem was that even when mom was mad she didn't 'seem' mad enough to alarm my father and so Dad had rolled himself a big fat blunt while we'd been on the coin hunt (not that it wasn't something he wasn't constantly doing anyway!) and as a result, he'd rolled just one roll of dimes in slow-motion, taking the time it took Mom and me to roll the rest.

I'd intended to get to the bank today to deposit the loot because it was the last day of the month and rent was due tomorrow but I got stuck at work for twenty-five minutes past my shift and because of that, I'd missed the bank. My mother said it'd be okay to get it deposited in the morning as the rent check wouldn't likely post until overnight tomorrow night.

This was gonna mean a tight upcoming few weeks. Luckily my mom was a couponer and my parents were survivalists so the pantry was stocked. We had *quite* the non-perishable food cache in the pantry and had shelves of crap food that could last forever along with first aid supplies and paper products that'd also last eons. Our KD, canned peaches, and Ramen stash alone could sustain a small town for weeks (slight exaggeration).

I'd pitch in extra for perishable groceries and had offered to pay the water bill when I got my pay in a few days so no lovely Starbucks Caramel Macchiato indulgences for a while -—if I ever got out of this gas station. I was having some doubts.

Then again, staring at the back of the beautiful biker? I could do that for a good while longer before getting impatient. I could stare at him for a good looooong time. Yep. I was in no hurry. No hurry at all.

The beautiful biker shifted with increasing impatience and then reached into his jacket pocket and yanked out a beaten-up looking cell phone and glanced at it, probably to check the time, and then stuffed it back into his pocket with increasing impatience.

In front of him was an old woman with her giant handbag on the counter and she was having lottery ticket after ticket checked. Most of them were winners, small winnings, either free tickets or small denominations and after each announcement of the winnings by the older distinguished-looking East Indian clerk that I had affectionately nicknamed (in my head only) Mr. Apu-Singh (after the Simpson's character Apu because he also had a mustache and a similar haircut but his nametag identified him as Mr. Singh).

Old Lottery Lady was taking eons to carefully consider her options for the next ticket she'd buy in the $1 ticket section. Too carefully. As if she had all the time in the world and there wasn't a growing line behind her.

Mr. Apu-Singh had started giving everyone in the growing line-up sweeping apologetic looks. I glanced over my shoulder and saw that there were about half a dozen people behind me. I was behind Beautiful Biker and he was behind Old Lottery Lady. The person at the back of the line was half in and half outside because there was no more room inside.

It was almost dinner hour, the tail-end of rush-hour and she had picked a terrible time to do all her lottery stuff. I mean, it looked like she had a stack of a dozen or so lottery tickets of varying types still to go. And many were scratch tickets and she hadn't scratched the sections off fully so poor Mr. Apu-singh had to scratch them to get them to scan. We were gonna be here all bloody evening.

My cell started ringing with the ring tone of *Gangnam Style* and it was loud. I'm talking l-o-u-d LOUD. It was Jenna's ringtone. Jenna is my best friend and she forbade me from changing that ringtone. I frequently did change it despite her stern orders. But she'd always get her hands on my phone and change it back. And every single time my phone rang in public I cursed her name, ready to die from embarrassment.

That song had been a hoot when it came out but it'd been years already. It was time to change it. Jenna disagreed. I tried to retaliate by changing her ring tone on her own phone frequently. Among the list of songs was: Tiny Bubbles, Tiptoe through the Tulips, One Eyed One Horned Flying Purple People Eater, and so forth. She won't get creative with me. No matter how many times I change it and no matter how many awesome songs I assign to her name, she somehow grabs my phone and changes it back to Gangnam

Style when I'm not looking. My little brother told me recently that she'd snuck in while I was asleep to change it back. I didn't know how she'd managed it *this* time.

We've been friends and neighbors since we were five years old and me and my family moved into the house next door to her, thereby lowering the property values for the whole street. As close as we are, we are worlds apart in some ways.

She wears expensive designer clothes. I opt for thrift shop chic or clearance bin deals. I'm blonde, she's brunette. I'm short, she's tall. Her parents' house is tidy and beautiful and well-tended upper middle class. Our house is an old farmhouse with zero curb appeal that brings down the property value of the entire street.

We're the only renters on that block and my parents decorate in eclectic. I'm talking tacky eclectic and wild. Hippie gypsy wild.

A dozen wooden wind chimes and metal lawn art that my father makes and sells amid wildflowers. Loads of wildflowers. It's like a jungle. And the messy garage's door is almost always open because Dad is always out there in his man cave because Mom won't allow him to smoke in the house and he's always smoking, nearly always entertaining one or more of his buddies, and usually playing 60-70's acid rock. It'd be embarrassing if I hadn't grown up with it as the norm.

Who am I kidding? It's still somewhat embarrassing, anyway. I feel like cousin Marilyn Munster with my stoner musician dad and hippie gypsy mom.

I'm not straight edged or anything but I think I'm a lot more conservative than the rest of my eccentric family. Jenna's family are conservative, quiet, businesspeople with carefully tended rose bushes. My family are wild, loud, mismatched, and crazy and artistic people living in a jungle of wildflowers. We often joke that the storks got our parents mixed up and should've given them Jenna.

At the harsh blurt of K-pop star PSY, Beautiful Biker glanced over his shoulder at me with that pierced eyebrow raised at my ringtone and my heart stopped at the sight of more of his face and his mouth. His mouth! Full beautiful lips. I had the craziest urge to suck on that pouty looking bottom lip.

I sucked in my own bottom lip in response as I fumbled for and then answered the phone, "Jenna. Can I call you back? I'm in line to pay for gas."

My eyes were still on his mouth. Absolutely transfixed on it.

"Where are youuuu, Ellie bell-belly bella?" she giggle-slurred.

Slurred? Was she drunk? It was 5:40 pm.

"Are you tanked, Jen?" I whispered, aghast.

Beautiful Biker's head was still turned, still aimed at me, only his body had turned more and now I could see all of his face. All of his incredibly handsome face.

Holy whoa.

My eyes moved from his mouth up to his eyes and his left eyebrow was still notched. The way his eyebrow jewelry sparkled was so sexy it made my heartbeat stutter. Was there anything about him that wasn't sexy? And his eyes? My God, they were seriously beautiful full on.

He smirked at me and then his eyes were on *my* mouth. Double sexy.

I licked my lips, not even thinking, betraying how I felt about his yumminess. Did he think I was flirting? I was *so not* being subtle about my ogling because it was impossible to be subtle when you were staring at the epitome of absolute sexuality. I felt the heat rise in my face.

"Maybe a 'lil tanked," The forgotten Jenna said in my ear and that was what she always said. A little crazy. A little tanked. A little bit of a pain in my ass.

I could just picture her with her thumb and index finger aloft with an inch between them, her dark wavy hair in her eyes, her big silly sloshed grin.

"Me and the girls went for drinks after work at that biker bar, Deke's Roadhouse. You know, the old Whisky? They've renamed and re-opened it and it's a total biker bar. You should see all the hotness here. Man! Come meet me. I wanna dance. And you're my favoritest designated driver in the whole wide word. World. Word!" she giggled.

Yep. Totally smashed. And less than an hour after her salon closed! They must've been doing shots. This happened often.

But I could totally relate to the hotness comment. She should see all the hotness in front of me.

"Sorry, Jenna. I'm busy tonight. Gotta go. Call a taxi, okay?"

"Awe, Belly elle-belly! Puh-leeease? All of us will fit in The Snotbox. We neeeeed you."

Drunk people were so annoying.

"I can't, Jenna."

"Come meet up later then; sleep over!" She meant her apartment, which she shared with her esthetician. She'd moved out of her parents next door two years back. Her apartment was above the salon and her parents had gifted her the whole building. Her Mom worked at a bank and her dad was in real estate.

"Can't; gotta hit the Citibank right when it opens and then I'm working a double shift. Whoopsie! Got another call, Jenna. Get Gatorade and Advil after your late night snacks. Call me tomorrow."

"Ella—-" she tried.

"Love you byeee!" I ended the call with over-the-top cheerfulness and then turned the ringer off and shoved the phone back into my purse and let the faux cheer seep out as I blew my bangs out of my eyes. I just knew she'd drunk dial me at least ten times tonight and I didn't wanna face it.

He was still looking at me. And he was now completely facing me.

And lottery lady was still sorting through her tickets.

Heat crept upwards from under my jacket up to my ears. I looked behind myself to see that the line hadn't gotten any longer, probably because there was now a line-up outside to get to the pumps. I also looked behind me thinking that by the time I was face-forward again I'd be again looking at his beautiful back and behind instead of trying to avoid his sexy tiger eyes.

But his eyes were still on me when I faced forward again.

Aye yai yai.

I smiled a little. Feeling more red creep up my cheeks.

His expression was assessing. His gaze piercing. He sucked his bottom lip in and his eyes very intentionally travelled from my pink and white Converse straight up the length of my skinny jeans, to my half unzipped army green utility jacket, which I'd commandeered from my dad, (who'd got it at an army surplus store eons ago), rather than buying it at Forever 21 like most girls my age. The jacket was *the bomb*, though; people always asked me where I got it).

Beautiful Biker's eyes stopped at my cleavage, lingering there for a beat (Yep, I know. Huge rack for a short girl! For any girl.) and then moved to my face. It probably happened quickly, despite feeling like time stood still while I also mentally assessed myself during his journey, although my self-assessment went from head to toe instead of the toe to head direction.

Long blonde hair with lots of curls, so much curl that every day was a crap-shoot as to whether it'd be a good hair day or a bad one. Today, thankfully, was a good one. Eyes that weren't green or brown, somewhere in the middle, hazel I guess (though the green did stand out when I wore this army green jacket), on the short side at 5'2 and a half. Big boobs, as previously mentioned, and kinda cute, I guess / so I'm told, but that's not necessarily a good thing because I look younger than I am, like everyone's little sister whose cheeks you wanted to pinch; definitely not sexy or sophisticated.

I always got carded going into the bar. Jenna tells me I look like a sixteen-year-old whose had her boobs done. Guys who crushed on me were usually nice guys, guys who worked in banks or offices, guys who went to church. Men who wanted a wholesome-looking girl next door type (but with big boobs), I guess. People tell me I look like Elisabeth Hasselbeck's cute little busty sister.

Am I wholesome? I think not. I swear like a sailor. I'm not a big drinker or dope smoker but I do like to party on occasion and when I do, I let my wild child loose. It's generally pretty memorable for all involved when I *do* let my hair down and that's probably why Jenna's always trying to get me to do just that.

I've dated a fair bit. I like sex. I like sex a lot, actually. I just haven't had many good partners. I bet I could be great in bed if I had the right partner. Unlike Jay, my most recent ex.

Jay told me I was the best lay he'd ever had because I tried REAL hard to make the sex good but I couldn't return the sentiment because Jay just didn't deliver. He couldn't find a clitoris with a labeled map of the vagina that had a big old bullseye on the clit! And yes, I'd shown him where it was repeatedly but he still didn't take the time to figure out what to do with it. I didn't just break up with him for bad sex. He had a lot about him that wasn't worth the effort.

But Beautiful Biker? Hmm. I bet *he* knew where the clitoris was. Just looking at him, I would bet he had no problem finding it. He probably had it thrown at him like crazy.

How sad would it be if a fine specimen like *that* was bad in bed? No, I couldn't think like that. I'd never ever have anyone that beautiful but I *had* to believe he'd be amazing.

I knew what to do with my clit. I started and ended just about each and every day with my hand or my Lelo battery-operated-boyfriend to it. Yep, I was a sexual being, for sure, even if I didn't look old enough to be legal. And looking at this beautiful man in front of me I now had spank bank material for months ahead of me.

I wouldn't even have to open the Tumblr app on my iPhone under the blankets and scroll my dirty pages while I diddled myself. I'd just have to picture him. The porn pages I followed on Tumblr wouldn't even come close to doing it for me after seeing this man fully clothed. *What on earth would he look like naked?*

My breath got caught in my throat and I awkwardly peered around him to see how lottery lady was doing. Mr. Apu-singh was getting flustered because now she was fishing through her purse, mumbling.

"Hey granny!" an older guy wearing mechanic overalls way in the back of the store called out grumpily, "You wanna hurry it up? Some of us got places to be!"

"Time to add a second register, Mr. Singh?" a lady's voice called out, not grumpily, really, light-hearted, probably to thin out the thickness of the air.

Mr. Singh answered, "So sorry!" and he was getting even more frazzled but he was the consummate professional. He didn't want to get rude with rude old lottery lady.

The old lottery lady then got her nickname changed because she transformed into Old Battleax. She glared over her shoulder at every person in line, one by one by one, (except BB, because he was still turned toward me) making sure we all saw that she was an old battleax and then announced,

"You can wait your turn. Right now it's *my* turn!"

Oh no. The air changed. People went from impatient to irate. Poor Mr. Apu-singh.

Beautiful biker's phone made an incoming text noise so his attention went to it and then he was texting, his eyes off me. Thank the Lord; I could breathe again. My heart was racing!

Huffs and sighs and rumbles and all-around misery filled the place until Beautiful Biker finally got his turn. When Old Battleax finally ambled out the door, every eye in the place must've been on her, except mine. My eyes were again on the back of the fine specimen in front of me. His attention was on his phone until it was finally his turn.

That fine specimen paid for his gas, bought a pack of rolling papers, asked for two packs of Marlboros, (He had a sexy voice, too. Deep, silky) and then he sauntered out, eyes landing on my chest briefly before he disappeared out of my life. Sadly, not having first thrown me over his shoulder to take me away and have his way with me. But he had a half smirk on his face as he passed me. As if he had a dirty secret. My face once again got hot but finally, it was my turn to pay for my gas.

I LEFT, CLIMBING INTO The Shitbox and driving the three remaining blocks to my house. The Shitbox probably used up $5 in gas in just that distance.

When I pulled into my driveway I noticed that a big black quad cab nearly new GMC Sierra was pulling in behind me. It stopped but kept idling, half in the driveway, half out on the street. And then I saw who the driver was.

Whoa. Beautiful Biker was driving that ride! What was he doing here?

Before I had a chance to do more than tingle, another guy, maybe my Dad's age, fit, with an interesting face was getting out of the passenger seat. He looked damn good for his age and he was absolutely a biker, too. On closer examination I saw that he had the same eyes as Beautiful Biker (his Dad?) and was just about as tall. He strolled toward me and stopped.

He said, "Sweet ride" looking at The Shitbox. He had a deep Sam Elliot-like voice, goatee, a tiny bit of grey around his temples. He had a bit of a Joe Manganiello thing going on, only he might be about 10 years older than Joe. He added, "Except for the pink fuzzy dice and the Betty Boop shit. That shit oughta be illegal in that ride."

I laughed, "Uh, thanks, but Betty Boop is my spirit cartoon and pink is my favorite color so... I guess you can call me a rebel," I shrugged. His face broke out into a very nice smile.

I was far from a rebel. Far!

"Spirit cartoon?"

"Like a spirit animal. But animated."

He chuckled.

I did love my Betty Boop shit. She adorned my front seats with red and black covers as well as was all over my steering wheel cover. And I had all sorts of other Betty accessories, too. T-shirts, coffee mug, slippers. A Betty Boop soap dish and hand cream dispenser in my bathroom, plus a huge Betty Boop overnight bag. In fact, birthdays and Christmases rarely passed without something Betty to add to my collection.

If I had to drive that Shitbox I had to at least put my stamp on it.

He shook his head disapprovingly and kept heading toward the garage. Dad was waving at both of us. I shut my car door and I tried really hard to not look at the driver, Beautiful Biker. But I did. And he saw me do it, too, before he pulled away.

SO, I'M ELLA FORKER and I live in a place called Boring and Responsible-ville. Well, that's not technically the name of the city but it's technically my life. Busy being responsible but bored. Same old same old. Not much exciting happens. Why? Because I'm probably too responsible and boring. I attract boring guys or losers. My friends aren't boring but I'm the responsible one of the group because I'm forever trying to stop them from dragging me into their myriad of hair-brained schemes.

My name, actually, is Elizabelle Isabeth Forker. Nope, not a typo. I know; it makes my brain a little scrambled, too. I'm the eldest of the two Forker children and my little brother is often mistaken for being my kid out in public because I'm 23 but he's five.

Mom wanted me to be named after her mother, Isabelle. Dad wanted me called after his mom, Elizabeth. Neither of my parents are real traditional and so they compromised on this crazy combination of two made-up hybrid names. Elizabelle Isabeth. Yep. But it could be worse. Thank God they didn't name me a hybrid of *their* names. Mom's name is Bertha and Dad's name is Robert. I could be Bertbert, which I joke all the time is their celebrity couple Brangelina name.

Mom, known to most as Bertie, calls me Ella or sweetie or Sunshine. Dad, known as Rob, rotates through a variety of nicknames. He'll call me Bella or Belly or Betsy or Elizzie or some other variation as well as a long list of pet names, and often it's a compound name. Unless he is pissed or serious, which rarely happens, but when it does he and Mom both call me by my full first name.

I seriously can't wait to get married. Mostly because it'll mean I can change my last name. I don't care what his last name is. I'm taking it. No hyphenation. Bye bye Forker! Whatever it is, I figure it has to be better than Forker. As long as he can find my clit and his name sounds at least marginally better than mine, I'm game. Okay, so I'm a ~~little~~ lot pickier than that but seriously…cannot wait to change this last name.

When I say it was rough growing up with a name like Forker, you might think you'd be able to imagine but you can't truly imagine the depths of my despair unless you have an equally bad last name, one that sounds like a curse word or a body part. Jenna always joked that it could be worse: I could be named Martha. Martha Forker. Or I could be a boy named Richard, called Dick for short. Dick Forker. People had fun with the Forker surname. Especially when my father once called me Dolly as a nickname shortened from his oft-used Baby Doll, in front of a few boys from my school. At that point, I started being known as Dolly Parton, Ella Parton, and several rather rude various to do with my Dolly Parton-ish chest and the Forker surname.

Shudder.

So, I'm not dating right now, unless you count my purple Lelo Ina 2. It cost me $180 and it was the best money I ever spent.

Ladies of the world, you deserve the orgasms Lelo can give you. I'm telling you the truth! I buy my clothes in thrift stores and clearance bins but

I would pay thousands for a Lelo if mine broke and they raised the prices two thousand per cent.

Other than my rechargeable and water-resistant boyfriend, I've just now decided to save myself for Beautiful Biker. Hah! Just kidding. But I wonder what *his* last name is? It's gotta be better than Forker. But if it isn't, maybe I'd settle for a worse last name if I could be Mrs. Beautiful Biker.

I'm not really looking for another boyfriend. My last break-up was a little bit ugly. Jay doesn't want to be an ex so it's been five weeks but it's as if we're still in the midst of breaking up. When I broke up with him he said that he was planning to buy me a promise ring, that he wants to get married, eventually. It is not happening. Even though his last name is Smyth, pronounced like Smith, the most benign last name ever.

Hmm, maybe a new guy would get Jay to finally back off.

So, why isn't Jay *the one* (besides the fact that he sucks in bed)? He's cute enough yeah, he's even kind of a broody hot, but in addition to being a bad lay, he got creepy-clingy when I started backing off. And he's cheap. And I mean like dirt-cheap.

Not in a frugal, saving money for a rainy day kind of way. I'm talking about him only dining out with coupons. I'm talking about only going to the movies on cheap Tuesday. For his Mom's birthday, he got her a cheap Groupon deal for a salon day. And he didn't even print it out and put it in the card because he complained that printer ink was so bloody expensive. He signed my name to the card for his mother and then the following week dropped, in conversation, that if I made it to an ATM I could maybe grab the $14.50 for my half of his Mom's gift. Seriously cheap. He has a good job in IT, makes decent money, and hoards that money.

I'm talking: asking if refills are free at restaurants and if they're not, getting more water added to the tea pot not just for a second filling but I once saw him go through four pots of tea with the same bag when we'd gone for an endless 3 hour all-you-can-eat buffet lunch.

We were there so long it was like he was trying to get two meals out of one. He also forgot his wallet sometimes (read: often. More than once is too often, am I right?) when we'd go out so I'd have to pay, which I don't mind, I'm all for equality, but those were the occasions we didn't do cheap dates so it was so bloody obvious that he'd forgotten it on purpose. And he also lives with his mother.

I know, I live with my parents, too, but I chip in, I help out. And I'll be on my own eventually. But Jay's mother cooks and does his laundry for him and I wouldn't be at all surprised if whenever he does get married, he just moves her in with his mother. And he doesn't even pay room and board at the age of 27. I help out at home by chipping in for rent and bills, groceries, do my share of cleaning, do 80% of the cooking, and help out loads with my little brother.

Jay was sex-obsessed but in a bad way because the sex was bad. I made the mistake of letting my kinkiness show a bit with him so he tried to be kinky, too, but he was bad at it.

So, we dated for three months and I ended it. That was about five weeks ago right after he dropped the three-word bomb. I didn't drop him as soon as he said he loved me but I toiled over it for four days after the fact. He'd been quietly pissy about the fact that I hadn't given it back to him but to me, it wasn't something I could just throw around.

I hadn't told a guy I loved him. I told my friends and my family that I loved them, I wasn't afraid of the four-letter L-word or anything like that but in a relationship I firmly believed it meant something, it wasn't throw-away. When he said it and I knew I couldn't return it, I knew it was time to move on. His quirks had annoyed me, he hadn't given me butterflies since our second date, and I was just over it.

How would I be open for love if I trapped myself in something that was going nowhere? So I ended it as politely as possible and now, five weeks later, he's still calling and texting good morning and goodnights (with hearts and kisses in the texts) and twice he's tried to list me as his 'relationship' on Facebook, messaging "Accept my relationship request if you want to try again.).

He also tried to dirty-sext me the other day. I'd be into that, totally into that, if it'd been when we were together and I knew there was the potential for a 'happy ending' with him but no. The texts that came through the other day were kinda gross.

"I have a craving for something juicy. I remember the last time I tasted your sweet twat"

Eww. Twat? Seriously? I'd replied with, **"Don't be a pig"**
Yeah, he'd tasted it. He'd stayed down there a good 30 minutes getting nowhere and being kind of creepy trying to dirty talk while he did it. I nearly fell asleep it went on so long.

"Want to meet up and ride me until I make you scream? Let me remind you of how amazing we can be 2gether."

Um, no thanks. I didn't even answer that one. He'd never made me do anything close to screaming.

I headed up to my room to drop my 500-pound (slight exaggeration but it seriously felt like it!) purse and charge my dying phone. Our rental is a big old house and we're good friends with the owner, Jed, who is like an adopted grandfather to me and my brother, so I know Mom and Dad have no plans to leave it, even if they could buy their own place.

We occasionally have to go digging in the sofa cushions to make ends meet but my parents are great. Everyone loves them. We have a big circle of friends. My Dad's parents are dead, never met them, but my Mom's mom, my Gran, is still around. She lives in a nursing home a few blocks away. She's a lot like my Mom, who has this sweet hippie gypsy thing going on. Gran still wears her hair long, wears bright colors with lots of accessories, and she's so sweet; everyone loves her. She's also a bit of a spitfire. She has loads of fire left in her.

I visit Gran at least a couple times a week. We'd have her live here with us but she refuses, doesn't want to be a burden. She's starting to lose her memory a little bit. She repeats herself often. I think that's why she's there instead of with us. She knows she's losing herself. I try not to think about it, just to visit her as often as I can.

I have an uncle, my Dad's brother the biker, but he's no good. Bad news. He's not welcome here. He was hardly ever welcome but started coming around even less once I hit puberty. I needed a bra at age eleven and everyone noticed but my uncle *seriously* noticed. I overheard my parents discussing him ogling me when I was 12 or 13 and it was one of the few times my mom went Momma-bear full throttle.

I heard her yelling that something had to be done before and then I didn't hear what the 'before' was but I knew she worried he'd do something about his fixation on me. Dad was yelling, too, at Uncle Willie, saying he'd 'fucking kill' Willie if he ever 'something' again (I didn't hear what the something was).

He always wanted me to sit on his knee. When I started developing it was even worse and he was very touchy feely and he watched me. Closely. Gross. He lives a few towns away but I occasionally see him around town as ours is a hub for shopping for some of the smaller nearby towns.

He always says Hello and tries to chat me up but I keep my distance, particularly since he stares at my chest when he talks to me. He has two adult sons, one a few years older than me, Chris, one my age, Jonathan, and while I get along fine with Jonathan, Chris is another douchebag-in-training and he's a prospect with my uncle's MC.

I loved my room. It was me. The rest of the place was quite cluttered with crafts and such but my space was totally me.

I'm in the walk-up attic on the third floor. It has a cool vibe; I love it. The inside door is hidden in the back of the linen closet on the second floor where there's a door that goes up these cool stairs into my slope-roofed third floor. I have built-in dressers and shelves as well as a built-in desk, vanity table with all my make-up, and everything fits nicely with my cool sloped ceilings.

I have a big king-sized bed with a huge pink eyelet comforter and about twenty pillows. I have twinkle lights wound around the brass headboard. It's spacious but yet cozy up here at the same time. I absolutely love it.

I have my own bathroom, decorated entirely in Betty Boop, and I have a cool black wrought iron spiral fire escape off a tiny little wrought iron deck that leads to the back yard.

Beau is on the second floor and he's got a massive play room beside his room as well as a bathroom. Mom and Dad's room is on the main floor.

This big old house is often busy so I like my quiet space up in my huge room that has a she-cave feel to it. But I also like that I can almost always wander downstairs or out to the garage and find some company. Sometimes we've got a dozen people for dinner. There are constant campfires and pot luck meals and it often then transitions out to the garage for drinking, pot-smoking (or pot cookie consumption), and jamming. Quite often Dad and his buds just eat dinner in the garage. Dad has a wood stove in there for the cooler nights, too.

Mom makes money selling her crafts online and she teaches a weird yoga-esque class called Namastwist, a play on words for her pretzel-like meditation class. It's a sort of hokey made-up mash-up of some stretching and breathing and chanting about positivity. But she has a slew of regulars and sometimes even has a waiting list. She doesn't charge a lot of money. It sounds hokey but Mom is the most genuine person you'd ever meet.

Mom isn't about money. She's very hippie-ish. Our house has a lot of beaded curtains and afghans that she's made in a variety of groovy color combinations. She has all sorts of cool tie-dyed pottery she's made all around the house.

We have an ancient floor model television and our décor is second hand shabby chic new-to-us furniture that comes from friends who upgrade, for the most part. People come and hang out and stretch and chant and usually stay a while after one of her classes.

Mom also has the most melodic singing voice so she and Dad do occasional gigs together in the local bars. She plays the harpsichord and together they harmonize so well that I swear they should've been a 70's duet and taken the show on the road but they would've been too young in the 70's and it was out of style by the time they got their act together so they just do it for fun, for the vibe, and for a bit of extra cash.

Dad is an amazing artist too; he sells his paintings, wind chimes, and metal art in her studio, which is in the back sun room of our house, as well as on eBay. Dad's pot-cookies are famous around these parts. He also makes and sells a variety of jams and sauces, some of which also contain cannabis (which he grows somewhere not far away and sells to close friends).

In addition to being a part-time cab driver and getting paid gigs for his band here and there he also occasionally does tattoos. Tattoos is where I think my baby brother Beau is going to go. Beau is already showing artistic signs. At five he already dabbles with drums and guitar and he's showing serious artistic talent when he draws.

Me? I'm not real artsy. I'm the most non-extraordinary / normal of the bunch with my job answering phones and taking orders in the cab office. I don't play any musical instruments, have a horrid singing voice. I can't draw well. I can cook pretty well and do most of the cooking but I wouldn't call that my talent. I don't really have a calling, at least not one I've heard the universe shouting out to me like my artistic parents.

I wanted to traipse around Europe after high school for a year to figure it all out but didn't wanna go alone and no one wanted to come with me. I was too chicken shit to go alone so I'm still here. I've waited tables, answered phones, and did a short stint as a receptionist in a lawyer's office, but he was a criminal defense lawyer and the stuff I encountered there made my skin crawl. We ended the working relationship amicably when I gave notice. Right now, I work about 25-30 hours a week at the cab company and I'm in between semesters for night school at a local community college where I've been taking business classes two nights a week.

I'm pretty good at business, good with computers, and I thought about moving to a bigger city for more adventure and job opportunities but my Mom had my baby brother Beau the year after I graduated from high school and I love the little monkey so much that I couldn't imagine missing watch him grow up. I also was a little bit afraid of adventure, even though I deep-down wanted it.

My Mom calls Beau her menopause baby. Beau heard her say that on the phone last week and whispered to me he doesn't think he has very big hands and doesn't know why he's a Man Paws baby. Beau says I'm the "the best big sister in the whole wild world" to use Beau's exact words. My baby bro *is* a handful, though. He keeps us on our toes. Last week he dyed his sandy blond hair green with Kool-Aid. We washed it a dozen times but it's here to stay for now. I offered to take him to Jenna but Mom didn't want to expose him to hair dye.

He also tried to tattoo himself with Dad's kit but thankfully Mom caught him in time and now keeps the tattoo stuff in the gun safe (my Mom is a pacifist but Dad still firmly believes in gun rights). Beau drew various pictures on himself with a red Sharpie instead. He still has remnants of the Superman logo on his little bicep. I'm guessing he's gonna have multi-colored hair, loads of piercings, and will wind up a tattoo artist in 15 years.

Beau calls me Cinder-lella because he says I look pretty enough to be a princess but I'm always doing work instead. Truth be told, the Cinderella part kind of fit. I do a lot around the house, a lot for Beau, work almost full time hours, volunteer at an animal shelter as often as I can, make sure to visit Gran at the nursing home every week and am often helping out while I'm there, am frequently called upon by Jenna and other friends to be their designated driver. I'm pretty much go-go-go all the time. And it saves me from the boredom that is my life.

I've always felt like I'm missing something but I can't quite figure out what that 'something' is.

I FOUND BEAU WATCHING cartoons. My Mom was in her studio; a big space where she did her classes and her crafts. I could hear her sewing machine going.

"Lella, Lella! Can you make me KD and hawdogs for Lupper?"

"Lupper, bud? Did you skip lunch today?"

"Yeah. I ate two breakfasts."

"Okay, sure but only if you eat a salad with it."

"Ermmmmmm...."

"C'mon, bud."

"Lella..." he kind of whined.

I folded my arms and gave him a stern look.

He slumped, "Okay. Only half-a."

"Okay, bud. Half a salad."

"Okey dokey, pokey." He was enthralled in his TV show while twisting Play-Doh around and around into loads of tiny worm-like pieces and dropping them on the side of the sofa arm. I knew what that meant. Lella would have to clean up later. Again.

I hated that stuff. It smelled gross and stuck to everything. Getting dried Play-doh out of the rug was never fun. I regularly chucked it in the trash but Mom or Dad or Dad's buddies would keep buying it for Beau.

"Dad!" I called out the kitchen door, which led to a homemade breezeway made out of green plastic siding that Dad had framed and put in. It opened up into the side of the garage where Dad had cut a doorway in. This way he could wander in and out of his smoking cave during bad weather without getting wet. It looked as bad as it sounded.

Dad poked his crewcut formerly blond, now mostly gray, head in, "Beautiful Bella! How was your day?"

"Good, Dad. I'm making Beau KD and hot dogs. You want some or you want salad and chicken?"

"KD and dogs sounds great, baby doll. Can you make a mountain of it? Deke and Jase'll have some, too."

"Got it." I always made a mountain when Dad and his buddies were involved. I knew who Jase was; he was one of dad's buddies who was frequently over jamming and hitting the bong. But Deke? Deke must've been the biker that my biker had dropped off.

My biker. Tee hee.

And that meant he was probably local so I would get to lay eyes on him again. I felt almost giddy about that notion. Even if I only got to see him from afar he sure was fun to look at.

I poked my head in Mom's studio. She was at her sewing machine, focused, her hair (long blonde curls, just like mine but hers fell to her waist and mine was about half way there), pulled back into a loose braid, a flowy bohemian broom skirt and beaded tank top on.

Nana Mouskouri was playing on Mom's 8-track. Yep. 8-track.

"Hey Momma."

She turned to me and beamed, "Ella! How are you today?"

"Good. Makin' Beau and Dad and Dad's accomplices some mac and cheese and hot dogs. Chicken and salad sound good for you and me?"

"Bless you. Yes."

I set Beau up with a TV tray and his favorite dinner (along with a small side salad and directions to eat it first so he couldn't pull the predictable 'I'm full' before the salad got touched) and a big glass of milk and then headed out to the garage to deliver food to Dad and his buds.

"Thanks Belle!" said Dad as he was weighing out some pot on a scale that was cleverly disguised in a CD case. The funny thing was that the CD case was of a hip hop artist, which wasn't a real good disguise when you considered the other music in Dad's collection.

"Sweet of ya, Ella honey," said Jase as I put the tray down on the table beside Dad.

Deke was sitting in one of the six lawn chairs that surrounded a beat up old coffee table, watching Dad.

I was pretty sure that Deke was Beautiful Biker's Dad. Uncle, maybe, but the resemblance was strong so I'd put money on him being his dad. Same tiger's eyes, dark curly hair, though shorter, similar body type. Deke had a bit of an older biker's body but still had some buff that hadn't quite turned to fluff yet.

"Why thank ya, Betty," Deke winked at me.

I smiled, "Gourmet. I forgot the linen napkins and we ran out of truffle shavings but I hope it'll suffice. I'll bring back the Ketchup."

"And the parmesan and Frank's Red Hot, baby doll?" Dad requested.

"Sure thing."

I checked on mine and Mom's chicken breasts, which were under the broiler, and grabbed the ketchup and other condiments for Dad and his buddies and headed back through the breezeway to the garage.

"Deke, this is my baby doll and pride and joy, Elizabelle. My baby belle of the ball. Calls herself Ella. Deke Valentine here's my new boss and a new buddy. I'll be workin' for his garage part-time and me and The Dubes'll be doing some gigs at his bar. Startin' Saturday night."

Valentine? How perfect of a last name was *that*?

"Really?" I knew Mom had been pushing Dad to bring in more money. Especially after his most recent purchase. She refused to let him fund his boat restoration project without bringing in more funds first. Mom was a hippie but she also had a head for numbers. We didn't live on much, she was frugal, but she did come down on Dad on occasion, in her gentle way, when there wasn't enough to cover everything and we had to go hunting under couch cushions to make rent.

But Dad wasn't a fast mechanic. He puttered. He was good at what he did but he liked to do it at his own pace. Case in point: The Shitbox. Case in point part deux: we had a dozen things around the house that needed to be fixed. Dad took eons to do stuff.

"Yeah, I'm gonna run him around, do some errands, courier stuff for the garage and bike dealership."

"Oh. Not a mechanic then?"

Deke spoke up, "Naw, little lady, I've got a full staff of mechanics. I lost my license to a DUI. Get it back in about two months. Asshole move on my part but there were extenuating circumstances. My boys're gettin' tired of ferrying me around. Your pop's perfect for the job, bein' a cabbie and all."

"Ah. I see. Well, it's nice to meet you, Deke."

"And you," he winked, "Got a feeling we'll see plenty of each other." His eyes twinkled. He was seriously good-looking for an older biker guy.

Dad reached into his beer fridge and passed Deke and Jase beers and then grabbed one for himself and sat at the table.

Deke grabbed the baggie dad had measured out and dropped a wad of twenties on the table by Dad. Dad stuffed them into his pocket.

"See ya!" I headed back inside, smiling at Deke.

I wondered if Dad had made up the rent money and if I didn't need to cart the ten tonnes of coins in my purse to the bank in the morning after all. We could have some serious Rummoli fun with that money thrown back into the kitty.

I went back to the kitchen to put my and Mom's warm chicken Caesar salads together.

Beautiful Biker Valentine?

Ella Valentine. Sigh.

I often tried on a cute guy's last name for size in my head or maybe even by writing it down and practicing my potential signature. But Valentine just might be my favorite so far. I couldn't wait to write that down. I'd put a little heart over the letter i in Valentine.

Dad strolled in to the kitchen, reaching for an unopened bottle of Frank's Red Hot that was in the fridge. I saw Beau's empty salad bowl sitting on the counter. It had a dark tinged liquid in it. What was that? I lifted it and got it under my nose. Chocolate syrup. Ugh. Well, get your veggies down however necessary, I guess.

"Dad? You got cash now for the rest of the rent?" I asked.

"Naw, baby doll, I owe for that primo herb Louie spotted me. What I sold to Deke is gonna catch me up. Didn't you and your mother sort the extra?"

I was a little bit pissed at that. Typical Dad. His pot-selling funded most of his side projects as well as his pot habit but when the family was in need, shouldn't his side project money go into the house instead of the garage? Well, not my problem, right? If Mom was okay with it, I shouldn't let it get to me.

"Yeah, I have to put the change in the account in the morning. So, uh, where do you know Deke from?" I asked casually.

"You a cop?"

I shook my head, "Not yet. But it hasn't been ruled it out as a career choice."

He chuckled, "He's a regular fare. He bought the whole block of land around the corner from the cab office and turned that old car lot and garage into a garage and bike dealership as well as re-opened Whisky's as Deke's Roadhouse. Been vacant a while, but business is hoppin' since Deke opened up a few weeks ago. I've done a few regular runs for them. Got to talkin'. Likes my primo herb, likes good tunes. He's prez of a motorcycle club that's just opened a charter here. Good contact to have."

I felt a bit of impending doom. Not because Dad was working with Deke, I knew my father wasn't a violent guy and wouldn't put himself in that sort of position on purpose but I was concerned partly because there was another MC around. They were a bit rough and my Uncle Willie was a member of the charter the next town over but they acted like our city was theirs, too. I wasn't sure how they'd take to another MC in this neighborhood. We lived in a medium-sized town in South Dakota and it was a place where motorcycle enthusiasts often stopped on their way to Sturgis. And some stayed a while. I could see how another garage and bike dealership would be a good addition to town. It was big enough with enough bikers around here and the neighboring towns to support some competition.

Dad was a nighttime cab driver and most of those had a 'don't ask; don't tell' kind of mentality with the seedy underbelly of the town. People liked dad but I didn't know if the Wyld Jackals would see his association with a new MC in a way that would put dad on their list of enemies. The Jackals had chapters all over the state and a few neighboring states and they weren't known for being friendly with other clubs encroaching on what they'd considered their territory. They had patched over the last club that tried to start up here a few years earlier and I heard that the club before that was wiped out a decade ago. Rumor had it that they refused to play ball with the Jackals and were executed. I didn't know if it was true but that's what local lore said.

"Their club friendly with The Jackals?"

Dad wrinkled his nose, "Not so much."

"Yikes," I said, "Careful, Dad."

"No worries, Belly." He kissed my temple, "This bunch is a good bunch. Wouldn't mind seein' them run the Jackals outta town, really, but mum's the word on that."

I nodded. "What's their MC called?"

"Dominion Brotherhood. Smaller club. Just a few chapters in North and South Dakota. Known as the Doms. Smart, though. Wouldn't be surprised if they grew. They're well-connected with some bigger clubs, too."

Dom. I felt tingly. I liked the idea of envisioning the beautiful biker in a dominating way. I wanted to envision him bending me over, grabbing my hair roughly. He'd be a man who would take control and take what he wanted. The idea of opening myself up to his whims? Phew. I hadn't had it yet. Not ever. But boy did it sound good. Some of my favorite Tumblr pages were sexy Dom/sub pages.

Dad headed back out to the cave and I got Mom and me our dinner, daydreaming about Beautiful Biker while I did it. She and I ate in her studio chatting while Beau played with Legos on the floor. I had bought him several Lego robot kits for his last birthday but instead of following the directions for each, in typical Beau fashion he got a big box and dumped all the kits in the one box and then proceeded to work on building a Super Robot.

After I helped him with his bed and bath routine, by shampooing his hair (he did the rest of his bath routine on his own and hated it if anyone but his Lella did his shampooing) and reading him his bedtime story, I headed up to my room.

I went to bed early. I Jilled off not to visual porn but to the porn playing out on a reel in my brain instead. I got myself off to the idea of BB, Beautiful Biker Valentine. I could swear I smelled the leather and the wind, felt his eyebrow jewelry against my thighs as I imagined him with his head between my legs. I fell asleep so blissfully sated that I forgot to put my Lelo away.

I WAS DREAMING I WAS in one of those motel beds I'd seen in the movies that you could put a quarter in to get the bed to vibrate but in the dream I was in the bed and Beautiful Biker's sexy hand with the eagle ring kept putting quarter after quarter in the machine.

I woke up feeling like I was buzzing. Shit! I'd rolled on the Lelo, and turned the dang thing on. But it was a good thing my B.O.B woke me because my volume on my cell was still all the way down so I almost slept in. I took my Lelo to my bathroom to clean it, planning to put it away but while I was washing it I got to thinking about Beautiful Biker and wound up taking the time I needed to start my day off right.

At full blast with visions of BB in my head, Lelo got me off spectacularly in about 45 seconds.

I WORKED FROM 9:30AM (right after I got to work from the bank) until 10:15 that night. And it was busy, as Friday nights typically were. The crazies seemed to be out in full force; it was pouring rain and everyone wanted a cab. People got irate at waiting. People threatened to start using Uber, which they were already doing so we had fewer cabs on the road than ever, and we used to put two girls on the phones at a time and now it was just one order taker at a time so if you ran to pee then you got an earful from people who hated sitting on hold. But in the rain, people wanted a cab NOW because they didn't want to pay surge pricing or whatever.

The rain cleared before the end of my shift and on the way home I realized I was driving dangerously close to empty. How on earth did that happen? I had only put in $20 the night before but it'd looked like I'd had almost a quarter tank when I got home. I'd only put $20 in because that left me with twenty bucks to my name until payday on Tuesday.

I'd only gone home, to the bank, and then to work. Either The Shitbox had a problem with the gas gage or someone had siphoned gas out. It was a gas pig but surely I had enough to get home, didn't I? I couldn't decide if I should take a chance or not so I decided to be safe and put another $10 in. I had plans the next morning to visit with Jenna at her salon so I stopped at Mr. Apu-Singh's gas station.

The place was empty when I got to the counter but a beat later two tweaked out skids were behind me. Yuck.

Don't make eye contact, Ella! It was never a good idea to let yourself get snagged into conversation with a tweaker. If I didn't make eye contact, I had a better chance of being invisible.

I heard one tweaker whisper to the other, "You go on out. Keep watch."

"Get me a Snickers," the other muttered on his way out.

Oh shit. What? I heard the jingling of the chimes as one guy left. The other? I could see him in the reflection of the window and he was around my age or maybe a bit older and he was sketchy. Like…sketchy dirty. He was wigging out on some kind of junk and he gave me an acute sense of impending doom.

He was standing too close to me. Way too close. And the debit machine was taking for freakin' ever to authorize my transaction.

What to do? I couldn't rush out. I couldn't warn Mr. Singh. Or could I? Could I somehow signal him so that he'd be on guard?

The tweaker wasn't feeling patient. He was practically buzzing with energy behind me, fidgeting, muttering to himself unintelligibly, and setting my teeth on edge.

"Cash, man. Fill a bag!" He blurted this all of a sudden, pulling out a big knife from inside his jacket and pointed it very close to Mr. Singh's throat.

Oh no! Tweaker's shoulder was touching mine.

Mr. Singh immediately made to reach below and Skid Tweaker yelled, in a ferocious cry, "NO! Hands where I can see 'em or I gut ya!"

Mr. Singh put his hands straight up and I knew, too, he'd been about to reach for a panic button.

Tweaker very suddenly hooked his free arm around my neck and hauled me behind the clerk's counter with him. My eyes went wide. Mr. Singh's eyes went wide. His hands were still in the air.

"Make the register open!" Tweaker pointed his knife in the direction of the cash register.

God, he smelled awful. My skin was crawling.

Mr. Singh's hands started to shake and he was shaking his head vigorously, "I keep thirty dollars only. Thirty dollars only."

"No. You got a safe, too. My brother knows a guy who used to work here. Open the till. Open the safe. Or I'll carve a swastika in this pretty blonde's cheek. Hey pretty thing. Don't fight. Be still and this'll be over soon."

He licked my face. Licked my fucking face! Ew!

I was speechless. I was scared shitless. And this guy smelled rank! Gross. Like seriously dirty laundry, body odor, and nachos. My cheek was wet and I felt disgustingly sick.

Mr. Singh opened the till and tweaker said, "Lift the drawer!" Underneath there was definitely more than $30 in there. At least four or five hundred dollars in fifties and one hundred dollar bills, which he obviously tried to hide between trips to his safe.

He got the money into a pile on the counter.

"The safe, too," Tweaker ordered.

"I cannot open safe. My manager only. He…"

The tweaker's arm tightened around my throat as the chimes jingled.

Oh no. The other tweaker? Oh wait. Nope.

Normally I'd say adding another unknown to this equation might be really bad and tweak the tweaker in a dangerous way but the chimes jingled because… yep, you guessed it; Beautiful Biker came in.

He looked as good as he had the day before, only today he wasn't wearing a leather jacket. He was wearing an army green Henley underneath a leather vest with an eagle emblem on the breast. It said 'Death' above the emblem and 'before enslavement' underneath. He had a wool gray beanie on his head and a big ass gun in his hand.

I could tell by the way he entered the space that he knew what he was walking into and he was prepared. Prepared as in carrying a drawn gun and pointing it in our direction.

Holy shit.

"Back away from her and leave." His piercing gaze was right on the tweaker.

I swallowed hard. Skid Tweaker had tightened his hold on me.

"The fuck're you?" Tweaker was trembling. But I didn't think it was fear. I think it was adrenaline, "A Dom?"

"Yeah, man. I am. Now. Make this easy for both of us. Let her go. Now. You go right now with no problems there'll be no retribution."

"Why d'you care? You got a stake in this place?"

"Not this place," Beautiful Biker replied, "Her." He jerked his chin in my direction.

"She yours?" Tweaker went wired.

He gave a definitive nod. "She is. Let her go. C'mere, Kitten." He said this, addressing me, but not taking his eyes off the tweaker, but he wiggled his free index finger at me. I was frozen in place, the tweaker still holding me.

Tweaker began to move us and walked me around the counter, his arm still hooked around my neck, only now it was in a brotherly way instead of an armed robbery taking-a-hostage kind of way, and he handed me off to the biker.

"My sincere apologies, man. I had no idea. No idea at all." Tweaker's demeanor completely changed and his hands were up in the air, though he hadn't put the knife down.

The biker swept me behind him with his free hand, his eyes and gun still trained on the tweaker.

"Go," he barked to the tweaker.

I wiped my cheek with my jacket sleeve. Seriously gross!

"No. no no, you can put that away. I'm cool. We're cool, man, totally cool." He was backing away from where we stood on the other side of the clerk's counter, waving his arms.

He continued, "Not to worry. My mistake. I seriously didn't know. My apologies, man. If I knew... see, she was just in the way. I was gonna wait 'til she left but shit was takin' for fuckin' ever. I meant no disrespect to the Doms. I know of your club. My uncle's neighbor's brother is a fully patched member in the Bismarck chapter."

"Oh yeah?" The biker didn't seem to relax or lower his gun, "What's his name?"

"Not a fuckin' clue, to be honest, dude," Tweaker answered, shrugging, "I met him once. We had beers around this fire. Did some shrooms together. Can't remember the dude's name but he was cool."

He was by the door now, still backing out. The chimes jingled as he was half way out the door, "No retribution?" then he stupidly muttered, "We can split what's in the till and safe, man."

"Fuck off right now," The biker told him matter-of-factly, "No retribution. You don't fuck off, we got problems."

I don't think the guy believed him. What he said next showed as much.

"Man, I'm tight with the Jackals, too." There was loaded silence, and then the tweaker added, "Just sayin'."

"Threatening me? Not a smart move, asshole," The biker declared.

I was trembling like a leaf. I gave Mr. Apu-Singh a hopeful smile but still felt filled with dread. The debit machine finally started to spit out a receipt for my transaction and Mr. Apu-singh leaned forward to fetch it but I knew he pushed the panic button as he did.

The tweaker didn't miss that either.

"Aw, fuck man. You stupid shit!" He started to move back in our direction, waving his knife at the clerk, "Why'd you trip the fuckin' alarm for?" And then he kicked over a display of four packs of Red Bull as he lunged back toward the counter, looking like he intended to use the knife in his hand.

"Doesn't matter. Cops were called before I came in," Beautiful biker said.

It was if the tweaker suddenly remembered the biker with the gun. He raised his arms defensively again but looked a little shell-shocked.

"You called the cops?"

BB took one step closer to him and conked the tweaker on the head with the butt of his gun, making the guy fall face-first into the pile of knocked over Red Bull cans.

Me, BB, and Mr. Singh all stood for what felt like a long moment, staring at the guy passed out on the floor amid the cans.

"There was another guy with him," I breathed, looking back toward the door.

"He ran," Beautiful Biker muttered.

The clerk was writing something down and then he quickly came around the counter and locked the door and taped up a sign that said 'TEMPORARY CLOSED. SORRY'

"Please to wait to talk to police," he requested.

The biker nodded and put his gun into the back of his jeans but kept his eyes on the unconscious guy on the floor. He kicked the knife aside so that it'd be way out of the guy's reach, if he woke up.

The clerk went back behind the counter and started to push buttons on a cordless phone and then was talking on the phone. I felt sick to my stomach. I went for the rest room a few feet away from me and not even shutting the door, ran water over paper towels and started wiping my face. There was a hand sanitizer dispenser on the wall. I pushed the button three times with a paper towel wad underneath and started frantically wiping my cheek.

The biker leaned back against an ice cream chest freezer and folded his arms across his chest and leveled his gaze on me.

I looked right into his golden brown eyes.

I could not swallow.

Police car sirens sounded in the distance and I let out a staggered breath.

Beautiful Biker's eyes traveled from my eyes to my feet and then back up.

"You good?" This time the assessment wasn't sexual. This was an assessment of my well-being. He looked pissed right off.

"He licked my face," I muttered. I was pretty freaked out. I was shaking.

Beautiful Biker clenched his jaw and his eyes narrowed.

"Please, have drink, both of you," Mr. Apu-singh invited in a somewhat heavy East Indian accent, "Go take a drink from cooler, complimentary. Thank you for waiting for police. They will need statement. Thank you, Mister. Thank you very much."

I shakily moved to the cooler and opened it and got a bottle of water. I looked at him, "Drink?"

He shook his head. He was working his jaw muscles, looking intense.

"Do you want a drink Mr. Apu... I mean Mr. Singh?"

"No thank you. What is your names? I am Mr. Singh," he stated the obvious.

"I'm Ella."

We both looked to the biker. His expression was hard. His eyes were on the guy on the floor.

We waited.

"Deacon Valentine," he finally mumbled, not taking his eyes off the guy on the floor. The guy groaned, looking like he was going to rouse. But his eyes stayed shut.

THE COPS WERE DONE taking our statements. One was talking to Deacon and I knew they were talking about his gun, and another talked to me and Mr. Singh, who thanked Deacon and apologized to me before the cop I'd been talking to said I could go.

Deacon was following a cop to his cruiser. He looked over his shoulder at me.

"Wait," he ordered. I nodded and pulled my car away from the gas pump and over to beside a motorcycle, which was parked in front of the air hose. It was the only other vehicle here so it had to be his bike. It was dark but based on the light coming from the store I could see it was a nice motorcycle. Sparkling with chrome. Fancy.

A moment later, paramedics were taking the tweaker on a stretcher into their ambulance.

I was shell shocked. Talk about nuts! A minute later Deacon *Beautiful Biker* Valentine approached the motorcycle beside me. I got out of my car. I said, "Thank you. That was really cool of you in there. Brave."

His expression was blank. He threw a leg over his motorcycle and started it up. His eyes were on me the whole time but his face wasn't welcoming further chit-chat. I didn't know why he'd asked me to wait. He obviously wasn't in the mood for discussion.

"Okay, well, see ya around. Thanks again," I called, feeling a little embarrassed. He probably couldn't hear me over the roar of his bike.

He jerked his chin up, motioning to my car with it; I guess he meant for me to go, so I waved and gave a bit of an awkward smile and then got in my car, locked the door, and drove away.

Deacon followed me home. Was he picking up Deke?

I pulled into the driveway. I glanced down toward the garage, which was set back a ways from the house. It was shut down. No lights on in the garage or the house. Dad's pick-up truck was gone. Dad must be out; Mom must be in bed.

I looked back at him. He was idling in front of the house.

I didn't know whether to say that his Dad wasn't here or not but it was probably pretty obvious what with all the lights being off so I shut the car down and got out and stood there, looking at him. He jerked his head toward my door so I probably frowned and then I just went to head inside.

When I got to the door, key in the lock, I looked back at him. He was still sitting there. I went inside and closed the door and locked it. The house was dark, Mom and Beau in bed, so I went right upstairs to the top floor to my room and turned the light on. I looked out the front window. He was still there, looking up at my window. And then he pulled away. It was as if he'd seen me safely right to my room and then just left.

I had trouble getting to sleep, my mind yo-yo'd between thinking about getting my face carved, about Mr. Singh almost getting hurt, and thinking about Deacon calling me Kitten, telling the tweaker that I was his.

I mean, it was obviously just a method of getting the guy to not carve a swastika in my face. But still. It was freaky. A freaky night. How brave was that of him to do that? He came in with his gun out and pointed and had called the cops on his way in so he clearly knew what was going on.

I could've woken my Mom and told her. I could've called my Dad. I could've called Jenna or one of my other friends. But I felt like I'd been inside a tunnel made of drum symbol material and it was still ringing and vibrating. So instead, I took a bath and got into a nightie and then I climbed into my bed and stared at the ceiling for what felt like hours before finally passing out.

2

It was Saturday morning and I was starting the day off with an eyebrow wax at Jenna's salon. I'd had weird dreams all night. First, nightmares with my face being carved by tweaker and then sexy dreams where Deacon was calling me Kitten and I was riding on the back of his bike. And kissing him. A lot. But then my face was gushing with blood in the dream so I woke up in a panic.

I slept terrible so wound up sleeping in. I hadn't put myself to sleep with my Lelo or my hand and I hadn't taken care of myself that morning, either, despite the sexy dreams. It was like I was afraid to do it, knowing I'd picture him and for some reason, I feared it'd be too intense. I couldn't handle anything remotely intense after the intensity of the previous evening. Not after hearing his voice calling me that name, not after seeing him with a gun, not after feeling the sizzle of the promise of his touch I felt when he pushed me behind him for safety. And certainly not knowing how to process him seeing me safely home, which was really very sweet.

I got up and the house was empty. Mom and Beau were off somewhere, likely the library -—their usual Saturday morning spot, and Dad was in the garage welding something and making noise. I poured a coffee to-go and then just waved at him as I left.

Jenna's salon was in the downtown strip, between a bakery and a health food store. The salon had three chairs and a little room for waxing and nails and she had one part-time stylist, the lady who used to own the salon who now rented a chair and worked only a few partial days a week, and an esthetician, Pippa, who I was also tight with.

Jenna had gone to school and got her BA in business but had also gone to beauty school and her parents, who had a pretty diverse portfolio, including some real estate, gifted her with the salon.

She lived upstairs with Pippa in a huge apartment that had a massive rooftop deck. They had a blast every day at work but they partied non-stop, it seemed. Jenna suggested I go to beauty school and join her here but it didn't feel like it'd be my gig. She even invited me to move in with them, saying that Pippa was planning to leave soon so she could move in with her boyfriend but that we could bunk in Jenna's room together in the meantime if I wanted to make the move now.

As much as I loved Jenna I suspected that working together and being besties might make me like Jenna less. As much as I loved her, she was a wild child, much wilder than me, who partied too much and constantly tried to drag me into trouble with her. She often succeeded, too! *She* was the one her mother warned her about. She belonged with my crazy family and I probably belonged with her "normal" conservative folks.

"So, get this!" She says to me as soon as I was in the door, bouncing up and down, her long wavy dark shiny hair bouncing along with her, "Thursday night I met this guy. Fuck, Elle, he was gorgeous! A biker. Hot biker. Hottest biker I've ever ever seen! You have got to see him. He's new in town and I made out with him at that roadhouse biker bar. Gave him my number. Cannot wait to see him again. Think I'm goin' back to the bar tonight to see if I can catch his eye. I'm a little bit in love, I think. Maybe in lust but love is definitely a possibility."

Hottest biker she's ever ever seen? Uh oh. My heart sank, "What was his name?"

"Rider. But maybe that's a biker nickname. I dunno. Met him right at last call. Wish I'd had more time. If I'd met him at the start of the night I bet I would've brought him home. Fuck, Ella. Best kiss I ever had."

"What does he look like?"

"Gorgeous. So fucking gorgeous. Long dark hair. Tall. Built. Tattooed. Totally my type."

"Since when is that your type?" Pippa piped up, coming out from the back room with a customer. She was gorgeous, too. She had straight dark hair with highlights and big brandy-colored eyes. She had a great body and was an awesome friend. Not nearly as wild as Jenna but definitely wilder than me.

Pippa's guy was completely clean cut, jock type, but a great guy. Well, now he was. He wasn't always a great guy but he had changed for Pip. Pippa was right though; I'd never seen Jenna go for the biker bad boy type.

"Since I laid eyes on Rider. Anyway, the new Deke's Roadhouse, used to be Whisky's? It's below the clubhouse for that new Dom MC as well and he's definitely one of them. Beside the garage and old Pontiac dealership? It's now a bike dealership. Maybe I'll be a biker broad. An old lady. Ha!"

Pippa and a girl, maybe a little younger than us, that she was ringing up with freshly painted nails cackled.

I looked down at my nails. They were kind of in need of a manicure. But I couldn't afford it this week so I'd have to do it myself at home.

"What's wrong?" Jenna was assessing my face.

She made out with my biker? I mean, he wasn't mine but...

"Nothing. Well, not nothing. The Circle J got mugged last night. A tweaker fuckboy skid held a knife to my face. Threatened to carve a swastika on my cheek. I got saved by a Dominion Brotherhood member who pistol whipped the skid mark into a pile of Red Bull cans. Had to give my statement to the cops and everything."

"You did? Holy shit!" She grabbed me and hugged me, "How horrible! Tell me everything!" She sat in the empty salon chair beside me, angling it to face me.

I told her everything about the incident, leaving out that I'd been crushing on the biker the day before and that I suspected it was the biker she'd made out with the night before. I had a captive audience of Pippa, the girl with the fresh nails and Pippa's next appointment, a girl named Andie we went to high school with who was also there to get her eyebrows waxed.

I was fawned over and Pippa insisted on giving me the star treatment with waxing plus manicure and pedicure after her client left. And then they talked me into going to Deke's Roadhouse that night to get my mind off my trauma. I'd cleaned out the change in my purse and added it to two lonely dollar bills to get my brows done but was living on next to nothing for the next few days until pay day.

I tried to get out of Saturday night at a bar, saying I didn't have money to blow at the bar, when Jenna stuffed two tens and three twenty dollar bills into my bra (she was handsy like that) and said she owed it to me from when I fixed her website up. I did that for free. I wasn't a pro but I dabbled and was pretty good with that stuff and she'd loved what I'd done with her site. I relented and then Jenna wanted to give me a wash and blow out, which she also insisted on doing for free.

Jenna wanted to see if she'd run into her biker again. I finally agreed, in part because I wanted to see if I ran into my biker. And see if my biker was Jenna's biker. I suspected he was. And that bothered me. But I had to know. When I'd told the story I didn't talk about what the biker who'd saved me looked like. I also hadn't said that I'd been in line behind him the day before or that he'd followed me home twice, once to drop Deke of Deke's Roadhouse off and the other time, for some unknown reason after the attempted robbery.

Dad would be playing at the Roadhouse, too, according to what he'd said the other day so there was that as an excuse to go, too.

Jenna snipped about two inches off my ends, adding a few long layers into my curly hair and before I knew it, she was flat ironing it for that evening. I usually wore it curly. Not like I had a choice. I'd tried doing blow-outs myself but my hair always returned to the curl or sometimes the curls completely rebelled against my attempt at taming and instead went to a dreaded frizz, usually within hours of a blow-out. This was the first time I'd seen my hair *that* bone straight and I had to admit, it made me look older than 16.

I dashed home after spending the whole afternoon hanging at the salon (I was there so long that Pippa even gave me a free Brazilian) and I dressed in tight jeans, high heeled black strappy sandals, and a stretchy black flowy top that had a halter neck but cut-outs to expose my shoulders and drapey material around the biceps. My eyes were done in smoky. I tried for winged eyeliner but screwed it up so after umpteen tries decided normal eyeliner would have to do.

I didn't have to be designated driver for a switch. Joe, Pippa's boyfriend, was a recovering alcoholic and so he was DD'ing for us. I was driving to Jenna's to meet there and get a lift to Deke's Roadhouse and then I'd crash on Jenna and Pippa's couch if Jenna brought home 'her biker' and would crash in Jenna's bed with her otherwise. I was planning to actually let my hair down for a change. Literally.

I needed to leave Boring and Responsible-ville for a night. Maybe it was having a knife held to my face that had me in the mood to live a little wild.

I'd live it up for a change. Unless, of course, Jenna hooked up with Deacon. And then instead of living it up I'd be crying into my rum and Coke. Suffering in silence, though, because I had no claim on him and wouldn't want Jenna to feel bad about hooking up with someone *that* delicious.

As I was on my way down the stairs, getting ready to head out the front door, my Mom stopped me.

"Wow, sweetie. Your hair!"

"I know! Jenna did it. This $200 flat iron. I'm SO buying one of these next pay! I'll do yours, too!"

She smiled but the smile didn't quite touch her eyes, which was odd. Mom smiled with her whole face, usually. She put her hand on my bare shoulder and said, "I heard about the robbery last night from Sue at the library. Why didn't you tell me?"

I took a breath and sat on the stairs, my eyes on my French pedicure, "I was processing. I didn't want to wake you."

"You should have woken me, Elizabelle."

"I'm okay, Momma."

"But, why didn't you tell me all day today?"

"You were out when I got up. I just... ugh. I just went to Jenna's salon. I meant to call. I'm just glad it's over and didn't end worse than it did."

"It must have been terrifying!"

"It was."

"Your Dad told me that Deke's son stopped the robbery."

"He did. How does Dad know?"

Confirmed. Deke's son; as suspected.

"Dad is at the roadhouse, setting up. I guess Deke told him. You were the only witness. Besides Mr. Singh?"

I nodded.

"Are you okay, sunshine?"

"I'm...yeah, I'm good. I was a bit shaken up last night but I'm okay."

"Deke said his son said that the robber held you at knifepoint. Had a knife to your face."

"Threatened to carve a swastika in it."

Mom clutched her long necklace, "Oh Lord!"

"I just wanna go out and let my hair down tonight. Me and the girls are going to the roadhouse. We'll see Dad play. Dance a little. Be silly. You should come. Get a sitter for Beau."

"It's okay, Ella. I feel like a quiet night in. I have a book to finish reading. I've been saving the last chapter for a quiet night. You have fun." She seemed more than a little bit shaken up about the robbery.

"I'll probably sleep over at Jenna's. I'll see how it goes."

"Okay." She looked concerned, "Just send a text if you do. Sure you're okay?"

"I'm good, Momma." I hugged her.

She stroked my hair, "Oh my! It's like silk!"

"I know!" I flipped my hair, "She put this Moroccan oil in it, too. I love it! It's like $80 a bottle so I might have to sell a kidney but I am *so* buying some."

I waved Bye to her and then ducked into the living room and kissed Beau on the top of his still-green tinged head. He was busy playing a video game and so focused I don't think he even noticed me. And then I headed off to Jenna's where Pippa did the winged eyeliner for me, adding this fiber mascara that made my eyelashes seem almost as long as Deacon's. My beautiful biker. Or maybe Jenna's beautiful biker.

Sigh.

DEKE'S ROADHOUSE WAS wall-to-wall people. Mostly, wall to wall bikers. It was loud and rough-looking but there were a fair few younger bikers in there. Some good-looking ones, too. Maybe because of Deacon I was starting to have an appreciation for these rugged-looking men in leather.

They hadn't done anything to spruce the old Whiskey up. If anything, it might've looked even rougher. But in Deke's defense, it'd only been open a few weeks and it'd sat vacant for more than a year.

There was a really long bar that must've had at least 50 bar stools running parallel, about twenty or so 4-seater tables, a wall with about half a dozen booths, a big dance floor, a big stage, and an area with half a dozen pool tables along with a small area for darts. The building was large and this place had a second storey that used to have some banquet rooms but now I suspected it was the MC clubhouse part of the place now as the outside staircase that led to the second floor from the parking lot led to a door with the club's emblem over the door.

My Dad's band was already playing when we got in. They were playing Hook, a Blues Traveler song that I really liked and Deke was up there playing harmonica while Dad sang. Dad did an awesome job of the song and always wowed people when he sang Blues Traveler because he sounded just like John Popper and could do all the fast parts in the song perfectly. This addition with the harmonica took the song from good to great.

I caught Dad's eye and waved at him. His eyes hit mine and he made a "Wow" face, as if he barely recognized me. I flipped my hair dramatically as me and the girls headed toward the bar for drinks. My Dad gave me a huge smile.

Before my smile had a chance to wane I saw *him*. Deacon. Beautiful Biker. And I was pretty sure he'd seen my entrance and dramatic hair flip.

He stood out amongst that sea of people as if there'd been a light shining down on him, an even brighter light in those eyes. He was standing at the end of the bar and his eyes were burning into me with so much heat that it felt like he was touching me. I tried to smile but I don't think it came across very well. I tried not to blush but failed miserably.

He was wearing a black button down shirt, dark button fly jeans, and black motorcycle boots. His hair was loose from the ponytail I'd seen him in before and he was clean shaven. He had a cool leather necklace with a black onyx stone on it that sat in the center of his upper chest. I could see ink from a tattoo peeking out of the half unbuttoned shirt but not enough to decipher what the ink was of. He had a bottle of beer by the neck and there was a tall and gorgeous redhead standing beside him, trying to get his attention. She was wearing skinny jeans, high heeled boots, and a leather bustier.

I looked to my side where Jenna and Pippa were and looked to Jenna's face for recognition. Her eyes were boinging. She slapped my arm and whispered something in my ear but the music and the crowd were too loud so I couldn't hear what she was saying.

I couldn't tear my eyes away from Deacon's. I tried again with the smile but his face was so serious that I felt super-duper self-conscious. His eyes moved down my body and it felt like every nerve in my body responded to it, as if it were a physical caress. He took a sip of his beer and then sucked in his lower lip and then his look turned to irritation as the redhead tapped his shoulder. He jerked as if repulsed and kept looking at me.

The redhead followed Deacon's gaze to me and she contorted her face into a sour look. She wasn't happy that his focus wasn't on her. I knew who she was. Her name was Paige. She had graduated from our high school two years ahead of me and she was definitely a biker hang-around. She'd dated a biker who was a member of the Jackals in grade 12. A few months back I'd seen my cousin Chris ride through town on a motorcycle with a Jackal vest on and she was on the back of it.

She put her hand on Deacon's shoulder, trying to get his attention but he shrugged her off as if she were an annoyance, a mosquito.

Pippa's boyfriend Joe passed the girls beers and me a rum and Coke. We all cheers'd and then I tipped my drink in Deacon's direction. He was still watching me and I tried again with a smile. He didn't return it. I shrugged and took a big sip and looked back to my friends. I would've bought him a beer as the least I could do to say thanks for stopping a junkie from carving my face but his expression didn't invite approach. At least I didn't think it did.

"You know him?" Jenna mouthed, jerking her thumb in Deacon's direction but doing it in front of her chest, her back to him so he wouldn't see.

I nodded and tilted my hand to say 'so-so'.

"Do you?" I mouthed.

She shook her head and then waved me to come to the bathroom. We left our drinks with Pippa and Joe.

In the bathroom she said, "You know that guy? He's absolutely gorgeous! I think he might be related to the guy I made out with Thursday night. The guy I made out with looked a lot like him. But his hair was longer. And he had a bit of a goatee. And green eyes. Gorgeous green eyes."

I felt immense relief. It showed.

"Oh thank God. I was worried it was the same guy you described. That's the guy who saved me from the tweaker at the gas station."

"No shit?" Jenna grabbed me.

"No shit," I confirmed.

"So you were hoping it wasn't the guy I made out with because you totally dig this guy?"

"Duh? Did you see him?"

She giggled and reached into her bag and produced her lip gloss. "He was looking at you like he wanted to eat you for breakfast tomorrow morning after eating you for an all-night snack tonight!"

I chuckled and checked my own make-up in the mirror, "That's not what I was getting but..." I shrugged.

"No, seriously, Ella. You crook your finger and he'd be on you like white on rice. God, if my biker marries me and your biker marries you and they're brothers, which they *have* to be, then you and me will be sisters. Fucking sisters. Finally!"

She bumped me with her shoulder and got dreamy-eyed.

"It's more like the other way around," I giggled, "He crooks his finger I'll just float in his direction, so strong will be the call of the beautiful biker. Let's go get our drinks. I know what's up next in Dad's set list and we don't wanna miss it!"

We got back out to the bar area and Deacon wasn't there. The redhead Paige was, though, and she was shooting lethal lasers from her eyes at me, as if my presence alone was what had made Deacon shrug her off.

I tried to ignore her burning lasers. Me and the girls got up close to the stage to show our support to Dad's band and sing along to Paradise by the Dashboard Light by Meatloaf. We were over the top with our sing-along and it was a blast, as always. Dad's bassist sang the female parts in a high pitched voice so the crowd ate it up because he managed to sound a bit like a woman without going off pitch.

When the song was over, Deke jumped up on stage and said,

"Better book these guys in every Saturday night if they bring their own groupies!" Deke motioned to me, Jenna, and Pippa. We threw our arms up and Woo'd really loud.

The drummer, Dad's friend Louie, who called himself Uncle Lou to me whenever addressing himself, called out "I'll take the hot blonde!"

He was joking, of course.

Dad leaned over toward his mic, "These groupies are off limits to the band! Particularly the blonde, as she's my baby girl."

There were hoots and whistles all around.

I felt the unmistakable feeling you felt when you were being watched. I looked around, wondering if Deacon's hot gaze was on me. But it wasn't Deacon. I spotted Jay Smyth, my ex. He was off to the side of the dance floor. Eyes on me. Beer to his lips. I had ignored his last three texts, one of which had come through that morning asking me out to dinner, as friends. Bullshit.

Jay looked a little rough but in kind of a hot way. He was definitely good-looking but right now he looked like he hadn't slept in days, but instead drank cup after cup of coffee. He was sporting about 4 days of stubble and his short dark hair was messy, like he'd just rolled out of bed. He was in jeans and a hoodie and he was drinking from a beer bottle, eyes on me, darkly. It gave me an unpleasant shudder. This was getting out of hand.

Dad announced that he and the band were gonna take a break and they switched to the jukebox so me and the girls were heading back toward the bar when Jay approached.

"Oh shit," Jenna muttered, "He came in to try to book an appointment for next week today right after you left. Like, immediately after. As if he was waiting for you to go. Pippa was on the phone with Joe and said you were coming with us tonight. He must've heard. Sorry, Elle."

The look Jay gave me was oily. He was right in my space all of a sudden. He lifted a hand and ran it through my hair, "I love it, Elizabelle. It's gorgeous," he said. I hated how he used my name. I'd repeatedly asked him not to call me Elizabelle but he'd paid no mind.

"Uh, thanks." I backed away from him and kind of cringed. I didn't want to give him any mixed signals whatsoever. He advanced toward me and reached his hand out, almost got my hand but then suddenly Deacon was there, at my side, arm around my waist, and he'd gotten right between me and Jay.

"Hey Kitten. Ready for another drink?"

Jay's expression dropped. Deacon leveled a look in his direction that'd make anyone quake in their boots. Jay took a step backwards.

"She's taken," he said to Jay, looking down at him. Deacon was at least four inches taller and a whole lot more muscular.

Jay looked like he was shitting himself but somehow mustered up some courage. He still stayed back, though.

Jay glared, "I know she's taken. By me. She's my girlfriend."

Deacon turned to look at me and arched that pierced brow at me.

I shook my head, "We broke up a month ago, no, five weeks ago, Jay."

Jay opened his mouth, about to plead his case I guess, but then we heard, "All good, baby doll?"

My Dad was in our space, looking at the stand-off between Jay and Deacon.

Dad knew Jay. He didn't think much of him.

"Hey Mr. Forker," Jay said to dad and extended a hand, "Great set, Sir."

"Cheers, Jay," Dad didn't shake his hand but put his hand on Jay's shoulder in a friendly way and continued, "EllaBella, here, tells me you two are done and it seems here that you're upsetting her so maybe it'd be good you didn't stick around for the second set, yeah?"

Jay looked ready to protest.

Dad was no slouch. He was six feet tall and trim but wiry. He had a super short grey crewcut and a trim goatee and really nice blue eyes. He turned women's heads and men liked him. He was pretty laid back but I'd seen him in a bar brawl or two and as laid back as he was, when he gave you a serious look, you felt it.

Dad looked at Deacon and held his hand out, "You Deke's son?"

"Yeah," Deacon shook Dad's outstretched hand. Jay was seething. It was palpable.

"Which one?"

"Deacon."

"Good to meet ya, Deacon. Rob Forker. You seein' my daughter?"

Deacon gave Dad a chin jerk. My guess was he wanted to help me ward off Jay but didn't want to out and out lie to my Dad since Dad was becoming friends with his Dad.

"Speak to ya a minute?" Dad requested, "Join me on the smoking patio?"

Deacon nodded and let my waist go but he'd squeezed my hip a little bit first. I was tingling. And confused.

"Walk you to your car, Jay," Deacon said and it wasn't a request. Deacon's head turned toward the bar and he jerked his chin at someone and then jerked his thumb toward the door. Jay downed his beer and then he gave me a look that I could swear meant that we weren't done yet. It was sort of sinister, even, making my skin a little bit crawly.

Jay followed Dad and Deacon outside and two large older bikers followed too, flanking Deacon. Bouncers?

"Holy fuck-a-luk!" Jenna whispered in my ear.

"Holy fuck is right!" Pippa agreed.

"Hey gorgeous, where've you been all my life?" A guy grabbed Jenna and gave her a dramatic twirl, and then dipped her.

He was gorgeous. And a biker. Yep, this guy *had* to be Deacon's brother. Definitely. He had long hair, as long as mine, not nearly as curly as Deacon's but it had a wave. He had a short neat goatee. He had blue-green, but more green than blue, eyes and wore a Dom vest and jeans with a black thermal shirt underneath. He and Jenna had almost the exact same hair. They looked like one of those beautiful brother-sister like couples. They would make some beautiful babies.

There was another guy with them, too, and I was guessing he was a third Valentine brother because he was also gorgeous. He had shorter hair but with a flop to it, kind of like a bit of a modern pompadour. He had the same eyes as Deacon and also wore a motorcycle vest. He looked younger than Deacon and younger than Deacon's brother but older than me and he was looking me up and down hungrily. He had a bit of a John Mayer vibe to him. Chin dimple, pouty lips. He ran his fingers through the thick flop of hair, pushing it away from his eyes and gave me a wink.

"Introduce me to your girls, babe," the one with Jenna in his arms said, "This is my brother Spencer."

"Pippa. Her beau Joe is at the dart board, in the red shirt over there." Jenna pointed to Joe and then placed her hand on Rider's chest, "Girlies, this is Rider. And this here, is Ella. And I think she might be about to be whisked away by your brother."

"My brother? Spence?" He looked behind him.

"I can definitely rise to that challenge," Spencer said flirtily and stepped forward.

"No, the other one," Jenna corrected.

"Deacon?" Both guys asked in unison. They both seemed surprised.

I smiled and blushed.

"Naw," Spencer moved in and put his arm around me, "You don't wanna try to date Deacon. He's not the dating kind. How about you give me a shot?" He ran his hand up the length of my bare arm.

He was cute. More than cute. If I'd seen him before Deacon, I'd definitely have given him a double-take, a triple-take even, but something about him put me off. He was drunk, or close to it; I could smell the booze on him, and he was acting almost predatory.

"Yo, Spence. Step back." Deacon appeared and said this to Spencer, stepping forward and getting right in his face.

"Hey, man. Why? I'm getting acquainted with this fine young fox here," Spencer looked pleased, almost smarmy, but he still backed away from me. Deacon's body language was seriously intense. I don't think Spencer had a choice but to back away.

"Whatever you think you're doin', it stops now." Deacon stepped forward between me and Spencer, making Spencer take another step back.

"Oh yeah?" Spencer challenged.

"Yeah," Deacon glared at him.

"And why is that?" Spencer pushed.

"You know why," Deacon stated.

"You stakin' a claim?" Spencer jerked his chin but it was a bit of a throw down, by the looks of it.

"That's right," Deacon said took a step closer to Spencer. Spencer took another step back. Deacon's deep voice reverberated in my chest.

Rider winced. My eyes darted to him and he looked almost stricken.

"No hesitation?" Spencer seemed surprised. Rider jerked in surprise, too.

"Nope," Deacon confirmed, "None." That feeling in my chest intensified.

"That cool with you?" Spencer asked me.

Jenna and Pippa were also gawking, mouths opened. Something weird was happening here and me and the girls were all a little flabbergasted at the intensity between these boys.

Rider's eyebrows were up high.

"'Cuz it probably shouldn't be..." Spencer said.

"Uh..." I started but before I knew how to proceed, Deacon grabbed my hand and started to walk. Having no real choice, I followed.

He took me down a hall past the bathrooms to a room marked "Private" and he pulled a set of keys from his pocket and aimed an attached key fob at the small panel below the door knob. The red light switched to green and he pulled me inside and shut the door.

"What was that all about?" I was a bit breathless. No, a lot breathless. Not from physically walking to that room, although my feet weren't used to heels this high, but more from being a bit shocked.

We were in a good-sized supply room. There were cases of beer, cases of soft drinks, and bathroom and cleaning supplies. There was also a small loveseat-sized sofa bed in the corner and it was pulled out and made up with pillows and blankets. He was standing there, his arms folded across his chest, looking at me like he was pissed at me, which made me more than a little bit annoyed. I didn't even know this guy!

"Savin' your bacon. Again."

"From your brother?"

"Yep," His eyes lit with amusement, though, so I didn't know what to make of it. His eyes traveled up and down my body.

"So that's three times now that you've pretended to be my boyfriend. The first time, to save me from that tweaker. Thank you for that. So much. I thank you and my face thanks you for not letting him carve it up. I should buy you a beer, at least."

"Not necessary."

"But thank you."

"You're welcome. Your father just thanked me." His expression was back to hard.

I hadn't talked to Dad yet about all of that.

I nodded, "And thanks for pretending with Jay. He's not taking the break-up well." I winced.

Deacon's expression went harder somehow. Way harder. He didn't say anything but his jaw was clenching.

An awkward moment passed while I watched the muscles working in his jaw. What was that all about?

"So, uh.. did you whisk me in here to save me from your brother? Is he that bad?" I laughed.

"You changed your hair," he said, instead of answering.

I felt heat creep up my face.

"Yeah, Jenna, my friend out there, the one on your brother's arm, did it. She's a hair stylist."

"Permanent?"

I shook my head, "No. It's not."

He nodded, looking pleased about that news, and shifted from one foot to another. His eyes moved to my cleavage.

"Uh…" I struggled, "Are we going back out, or? I'm sure your brother took the hint. Is he not a good guy?"

He moved closer to me.

"No, he's a good guy. When he's not drunk and movin' in on someone I wanna move in on."

"Oh."

Um, wow.

He took a step closer still and I backed up against the door.

"You're blockin' the door," he said softly.

"Oops." I went to move away but as I moved to the left his right arm came up and his palm rested against the door, blocking that direction. I went to move to the right to clear the door and his left hand came up the same way. He had me caged in.

I could hardly breathe. And he was obviously trying to make some sort of point right here, right now.

"Now I'm pinned against the door," I informed him, "I can't go anywhere."

His lips tipped up a bit, like he was fighting a smile, "I know."

I didn't know how to respond to that so I didn't. I could hear the distant tinkling of glasses, the bass of the music. And I was here, caged, in a room with a sofa bed that was all made up and I was alone with the Beautiful Biker who saved my face from a drug-addict with a knife. He was just staring at me, intensely. Not moving away, not moving in. Those tiger eyes just kept roving my face.

"Why do you keep pretending to be my boyfriend, Deacon?"

He closed his eyes for a second and let out a breath. He looked like he was warring with something.

And then he said, "Maybe I'm thinkin' that's what I'd like to be."

I watched his lips form those words and my heart tripped over itself.

Holy shit.

He kept going, "Maybe I've been thinking about it non-stop since you looked at my mouth 2 days ago just like you're doin' right now," he said, huskily.

"Now I've got a question for you," he said.

I just stared.

"How come, Kitten, every eye in this place is on you, watching you, but you look at me like I'm the only man in the world?"

My heart started to race. There was a click and the door started to open against my back. Deacon pushed on it so whoever was on the other side couldn't get in.

His gaze was heated.

I was chewing my lip, my eyes traveling over his gorgeous sculpted face and area his almost half opened shirt revealed.

"Deacon?" We heard a guy call in and there was pounding on the door.

"Sorry," he said to me as he pulled me away from the door by my wrist and opened it just a little, "Gimme a minute, man." He still had my wrist.

"Know you're in there with a chick and sorry man, but need your help. It's urgent."

"Fuck. Okay. Two seconds." He shut the door and looked at my mouth. His hand let go of my wrist but his fingers laced with my fingers. Tingles crawled up my spine.

"I'll be back. I'm takin' you home."

I shook my head, "I'm supposed to stay at Jenna's."

He shook his head, "I'll drive you there. They stayin' till close?"

"Most likely."

"I'll be back for you. Wait for me." He let go of my hand but caught me by the waist and we left the supply room and headed back into the noisy bar. Dad's band was getting geared up to go again. Jenna, Rider, and Spencer were all by the bar and two other younger bikers were with them. One of them was blond and kind of cute. The other was a big red-headed guy, around my age, but he had to be close to seven feet tall. He already had a huge biker gut and long beard but he had a baby face. They both looked at Deacon and me and smiled. Rider whispered something to Jenna and she giggled. Deacon leaned over and said something to Rider. He nodded.

"Scoot, Bronto, this is Ella. No one bothers her. I'll be back for her."

"Ella!" Bronto was the big guy and he reached out and engulfed me in a big hug. He transformed from scary biker guy to big teddy bear.

"Scooter," The blond cutie biker shook my hand. I was still in the teddy bear's embrace, "Well, it's Scott, actually, but Scoot or Scooter works. This here's Ted. But we call him Brontosaurus. Or Bronto. We're prospects with The Dominion Brotherhood and it looks like Deacon has assigned us with Ella duty."

I giggled, "You poor thing. I tend to be a handful after a couple of those," I gestured to the shot glass in front of Spencer.

Spencer rolled his eyes and took a swig of his beer and then downed a shot that was in front of him. He didn't look pleased at all. But then he said, "Well then let's get you shift-faced," with a sneer.

Jenna was very cozy with Rider. Pippa had gone over to the dart board with Joe but they were on their way back toward us.

I was thinking about the fact that I'd just nearly gotten kissed by Deacon. My nipples and lips were all tingly.

"Let's grab a table," Spencer said, downing another shot, and we all moved to a big table.

"We'll need more drinks," Spencer then said, "What're ya drinking, Ella?"

"Rum and coke. Thanks," I said, "'Cuz this place has no Pepsi."

"Rum and Pepsi doesn't sound right," Pippa said.

"But it tastes way better," I informed her.

"Get a round in, Scoot." Spencer said, throwing a few twenties at Scott and pulled out a chair for me to sit down. I sat. He winked.

Rider shot him a dirty look.

Spencer ignored that and sat beside me, leaned over, throwing his arm around me, and said, "You like my brother, Deacon?"

I shuffled uneasily, "We've just recently met but yeah, I like him so far."

He nodded cockily, "Alright, well when he's through with you, I'll be waiting." He ran the back of his thumb over my bare shoulder. I winced.

"Spence…" Rider muttered, "Stop."

Jenna gave me a pointed look. I'm sure I looked flipped out or something.

Spencer ignored Rider and continued, "Our big bro isn't real big on commitment. You look like a nice girl. Your friends over here said you got all sex kitten'd up for tonight but that you're usually a nice girl so I'm just laying it on the line. Deacon is a dawg. Me? I'm in the market for something a little longer-term than he is and I have no problem with my brother's leftovers so long as they're nice girls—-"

"Spence, quit!" Rider clipped, "Pay no mind, Ella. Add alcohol to Spencer and it's instant asshole."

I was a little flabbergasted. Scott returned with a tray of drinks so I took a big sip of mine.

Dad's band started playing again. I sat quietly, watching the show, sort of stuck in my head, thinking about Deacon.

Was all that in the office just a line to get me to have sex? Was that all he wanted? Sex with me in a supply room on a sofa bed? Did he feel like I owed him that because he saved me the night before, maybe? Was I gonna be expected to pay back his kindness in flesh?

Someone brought me another drink before I was barely into the one in my hand. I decided to catch up and get my mind off the track it was on. I was empty before anyone else was. So I got up and went to buy a round and Scott and Bronto followed me and then they wouldn't let me pay. Scott carried the tray back to the table. I drank that drink. And then another. And then I did two shots with Scott and Bronto, busting a gut laughing along at their jokes. They were good guys.

Conversation happened around me as Spencer and Scott joked about some party that they'd been at the night before, talking about how some girl got hammered and threw up all over the place. Jenna and Rider started making out hot and heavy. Dad's band started playing Journey's Open Arms so then Pippa and Joe plus Rider and Jenna got up to slow dance.

Pippa and Joe had been dating for two years, other than a six-month break, and they had plans in two months to move in together. They sang to one another and held each other and I was smiling watching them, seeing how much they loved one another.

Pippa was a bit drunk but Joe was completely sober. He'd stopped drinking when he got really drunk last summer and clocked Pippa in the face. He had apparently blacked out and remembered nothing. Pippa's brother had put Joe in the hospital. Broke his jaw.

Joe gave up the booze and begged her for another chance. She wasn't too quick to give him that chance; he had to work for it. Pippa finally forgave Joe after he'd been six months clean and they'd been going strong ever since.

Spencer put his arm around my chair again and talked loudly over the music, right in my ear, "I'm sorry if you think that was an asshole thing of me to say, earlier, Ella. I just don't wanna see my brother hurt another nice girl. There've been too many already."

I winced. Spencer was very hammered.

"That's okay." I moved my chair a few inches away. I saw Bronto and Scott exchange uncomfortable glances.

Spencer continued, trying to gain volume over Dad's singing, "It's just that he's either a dirty dawg or he's a psycho. He gets possessive, jealous. One or the other. Either he's in it just for a quick dip or he's possessive as hell. So, girls have no chance. Nooooo chance. You get caught in his web and you're either eaten for breakfast by a big bad wolf spider or you're in prison."

"Hey Spence?" Scott moved from the other side of the table to us, "Wanna get your ass handed to you over a game of pool?" Scott was attempting to do damage control.

It had to be awkward. Deacon asks them to make sure no one bothers me and they have to save me from Deacon's smashed drunk brother talking smack and throwing him under the bus.

"Naw man, I'm havin' a conversation here, Scoot. So why don't you just...scoot!" Spence said and then his index finger traced my large hoop earring.

"I think I'm just gonna go home," I said, feeling sour. I got to my feet.

"Deacon said you were waitin' for him," Scott said, "Texted two minutes ago and said he was on his way back."

"I'm getting a headache. I'm just gonna go home." I looked out at the dance floor. Jenna and Rider were making out. Pippa and Joe were making out, too. This song...

I felt a little bit choked up.

Dad was in the middle of a set and my car was at Jenna's. Jenna had given me eighty bucks so I could come out and not mooch so I guess I could pay for a cab since no one had let me pay for any drinks tonight. But I didn't really like the idea of waiting for a cab here. Maybe I'd just head over to the cab office. It was just a few blocks away.

I grabbed my purse.

"Hey? Where ya goin'?" Spencer asked, standing up and getting in front of me.

"Home."

"Awe, man. Was it what I said? 'Cuz I didn't know you were that sweet on him, babe. He's just bad news for a girl like you so I had to warn ya."

"Excuse me." I squeezed around him.

"I had to warn her," Spencer was telling everyone but no one was paying attention. Scooter-Scott and Bronto were looking at me.

"Ella, if you have to go, I'll take you home," Bronto said, "I've only had a few drinks. I'm good."

Scooter-Scott grabbed his phone from the table and started thumbing at it.

"It's okay."

"Serious. Deacon would have my balls if I let you go out into the night all alone."

"Sorry, Bronto. I'm sure you're more teddy bear than T-Rex but I also don't know you. I'm not in the habit of taking rides from people I don't know. No offense."

"Shit," he muttered but nodded. His facial expression was reasonable. He knew that what I said made sense.

I'd had four rum and cokes and had drank three drinks at Jenna's before we got there plus a few shots and I was feeling absolutely no pain.

I waved at my Dad as I exited, putting my purse on, cross body. He smiled and waved, without missing a beat.

He probably thought I was sober and had my car or at least a ride. I was usually a responsible person, I was the epitome of responsible, so he had no call to be concerned. I got outside and there were a bunch of guys congregating, smoking cigarettes outside the front door. Most of them were bikers.

"Aren't you a sweet little thing?" An arm hooked around my waist.

It was a tall biker with a long beard and a man bun. He wasn't that much older than me.

Ugh.

"Excuse me," I pulled out of his grasp.

Someone said, "Rob from the band's daughter."

Someone else called out, "And Deacon staked his claim, man. Don't."

"Where ya goin'?" I heard a sort of familiar deep voice call out. It was Deacon's dad. He'd been in with the group of bikers smoking and was now emerging from the crowd, which parted for him.

"Hey Deke. Just goin' home," I waved him off.

"Hold up." He put his cigarette out in a planter filled with sand by the door.

"Where's that sweet ride, Betty?" Deke looked very much the MC president, wearing a leather Dominion Brotherhood vest with his jeans and motorcycle boots.

"Oh, it's at my friend's. I left it at her house. Let my hair down tonight." I flipped my hair with my hands. Not flirtily. I did it like it'd been a waste that I was sorely disappointed with.

"So, how're ya getting home? Your friends are still inside." Deke looked concerned.

"I'm good. No worries." I started to walk faster.

Deke caught my elbow, "Hey, hold up, Ella."

I stopped and let out an exasperated sound. The fresh air was doing my head in. I was way drunker than I'd realized. And my feet were killing me. And Deacon's dad had gone from his usual playful manner toward me to the far-more-serious father-figure demeanor.

"Word's travelin' that Deacon says you're his. And sure as shit he wouldn't want his woman shitfaced, all dolled up, and walkin' home alone in the dark."

I waved my hand, "Oh, I'm not his woman. It was just pretend, and I'm only goin' a few blocks."

"Pretend? That doesn't sound like my son."

I waved my hand, "Bah! He just said it to the tweaker at the gas station so he wouldn't carve a Nazi symbol into my face. And then...what was it? Oh! Then he said it again to my ex-boyfriend because he won't leave me alone. Guy can't take a hint. But I don't know how Deacon picked up on that." I shrugged, "And then one more time when your other son tried to flirt with me. Not the long-haired one. He's with my friend. The short-haired one that has the beautiful tiger eyes like Deacon. And you. You have those eyes, too, did you know that? Course you knew that. Duh."

Deke smiled.

"But yeah… it's just pretend. 'Cuz apparently he's a dirty dawg who prolly changes women like underwear, so yeah. Betty don't play dat." I giggled, "I'm goin' home. G'night, Deke. Boop boop be doop." I pointed my index fingers like guns at him and then giggled at myself and went to leave but he caught my elbow again.

"Just a sec, little lady."

I let out an exasperated sigh, "What now?"

"First, you're Rob's little girl so I can't let you go off in the middle of the night on your own like this. Second, my son's staked a claim with you that ain't pretend, you got it in your head that it's a game but I know my boy. Deacon doesn't play those games. Third, I'd be a pretty shitty fuckin' human being to let a pretty young girl or any female for that matter head out into the night on foot when she's shitfaced. Let me get you a lift."

"No, no. I'm good. Honestly. The dinosaur guy offered but I don't get in cars with strangers. I can walk."

"You're not walkin'. And it won't be a stranger. You're among friends."

The sound of motorcycle pipes drowned out the sound of Dad's band. The motorcycle pulled up to a parking spot pretty close by the door. Deacon.

Ho boy. He was hot on that bike!

"Man, he looks hawwwwt on that bike," I told Deke. He gave me a big smile. He thinks I'm funny.

Deacon climbed off, removed a helmet, and his eyes moved from the crowd over by the door to me and his Dad, about fifty feet away, very clearly in a little bit of a stand-off that had a captive audience.

He was coming over. And his face looked hard, pissed off.

"What's up?" he asked us both.

"Betty Boop over here is tryin' to walk home. I'm trying, yet failing, to convince her that it ain't happenin'. Good you're here, son, because I was about to haul her over my shoulder back inside since she's full 'o sass but I'm thinkin' that's a job you'd rather have."

Deacon frowned at me and folded his arms over his chest.

"Where you goin'?" Deacon asked me.

"Home," I grumpily replied, folding my arms just like him.

"You're smashed."

"So smashed!" I agreed, "But not so smashed to fall for the line of a dirty dirty dawg." I wagged my finger at him like the naughty bad dawg he was.

He looked at me like I was from outer space, "What?"

"I'm goin' home. Bye all!" I waved at the crowd of bikers behind us. I heard laughing.

I started to walk off. He was suddenly in front of me and his hands were on my shoulders.

"What's the problem? Did someone piss you off, harass you?"

"I'm just bein' proactive. Protecting my heart," I moved past him and started walking faster. Not much faster, though, because stupid shoes!

"Slow down, Kitten. Tell me what happened."

"Nothing happened. I'm just not sticking around for no good reason." God, I loved that he was calling me Kitten again. But I couldn't love that. He probably had a whole litter of kittens on the side.

"No good reason? I asked you to wait for me. What about that says 'no good reason'?" He caught my elbow and made me stop.

"Hmpf! Yep, I'm not gonna be the runt of your litter, that's for sure. These stupid shoes!" These shoes had to go if I was gonna get past him.

I leaned down and unbuckled the strap on one and kicked it off. It went flying across the parking lot pretty far away and it landed on the windshield of my Dad's pickup truck. Phew. It could've landed on someone's motorcycle!

"Phew. That was close."

I leaned down and unbuckled the other shoe and then gave a big kick and the shoe sailed through the sky and landed in the bed of Dad's pickup truck.

"Score!" I jumped up and punched the sky, "Shoe shot put champion of the world. Wooooo!"

I looked behind me because there was laughing coming from the smoking area.

"It's okay! It's my Dad's truck! Hey Deke!" I yelled, bending over, as if that'd help my voice carry further.

"Yeah?" He was amused. I was amusing. I'm amusing when I'm drunk. I giggled, pleased with myself.

"Will you ask my Daddy to take care a those for me?"

"Sure thing, Boop," he said and gave me a salute.

"What the fuck are you doin'?" Deacon asked me. Unlike the rest of the people in the parking lot, he was not amused.

"Is your name after your Dad? Is Deacon short? I mean, you're not short, you're tall. I mean, is Deke short for Deacon?"

"Yeah."

"You don't seem like a Deke. You seem like a Deacon."

He shook his head, a little bit amused, "That's 'cuz I *am* a Deacon."

"Did you know a Deacon is an ordained minister of some sort?"

He nodded, "So I've heard."

"You're not *that* kinda Deacon. A minister. You're reportedly a dirty dawg."

His eyes narrowed, "Excuse me?"

"I'm not that kinda girl, Deacon. Even if you're beautiful and big and strong and heroic. And fucking beautiful with the longest eyelashes I've ever seen on a man," I leaned forward and put my hand on his chest, "Yeah, I know I said beautiful twice. It bears repeating. For a minute there I thought maybe, yeah, I could do just a fuck because maybe you'd be the first guy to actually find my clit. But... then I thought...oh fuck. Did I say that out loud?"

I leaned closer to him as I asked this. His chest was rock hard. Yum.

"Yum," I said and dug my nails into his chest a little, looking at my hand.

He was looking at me with an astounded look on his face.

I heard more laughing. Maybe I was louder than I thought I'd been.

"Shhh, Elizabelle!" I admonished myself out loud, making a loud shhh sound with my index finger against my lips.

"Get over here." He grabbed my hand and we were walking further away from the building and the crowd.

As we were walking, to whereabouts unknown, I kept talking.

"You're walkin' too fast. I've got no shoes on. But you should know that I thought about it for half a second and thought, so what? People have casual sex all the time. I should just have some fun. Right? I've had casual sex before. Why is it bothering me so much that you're just after one thing? But you know what? I can't do this."

He glared at me. We stopped in the far corner of the parking lot for the bike shop and garage instead of the bar, which was next door to the garage. We were in front of that big GMC Sierra.

"Ouch. I shouldn't have took my shoes off. Shouldn't have worn heels. Really, shouldn't have even come out tonight."

"Can't do what?" he asked impatiently.

"What?" I asked.

"You said *I can't do this.* Can't do what?"

"Oh. Can't do a casual fuck with you. Because one look at you and I knew that if you gave me the time of day, I'd prolly fall and if you turned out to be a dawg and didn't catch me, I'd go splat." I smacked one palm against the other, "Splat would go my heart. I don't like the sound of that. So, uh, sorry. I'll just tell ya now, don't waste your time on me because I can't put my heart on the line like that. Not with you. Can't be a no-strings bed buddy. I'm sure Paige is still in there and she is a total biker bitch. She'd be happy to go for a ride, if ya know what I mean." I nodded at my own sage advice.

The truck beeped and Deacon opened the passenger door.

I was standing there looking at the door feeling that horrible feeling you feel when you're smashed drunk and have no filter but are suddenly acutely aware of all the verbal diarrhea that's just come out of your mouth.

Oh shit. Ella? I chastised myself. Shit. What a dummy.

"Get in," he ordered.

"What? Why?"

"I'm driving you home."

"No. You don't have to."

"You're not walking home in the fuckin' dark, pissed drunk, with no goddamn shoes on, Ella. Get in the truck."

"I'll just take my big stupid filter-less mouth back inside and find my friends."

"Get in the truck now, Ella."

"You're mad at me."

But I really like it when he says my name. Almost as much as when he calls me Kitten.

He rolled his eyes. His beautiful tiger's eyes.

I am SUCH a dummy.

"Sorry for callin' you out. I just have a zero bullshit filter when I'm drunk. So yeah. You don't have to drive me home. You can go in there and..."

"You're not walkin' home."

"Okay, I'll go talk to Joe, Pip—-"

"Get in the fuckin' truck!" He was pissed.

I glared at him and put my hand to my waist, "Uh, I don't know who you think you're talking to, but..."

He put me in the truck. He lifted me up by the waist, making me squeal, put me in the truck and buckled my seatbelt.

He slammed the door. I was hyperventilating.

He rounded the truck and got in.

"Hey! What're you doing?"

He started the truck.

The truck squealed as we spun around and drove up to the door. Deacon hit the button to make the window roll down. Scott was outside with the crowd of smokers.

"Scoot, tell her friends I've got her."

Scooter gave him a nod and put his cigarette out. I saw Deacon's dad smiling big, standing by the door.

"Who told you I was a dawg, Ella? Spencer?" Deacon was pulling out onto the street.

"I ain't sayin'. I don't wanna start trouble between brothers."

He rolled his eyes, "Fuckin' Spence."

Oops. I guess I gave it away.

I was feeling regret. Regret at my big fat mouth. And I was feeling sleepy. I hadn't slept great last night, barely ate anything that day, and drank way more than usual. I yawned and shivered.

I FELT FINGERS TUCK my hair behind my ear. I guess I'd fallen asleep.

"Hi," I sat up straighter. We were in my driveway already.

I leaned into the hand. It was holding onto the part of the seatbelt that came out of the car.

He let go and cupped my jaw and his thumb stroked across my cheekbone. It felt nice.

"Wake up, Kitten."

"That feels nice."

"Yeah?"

"Isn't my hair soft?" I asked sleepily, "This oil Jenna put in is the bomb."

"Yeah, it is. C'mon. Up." His voice didn't sound mad anymore.

"I'm home," I muttered.

"Yeah, let's go." Then after a minute I felt the air on my face. He was lifting me out of the seat and carrying me toward my door. I snuggled in. He smelled good.

He was strong, too. I put my arms around his neck and could feel the muscles everywhere.

"Yum." I said.

"Where's your keys?"

"Door's prolly open," I mumbled.

I felt like I was floating as he carried me to the back of the house.

"That your bedroom up there?"

"Mm hm."

"Just your room?"

"All mine." I yawned.

"Tell me that door up there's locked."

"Yup. It is. I have a key to that door. But I don't think I can walk those steps. I drank a little bit too much. Too steep and bendy. I can go in the other door. Hey, this is three days in a row you came to my house with me."

"Find me the key, Kitten." He started to climb the iron staircase that led right to my room.

Oh wow. Was I gonna have a bad boy biker in my room? Wahoo! Wait. What?

"You should just take me to the kitchen breezeway door. Mom'll have left the door unlocked for Dad and I can just go upstairs."

"We're here. The key?"

I fumbled with the front zip of my purse, which, thankfully was across my body or I'd have lost it somewhere. I passed the keys to Deacon.

"There are a dozen keys on this thing."

"Betty Boop key," I snuggled in, "Beside the key to The Shitbox." I heard keys jingling. It was dark. He probably couldn't make out the keys.

I heard the door open. He figured it out. He figured it out in the dark with me in his arms.

"My hero," I think I said it aloud.

The door shut and a minute later I was falling. He dropped me on my bed. It was actually kind of not so gentle. I say, "heyyyy" as I bounced.

A light was flicked on. He dropped the keys on my desk and glared at me.

"Lock the door, Ella. It wasn't locked."

"Yep," I grumbled.

"Lock this fuckin' door, Ella!" His voice was angry.

"Okaaay! Such a growly tiger. Rrr." I growled back at him but I didn't move. He was mad at me. I didn't care. Might as well be mad at him, too. I just wanted to sleep. So I climbed under the blanket and turned my back to him.

3

I had the MOTHER of all hangovers. And I deserved it. I made a total ass of myself the night before. When I got my eyes open I had two thoughts that overshadowed the flashbacks of the night before. Well, two thoughts beyond the fact that I was never ever drinking again. (Oh, I know; that's what they always say. But we always mean it, don't we?)

Those two thoughts were my primary directive at the moment:

1. Advil.
2. Gatorade.

The shame could wash over me after I got this nasty-ass taste out of my mouth. I had a little mini Coke fridge under my desk that was big enough to hold a dozen drinks. It'd been a joke gift from Jenna because I was a staunch Pepsi drinker. I hoped there would be a Gatorade in it. There was. Hallelujah. But I had zero Advil in my medicine cabinet. I caught a glimpse of my reflection and my hair still looked fantastic. That flat iron was a miracle worker! But my smoky eyes? Yikes! Rocky Raccoon.

I felt like garbage. I got a make-up removal moist towelette and swiped my eyes as I made my way down to the main floor, every step painful, still in the clothes I wore last night.

My Dad was in the kitchen, frying bacon.

"Good morning Beautiful Bella Ella! How's your head?" He said this all real loudly in my ear.

"Ow. Not nice." I opened the kitchen cupboard where my Mom kept medicine. She didn't like prescriptions much, was big on herbal remedies, but usually kept Advil in the house. There weren't any. Only children's Advil. I looked at the label and saw they were 100mg cherry chewables. I popped four and chewed them and then wiped my other eye with the make-up wipe and tossed it in the trash.

Beau galloped into the kitchen, his blond-green hair all spiked up with gel. He was dressed and ready to take on the day.

"Hey baby bro," I muttered and took a big swig of Gatorade.

"Morning! Ten bacons for me, Dad. You missed a bunch of black stuff on yer face, Lella."

"Aye aye, Captain," my father saluted him and returned to the bacon.

"So...we've got a bit of ground to cover, baby belle."

I grabbed a paper towel square from the roll, wet it and winced, "I think I need to sleep it off a bit longer first, Dad." I went back to wiping my eyes. Beau was right. How on earth did I still have this much make-up on my face?

Dad flipped some bacon and put the tongs down on a spoon rest and looked at me with a serious look on his face.

"Elizabelle," Dad said.

Beau left the room, calling for Mom, "Lella's in trouble, Mom!"

Uh oh. Dad didn't give me that expression too often and didn't call me Elizabelle too often and Beau, at his tender age, already knew how to read that from Dad.

"Dad, can I just go get a few hours' sleep first?" My voice was kind of whiney.

"Okay, but after you do, we should chat about how you were held at knifepoint and didn't think to tell your Mother or me about it." Dad lifted the tongs and flipped some bacon over.

"I was just processing it. Word got around fast." I shrugged, "I would've told you."

"And I would've also said we needed to have a chat about Jay Smyth. I don't like how he's hasslin' you. You scraped him off weeks ago and the way he keeps sniffin' around makes my skin crawl. He's driven by the house slow-like a bunch and I don't like how he showed at the bar last night." He reached into the fridge and pulled out the milk.

I nodded, "I know."

"But since you're now exclusive with the third in command of the local chapter of the Dominion Brotherhood MC I'm now guessin' that Jay'll be a non-issue." Dad reached back into the fridge and pulled out a carton of eggs and put them on the counter.

I shook my head, "No. That's not true."

"No? Not what I hear."

"Do you disapprove of me dating a biker?" I asked, feeling myself getting very defensive.

"Not a bit. I quite like the idea of you datin' Deke's son."

"Well, I'm not dating him. It was just him trying to get Jay to back off for some weird reason and…well… I'm not."

"Well, baby doll, that's the thing. Actin' like I hear you acted at the roadhouse last night, you probably won't be."

I rolled my eyes.

"Guys in that life classify women in a few different ways, Elizabelle. There's the ones you have fun with, the ones you avoid, and the ones you settle down with. Last night you were actin' unlike yourself. First maybe you were one of the first, then from what I hear, you were definitely actin' like one of the second."

Who was this guy and what had he done with my laid back father?

Was I actually getting dating advice on how to snag a biker boyfriend? Was he seriously unhappy that I might've blown the chance at getting one?

"Am I in the Twilight Zone?" I asked him.

He shook his head, "That family had clout where they were from and they'll quickly have it here. You could do a lot worse. He's about to become next in line to become chapter prez. That's a profitable company they're building, too. They do custom bikes, sell a lotta Harleys and their garage is hoppin', too, already … even though they've only been in business here a few weeks. The way the Roadhouse is packing 'em in? And they're bikers, to be sure, but they aren't scum like the Jackals. And what I hear about Deacon—-"

"Maybe you'd be better to pick some aspirations for yourself rather than wanting to marry me off into a family with money, Dad."

He looked at me like he was sorely disappointed in me. I'd never seen my father look at me like that. My heart sank. I'd never talked to my Dad like that, either. So, evidently Drunk Ella was entertaining with zero filter but Hungover Ella? Hungover Ella was a bitch.

"I have no desire to marry you into a family for money, Elizabelle."

Fuck. Three Elizabelles in a row.

He kept going. "But it seems like he has his shit together and knowing you, I know that you'd settle for nothing less. His old man's proud of that boy and all he's accomplished so far. But I can't say it wouldn't help me sleep better at night bein' a father with my girl hooked to a guy who'd look after you, keep you safe."

I rolled my eyes. Dad wasn't done. His face took on a fierce expression after my eye roll.

"Like the kind of guy to pistol whip a junkie who'd put a fuckin' knife to your beautiful face. The kind of guy to get that creepy fuck to leave you be. The kinda guy to get you home safe when you were smashed drunk in the street barefoot and makin' a fool of yourself."

Ouch. I winced. All of that stung. Bad.

My Mom was now leaning in the doorway, witness to the lecture. Her eyes were on me and they looked disappointed, too.

Double uh-oh.

"I got drunk. I acted stupid. I don't do stuff like that all the time. Gimme a break. I'm usually the most responsible and boring 23-year-old in the world," I took another swig of my Gatorade.

Mom spoke up, "Elizabelle, and you also didn't tell your family that you had been at an armed robbery, held at knifepoint the day before you went out and acted unlike yourself so we're a little concerned and hoping that you aren't on a road to destruction after something bad happening to you."

I shook my head, "No, Momma. I'm okay. Honest. Right now I just have a hangover. I need to sleep."

Dad turned his back and started transferring bacon from the pan onto a plate lined with paper towel.

Mom hugged me as I went to pass her. I gave her a squeeze.

"I'm okay, Momma. I just drank too much and acted like an idiot in front of a hot guy. I'm sure I'm not the first."

"Are you dating Deacon Valentine?" she asked.

"I don't think he's the dating kind."

She smiled, "Don't be so quick to write him off."

I shrugged, "I'm gonna lie down. Sorry you guys are worrying about me but I'm cool. No worries, okay?"

She nodded.

"Okay, Daddy?" I called out.

Dad gave me a smile, "Have some bacon and eggs with us, then a nap. Perfect hangover cure other than hair 'o the dog."

I shook my head, "Naw. I need to just lay down. Maybe later. Except the hair of the dog thing. We'll call that one never. Sorry for bein' bitchy, Dad."

"I'll save you some bacon," he said with a chuckle, "If I can stop your brother from eating all of it."

"He really is eating far too many processed meats. So many sulfites," Mom muttered.

I nodded in agreement but was daydreaming about Deacon talking about saving *my* bacon.

I made my way back up to my room and grabbed my phone from my purse and opened my texts.

"You okay?"

that was Pippa.

I also had a text from Jenna.

"Call me! We NEED to talk about Deacon."

I replied to them both saying I was sleeping it off and would text later.

An earlier text was waiting from my boss at work asking if I could come in that day and cover the phones. The text had come through at 6:00 AM. It was now 12:10 pm.

I texted back, **"Hi Lloyd. Sorry, just got your msg. I'm not feeling well today. See you tomorrow. Hope you found someone else."**

A text came back saying, **"You're not on schedule tomorrow. Come by the office during business hours for your updated schedule."**

That was weird. I *was* on schedule for Monday and Tuesday, plus Thursday and Saturday when I'd last looked.

My boss was the sort who'd cut your hours if you didn't answer a text to come in to the office to cover for someone. It'd never happened to me before because I was Miss Responsibility. But I'd seen him to it to others, plenty. Shit.

I replied to say **"Ok"** and threw myself back on my bed.

I'd always been super-reliable. I regularly covered shifts at a moment's notice. More than once I'd stayed late and worked a double shift when someone hadn't shown up. The one time I don't answer a text immediately and he decides to cut my hours? Total jerk off.

I didn't fall back to sleep. I laid there wallowing with my headache and my regrets for a while.

I got another text.

"Hey Ella."

It wasn't someone in my contact list but the number was local.

>**"Who is this?"**
>**"Spencer Valentine."**

I bolted upright in bed.

"Hi"

What the heck? I waited a few minutes. Finally, another text dinged.

>**"Your friend Joe got me your number. I just wanted to apologize for being an asshole last night. I shouldn't have mouthed off about my brother. It was BS. Forget everything I said. If it makes you feel better, I'm paying for my assholery with a killer hangover. And a black eye & fat lip."**

I replied,

>**"Hangover over here too. Don't worry about it. Thanks for apologizing. Have a good day."**

Black eye? Fat lip?
He replied with

>**"605.555.7399. That's D's number if you want it. See ya around."**

I replied,
"Thx"
and then put my phone down.

I stared at the ceiling for about a year or two (or so it felt. It was probably more like 2 minutes) and then typed out a text to Deacon.

"Thank you for getting me home safely last night. Sorry for the drama. That's not me. I don't usually drink so much. I'm paying for it today. Anyway, thanks. This is Ella, btw. In case you drove any other shoeless drunk girls home last night. LOL. Spencer gave me your #"

I hit send and saved him in my contacts under *Beautiful Biker*.
I stared at my phone's home screen for a few minutes.
He didn't text back.

I went down to the second floor and took a shower (my shower was broken. Another thing on Dad's long to-fix list) and when I climbed back up the stairs I could faintly hear Gangnam Style playing from my bed. As I was drying off I heard a text alert so bolted for the bed. It wasn't a text from Deacon. It was a text from Jenna stating that my car was on its way. She'd called twice.

That was odd. I had my keys. I lifted at my keychain. My car key ring was missing.

"Where's my car?" I called Jenna and said this before she even got the word Hello all the way out of her mouth.

"Duuuude. Where's my car? Haha. Well, hello to you, too, bitch."

"Sorry, Jen. Feelin' rough. I blame you and Pip. My car?"

"Isn't it always my fault when you have a hangover? Haha. Deacon picked it up. Rider and Joe followed him there with Joe's car and Deacon's bike. Rider spent the night, Ella. Oh. My. God. Omigod! I think I'm a little bit in love. I think I've met the father of my future children."

I looked out the front window. My car was being backed into the driveway. I moved to the side window, Deacon was getting out of the driver's seat, shutting the door, and he was talking to my Dad. Rider got off a motorcycle and shook hands with Dad and then clapped Deacon on the shoulder and then he got into Joe's car, which was out on the street.

Holy shit.

"But listen, Ella, I need to talk to you about D—-"

"Oh. That's good. Listen, I'll call you back," I cut her off and hung up distractedly without giving Jenna a chance to say anything else.

I watched Joe's car pull away.

Dad and Deacon talked for a moment and then Deacon followed Dad into the garage. I ran into the bathroom and looked in the mirror. My hair was wet, wild, and curly; I was in a towel. I quickly changed into a pair of button fly jean shorts and a black tank top and tied my hair back into a sloppy high bun. I heard motorcycle pipes. Shit. Was that him leaving or someone else arriving? I threw on sunglasses and then swished mouthwash while getting into a pair of flip flops hurriedly. I spit it out and then unlocked and dashed out my bedroom door that led to the back stairs and then trotted down to the driveway.

The motorcycle was gone.

I stepped into the garage. Dad was loading his bong. Alone.

"Hi Dad."

"Oh hey, baby doll. There's your car key." He pointed to the table where my key sat.

I picked it up and looked around.

"You missed Deacon," Dad said, lighting up.

"Oh. Did he ask for me?"

Maybe Dad told him I was still sleeping it off.

"Nope," Dad said on his exhale, eyes active, watching for my reaction.

I tried not to let my expression drop.

"Okay." I didn't make eye contact, even though my sunglasses probably hid my disappointment. I headed back up to my room and checked my phone.

Nope, no return text. I compared the number against the number Spencer had sent me. I hadn't sent the text to the wrong number.

Okay then. Nice enough to return my car to me, obviously having planned to do so when he slipped my key off my keyring last night, but clearly too pissed off to speak to me or answer my text. Weird.

Why would he care to bring my car to me? I'd made an ass of myself. *I* wouldn't have brought my car to me.

I saw my keys on my desk so moved over, ready to add my car key back to my key ring.

That's when I noticed that my Betty Boop key was missing. I had a stupid amount of keys so I had them separated by smaller rings. I had the 2 main floor keys for the house on one ring. Dad's man cave key and the spare key to his truck on another, a ring with a key for the cab office, and another ring with the key to Jenna's salon and her apartment. Everyone wanted me to have copies of their keys. Why? Probably because I was the most responsible person everyone knew. Just the week before I turned down copies of keys to the local animal shelter because my key ring was getting so freaking heavy.

I kept my car key and my bedroom Betty Boop key on the same ring. The car key was returned not on its usual ring and the Betty Boop key was nowhere in sight.

What on earth was Deacon doing with my room key? Maybe he took it off to lock the door on his way out and forgot to give it back.

His voice "Lock the door, Ella," rang in my ears. He'd said that the night before. Did he take the key to lock up because I was passed out?

The idea of him having a key to my room gave me a bit of a thrill. Okay, more than a bit. But he wasn't returning my calls so maybe he just forgot he had it. Or maybe he lost it. But he would've had to have taken the car key off the ring with the Betty key to give it to my Dad on its own like this. I twirled my keys, lost in thought. *Hmm.*

GANGNAM STYLE BLASTED twice that afternoon and I ignored it both times with a glare at the phone and then I didn't answer another text from Jenna that said to call her.

I also got a text from Jay that said,
"I need to talk to you. Can we meet for coffee?"
Blah.

Fuck off, everyone, and let me die of my alcohol poisoning and mortification in peace!

I CAMPED OUT IN MY room all day, alone with my mortification. Mom came up with some herbal tea and told me she, Dad, and Beau were going to a *movies in the park* thing where you brought blankets and they played on the side of a whitewashed building. I usually went to those things, often volunteered at the popcorn and drink stand for them, but I said I felt like a quiet day in. I closed all the blinds and put my TV on and napped and then watched a few episodes of Outlander, perving on Sam Heughan, and then around 8:00 at night, I wandered downstairs and made a bacon and tomato sandwich with warmed-up leftover bacon. My family was all still out.

I texted Deacon,

"It's Ella again. Thank you for bringing my car over. Do you have my room key, btw?"

He didn't answer me. After eating, I crashed early.

I WAS DREAMING THAT Deacon's face was beside me, on one of my pillows.

I smiled, "Hi."

He wasn't smiling.

Uh... wait.

I wasn't dreaming.

I was awake. He was in my room. In my room! He was in my bed with me. Me!

(Am I adequately conveying my shock? I doubt it.)

He was on top of the covers, laying on his back, his head on my favorite frilled Betty Boop pillow, one knee cocked, his wrist casually resting on that knee and holding my remote, flicking through channels on my muted TV. I sat up, gasping, heart racing. My clock radio said it was 12:46 AM.

He hit the *off* button on the TV remote, put the remote down, and put his hands behind his head, a serious look on his face. My twinkle lights were on, adding a soft glow to the room.

"What the fuck?" I breathed and my eyes traveled the length of him.

He held out my key. I opened my palm. He put it there. I stared at it, trying to clear the cobwebs from my brain.

I put it down beside me on my bedside table and my hands went into my hair. I still hadn't gathered my senses.

"You make it a habit to crash when you've lost the key to your room?" He looked a bit pissed.

He was right. I should've propped a chair up against the door or something.

"Uh…"

"I made a copy," he told me, fitting his hand back behind his head, "but you need a deadbolt and a chain."

I gawked, mouth open, "Why?"

"So you can keep out fuckwad perverts."

"And broody bikers?" I challenged.

His lips twitched. He was fighting a smile for a second but it didn't look like it was too difficult. It looked like his desire to be broody won out.

"Why did you make a copy?"

"So I can lock up after you pass out after getting sauced without keepin' yours," he said, matter-of-factly.

I wasn't planning on getting sauced and passing out like that again. And why would he expect to be there?

He continued, "Or, so I can get in. We're having a little chat right now and after the chat, you tell me whether you want it back or not. You want it back, it's yours."

He still looked pissed off.

"Why would you need to get in?" I asked.

He sat up and reached for me and then his hands were both holding my face. His nose touched the tip of my nose.

My heart stopped.

He tilted his head and then moved in for a kiss. His soft lips touched mine gently and then he backed away, still holding my face, watching me. I wanted more so I leaned forward and touched my lips to his and then went to lean back but he tightened his grip on my face and the kiss went crazy. Like, seriously hungry.

His mouth opened against mine and his tongue caressed my bottom lip and then it dipped inside as his fingers on one hand gripped the bunch of hair in the sloppy ponytail / bun. His lips were soft, strong, and he tasted good. *So* good.

God, I hoped I didn't taste bad.

I moaned and then both of my hands were flat against his chest. Man, his chest felt good.

This was the best kiss I'd ever had. He kissed me like he'd been dying to taste me. He kissed me like he had every right to. He held my face like I was precious and treasured, a precious treasured girl that he was going to fucking devour. *Holy shit.*

He was wearing a white long-sleeved t-shirt and dark button fly jeans with a black belt and big silver buckle, dark socks. His hair was loose, not in a ponytail or bun and I wanted to touch it. He was kissing me so it occurred to me that I *could* touch it!

I got both hands into it and then I climbed up, straddling him and his hands let go of my face and moved to my bottom. His hair was very soft. I tangled my fingers in and went for his mouth again. His face was a little scratchy and it felt fucking great.

He pulled me tight against his crotch and he was rock hard and that hardness was exactly where I wanted it. He pulled the elastic out of my hair a little bit roughly, making me gasp. He held the length of my hair in one hand while his lips and tongue ravished my throat. My head rolled back and my mouth was open as air rushed out of me. I felt the five o'clock shadow of stubble on his face as he nipped and kissed my neck and my earlobes and I let out another long breath and then kissed his eyebrow jewelry. That was when my top jean shorts button released and I was put on my back.

He was hovering over me and then he got up on his knees between my legs. His hand worked all subsequent buttons on my shorts undone in a flash and the other hand went up into my tank top, yanking my bra up so that he could cup one of my breasts. His thumb moved across my nipple and I let out a huff. I looked into his eyes and they were on fire. Even in the dimness of the room lit by just the TV and the twinkle lights that were wound around my headboard, I could see them and they were like amber molten lava.

He notched a brow and looked at me, like he was assessing my face, assessing whether or not he had permission to go further. I licked my lips and he obviously took that as an affirmative reply because then his mouth was on mine again.

He rolled over onto his side, propping his ear on his hand, his right hand diving into the undone jean shorts, into my panties, and he immediately found my clit. Holy fuck, did he *ever* find my clit! He didn't move past it. He stayed right there and then he started to work it. I made a squeaky noise kind of like an "Eee"

And then I went, "Oh" and my mouth stayed opened in that *o* as the sensations took over. He leaned right over my face while his hand worked inside my panties, multiple fingers gliding over that beautiful knot of nerves that had somehow managed to elude every other guy who visited the vicinity and then Deacon Valentine, Beautiful Biker, gave me a big smile. A big BIG totally *gorgeous* smile. The first big one he'd given me and I swear to God it was so amazing it took my breath. I thought before that he was the most beautiful man I'd laid eyes on and at that instant I decided I'd known nothing of the beauty he could show me until he'd shown me that smile.

I could fall hopelessly in love with that smile. He was seriously attractive and he was going to give me an orgasm. A ginormous one! I knew, right then, that my life was about to be permanently altered.

My back and neck both arched as he worked my clit, going round and round in tiny circles, while watching my face. I tried to roll into his body, so I could bury my face in his chest and just let the sensation take over, but he shook his head and the smile vanished, "Stay there," he commanded, "I need to watch you come." He stared into my eyes and took his hand out.

Him saying that was super-duper hot. But why did he take his hand out? Oh no! Why was he stopping?

He yanked my tank top and bra up high, leaving my boobs completely exposed, "Fuck, gorgeous," he muttered, eyes on my boobs, and then he yanked my shorts and panties down and off, "Spread wider for me, Kitten," he ordered and I was in such shock that I did not move a single muscle. I couldn't. I was paralyzed from the brain down.

He took both thighs and spread them himself, kneeling between my legs, and then he leaned forward and his fingers were back on the bullseye. He began going faster on my clit and then drove fingers inside, continuing to work my clit with his thumb, staring at my pussy intently, chewing that bottom pouty lip.

He leaned over and then his mouth closed in over my right nipple and he sucked, hard, continuing to work magic down below.

Completely pure magic.

Holy freaking crap! The combination of things: his fingers, his mouth, his eyes on me, me being naked (while he wasn't), spread-eagled, and fully exposed, and it being HIM...I started to come. Holy mackerel... an orgasm, *not* by myself!

He released my nipple and kept his fingers working, watching as I came so hard that my legs shook right through it. It was so fucking hot. It was the single hottest moment of my entire life having him watch me orgasm, a sexy look on his face as he took me there and then his lips were on mine again mid-climax as I shuddered and moaned right into his mouth.

I tried to close my legs. Too much. Too much sensation. But he didn't allow it. In fact, before I realized what he was doing, I felt very different sensations down there. His mouth moved down to my stomach, trailing kisses all the way, and then his mouth was there. THERE!

His mouth was on my clit while his fingers continued to thrust inside me over and over and over and then I hit another level of nirvana.

If it was possible to die from coming too hard, I was dangerously close to the blinding white light. I cried out loudly and then put both of my hands over my own mouth to drown out my noises. He got back up on his knees, pulling my bra and tank top down to cover my boobs. He got up, leaned over, and then shimmied my panties back up on me, tossing my shorts to the nightstand.

I was panting, trying to recover, shaking all over, and not sure if I might've felt a little bit mortified by reacting so much to all of that.

He moved my palms away from my mouth and then he kissed me passionately and then pulled the blanket up over me and sat on the edge of the bed and started pulling his boots on.

I was trying to catch my breath but I was starting to panic. He was leaving? Leaving? What the fuck?

He leaned over and kissed me on the mouth again, his hand cupping my jaw.

"No. Don't think that way."

He knew I was panicking. It must've been all over my face.

I shook my head, confused. I was about to ask questions about where he was going, about why he wasn't letting me take care of him, too. About to declare devotion to my dying day, surrounded by our great grandchildren...

"Can't stay the night with this bein' your parents place; I'd love to stay and hold you at least 'till you fall back to sleep but I've gotta run. Never planned to stay this long."

I stared, dumbfounded.

"Couldn't help it, though. That was your preview of things to come. Now you know that I can, in fact, find it."

I was wide-eyed. Oh, he found it alright! I don't know if it'll ever be the same!

He smirked arrogantly. But he had the right to be arrogant about "finding it". Holy moly.

"Pick you up tomorrow night at six. Take you for a ride, get something to eat. But two things."

I was all ears. My legs were still shaking and I was pretty sure my cookie was still having some sort of wild contractions, but I was all ears. I also couldn't speak so had no choice but to be all ears.

"One: pull a stunt like last night again and your ass'll be so red it'll be a long time before you sit down without feeling my hand."

"Uh...wh—-"

He leaned in real close to my face, "Two: I'm no dirty dawg. I don't fuck around when I'm exclusive with someone. I haven't had the desire to be exclusive in more than three years. Until now. With you. You want that with me?"

I was dumbfounded. I closed my mouth, which had still been open from when I'd tried to react to the *ass'll be red* comment.

"You want me, Ella?" he demanded to know.

I nodded, speechless, but very enthusiastically.

"Good." He gave me a quick peck on the lips, "You want the key back?" His index finger curved under my chin. He reached into his jeans pocket and held a key on a ring up, dangling it from his finger.

I shook my head vigorously. No way, Jose.

He gave me another big smile and then another kiss, this time longer and sweet. So damn sweet.

I melted. His hand was in my hair and his mouth had moved away but only an inch. I blinked at him, in a total daze.

"Good. That means you acknowledge right here, right now, that you're mine. Just mine. And no one fucks with what's mine. Never. They do, there are consequences. While you and I get to know each other, you hear something about me that I haven't yet shared, you talk to me about it. You don't jump to conclusions like last night, no matter what you hear. And chances are, you'll hear at least some shit before I get a chance to share so you talk to me about it. You don't bail. You talk to me. That's the deal. Can you deal?"

He stood up and shrugged on his leather Dom vest, which had been on the stool in front of my little brass vanity table.

"I think so."

"No, Kitten. Can you deal?" His expression was hard.

I nodded.

"Good. Go to sleep. See you tomorrow at six." He came back to me and kissed me hard on the mouth, slipping the tongue, and then he broke away and left via the fire escape door and I heard a key go in as he locked the door from the outside with his own key.

Aye Carumba!

His version of asking a girl to go steady was pretty dang spectacular.

4

I'd been deconstructing last night all morning while getting ready for my day and I didn't know if I was still coasting on the adrenaline of non-self-induced orgasms or not but my brain was going about a million miles a minute.

I was getting coffee, taking my little brother to the school bus stop at the end of our street since Mom had an early morning Namastwist class with a motley crew of about a dozen people, and then I was heading to the taxi office to find out what was what with my schedule.

I was thinking about Deacon. I was thinking that it was Monday morning and I had somehow found myself in a new and exclusive relationship with a beautiful biker that I'd only had a series of several sentences worth of conversations with since Thursday night and we hadn't even really talked much Thursday or Friday or Saturday, really.

And although he'd done most of the talking Sunday night, because I'd been sleep-dazed and then post-orgasm-speechless, I still knew pretty near nothing about him.

But I'd agreed to be in an exclusive relationship with him. He'd called me 'mine' and wow...the feelings that evoked? Yowza! I was still processing it.

I didn't know much. Not where he lived, how old he was, what he did for work...although I could guess he worked with his father. But I knew next to nothing.

What I *did* know was that the biker was beautiful, for sure, and that I somehow magically gained his interest.

Me.

Cutesy little Ella Forker.

How?

Why?

It was more than a little bit surreal.

I was also thinking that he'd given me a multiple-type orgasm last night that was so amazing that if I were artistic like the rest of my family, I could write songs about it. Now that I'd had a guy actually take me to orgasm, how could I ever go back to the sort of sex I'd had before. *How?*

And he was beautiful, for sure, but so far he'd been mostly serious, very serious. Broody, even. And I was also thinking that he was super bossy. He'd bossed me around. He'd stolen my keys, made his own copy of my bedroom key, and threatened to give me a spanking. And that'd freaked me out but made me tingle, too.

Okay, so I had secret erotic spanking fantasies so I wasn't totally against that idea but he didn't know I had those fantasies. I also didn't know if the spanking would be erotic in that it'd come with a happy ending. But I had decided I was making a rule. If I was getting a spanking it'd better come with a happy ending.

I wondered if I'd have the nerve to communicate that to him without being fueled with liquid courage. I tingled harder at the potential for kink but shook it off and tried to get my brain to stay on the logical train rails.

So yeah, he'd made a key but it wasn't like he'd kept that secret and he'd offered to return the key, so while making his own copy was forward of him to do, it wasn't like I didn't have a choice. And I suspected he took my keys to lock the door *and* bring my car to me, which was really kind of sweet.

And that beautiful smile he'd given me?

Oh.

My.

Good.

Gravy.

Tonight I had a date with him. Woot woot! But then again there was all the stuff his brother had said about the whole spider web thing and a girl either being eaten for breakfast or in prison. That was weird. A little scary, too.

But I'd spilled my guts with the whole embarrassing *heart going splat* conversation so he knew where I stood on that front. And he had given me that spectacular happy ending last night without getting one himself and I'd have been perfectly willing to give him one but he declined, probably to show he wasn't the dirty dawg his brother had painted him to be.

I was feeling a little bit apprehensive about all of this. What about me in those few brief meetings made Deacon Valentine want to be exclusive with someone, that someone being me, for the first time in three plus years? And should I pay attention to Spencer's warnings? Yeah, he'd taken them back but what about that saying?

In vino veritas.

But even more than the feeling of being apprehensive, I was feeling butterflies. Butterflies about the potential of a relationship with a hot and mysterious guy. Why shouldn't I see where this went? Yeah, it could land me in heartache but wasn't it worth taking the chance if there was a possibility that it could be a happily ever after instead of a bloody splattered mess? I spent all my time in Boring-ville but maybe that was my fault, too.

Here, I finally *finally* had a chance to take a detour off Boring street to go to somewhere potentially exciting. But was I too chicken to actually take it?

He had a great last name and he knew how to find the elusive *love button* as well as what to do with it. My father's list of reasons to date him was also a pretty good list. Brave, protective, together. Dad had said that the Doms weren't a scumbag MC but was everything as it seemed?

And alpha male sex was definitely my fantasy. But could I handle it if it were my reality? Fantasy and reality were very different. It felt safe staring at images of my fantasy on my phone screen under the blankets with my Lelo in hand. *That* was safe. I didn't need safe words or to worry about a thing when I was just fantasizing.

I got in my car and turned it on and something wasn't right. I quickly realized that beyond the fact that my seat had been adjusted to where my feet could no longer reach the pedals, my Betty Boop driver's side stuff was gone. The seat cover and steering wheel cover were both gone. So were my fuzzy pink dice. My passenger seat still had the cover on.

Oh. My dice were lying on the passenger seat. I grimaced.

I guess Deacon Valentine didn't wanna be seen driving with his beautiful hands and his fine ass on Betty Boop stuff.

I returned my dice to their rightful home over the rearview mirror and turned the ignition. My gas tank was reading as full. I gawked at the gage.

Maybe it *was* off kilter. I flicked the glass in front of the gage. The needle stayed put.

I'd be taking a chance driving it assuming it was full when it might not be. I didn't have AAA if I broke down and couldn't afford a tow truck. I grabbed my phone from my purse and stared at it for a minute, chewing my thumbnail. Finally, I hit the number assigned to Beautiful Biker.

It rang and my heart started to race.

"Hello?" he answered. He sounded sleepy. His voice sounded very sexy. VERY sexy.

"Um, hi."

"Hey, Kitten. It's fuckin' early."

It was. It was not quite 8:00 AM. But he didn't sound pissed off.

"Sorry to wake you up."

"It's alright. Gotta get to work anyhow. What's up? Get yourself in trouble again?" He made a growly sound as if he was stretching. I felt a little tingle. I wondered if he slept in the nude.

Oh wow.

I'd get to see Beautiful Biker Deacon Valentine naked at some point if this thing was really what it seemed like it was going to be. The little tingle turned into a big one.

"Kitten?" He took me out of my daydream.

I wondered what the Kitten nickname was all about, too. But I freaking loved it.

"I, uh, I was just wondering about my car. It says it's full but my gas gage might just be acting up so I didn't wanna just drive it too far in case..." I flicked the glass again.

"I filled it," he stopped me from rambling.

"Oh. You didn't have to do that."

It must've cost him at least $100 to fill the beast. I'd never ever filled The Shitbox so I didn't even know how much gas it even took. I only knew that I was constantly putting $10 or $20 in it or maybe $40 on payday but that didn't ever last too long.

"That's alright," he said with a little yawn.

"Well, thank you."

"You're welcome," he said.

"I'll pay you back on pay day. I get paid tomorrow."

"No you won't. It's just gas."

"Um, it was a lot of gas."

"You're not paying me back. Anything else, babe? Need to grab a shower."

"But Deacon..."

"Ella, I did it. Didn't want you to have to go back to that gas station so soon after what happened. You didn't ask me to do it. You're not paying me back."

Okay, then. I couldn't exactly argue with that logic and that was awfully sweet. So instead I said,

"Thank you, Deacon." I meant it.

There was dead air for a second and it felt weighty.

Finally, I broke the silence, "Um, did you take my Betty Boop stuff off?"

He chuckled and it was a pretty awesome sound.

"No way was I driving your ride with that shit. That shit oughta be illegal in a ride like that."

"That's what your Dad said to me."

"The man knows what he's talkin' about."

"But...did you throw it away?" My heart sank at the same time as butterflies flipped in my belly at his sexy laugh and the sound of smiles in his voice.

"Back seat."

"Oh." I smiled and looked over my shoulder. It was all there.

"Where're you off to?" he asked.

"I gotta go in to work to talk to the boss. I was supposed to work today but he said I'm not on schedule but to come see him. Hopefully I'm not getting fired. Then my day is free. I might pop into the nursing home to visit with my Gran. You?"

"Working 'till around five, five thirty."

"Where do you work?"

"The garage next to the bar. I'm a mechanic."

"Oh."

"I run it. Dad runs the bike shop and the bar. Rider works in the garage with me. Spence does sales for the bike dealership."

"Ah. You just have the two brothers?"

"Besides my MC brothers, yeah. And a sister. She's just turned 19, the youngest. She lives in Sioux Falls with our mother. Parents got divorced last year."

"Oh. How old are you?"

"28."

"I'm 23," I told him, "Even if I look sixteen."

"You do *not* look sixteen." He sounded a little disgusted.

I laughed.

He was quiet.

"Uh, do you wanna know where I work?" I asked.

"I already know where you work," he replied.

How did he know that?

"Oh. How'd you know that?"

"Cab company's around the corner from us. I've seen your ride parked there for the past few weeks."

"Oh. Not easy to blend in with The Shitbox."

"Shit box? *That* is no shit box."

"That's debatable."

"You're shitting me, right? Popped the hood and that car is mint. Drives like a fuckin' dream."

This time I was quiet. I guess he liked my car.

Finally, he broke the silence, "So I'm working, then I'm grabbin' another shower and picking up my girl for a ride on my bike around six and taking her for some food. Dress for the bike. Okay?"

My face split into a huge smile, "Okay."

His girl? Swoon.

"And then…" His voice went husky, "Maybe I'll be gettin' lucky. We'll see how the date goes."

"I think the odds are in your favor so far," I whispered, loving the husky tone in his voice. Loving it *a lot*.

He let out another little chuckle, "Good to have that to look forward to. But just sayin', if you decide that's a little too fast for you, I'm okay if we just chill out tonight. But I do plan to kiss you a lot."

"Good to know."

"And if you want to make sure last night wasn't just a fluke, I could show you I've got it in me to find it again..."

There was now a teasing tone in his voice.

I laughed. "Have a good day, Deacon."

"You, too, Kitten. Stay outta trouble."

"I'll try, Tiger. Bye."

He laughed again, "Bye."

I ended the call, put my phone down, and smiled huge. So huge, my face hurt.

I HAPPILY SANG AND car-danced all the way to the cab office. Katrina and the Waves' Walking on Sunshine came on the radio and I belted it out totally off-key and at the top of my lungs.

I passed the Valentine block, on purpose. Normally my route didn't take me by it. The garage, sandwiched between the bar and the dealership, was open and I could see people working. There were also half a dozen bikers standing outside in a circle, Deke being one of them, looking like he was leading some sort of pow wow. He waved as I passed. I waved back. Again, I couldn't exactly be incognito in The Shitbox.

I got into work and popped my head into the control room, where the switchboard and dispatcher desks were, and I waved at the dispatcher and order taker on my way to Lloyd's office.

But the order taker was Lloyd's wife, Debbie. Weird. And the phones looked like they were lit up like a Christmas tree. Either it was a busy day or Debbie was super-duper slow. Considering she didn't usually work the phones I'd bet it was the latter.

The schedule was posted on Lloyd's door and he only had me listed for Wednesday for 6 hours. I'd previously been scheduled Monday, Tuesday, and Thursday and my shifts were always 8 or more hours. What the heck? At least I wasn't fired but *really*?

He told me that the company was hurting and that everyone's hours had been cut. But his wife was listed on the days I'd previously been scheduled. He'd said she'd covered for me on Sunday and took to it like a natural. Sunday hadn't even been my shift so it was as if I was being punished for not covering Deanna, a single 20-something Mom of two kids, who was the one who was scheduled Sunday. I noticed Deanna wasn't on this week's schedule at all. I didn't ask if she'd been fired.

Debbie had never worked the phones before. She did payroll and occasionally helped Lloyd in the office, but now it looked like she had at least 30 hours on the phones this week.

I was *not* impressed. He told me that until business picked up I'd probably only get 1-2 days a week but that he'd appreciate it if I'd be on call in case they needed me. Yeah, right. And I'd bet money if I didn't come running at his call I'd lose even more hours. Ugh.

I knew the company wasn't doing great but it was also blatant nepotism at work here. I kept my cool and left the office and heard my text alert go off.

Beautiful Biker:

"Call me when you finish at work."

I called him from The Shitbox before I left the parking lot.

"Hey babe," he answered, "You done already?"

"Hi. Yep, I am."

"What happened?"

"Ack, my hours have been cut. I'm only working Wednesday this week. The company is in trouble. I'm gonna start looking for a new job."

"Sorry about that, Kitten," he said.

"Thanks. You get to work already?"

"Already? I live here. Come over."

"Yeah?"

"Yeah, I'd like a good morning kiss."

"Want me to stop and get coffees?"

"No, just come over. We have coffee here."

"Decent coffee?" I pressed.

"Yeah, it's good. You a coffee snob?"

"Little bit."

"I think it's good. And if not, the kiss'll make up for it."

"I've been kissed by you so I believe you. Be there in two minutes."

"Good," I could hear a smile through the phone, "See ya in a few."

When I walked up to the garage, which was between the bar and the bike dealership, the two big bay doors were open, and he was walking toward me, wearing blue coveralls but the sleeves were tied around his waist. The parking lot no longer crawled with bikers. He wore a white wife beater and had his hair in a ponytail at his nape, a navy blue baseball cap on backwards. He came toward me, wiping his hands on a red bandana, looking like he was almost strutting the runway of a Magic Mike show.

Holy hotness!

His brother Rider came out, too, sporting a low man bun and coveralls, but his were way dirtier and completely on. Rider also had motor grease of some sort on his cheek.

Spencer was standing there, too, dressed in jeans and motorcycle boots but with a green button-down shirt, opened half way down, showing off his tatted chest and a few leather necklaces. Spencer's face was a little bit sour. He had a black eye and a slightly fat lip. Oh yikes. He wasn't kidding. Did Deacon hit him?

Even with the bruises, Spencer looked good. All three Valentine boys were beautiful bikers and certainly had good genes. Deke was handsome, for sure, and looking at these boys I'd bet their mother was a knockout, too.

Deacon approached me and when he got to me he dipped and grabbed me by the hips and lifted me and planted a big and beautiful wet one on me. My hands went right around his neck and I bent one leg and my flip flop fell off. I went for the gusto.

"Wow," I said, against his mouth when we came up for air and he smiled and set me on my feet. Did I say that out loud? Oops. His hair was a little damp from a shower. He smelled really really good. I staggered a little, getting into my shoe.

Rider had a big smile on his face. Spencer didn't.

"Mornin' Ella," Rider greeted.

"Hey, how are you?"

He smiled, "Can't complain."

"Jenna's not complaining' either," I winked at him.

He smirked. He was seriously hot. Jenna was a lucky duck.

"Hi Spencer," I said.

"Hey Ella. Gotta open up. See you all later." He walked to the building next door, a small car dealership that had a bunch of gleaming motorcycles in a showroom.

"Coffee?" Deacon asked me and grabbed my hand.

"What's coffee again?" I asked, still a little bit dazed and gave him a smile.

He squeezed my hand, wearing a big smile, too. I followed him inside, holding his hand. It was big, warm, and felt strong. I felt tingly.

There were two bikes being worked on in there plus two cars up on hoists, and a glassed in office and waiting room at the back where there was a sofa, television, and coffee maker.

"So, you live here?" I asked.

"I stay in my fifth wheel out back. Dad, Ride, and Spence live above the bar in our temporary clubhouse for now. I like my space. I'm shopping for a piece of land. I'll probably move my trailer there and take my time and build a place. Spence just made a pot of coffee. How do you take it?"

"Cream, two sugars." I liked how chatty he was being.

"Same as me," he noted.

"Hmm. Did you give Spencer that black eye?"

My phone dinged.

I lifted it from my purse and looked at it. Another text from Jay.

> "It's very important that I speak to you. Please can you meet me for coffee at Dutchie's at 10:30? V V important Ella!"

I wrote back,

> "Fine. I'll be there but I'm busy today so it'll have to be super quick."

I wasn't busy until after, for my date with Deacon, but I didn't want to give Jay more than a few minutes of my time and during that time I planned to tell him I had moved on and to stop calling me.

I blew my hair out of my eyes and stuffed the phone back into my purse. Deacon was stirring my coffee with a stir stick. He passed it to me and sat down on a leather sofa.

I sat beside him. "Thanks. Did you?"

"Hit Spence? Yeah but he swung first. Something wrong?" he asked.

"You don't have a black eye." I noted.

"Nope," he gave me a grin, "A, I wasn't shitfaced. B, got better reflexes than Spence, especially drunk Spence."

The phone made another noise and I glanced at it and it was a happy face from Jay. I rolled my eyes.

"What's up, Ella?" Deacon pressed.

"Oh," I shook my head, "That was that ex, Jay. The guy from the bar the other night. He wants to meet me for coffee this morning. He's been harassing me for weeks so I said yes. I'll just get him off my back. Make sure it's clear."

His eyes narrowed, "I made things *real* clear for him Saturday night."

I shrugged, "Well, I'll make sure he gets it."

"Uh, no. You won't," he said, "I'll come with you and I'll make sure he actually gets it."

My eyes went wide, "Whaaaat? No. That's okay. I mean... I don't want that."

He got close, super close, leaning over, and his arms flexed. I eyed the tattoo peeking out of his wife beater on the right side of his chest. It was an intricate-looking wing. Deacon's right shoulder was of the American flag that covered the entire cap of his shoulder but his other arm was ink-free, except for a thick black ampersand on the inside of his forearm. The style of ampersand that looked like a capital E, which was kind of cool if you considered that my name started with an E.

"He's pushing his luck. He knows you're with me and he's still harassing you."

"I'll just go find out what he wants. It's a public place. I've been tired of his constant texts and calls anyway so I'll make it clear that it needs to stop."

"Your father told me he keeps driving by your house, too."

"Dad told you that?"

"Yep. Enough is enough."

"Okay, I agree, but you and I have just started seeing each other and I'll handle this."

He shook his head, about to protest but I put my fingertips to his lips. God, he was sexy. I felt tingles shoot straight up my arm from where my fingers were connected to him.

"No, seriously. If he doesn't get the hint after today, I'll give you free reign."

He kissed my fingertips and then pulled me close.

"No one fucks with you, Ella." There was intensity in his voice that was kind of serious. His left hand was around my waist, cupping my hip. His right hand cupped my jaw.

I looked into his eyes.

"I mean it," he told me.

I nodded, "I believe you. You proved that when you saved me from that tweaker and you didn't even know me. Now that you kind of are starting to get to know me, I *really* believe you."

He sighed, "I wanted to put a bullet in that fuckin' goof. If you'd shed one drop of blood, I would've."

My eyes bugged out. And despite the fact that, yes, that tweaker was seriously dangerous and did, in fact, have a knife to my face, Deacon's manner right now sent up a red flag for me. A big red flag that made Spencer's words of Saturday night ring in my memory.

I moved away and sipped my coffee.

"Something you need to know about me," he muttered, moving closer.

I looked to his face.

"I lost someone once. To something really violent. So, I'm protective, Ella."

I swallowed hard, thinking *Yikes*.

"Not ready to talk about that right yet but we'll get to it. I know we've just met but I really don't like the way that fuckwad ex looked at you. He's bad news. And that's not just me being protective."

"I'm sure he's harmless, Deacon. He's just—-" I was about to say persistent but Deacon cut me off and moved closer at the same time, right in my space. I couldn't move further down the sofa; I was at the arm. His arm curled around my waist again. He gave me a squeeze and his mouth was to my temple. He pressed his lips against it and then said,

"Wasn't plannin' on sharing this but you need to get why I don't want him around you. Before I met you, I overheard that guy having a conversation that I now know was about you."

"What?"

"He was talking in a diner with one of his buddies. I didn't know it was about you at the time, hadn't met you yet. I was eating breakfast and reading the paper alone in the booth right behind him, my back to his back, and for a good long while he talked about the girl who'd just broken up with him. I didn't like what I heard. Set my teeth on edge not even knowing him or who he was talking about but it was sick. Stalker sick. I put two and two together when I saw him talking to you Saturday night and you said you'd broken up weeks ago. I don't want you to meet up with him. I think you should steer well clear, Kitten. Any guy who'd share details like those and in the same breath talk about getting you back?" Deacon shook his head, his face filled with disgust.

My whole body jerked. Yikes. "What did he say about me?"

Deacon shook his head, looking torn, not letting go of me, "If I tell you what he said, you're gonna think it's why I showed an interest in you. It won't paint me in a good light. And more than that...this is shit no girl wants to hear, Ella. Trust me on that."

I bolted upright. He got to his feet, too.

"Tell me," I ordered, ready to walk out the door otherwise.

Deacon looked to the ceiling and then put both palms on my arms and said, "He talked about you dumping him but said he was gonna get you back at any cost because you were the best lay he's ever had. That you were wild in bed. That he's been with dozens of girls and none of them hold a candle to you. He went into explicit detail. Worse than your average locker room shit and that's all I'm sayin'."

I frowned and lifted my palm to signal him to stop.

Gross. Jay was like a nympho. But a bad nympho because he was bad in bed. I tried to compensate by putting my all into it, hoping he'd reciprocate, pick up on some cues. He didn't. But he wanted sex all the time.

"You're right. This doesn't paint you in a great light."

So, what? Mystery solved? That's why Beautiful Biker who was so out of my league it wasn't funny was interested in cutesy little Ella? But he could've had me already and he hadn't, though. Why? What was his game?

"I was already interested before I saw him at the bar approaching you," he interrupted my thoughts, seeming to read my mind.

I folded my arms across my chest and sarcastically retorted, "Yeah. Okay."

"I've seen you around."

I rolled my eyes.

"I saw you get in your car at the cab office a few times while I was driving to or from the garage. Your ride stands out. You caught my eye; you've got a great rack, Kitten. Fantastic ass. Gorgeous hair. I've always had a thing for short girls with all you got goin' on. So when I saw you at the gas station, I'd already set eyes on you a few times. And you were eye fucking me in that line-up."

I let out a breath and folded my arms. "I'm not *that* short. You're just really tall. And I wasn't eye-fucking you."

He reached for me and pulled me onto his lap, took my folded arms apart and wrapped my hands around his neck.

"You're short to me when I got at least a foot on you, probably more. And yeah, you were. The way you looked at me? Fuck. No other word for it. And you're *real* good at it." His hands moved down my arms.

I blushed. His eyes were dancing playfully as he smiled at me.

His fingers tangled into my hair at the back of my head and he stared even deeper into my eyes, "First time I saw you, you weren't even in your car. It was well over a week ago; I was at the animal shelter and you were there, rolling around on the floor with a bunch of kittens crawling all over you, gigglin' your sweet ass off, all these sweet curls fanned out on the floor with your knees up, little cut-off shorts on. You didn't see me. You've got a great laugh, great smile, Kitten. I stopped in with my Dad. Our shepherd got picked up, he wanders, so we went in to get him. Saw you and you were like sunshine with that giggle and all this hair." He fisted my hair in one hand and rubbed his nose against mine.

I loved that dog. I'd played with him the day he'd been brought in. He was a great dog. And he'd cried at the kittens, wanting at them so badly. They kept him separated and one of the shelter workers had said that he'd eat the kittens for breakfast but I knew he would've made friends. He was crying because he wanted to play with them.

"Is that why you keep calling me Kitten?"

He gave me a heart-stopping white smile but didn't reply. Instead he continued, "And when I saw your ride again at the gas station Friday night I was passing by but decided I'd go in to get a pack of gum or something just so we could eye fuck again. But then I saw that motherfucker with his hands on you and a knife to your face through the window." He let go of me, looking really pissed.

I winced and let go of his neck and stood up again and took a few steps back.

"I've seen you a few other times, too, around town. Couldn't take my eyes off you. Do I need to keep workin' at convincing you I was already interested before I knew you were the girl that fuckwad jackoff was talkin' about?"

"No," I said this quietly and stared at my feet.

He got up and his motorcycle-booted feet came closer and then he tipped my chin up with his index finger and thumb and looked me in the eye.

"Why do you keep retreating?"

I shook my head and shrugged.

"And as pissed as I was that my brother warned you off, which was because he wanted to tap your ass himself Saturday night, you looked fuckin' gorgeous, you cracked me the fuck up. You're cute when you're smashed."

"You seemed pretty pissed."

"I wasn't pissed you were smashed. I was pissed that you were gonna take off and ditch me when you agreed to wait for me, because of what Spence said. I was also just workin' out how to make my play and didn't wanna make it when you were shitfaced."

"You sure shocked with me with your play Sunday night."

He raised his eyebrows, "In a good way?"

My eyes went wide and I got goosebumps and felt a little bit of heat flood my panties, "In a very good way. Like you couldn't tell..." I rolled my eyes.

"I've gotta kiss you. You gonna knee me in the balls or is that alright?"

"Why would I knee you in the balls?"

"You're full 'o sass right now."

"Why would I knee you in the balls when that might put you out of commission? That's be like kneeing myself in the balls."

He cracked up laughing and then was kissing me, laughing against my mouth and then he said, "You're funny."

I smiled and I nodded a little and then he revved it up a notch and was kissing me breathless; one hand was on my bottom, the other slid up my side and his thumb grazed the side of my boob, making heat and wet flood my panties. I made a whimpering sound. Man, his lips were soft and strong at the same time.

I heard a manly Sam Elliot chuckle.

"Mornin' Deacon. Betty."

We broke apart but Deacon put his arm around me.

Deacon's Dad approached the coffee maker.

"Um, hi. How are you?" I asked cheerily, hoping my face wasn't as red as it felt. It was probably redder.

"Not bad for a Monday. Though not havin' as good a Monday as my namesake."

I laughed.

"How're you, darlin'?" He had a big infectious smile.

"I'm good. I just came by to say Hi. I work around the corner at the cab company. Well, sort of."

"Sort of?" Deke poured a little bit of milk and then a whole lot of sugar into a big #1 Dad coffee cup.

"Well, yeah. I had just about full time hours but they just cut me to a day a week. I'm gonna hit the classifieds, I think."

Deke looked thoughtful for a second, "We could use another waitress at the roadhouse. Or..."

"No," Deacon said firmly and shot his Dad a dirty look.

"I have waitressing experience," I answered excitedly.

I bet the tips were good.

"No," Deacon said again and squeezed my hand. I looked at him. He was shaking his head.

I frowned and shook my own head quizzically.

"We'll talk about it later. What time did you agree to meet the jackoff?"

"Ten thirty. But..." I started.

"I'm steppin' out for a few hours, Dad. Takin' Ella to breakfast; doin' a bit of pest control. Be back at 11:30 or 12."

"Right-o." Deke said and wandered out, giving me a smile as he left.

Things were so crazy my head was kind of spinning!

"Leave your car here, we'll ride," Deacon said as he kicked off his boots and climbed out of his coveralls. He had on jeans underneath. He fetched a button-up grey shirt from a hook in the coffee area and put it on over his wife beater and rolled up the sleeves, and then threw on his leather Dom vest and got his boots back on and reached for keys hanging on a hook by a desk at the back of the garage. Rider was sitting at that desk texting with a sly grin on his face.

"Doin' something with Ella, Ride. See ya in a few hours, man," Deacon said, tossing the baseball cap on the key hook.

Rider gave a two finger wave without looking up from his phone.

Deacon grabbed my hand and we walked to the bike dealership.

"Where are we going?"

"Getting you a helmet," he said.

I was sort of still whirling inside so I just followed him.

We walked into the bike dealership and there was a sexy blonde receptionist decked out in biker babe clothes.

She smiled at Deacon, "Good morning, Deacon." She fluttered her eyelashes at him.

"Hey, Trina. This is my girl, Ella."

"Hi," I smiled.

She smiled at me but it was fake. She looked at me like she tasted something foul. She was very busty with bee stung lips and a whole lot of make-up on.

"Hey, Ella. Good to meet you," she lied. She was sizing me up and finding me lacking, "Thought I was your girl, Deacon?" she batted her eyelashes at him again and said it in such a way that I could tell she wanted me to think she had a thing with him.

"I'm grabbin' a helmet. I'll leave the tag with you and you can ring it up, bill me, alright, Trina?" He didn't answer her question and gave her a look that, if he'd given it to me, would have me quaking in my flip flops.

"Sure, babe," she smiled with teeth at him but her smile didn't touch her eyes.

Spencer wandered over to the reception area.

"What's up?"

"Grabbin' a helmet for Ella."

Spencer looked me up and down with what looked like a hungry look on his face. It made me feel really self-conscious.

Sheesh, this environment felt toxic!

I was wearing jeans and a white peasant blouse with flip flips. My curls were everywhere, sunglasses on my head. Not looking like the "sex kitten" of Saturday night but he still looked at me like I was eye candy. Deacon's hand gave mine a squeeze and I looked up at him. His eyes were on his brother and they were cold.

Tension levels were high so I wanted to cut through it.

"Got any pink ones?" I asked.

"C'mon," Deacon led me deeper into the showroom, past the bikes, to a wall filled with helmets. There were also racks of leather jackets, t-shirts, jeans, leather chaps, belts and belt buckles, motorcycle boots. If I was gonna be a biker's girlfriend, maybe I ought to think about getting some gear. Maybe the next time I got a decent paycheck I'd stop in.

Deacon lifted up a metallic pale pink helmet and notched his left brow at me. His eyebrow barbell gleamed. I smiled at him, feeling starry-eyed at his beauty. The helmet was pretty but I moved toward a black helmet with some fuchsia swirly flames on it and a fuchsia skull with a Hello Kitty-type bow on the side of the skull. It was pretty cool and it was kind of more me.

"That the one?" he asked, smiling at me, making my belly flutter. He looked amused and shook his head, "Cute but badass?"

I beamed and nodded, "That's me. Cute badass kitten. Except the badass part."

He gave me a big smile and kissed the side of my head, hooking an arm around my waist and giving me a squeeze.

"What kind of helmet do you wear?" I asked.

He pointed at one, "I only wear a helmet on long runs or late at night. Not when I'm just bootin' around. Like that one."

The one he motioned to was black, it looked old school, like an army helmet. It looked like it was covered in leather. It was badass. The pink and black helmet was not a *real* badass helmet. But if I had to wear one, it was kinda me.

"You, though, you'll always wear a helmet."

"What?" I asked. That was kind of a double-standard.

He pulled the tag off the pink and black helmet.

"I think I can decide that for myself," I gave him a dirty look. He smiled but it looked a little bit dangerous, as if I'd just challenged him to a dare. Something about that dangerous smile got my motor running. Vroom. Seriously running.

"We'll pick ya some boots, too," he said nonchalantly.

I searched his face and then I guess it took me too long to respond because he said, "Shoe size? I'll pick."

"Seven," I answered and watched him crouched, rifling through boxes against the wall.

"So you don't want me working at Deke's Roadhouse..." I started to ask.

He shook his head, "Let's discuss that tonight."

Yeah, we were new so maybe it wasn't a good idea for me to work for his dad. If things went bad it could make things awkward.

WE GOT TO HIS MOTORCYCLE and in addition to my new helmet I was wearing black Harley Davidson socks with orange heels and toes, and I had some very cool black motorcycle boots, on, after Deacon insisted on buying them for me.

And like the man that rode it, his bike was also very sexy.

"This... is... gorgeous!"

"Thanks. Like bikes?"

"Love bikes."

"Good," he said, "Got four."

"Four motorcycles?" I asked.

He smiled and shrugged, "Yep. Two Harleys, A Boss Hoss, and a Triumph. Gotta represent in this business when you sell bikes."

"Which one is your favorite?"

"My original fat boy. Not near as sweet-looking as this but it was my first. Meant a lot to buy that. Bought it when I turned sixteen with money I saved up and then fixed it up. It isn't here. I gotta go back for it soon. Nothing I ride feels as natural as that one. Like it's an extension of me."

"I can't wait to see it," I said and he kissed me and put the helmet on my head.

"Can't wait for you to ride it," he said this low, sensually, a definite double entendre. I grinned wide. He did too, but he looked toward his boot as he kicked the kickstand up, "Maybe you can come back with me to get it. Road trip. Meet Jojo, my sister."

I smiled.

The Harley had a long chopper style front and it was black, loads of chrome, and had some dark blue flames painted and a bunch of blue lights on it. I'd been on the back of bikes a few times but never with a guy that I was so giddy about wrapping my arms around. It wasn't a long enough ride to Dutchie's diner, just about two minutes away, but it was still awesome to be on the back of Deacon's bike, my arms around him.

We got into the restaurant and had almost an hour to kill before Jay was due to arrive.

Deacon held my hand walking in and all eyes in the place were on us when we got inside. Given that the Dominion Brotherhood MC patch was new around town I was sure Deacon got double-takes everywhere he went. Add to that how good he looked, and there were probably double-takes for a myriad of reasons.

We grabbed a booth and the waitress came over, "Mornin' Ella. Deacon. How's tricks?"

Our waitress, Laura, was about 40 or maybe mid 40's but holding her age really well. She had been at Dutchie's years and remembered everyone's name. She already knew who Deacon was but that didn't surprise me. Considering Deacon's father owned a whole block with three businesses it'd garner some attention around town.

"Hey Laur... coffees and menus, please," Deacon said, "Be right back, Kitten." He kissed me quick and disappeared into the men's room.

She winked at me, "Good goin' Ella. Caught yourself a tiger by the tail."

I grinned, "That's a very apt observation, Laura."

She winked again, "Oh yeah. Good goin'. Couldn't've happened to a more deserving gal." She gave my shoulder a squeeze, "I know Deacon's dad Deke. Know him *real* well. Used to hook up with him years ago when I lived in the falls, before my life went to shit, which happened around the time Shelly, Deacon's mother became Deke's old lady. She got preggers with your new man and took his Daddy off the market. Wish it had been me. Woulda kept hold of that tail..." she shook her head with regret.

"You single?" I asked.

"I am these days," she said wistfully, "You need biker broad lessons just let me know. I know my way around that life. It can be a little bit overwhelming when you first adjust. Don't hesitate to call me if you need an ear to bend."

"I may take you up on that. He didn't bring Deacon's mother here to Aberdeen, though, so maybe it's time for you to go tiger-hunting?" I gave her an encouraging eyebrow wiggle.

She smiled, wiggling her own eyebrows, "I'd heard something about that. Heard a coupla things about the Valentine boys and it's all good. Maybe I will," and then she sashayed through the double doors that lead to the kitchen.

Deacon was gone a while so I browsed the menu and then scrolled through Facebook on my phone.

When he finally came back he had a hard look in his eyes until he realized my eyes were on him. His expression cleared.

"What's wrong?" I asked.

He shook his head, "Just club stuff. Got a call in the john."

Laura came back over and poured us coffees.

When she was gone I leaned over and asked in a low voice, "So, club stuff? Is your club a 1% club?"

"Someone sew a 1% patch on my cut when I wasn't lookin'?" he teased.

"Didn't look very closely," I admitted, while doctoring up my coffee the way I liked it and letting my eyes rove over his vest. I'd seen Dominion Brotherhood MC over the back on the top and Aberdeen on the bottom with their emblem of a motorcycle with wings as the graphic. The Aberdeen looked newer than the top patch. I guessed it used to say Sioux Falls. On the front was a smaller version of the patch, a set of wings over his left side, and embroidered S with an ampersand and T.

He shook his head, "We're not what you'd call squeaky clean but we're also not TV bikers."

"I see. My father says you're third in command."

He nodded, "Might as well be second, really. My father is charter prez. He was VP back home. His new VP is still getting organized to move down from another location but that VP will help him set up here and then start his own charter in about a year, maybe less; then I'll move up to VP. I'm Secretary and Treasurer."

"Is that a lot of responsibility?"

He shrugged, "We're still a small charter. Still getting set up but anticipating growth over the next few years. Anything I tell you about the club isn't for public consumption, not even your best girls, by the way. As you and I get to know one another, like I said, you'll hear things. I'll always be honest with you, Ella. Just be sure you really want the answers to the questions you ask me, okay?" His face was serious. A bit too serious. Iciness ran through my veins.

"What does that mean?" I asked.

"I'm a biker," he said with a shrug and then he dumped his creamer into his coffee.

"Do you have a criminal record?" I asked.

"It'd be better if we have this talk somewhere private," he replied, reaching across the table and grabbing the sugar. He spooned his sugar in and then took my hand into his and his thumb skated over the backs of my knuckles. Those sexy hands I'd admired just days ago were caressing mine. Last night they'd been all over my skin. Trippy.

"After this is over, I'll get you back to your car, then I've got something to do. I'll pick you up tonight and then we'll talk."

His tone was dismissive and ornery. I didn't really like it.

My eyes narrowed, "Bossy much?"

"Very," he replied but his eyes were playful.

"Just getting this on the table right now...not crazy about bossy, Deacon." I advised haughtily, hoping this wasn't going to be the shortest relationship in history. Hoping that he wasn't going to put his foot in his mouth and make me want to bolt.

I wasn't just interested in him because of the way he looked. I was interested in how protective he was but I was also interested in why he might be interested in me. He was a mystery. An extremely attractive mystery who had given me a spectacular happy ending last night but I wasn't just thinking with my cookie; I really wanted this to not be over before it got a chance to get started. Something in his eyes, the way he carried himself, it all appealed to me. There was depth there. I could feel it in the way he looked at me, the way he assessed me.

How did I feel about people living outside the law? My dad sold pot. He also worked for cash under the table at times. I'd never so much as shoplifted in my life and I didn't have a criminal record.

I could get behind vigilante justice. I believed in individual rights and freedoms and was fairly open-minded but yet traditional at the same time. I believed you should pay your taxes and work hard. I didn't think the government should control you and I also didn't think you should expect them to take care of you when you were capable of taking care of yourself. I wanted everyone to have equal rights.

Could I be in a relationship with an outlaw biker? Maybe not. Could I be in a relationship with a biker who lived on the fringe of the law? Maybe.

Could I be in a relationship with an alpha male who was a little bit bossy. Probably. I was the kind of girl who could see herself as a submissive in the bedroom but an equal partner out of the bedroom. All that bedroom stuff sounded fantastic in theory but could I really do it? That remained to be seen. And maybe Deacon would or wouldn't be into that but what I'd seen so far, he was looking like someone I very much wanted to submit to sexually.

But if he was bossy to the degree he tried to control me and subdue me and / or didn't value me as an equal in the relationship? Nope. NO WAY.

"Then I'll just put on the table that it's how I roll," he took my hand and gave it a reassuring squeeze, "But take my hand, kitten, and I'll never steer you wrong." He said it like a vow and his eyes twinkled.

I took a sip of my coffee and searched his face. Tingles worked through me.

"Million miles a minute?" Deacon asked and sipped his coffee.

"Pardon?" I asked.

"Your brain?"

I studied him carefully, "That's how it rolls."

He smiled. Laura returned with her notepad and pen at the ready. She looked at Deacon. He jerked his chin in my direction. Laura waved her hand dismissively, "Oh, I know what Ella wants. She always orders the same thing when she's here for breakfast. Strawberry shortcake waffles, crispy bacon."

"Shortcake?" Deacon winked at me.

I rolled my eyes.

"Is that right, Ella?" Laura asked, "Or is it a blue moon?"

I passed her my menu, "Yup, the usual. Can't not have them. They're just too good to resist."

"And for you, Deacon?"

"Bacon and eggs, eggs over medium. Bacon not crispy. Home fries crispy."

"Got it," Laura scratched out the order on her pad, winked at me, and then sashayed away.

I chewed the inside of my cheek thoughtfully.

Deacon reached across the table for my hand. My heart swelled. He smiled as his fingers caressed my knuckles.

"So, what made your family relocate here?" I asked.

"Opportunity. Our MC wanted to branch out and we have a few things to clean-up. Long story. Not a story for today. Dad would've moved up in another couple years to prez, Rudy's near ready to retire, but Dad wanted the challenge and the change of scenery. Things were tense with my mother after their divorce and he saw the business opportunity for the club and for himself personally, really liked the idea of buying the three businesses when he scouted this location and so we decided to make the move."

"You didn't mind relocating?"

"I was up for adventure; always up for adventure," He smiled.

I smiled back.

My phone dinged a text alert.

"Sorry. Gotta cancel. I'll msg later."

"That was Jay. He canceled," I said while typing out an 'Ok' to Jay's text.

Deacon's eyes narrowed.

He looked over at my phone and read Jay's message.

"He gets in touch, you tell me. You don't meet up with him without me."

"No arguments here." Talk about creeped out!

While we ate he asked questions and I told him about my parents and my little brother, shared about my job, night school, about my work at the shelter, told him about Gran. I told him I didn't know what I wanted to be when I grew up, even though I was kind of already grown up. He seemed to be paying attention to all I'd said, seemed to care.

"How about your family? You said your parents split up recently?"

He shook his head, "They've been goin' through the motions for the whole marriage. She's the epitome of a nagging spoiled rotten wife. She drinks heavily, spends heavily, argues with him endlessly. She's self-centered, rode all of us on a constant basis. Miserably negative person. Cheated on him. I'm surprised Jojo stayed. Seriously don't know why she didn't just come, transfer schools. Without us boys as buffers I'm bettin' she'll make the move soon. When she finishes with school. When she finishes school Dad'll stop paying for everything and Mom'll find some other guy to leach off so I think Jojo stayed and is puttin' up with shit 'cuz our mother guilted her."

"Got a big family other than your parents?" I asked.

"Not on Mom's side. She was an only child. Dad's side is a big family. He's third oldest in a brood of fourteen."

"Holy moly! Any twins or triplets?"

"Nope. We grew up in Sioux Falls but Dad's family is mostly in the Denver area."

"Whoa. And you, single at 28. No girlfriends in three years?"

"Nothing exclusive," he replied, finishing his last corner of toast with jam on it. He'd completely polished off his breakfast, every single bite.

"Why?" I asked.

"Why?"

"Yeah, you've been around plenty of women, I'm sure, and looking at you I bet they practically throw their panties at you. In three years none of them have been worthy of exclusive?"

"Nope," he replied and didn't even smile at my joke.

"Okay, then allow me to re-phrase. Why me?"

"Another discussion for private time," he winked at me.

I twitched my lips and narrowed my eyes, "So you're bossy and evasive."

His smile went huge, "Not evasive. I'm bossy and I'm private. This is a busy place. Never know what kind of ears are perked around you in a place like this. This was where I heard that fuckwad talking to his buddy about you, in fact. We'll talk later in private and you can ask me whatever you want. You want to crack this nut completely during our first meal together?"

"Not completely," I said.

But, I did want to know what I was getting myself into. And I couldn't help but think 'Why me?'

What was it about me that made him want exclusive when he had barely tested the waters with me? Why didn't he try a few dates first? Why demand exclusivity when he barely knew me?

He leaned over and kissed my hand and then signaled to Laura for the check.

ABOUT TWO MINUTES LATER, we walked out hand in hand but as we approached his bike I heard the roar of motorcycle pipes.

Across the street and a few doors down from the restaurant there was a smoke shop and it was owned by a friend to one of the Jackals. There was no clubhouse in this town, they were based just outside of Ipswich, not far away, but with how close the next town was, it was a given that they'd be here often. And they often hung out in that smoke shop or above it, in the apartment the owner lived in.

Four of them pulled up right then and didn't pull in front of the smoke shop. They pulled up directly opposite to the restaurant. Their eyes were on us. When the tallest took his helmet off I recognized him as my cousin, in full biker gear, with a Wyld Jackals leather vest, the emblem of a rabid dog.

Shit.

His eyes went from me to Deacon to me again. I felt Deacon's grip on my hand tighten and then he was in front of me, shielding me. My cousin crossed the street, "Lizzie," he called out, as he approached us. The three other Jackals stood in front of their bikes, arms crossed over their chests, sending over serious badass vibes.

When we were kids he used to tease me by calling me Lizzie the Lezzy or Lezzy-belle. He'd always been a jerk.

"Hey Chris," I said, peeking around Deacon and trying to be friendly but not fake, which was hard because I felt fake greeting him. I did *not* like him.

Deacon was on alert; I could feel the tension and threatening vibe emanating from him.

Chris was almost six and a half feet tall. He was even a bit taller than Deacon. Chris was only 26 but he had a beard, longish blond hair, and was more than threatening-looking. He was channeling an angry Jax Teller from Sons of Anarchy vibe with a dash of Brock O'Hurn. Chris had a mean-looking scowl on his face.

Deacon had bulk on Chris, Deacon more buff but Chris still looked strong -—like a contender. And the three other guys across the road all looked intimidating to me as well.

"Haven't seen you in a while," Chris said.

"Nope," I replied plainly and moved to Deacon's side. Deacon glanced sideways at me, looking unhappy.

"What kind of company's this you're keepin'?" He jerked his chin at Deacon and when I glanced up at Deacon's face, it looked like he was about to shift from careful control to explosives about to detonate.

"Deacon Valentine, Christian Forker. Chris is my cousin." I paused because I didn't know if I should introduce Deacon as my boyfriend.

Boyfriend didn't sound right. Deacon, the beautiful biker, was too much man to be referred to as a boy.

"And Valentine Junior here is your new man," Chris finished for me, "Rumors are true, then." And he looked at Deacon as if he was something Chris'd scraped off his shoe. Gosh, word traveled fast.

"Gotta say, consortin' with the enemy isn't looked on too fondly by my Pops, Lizzie."

I shrugged, "I still hate being called, Lizzie, Chris-toff." (he hated being called Chris-toff when we were kids. He hated Christian, too, but I chose Chris-toff the Jerkoff in retaliation for Lizzie the Lezzie), "That hasn't changed. And considering that we're not a close knit family, never were, it's actually none of your business who I consort with. And I know nothing about Wyld Jackals politics and don't wanna know, so... whatever."

Deacon took that as a cue to step in front of me again and he blocked Chris's face and reaction from my view.

There was a beat of loaded silence as the two bikers faced off without exchanging words.

"Deacon," I whispered. I didn't like this vibe. I also didn't like that Chris's biker buddies looked like they were itching to wade in here.

"Ella and I have somewhere to be." Deacon grabbed my hand and moved closer to his bike and grabbed my helmet.

Chris stood there and glared at him while he put my helmet on but said to me, "You tell Uncle Rob that my father wants to see him. He's not returnin' calls. If he doesn't call my dad tonight, we'll have to pay a visit tomorrow instead of waiting for an invite."

Deacon got onto the bike. I climbed on the back and wrapped my arms around Deacon's waist. That made Chris's lip curl.

"Not cool, Lizzie. You on the back of his bike could be construed as a direct insult to the Jackals."

"Since I have no relationship with the Jackals or you and your father, I don't see how I could be insulting anyone."

"Your father and my father'll talk about this," Chris said, "I'll be seein' you around, little cuz. You, too, *Junior*." He said 'junior' the way he used to say "Lizzie the Lezzie."

I could feel the tightness of Deacon's body but he didn't say a word. We sat a second, while I imagined he must've glared at Chris and finally, Deacon started up the bike and we pulled away. The other bikers across the street were all glaring at us, looking seriously intimidating.

When we got back to the garage parking lot where my car was, I got off first and took my helmet off. Deacon was glaring at me.

"The fuck?" he bit off.

"Huh?"

"You think it might've been a good idea to share that intel?"

"That... intel?"

"That you've got blood in the Jackals? That Fork is your cousin?" He was looking at me like I was an idiot.

I frowned. "My uncle is a member, not even in this town. I knew Chris was prospecting but I guess he's a full member by now. Chris isn't around here much; we don't hang out. No family reunions or anything like that. My dad doesn't get along with my Uncle Willie. We almost never see them. Maybe in town in passing occasionally, but they don't even live here. They're just outside Ipswich. I didn't even know Chris was known as 'Fork'. That's how out of the biker news loop I am."

"Fuck." Deacon took my hand and walked me to my car.

"What?" Harsh much?

"Gotta talk to my Dad about this shit. I'll call you later, explain later." He opened my door, which I'd left unlocked, and motioned for me to get in.

"Tell me if anything happens, between now and when I see you, with the Jackals or that fuckwad ex, alright? Avoid them. All of them."

"Alright," I whispered. I felt like I was missing something.

He looked seriously pissed.

"Deacon, I'm no biker broad. I don't know how these things work so if I've made some misstep it's because I don't know the rules."

His expression softened.

"I know, baby," (I tingled at that) and then his teeth clenched again, "Got shit to do. I'll pick you up at your place at six." He leaned over and his mouth was on mine, one of his hands on the roof, his fingers on his other hand in my hair and he laid a hot and heavy kiss on me. So, I guess he was pissy but kissed me to show me it wasn't *at* me?

Before I could recover from it, he slammed the door shut and slapped the top of my roof and motioned for me to go and then he stepped back.

In a bit of a fog, I pulled out and drove down the road. Two seconds later, Gangnam Style was blaring from my purse. I fumbled for it when I hit a red light and hit speaker.

"Hey Jen."

"Bitch! I need to talk to you! You off work?"

"Not working today. What's wrong?" I asked her.

"Salon. Now! Get over here immediately. You've been dodging me."

"Fine. Five minutes." I ended the call and drove the short jaunt over to Jenna's salon.

"OH MY GOD WHERE HAVE you been? Gimme one good reason I shouldn't bitch slap you and advertise for a new best friend?" That's how Jenna greeted me as I walked into the salon.

She ushered me to a salon chair and sat me down and immediately picked up her flat iron before I had a chance to reply to her greeting.

"Goodie!" I started to clap.

"No!" she waved the red hot iron at me with anger on her face, "You are in *so* much trouble!"

"Why?"

"Because. I have a zillion things to tell you and you've been dodging me."

"About you and Rider?"

"Well, you suck as a friend for not letting me wax lyrical about him but about you and his brother, most of all. I have the goods!"

"The goods? What goods?"

She started to pull the iron through my hair and I watched it transform from flyaway and very curly to sleek and smooth.

"The 4-1-1 on Deacon Valentine." She shook her head, "Sweetie..."

I smiled, "He's beautiful but I know... he's kind of a broody alpha and I have been in a bit of a fog amid some amped circumstances..."

"And he's got a quite a history," Jenna shared.

My eyes widened. I wasn't sure if I wanted to sit and listen to this or not. Deacon had told me that I'd hear things. The day had been a little unreal so far with all he'd said, with the scene with Chris. I needed to go home and sort it all out in my head before adding more crap on top of all that was already piled on me.

"Listen," I halted her with my hand, "He told me he had stuff to tell me and we haven't had much of a chance to get to know one another yet so I don't wanna listen to rumors about—-"

"I hear he's extremely jealous," Jenna interrupted me, "Word is that he put his last girlfriend in the hospital for cheating on him. You'd make sure I knew that if you had that information about a guy I was seeing. Wouldn't you?"

I pulled my lips tight.

Oh god. No.

"I don't know how serious you two have gotten yet but you needed to know. He's also done time over something to do with one girlfriend with some violent payback with her brother or something and he almost went down for putting another girlfriend in the hospital. He's apparently crazy jealous and possessive. He goes stalker crazy over women he stakes a claim with, according to Spencer, and since he did that staking a claim bit with you, I thought you oughta know all this pronto. So I've been trying to get ahold of you but again...you've been dodgin' me."

"All you're saying is based on what Spencer told you?"

She nodded, "It's what Spencer told Joe. We all partied at my place after the bar and they stayed up late. Pip passed out and me and Rider went to my room." She paused, smiled, and then continued, "But I'll fill you in on that later. I'm a little bit in love, I think. Anyhow, Spence and Joe hung out on the terrace smoking around the chiminea. Joe said Spence was trying to score some blow but Joe said he couldn't help him out. Can you say *loser*? Anyway, Deacon showed and beat the snot out of Spencer. Joe didn't know why, said Deacon kept telling Spencer that *he* knew why and Joe got the impression it was 'cuz Spencer was into you at the bar and maybe made that a little too obvious. Almost threw him off the roof terrace. Fucking dangled him by his ankles until Spence pleaded for mercy. It was seriously extreme, according to Joe. Joe tried to defuse the situation but Deacon acted like he wasn't even there. He was so focused on terrorizing Spencer."

I swallowed hard and then asked, "What about Rider? What does he say?"

"Rider and me have nothing to do with that and I don't want what we have colored by this so I'm telling you, on the side, keeping that separate. I haven't said anything to him."

"Maybe you should ask Rider about it. There's some sort of rivalry between Spencer and Deacon and maybe Spence is just out to fuck Deacon over."

"Just wanted you to know the information I had before you got in too deep. How deep are you? You went home with him after the bar but then he was at my place beating up his brother not long after. Don't tell me he's another minute man..."

"He dropped me off and that was it. I was absolutely wasted so nothing happened. I just passed out. But he came over last night."

"Yeah?"

"Yeah. He, uh, had swiped my room key and I woke up with him in bed with me." I felt my face get hot.

"Holy shit. That's sizzling fuckin' hot!" That was Pippa who had wandered to the cash register from the back room with a customer.

"That *would* be hot," said Jenna, "Mighty hot. *If* it weren't for all this other stuff. However, Joe said Spencer told him after the scrap that Deacon is a controlling asshole. When he gets his hooks into a girl, he's over the top. Case in point, the girlfriend with the broken nose and two broken ribs not to mention stitches on her face from where Deacon's ring ripped her cheek open. Spence also said some other girl left the country to get away from Deacon. That's how smothering he was."

I felt sick.

"Did you have sex with him last night?" Jenna asked.

I shook my head, "We fooled around. He got nothing out of it. I got... I got all of... it."

Jenna's mouth dropped open.

"He came in, told me he wanted to be exclusive, told me not to listen to what other people say without talking to him, and he gave me an orgasm. Well, two. But at once. It was like two smushed together."

"Since then?" Jenna asked. Pippa's eyes were boinging.

"I went to see him this morning, we went for breakfast. He wanted to deal with Jay."

I filled them in on what Deacon had said about Jay and they were both freaked right out.

"So is Deacon a stalker who's going to get rid of your other stalker?" Pippa asked.

"Maybe Deacon isn't really a stalker," Jenna said, "Maybe Spencer was embellishing."

"Maybe Spencer is a coke head with delusions," Pippa offered.

"Broken ribs and nose plus stitches from his ring? Does that sound like it could have a reasonable explanation?" I asked.

Jenna and Pippa both looked at one another and then at me. Jenna blew out a long breath, shaking her head.

"And today my jerk off Jackal cousin shows up and tries to have a show-down in the street because I'm on the back of the bike of the enemy."

"Your hot biker cousin?" Pippa asked.

"Ew," was my reply.

"Being your cuz doesn't change the fact that Chris is hot, Ella," Jenna informed me.

"Puh-lease. Spare me."

"He looks like an angry version of that hottie that does all the man bun videos. Yummy." Pippa called out from the back room."

"Don't," I put my hand up, "You just ruined the man bun hottie for me. Thanks a bunch."

"Ella, this Boring and Responsible-ville road you call your life has taken a sharp detour," Jenna told me.

"I'll say!" I agreed.

Jenna got interrupted with a phone call so I texted my father to give him the quick low-down about Chris.

"Dad, Chris saw me with Deacon and started spouting about it being an insult to the Jackals. Uncle Willie is threatening to visit if you don't return his calls."

Dad replied to say,
"Ok. See you at home and we'll talk."
I told him I'd be home in an hour.

Jenna finished doing my hair and started to wax lyrical about how amazing Rider was in bed but I was quiet, zoned out, pondering all I'd heard. I was a bad friend for not getting swooped up in her excitement with her but I think she understood. I apologized before I left but she gave me a tight hug and told me to watch myself, saying she'd feel things out with Rider if she could do so in a way that wouldn't put their newfound thing in the middle.

Part of me wanted to give Deacon the benefit of the doubt like he'd asked me to do, to give him an opportunity to confirm or deny the story about hospitalizing the ex.

But another part of me wanted to run screaming in the other direction because if he was really that possessive and violent then I could be in big danger. I had no idea what to do. Blow him off? Take off out of town for a few months so he'd forget about me? I needed time to think.

5

When I got home, Deacon's pickup truck was there so I wouldn't be getting time to think just yet. I hesitated, thinking about leaving, but Dad saw me through the window. I went inside and found my parents in the kitchen with Deke and Deacon.

"Hi," I stepped in, kind of freaked out but trying to hide it.

Dad smiled and motioned to the table toward an empty chair beside Deacon.

"Hey Ellie-girl. Take a load off."

I sat down at the opposite end of the table instead, and smiled at Deke and then Deacon, who was looking at me strangely. I looked down to my lap.

"You okay?" Deacon asked me.

I nodded and then looked back to my lap.

"Something else happen with your cousin, your ex?" Deacon asked.

I shook my head, "No." My throat was scratchy. I cleared it.

"Sweetie, drink?" Mom asked. I nodded and she poured me a glass of juice. I'd actually felt like a beer, like everyone else had, but let it go. Mom forgot I wasn't still six years old at times.

"Deacon filled me in," Deke said, "About the run-in with the Wyld Jackals this afternoon. He said that Fork was threatening to come by about it so I figured I'd get over here and see what was what by talking to your Dad."

I nodded.

"The Jackals are not pleased that we've set up shop. There's history between our club and theirs. Things have escalated in the past year in an ongoing feud between the two clubs and we want them dismantled. There'll be moves happening in nearly every city where there's a Jackal presence. My chapter's the first to set up a brand new charter near them in an effort to get to a common goal we have with a few other MCs who will be workin' together to bring them down. I'm telling you this because your father is a friend to the club and because you're with my son. When it was shared that Deacon had claimed you as his, the buzz started and it seems that escalated hostilities. As a result, Fork, among others got told to show here more often, to make a statement and further upset the apple cart. They know we're here so they've been lookin' for something to start shit about."

I winced.

"He's fresh, only been patched a year, but he's trouble with a capital T. So's his old man."

We all knew Uncle Willie was trouble.

"Had I known your father was Wild Will's brother sooner I might've handled things differently. Will Forker's a lower-level member. Not a decision-maker. Or he hasn't been. But it's lookin' like your association with Deacon, your Dad's association with the club, that might change things."

I nodded.

"And that ain't good. We need as few wild cards as possible to shut down these guys. I want you to keep Deacon posted about anything said to you or anything you see or hear to do with the Jackals. They may approach you again. If they do, you tell Deacon immediately. Give them no information about us. Give no info to anyone who asks. Be aware that they may be trying to glean intel from women of club members through other broads. Get me? As we assess the threat, be watchful." He put his index finger to his nose, "That okay by you?"

I nodded again.

"Good girl. Rob, go for a smoke?" Deke asked and stood.

"Thank you for the drink, Bertie." He squeezed my Mom's hand and kissed her cheek. She smiled.

"Nice to see you. And good to meet you, Deacon," she said smiling big at Deacon.

Deacon reached over and shook her hand and put his other hand over the top of her hand and gave her what looked like a genuine smile. A beautiful smile. My heart twinged with pain at his profile, his long eyelashes, his strong hands. Mom moved out of the kitchen and Dad and Deke left via the kitchen door.

Deacon looked to me and his mouth opened, about to say something, but then Beau was there, skidding to a halt on floppy socks, stopping right in front of Deacon.

"Holy moly, you're big!" He looked up at Deacon.

Deacon looked down at Beau, "And you're not. Not yet. Who are you, little man?"

"I'm the future Big Bad Beau Forker. For now I'm just Beau."

"Well it's good to meet you, Just Beau."

"Are you Lella's boyfriend?"

"Yep."

"You're tall."

"Yep."

"Lella's not."

"Nope. But she's real pretty."

"I think so, too. Lella's boyfriends need to bring me stuff when they visit. You butter me up and I talk you up to her. That's how it works."

"Is it?" Deacon looked like he was fighting a grin.

"Beau!" I exclaimed, shocked.

Beau looked at me and gave me a 'Leave this to me' look.

"Absolutely," he told Deacon.

"I'll try and remember that."

"Ask Lella what I like. She knows. She's knowed me my whole life. And she picks the bestest presents."

I nodded, "Okay, bud. That's enough extortion for today. Pull your floppy socks up so you don't trip."

"Bye!" he waved and halfheartedly pulled his socks up not nearly enough and then dashed to go but then skidded at the door and turned around to face Deacon, "Don't go kissing her. Not unless you buy her presents, too." And then he dashed off.

Deacon looked highly amused.

I chewed my lower lip and started fidgeting.

"Speaking of which, didn't get a hello kiss from you," he muttered and then took my hand and pulled me to standing.

I gave him a half a smile but I was stiff.

He leaned over and walked me backwards until my back was against the wall, "That'll be a rule, Kitten. You see me? You come to me so I can kiss you." His hands went into my hair and then he said, "I gotta go; be back at six." He touched his lips to mine briefly.

I nodded.

His eyes searched mine, "You alright?"

"Mm hmm."

"Something else happen? He text you again?"

I shook my head, "I'm kind of not feeling so hot. Maybe we should skip tonight."

He searched my face, "What's wrong?"

"Just not..." I put my hand over my stomach, "I have a little bit of a headache and..."

"Headache or stomach ache?" he looked at my hand on my belly.

"Uh, just, really, uh, not feeling good in general," I stammered.

He kissed my forehead and his hand caressed mine on my stomach. That was sweet.

Gah.

I stiffened.

"Why don't you rest up and then I'll text you in a few hours and see if you're feeling better."

"Okay," I nodded.

He kissed my lips again briefly, "Talk to you later."

And then he was gone.

I went upstairs to my room and laid on my bed and stared at the ceiling, feeling sick. Not a headache. Not a stomach ache. Sick at heart.

This had to be over before it ever even got started. I was totally freaked out by everything that'd happened. There was no way I wanted to get into a relationship with someone who was abusive. It was heartbreaking, though. I'd been so excited about the possibilities. I'd been so smitten. But not so smitten to ignore those warnings. No way.

AT 5:15, I WAS SITTING in the kitchen, at the table, keeping an eye on the dinner I was cooking for us, reading the small classified section of the newspaper and trying to get my brain to shut off. It'd been going round and round, ever since I saw Deacon's truck pull away.

Deacon sent me a text,

"how you feelin?"

I waited until 5:45 to answer. I replied,

"I'm sorry. I'm in bed, not feeling good. Sorry but don't feel up to going out tonight. Sorry"

After I hit send I realized I'd said sorry three times. I certainly was sorry. Sorry that my beautiful biker boyfriend was no longer. I changed his name to Deacon, knowing that after a few more texts and excuses to avoid seeing him I'd just be deleting him.

I put my phone down on the counter and heard Dad coming in, Deacon and Deke following him and dad was in mid-sentence, "makes it fanfuckingtastic. Puts a pound of shredded cheese on it with all these spices and sliced tomatoes and puts it under the broiler. Two more for dinner, Belle."

I was standing there with a stack of plates and Deacon was putting his phone back into his pocket as he came into the kitchen. He'd been reading my text. For sure. The text saying I was in bed. Damn it. I knew they'd left. I'd seen Deacon's truck go. When did he get back?

"Deacon popped by to pick up Deke and run him home before your date but figured you always put on a mountain of pasta when you make it, baby doll, so it'd be no hardship to feed the boys."

I was frozen in place, my eyes on the floor.

"You alright?" Dad asked.

"No," I whispered. But I don't think he heard me.

Deacon's eyes were on me and they were burning into me. His jaw was clenched.

I closed my eyes and took a big breath.

"Bertie! Beau!" Dad called and sat at the table.

"Sit down, boys." Dad motioned to the table to two empty spaces and then went into the cupboard and pulled out two more plates. Our little family of four had a table for eight because we so often had company.

He put the extra plates down and reached into the cutlery drawer. "You alright, Tinkerbelle? You're white as a sheet."

"I have to go lie down. I'm not, I'm not feeling well." I pushed past Dad through the doorway and ran up to my room.

Less than a minute later I heard a vehicle start up. I looked out and Deacon was pulling out. I let out a big breath.

I HID OUT IN MY ROOM for the next hour until there was a knock at my door.

"Come up." I called, knowing it was my Dad because it was his signature knock.

"What's up, baby doll?" he asked, climbing the stairs.

"Is Deke gone?"

"No, he's in the cave. I'll run him home later. Deke stayed for dinner but Deacon said he had to take off. He left suddenly. Right after you dashed upstairs. Everything alright?"

I nodded and shrugged.

"What's goin' on?"

I let out a slow breath.

"Elizabelle."

"He's intense. He's been kind of over-the-top intense. But then today I heard some stuff about him and it's the kind of stuff...I'm not sure I should be seeing him. And then all this stuff with Uncle Willie and Chris?"

"Sweetheart, I know you like your life to be a well-oiled machine, but let your old Dad give you some advice. Sometimes it's good to go off course. You heard that old saying, go out on a limb; that's where the fruit is. Right?"

I nodded.

"And don't believe everything you hear. That family's new to town. If word has traveled it's more than likely a case of broken telephone. And you know how convoluted the conversation can get with that shit. And with the Jackals in the equation, don't trust nothin' you hear without confirmation from the horse's mouth. They're gonna try to kill the credibility of any Dom.

They're in a feud, baby doll."

"I know, Dad. I'm just freaked." I wasn't about to explain it was a Valentine spreading word about another Valentine.

"Freaked?"

"Yeah. Everything has been really intense the last few days. It's a lot to wrap my brain around."

"I got a good feeling about these guys, Elizabelle. I'm not asking you to do anything you're not comfortable with, not trying to push you into a relationship with him, but the way I saw your eyes light up when you saw him at the roadhouse Saturday night? The way you're twisting yourself in knots now? Maybe you're just a little scared to leave your comfort zone."

I hugged my pillow closer. Dad knew me, for sure, but he didn't have all the facts here.

"If you're interested in giving it a go with Deacon, why not give him a chance to confirm or deny these rumors? Do you wanna share them with me?"

I shook my head. If they weren't true, I certainly didn't want to spread them.

Shit. If they weren't true, I was giving up the chance of being with the beautiful biker. I'd already thrown away my chance of being on his bike tonight, getting answers to my questions. I was torn between feeling like I was being childish and feeling like I was playing it smart.

Would he really admit to me if he'd put his girlfriend in the hospital? There wouldn't be any possible excuse that I could think of that'd justify that sort of violence against a woman. And even if Spencer was a bit jerky, surely he wouldn't fabricate all that; would he?

"I'll leave ya be. Just remember, there are two sides to every story," Dad advised.

I nodded, "Thanks, Dad. Do you think things are gonna be nasty with Uncle Willie?"

"That's not yours to worry about, punkin. I'll deal with my brother." Dad got an angry glint in his eye that I, thankfully, didn't see too often.

"Just keep mum about all that. Nothing goin' round. Not to your girls, even. What we discuss with the Valentines has to stay quiet. No telling tales. That's lesson number one in dealing with bikers."

"Of course," I agreed.

He leaned over and kissed the top of my head and then he left.

My text alert went off.

It was Jenna.

> **"Where r u?"**
> **"Home."**
> **"So you didn't go out on your date?"**
> **"No. Not feeling well. Turning phone off. I'll call you tomorrow."**

I turned the phone off before I had to hear an alert she'd replied, or worse, that she'd called. It wasn't the truth that I was sick but it wasn't exactly a lie, either. I just didn't wanna talk about it. I didn't want to get talked into seeing Deacon and I didn't want to get talked out of wanting him, either.

I took a bath and then snuck downstairs and got some pasta from the kitchen and warmed it up but I couldn't get more than a few bites into me before I gave up, took my bowl downstairs, and then went back upstairs and decided to crash for the night, hearing a bit of noise outside.

Dad and Mom were having a campfire singalong with some of their friends. Someone was playing guitar. It was a Monday night but at the Forker household it was almost always like it was a weekend.

Before I did go to sleep, though, I decided to prop the chair from my desk under the doorknob.

And then I dreamt about him. In my dreams he smiled his gorgeous smile at me, touching me, taking me for rides on his bike, and then making love to me. I woke up suddenly, disoriented, and I heard a noise.

Shit. What was that noise?

I huddled under the blankets, realizing that it was the door. I heard the key get pulled out and then the noise stopped.

He tried to get in and found the door jammed so gave up. And hopefully he'd just give up on me. And I could move on and forget his beautiful tiger's eyes, his touch, the promise of what might've been. I tossed and turned most of the rest of the night.

I GOT OUT OF BED SUPER early and headed to the animal shelter and spent about five hours there, cleaning cages, giving the homeless pets as much love as I could give. Early afternoon, I visited my Gran's nursing home but she had a group outing planned so I only got to spend about half an hour with her.

I drove to the next town over and spent the afternoon in the library, re-reading a book I'd read a dozen times. I left my cell phone in my purse in the car the whole day, didn't even look at it until after-hours in the library parking lot.

When I got to it, my screen was filled with notifications.

"You awake? Open the door."

That was Deacon the night before.

"Can you cover midnight shift on Friday?" Lloyd.

"Call me." Jenna.

> **"Need to talk to you. NEED NEED. K? Hurry. It's about Deacon"** Jenna
>
> **"hey girlie. wanna see a movie tonight?"** Pippa.
>
> **"Can we meet for coffee today at 10:45?"** Jay.
>
> **"Guess you are busy. Msg me."** Jay again.

"Call me ASAP." Deacon.

Deacon's most recent message had been sent in the afternoon. He'd also called me twice. It was now 5:30.

There was a quick rap on my window. I jumped about three feet, dropping my phone. Deacon was standing beside my window, a scowl on his face.

I rolled it down as I reached for the phone under the gas pedal.

"What the fuck?" he bit off.

How did he find me?

"What?" I asked. I must've been staring open-mouthed at him.

"You're avoiding me."

"I..." I had no response.

"I've been flipped the fuck out."

"You tracked me down?" I was in shock.

"That fuckwad ex, the shit with the Jackals? You vanish? Of course I tracked you down."

"I'm fine."

He shook his head, eyes narrowing, and folded his arms across his chest, "What did it? Did my brother say something else to you?"

"Not exactly."

His left eyebrow went up.

"What, exactly? What *exactly* was it that made you lie to me yesterday about being sick, lock me out of your room, and then avoid me all day? Hiding out in a library 15 miles away?"

He looked pissed. Scary pissed. Like a fire-breathing dragon.

My heart started to race and I started to tremble, "Listen, I don't think we should see one another. It's probably best with all this Jackal stuff that we..."

"Oh, you're gonna pretend it's that? Be straight with me at least."

I shook my head, "All this is too intense too fast, Deacon."

"Don't bullshit me. Have the decency to tell me to my fuckin' face what your problem is. Unlock the passenger door."

"What? Why?"

"So I can get in and fuckin' talk to you. Why else?"

"No, uh..." I turned the ignition.

"Ella, what the fuck?"

I shook my head, "Sorry, Deacon. This just isn't a good idea. Let's just leave it at that. I gotta go. Sorry."

I backed up and left. I left him standing there staring at me.

My whole body trembled for the entire ride home.

I got into the driveway and was grateful that it looked like no one was home.

I got into my room and threw myself on the bed and started to bawl. I looked at my phone. I didn't want to call Jenna or Pippa. I certainly didn't want to meet Jay for coffee.

I didn't want to talk to my parents about this. Mom was a gentle soul. She'd worry. Dad was convinced that the Valentines were stand-up guys and he wanted an in with them, he worked for Deke. I didn't know what to make of Deacon finding me a whole town away but that, along with all the other stuff? Letting himself into my room, making a copy of my key, and the stuff I'd heard about him from Spencer and from Jenna via what Spencer had told Joe? I hoped he got my message and would just leave me alone.

I heard a vehicle squeal outside, heard a slam, and then heard the fire escape stairs being climbed. He knocked on my outside door.

Fuck.

"Open the door, Ella!" Deacon called in.

I could see him through the blinds. I should've closed them. Shit.

I got up and went to the door but didn't move the chair.

"Deacon, I'd like you to just leave my room key on the step there, please, and go."

"Who said what to you?"

I shook my head. His eyes blazed at me through the window.

"Just tell me," he said, "Let me in. I'll give you the key. Just give me two minutes of your precious fuckin' time."

"Just go, Deacon," I told him.

"Why are you crying?"

I wiped my eyes. Shit.

"Come outside then; talk to me out here."

I shook my head.

"Not goin' till you talk to me," he said with a stone cold expression in his eyes.

"Fine," I relented.

I walked down the inside stairs and went outside and met him at the back side of the house. He was sitting a few steps up on the staircase that led to my room, putting us at eye-level.

I approached him. He handed me my key.

"Thank you," I said, and put it in my jeans pocket and he grabbed for my hand. I pulled back and he caught my wrist.

"I deserve to know why you wanna end things. Don't you think?"

"Let go of me," I demanded.

A muscle ticked in his jaw. He let go.

"Something to do with me's got you cryin'. I don't know what I did. I suspect I know what someone else did, though. Big fuckin' mouths."

I took a big breath and said, "I'm crying because we are over before we even got started and I was very much looking forward to getting started but I can't be in a relationship with someone who…" I dashed tears off my cheeks with my sleeves.

"Spence," he said through gritted teeth.

"Hits women. I heard that your last serious girlfriend wound up in the hospital. Your ring tearing up her face. Her ribs broken. Her nose. Because she cheated on you. I'm not okay with cheating but I don't think that sort of violence is okay. Ever. Also heard that you've got a long history with violence, that you've done time due to something violent to do with another girlfriend years before that."

His eyes flashed with anger.

"You were talking violently yesterday and it set off alarm bells. You sneaking into my room, making a key, that sent up a warning. The stuff you said about Jay? More red flags. Not because of what you overheard but because you're interested in me probably because of *what* you heard him say. So, add to all that the drama with the Jackals and this just doesn't seem like a good idea. All the other stuff on its own doesn't seem like a good idea but domestic violence? That's not a warning bell or a red flag; it's a *do not pass go* for me. Deal breaker."

He stood up. I took a step back. There was serious animosity rolling off of him.

"I told you that you'd hear things," he said accusingly, "You agreed to talk to me before jumpin' to any conclusions."

"You're right about that. But not a lot of wrong conclusions to jump to when a girl winds up with broken bones and stitches in her face, Deacon." I took another step back. He took another step toward me.

He shook his head, "Actually there is. She fucked my brother."

"Ah, and that makes it justifiable?" As if that made it okay to put her in the hospital, "We never got a chance to get started but sadly, we are not gonna get started, so you owe me no explanations, no nothing."

Deacon continued, giving me a dark glare, "I wasn't done talking. Let me finish."

I swallowed. My blood ran cold at his glare, his tone of voice, the entire vibe of this situation.

"Emma was fucked. Crazy bitch. Fucked my brother after we had a dumb little spat to get back at me so I'd ended it with her. She decided to fuck Spence again, in my bed, wanted me to catch them. He was fucked up on blow, half dozed, and he'd always had a thing for her and an even bigger thing for tryin' to stick it to me. When I tried to kick them out, not giving a shit that they hooked up, just wanting my bedroom back, she got pissed that I wasn't pissed about her fucking Spence and fucking whacked me with a crowbar, jumped me. Jumped on my back and started wailing on me. I threw her off, self-defense, and she landed on a table, cracked her ribs. Spence wakes up to her screaming and sees it, not knowing what happened, and he and I get into it. He hits me. I haul off to hit him at the same time as she comes at me again from behind and my elbow caught her nose. She goes mental, grabs my wrist with both hands. I tried to shake her off and my fist caught her cheek in the scuffle. It wasn't intentional, just had to get the rangy bitch off me. She was in the hospital overnight and it was all her doing. She was a whacked crazy bitch. I only dated her a fucking month. This was five or six years ago. Two years back she killed her old man. Took a baseball bat to his head, when he was in bed sleeping. She's doing 25 to life for murder one. Spence knows the true story. Why he's twisting it to fuck me over is just another example of his sour grapes. He saw you, wanted you, and I'd already claimed you. He was drunk and got pissed off. This is classic Spencer."

Yikes. I clutched my throat.

"Spence is a fuckin' alcoholic. Alcohol fuels his jealousy of me. When he gets hammered he shoots his mouth off. He had a crush on my last serious girlfriend but she knocked him back and pursued me instead. I had no idea he had a thing for her until she and I were serious so no, I wasn't about to back off at that point. We split up when she decided to go to school in France, live a little wild before settling down. I tried to talk her out of going, even suggested going with her, having that adventure together, but she said I was smothering her. Spence carried a torch for her, was always in her ear about me. He hated that she was with me and threw her leavin' me in my face every chance he got. Has been spreadin' around to any girl that'd listen that I'm a smothering jealous boyfriend. I won't deny I'm protective but I'm never violent against a woman."

I let out a breath.

"And as for doing time, I lost a girl when I was 17, she was 16. She was killed by her dumb fuck meth head stepbrother who, we figured out after the fact, traded time with her for a meth fix. He let his dealer and the guy's buddies behind closed doors with her for an hour in exchange for a score. They gang-raped her and filmed it. He got into a scuffle with one of the bastards over how much dope he'd get for it and pulled her Dad's shotgun. Had a scuffle and fought with the dealer over the gun. Gun went off and she got shot in the face. He got a hot shot lawyer and fed them a story and managed to get off, bullshitted his way out of it, acting like she got caught in the crossfire when he was trying to save her. But I found out the truth. Found out the truth in a really fuckin' rotten way. The stepbrother didn't give two fucks that he was responsible for killing her. I waited outside the courthouse for him and beat the fuck out of him, beat him to within an inch of his life. She couldn't even have an open casket at her fuckin' funeral because the asshole blew her face apart. So I smashed *his* face in, wishing he was in jail getting ass raped for what he did to her. I did time for that. I was a teenager; it was my first offence. Dad hired a good lawyer. The records were sealed. I moved on with my life. Unfortunately, I moved on to one fucked up bitch after another until I couldn't take it anymore so I stopped letting things get serious."

I blew out a long breath.

"But then I see you and something about you... I keep seein' you. I hear things, not talking about the things that fuckwad ex said. I hear people talking about you volunteering at that animal shelter, old folks' home, about how much of yourself you give. Laura at the diner pointed you out to me one day, too. Caught me staring at your ass as you walked down the street because I'd already seen you a few times and she told me you were sweet, did all sorts of volunteering, did a helluva lot for your parents helping out with your little brother. I keep seeing you and you're gorgeous. And then you finally see me and the way you looked at me? Fuck. Like I'm the man you wanna spend the rest of your life pleasing. And then you're sweet and cute and I think, fuck, maybe. Maybe I'm ready to try this shit again. Then of all fuckin' things a meth-head fuckin' junkie puts a knife to your face and I get infuriated that another junkie might damage a girl's face on my watch, that he might take away my shot to see if you were different. The next day I find out the fuckwad stalker pervert I overheard in the diner was talking about you when he said all that whacked shit so I get protective because I give a shit. And bad on me, right? Because now you think I'm the stalker. Rumors start circulating and you listen to them without giving me the respect of askin' about them. You're not different. You're just as fuckin' jacked as all the others. Why the fuck do I keep doing this to myself?"

He walked past me and got to his truck and put his hand to the handle, "If you hear one thing I say to you, Ella, hear this: Stay away from that fuckwad Smyth. He's the type to keep you in a pit in his goddamned basement. Have a nice life, Kitten." He got in and peeled away with a screech.

I felt faint. I lowered myself shakily and sat on the bottom step. I sat there for I don't even know how long. Dumbfounded.

All his words and actions so far washed through me, until finally I got to my feet and went inside. I stared out my bedroom window for ages. Heartbroken. Kicking myself in the ass because I fucked up. I fucked up huge.

Stupid stupid stupid.

And then I made my decision.

I took a shower, putting my hair in a shower cap to protect Jenna's flat iron job, and changed into a pair of jeans and a t-shirt. I grabbed a backpack and threw a change of clothes and my toothbrush and make-up bag in it and then headed down to the kitchen to leave a note for my parents saying I'd be back tomorrow after work. They'd left a note that they'd gone to a kinder-jam session with Beau.

I'd never been this apprehensive about a relationship in my life.

I'd also never ever been this attracted to someone and had not ever, not once, felt this much regret for playing it safe before.

I'd made him think I wasn't worth it after he'd thought maybe I *was* worth it. After all he'd been through! What I'd seen, the emotion that came when he said those things to me, it had gutted me.

I had to find out if this was salvageable. His past, the hurdles he'd faced, and that he wanted to move past it with me? Me!

It had made me want him more than ever.

I wanted to be worth it to him with a fierceness I didn't know I was capable of.

6

It was dark when I got to the Valentine block.

I wouldn't have expected the Roadhouse to be super busy being a Tuesday night but it was as if it was Saturday night. There were plenty of motorcycles and cars and about a dozen pickup trucks outside as well as at least two dozen or so men outside Deke's Roadhouse smoking.

I saw Deacon's fancy Harley, parked toward the back of the garage, so I parked there and then walked toward the back, which had a forest bordering the parking lot. Directly behind the garage, I saw a camper hooked to a pickup truck and there was a light on.

I started to make my way that way. But, when I got to about twenty feet away, the door swung open and Trina, the receptionist from the dealership, was coming down the stairs. She was straightening her tank top. She had sex-messed hair and even in the dimness of the parking lot I could see that her lipstick was smeared. She spotted me as I halted mid step, and gave me a smirk, wiping the corner of her mouth with her thumb.

My stomach churned as I spun around to head back toward my car. I had to stop myself from running.

Fuck. Fuck, fuck fuck! My heart. In. My. Throat.

I couldn't even process all I was feeling at that second other than the fact that I fucked up but not hours later he's with someone else?

God...

I got to The Shitbox and Deacon was leaning against it, his arms folded across his chest. My heart plummeted back down to my stomach. I was confused.

"I... is that your trailer?"

I jerked my thumb behind me.

He shook his head, "Nope."

"No?"

"Trina and her old man's."

"Oh. Where's yours?"

He jerked his chin toward the bar. "Back there. What are you doing here?"

"Can we talk?"

"Isn't that what we're doing?" His eyes were cold, hard.

"I made a mistake," I said carefully and then started talking quickly, "I jumped to conclusions. I promised you I wouldn't but then I did and I'm sorry. Things are just a little bit intense. Understatement. A lot intense. I'm used to living in Boring-ville and the past few days have been such a departure from boring I should've gotten some kind of a warning." I laughed a little. It was a nervous laugh. There wasn't a single thing funny about any of this.

"I don't need some warped version of my past dragged up and thrown in my face. It haunts me enough as it is." His hard expression didn't budge.

"I bet," I said, "And I apologize. But in my defense, I don't know you and you're pretty intense and I—-"

He shook his head, "Intense? You have no fucking clue after barely five minutes with me how intense I am. You ain't seen nothin'. Run along 'n head back to your boring safe life. I don't do boring, Ella. The Doms have started this chapter and my family's started three new businesses all at once in a new place where we had enemies before our boots hit the ground. Gotta have my head in the game; the last thing I need is some jacked crazy bitch fucking my life up or breakin' my heart because she can't handle my brand of intense. You're saving me a whole lotta trouble. I appreciate you showin' me who you are early on. Now I don't have to worry about keeping you safe on top of everything else."

Ouch.

His icy glare was still on me, locking me in place. It felt like an eternity of staring at one another but despite his hard glare, I saw so much depth. So much that I *wanted*. He was intense, for sure. Part of me wanted to turn tail and run. But I refused to give in to that urge. I knew, bone deep, that this beautiful biker in front of me was worth the risk, worth going out on that limb and stepping out of my comfort zone.

"I'm sorry," I whispered, "I fucked up. If you could just put yourself in my shoes—-"

"Told you this'd happen and asked if you could deal. You said you could. You couldn't. The end."

"I didn't know what I was agreeing to," I whispered.

"And now?" he challenged.

"Now I see that I misjudged you and I want to explore this with you. I don't want it to be the end."

He looked at me like I had a whole lot of nerve.

"I want to be with you, Deacon. I'm not jacked up and I'm not crazy or a bitch. I didn't know. And I'm just a little bit chicken shit."

He stared, flexing his jaw muscles, his chest was heaving up and down with his big breaths, then he was flexing his fingers, as if he was getting ready to do battle.

"You wanna know what a girl has to be ready for in order to be with me?" he bit off.

I nodded but I was terrified of what he might say. I was terrified that he wasn't going to give me another chance. I was also paralyzed with fear that if he did, my life would be scary, crazy, out of my control. Out of my comfort zone.

I'd joked about wanting to court danger. Wanting to be kinky. Wanting excitement. But the truth was that I was in Boring-ville because it was safe. I used my responsibilities as a crutch. In the back of my mind, I knew this about myself.

I was like Marilyn Munster because I chose to be. Taking a leap with Deacon would be scary but maybe exciting, exhilarating, erotic.

God... I *had* to get him to give me another chance.

"My woman? She'd have had to deal with bossy. Or boss back until we found middle ground, which I suspect you coulda done, based on the sass I've seen from you so far, which I liked. But you gave up before we even had a chance to see if what we have has staying power. I need to claim a woman in a way that means she knows it means I keep her safe from fuckwad stalker perverts and junkies and whatever threat comes along. And threats do come along when you're tied to a biker. But I do not do Boringland or whatever the fuck. I find myself in a place like that, I get the fuck out. I want wind and winding roads and to enjoy the ride. I want to go places where I can fuck sweet one day and fuck hard the next day and enjoy every goddamn minute possible. Haven't had a lotta reason to laugh in the last few years and for the first time in a while I find myself wantin' it. My girl's gotta be there for the hard times in order to deserve the good. I also want someone who will let her sexual freak flag fly with me. Let me let mine fly with her. I was interested in you before I heard what that fuckwad said and sick as it was that he was sharing that, it did open my eyes to you even more than they were opened, and they *were* opened, because it sounded like we'd be compatible in the sack. After you do time and live behind bars, after you lose someone to tragedy but find it in yourself to move on from that you decide what you want and what you don't want from life. I know what kinda woman I want. I know what kinda woman I don't want. I live hard. Someone fucks me over, I fuck them back harder. No one but no one fucks *her* over. If I'm not goin' it alone, and big if, 'cuz I'm not settling for some crazy bitch who doesn't trust me or who wants to tame me to make me live in Boringland or Miseryville like my ma had my dad in. I want a woman I trust, who trusts me and knows I will move goddamn mountains to keep her safe and give her everything she wants. If I can't have that, all of that, I'm not doing it."

"I want that," I whispered. Tears were streaming down my face. God, I wanted it so much. "All of it."

The emotion on his face, his beautiful beautiful face? God...

"Unfortunately, you have a problem handling intense. I'm intense."

"I'm scared. Yes. But the way you just laid that out? I've never wanted anything so bad in my whole damn boring life, Deacon. I never knew what the heck I even wanted in life before. But I want that. All of that. Please just give me one more chance."

He watched me throughout that whole speech. I don't know what my expressions said but if they said half as much as I felt, he had to know that I wanted it more than anything. As crazy as it might sound, that gaping hole of emptiness I'd always felt? The not knowing what about me was special or unique? Right now it felt like if I had someone like him I might have a chance of actually finding what made me happy.

He prowled toward me, looking angry so angry I was about to have a heart attack. I took a step back.

"Stop," he ordered, "And listen to me."

I stopped. My heart felt like it was about to take flight.

"Not one more chance," he said and my heart sank and big tears fell down my cheeks. But then he kept talking. Two inches away from me, not touching me, but close enough that I could feel his body heat.

"You're in this with me? You're in this there are no limits to what I do for you. A million chances if your heart is in the right place. You fuck up, I forgive you a million times if I need to. But you never ever cheat on me and don't lie to me. I'll never cheat. I'll give you all the truth you want. Never hurt you. I will protect you. It'll be unconditional as long as you're only mine and have a mind to making me happy and not trying to make me be someone I'm not. I will fall deep for you and give you everything I can give you; I know I will. I've already started falling, Kitten."

Oh my good God. Was I dreaming?

"So many things about you...fuck, can't get you outta my head. You gotta be ready for intensity but know me and my MC will put ourselves in the line of fire to keep you safe. I just need you to be you but take my hand, trust me with the lead, and take me as I am."

Was he for real? Please let him be for real.

"Yeah?" he asked.

I nodded, "Yes."

"You sure?" He held out his hand.

"Totally sure." I reached for his hand and when he took mine, he gave it a reassuring squeeze, and then his eyes sparkled and he bent and put a shoulder to my belly and hauled me up and over his shoulder and whacked my ass. I shrieked in surprise.

And then he walked past the bar. The smokers out front were hooting and howling encouragement.

"Atta boy, Deacon!"

"That's how ya lay a claim, brother!"

He strode to the far corner of the parking lot and back past the concrete and then carried me down a narrow wooden staircase leading into some woods and when he set me on my feet we were in front of a fifth wheel. It was lit with some solar garden lights outside and there was a picnic table outside the door. It was dark otherwise. This was tucked away.

"I have a bag in the car," I told him.

"A bag?"

"An overnight bag. If you want me to stay tonight..." I said.

"You're staying," he answered, "I'll get it."

And then he unlocked and opened the door and hit the wall, turning lights on. He signaled for me to step in ahead of him.

I pushed away my fears and the little voice warning me about him, warning me that he was too much man for little ole me, and as I took that little step into his place, it felt like a huge step. Huge.

"Be right back, grab us drinks," he told me and shut the door behind me. He hadn't lost any of the intensity from his speech. I took a big breath and took the space in.

Wow. This trailer could house a rock band. It was lush.

It was clean, spotlessly clean and modern inside and decorated in earth tones with a three seater plush chocolate brown sofa, a small granite booth style dining area that'd seat four, and the kitchen had a tiny island with a double sink and cook top. There was even a dishwasher. It was all sparkly granite and shiny stainless steel. The wall had a built-in cherry wood entertainment center with a TV, stereo, and a PlayStation.

Past the kitchen area were two steps, steps that looked like drawers. I climbed them and found a cute and modern but small bathroom with shower, toilet, and sink, and beside that was the bedroom. It was small, mostly just a double bed and the bed wasn't made, but it looked comfortable with a built-in bookshelf over the padded headboard and a mirrored closet. This space was totally big enough to live in and other than the bed being unmade the whole place was as if it was in a showroom, ready for prospective buyers.

I went into the bathroom and checked my face. I had mascara under my eyes so I cleaned up.

I opened the fridge and it was stocked with beer and cans of Coke and two quarts of milk but had zero food, unless you counted a bottle of ketchup, bottle of chocolate syrup, and a giant yellow bag of M&Ms. I grabbed two beers and moved to the seating area and sat.

I heard the door open and Deacon stepped in and tossed my backpack and purse on the floor.

I stood up.

He took me in from toe to head and then moved in my direction, his face still holding intensity. I resisted the urge to retreat.

When he got to me, I cautiously put my arms up around his neck and got up on my toes.

He grabbed my thighs and hefted me up. I wrapped my legs around his waist and I kissed him.

He walked me up to the bedroom and laid me on the bed and then he leaned back, breaking our lip lock, and threw his t-shirt off.

His chest was beautiful. Above his right peck was an intricate and detailed angel with long flowing hair and spanned wings that were very similar to the wings in his MC's emblem. It was breathtaking. In tiny letters underneath it, it said, *Rest in Peace*

I got up on an elbow and leaned forward and touched the tattoo.

"Is that for her?"

He looked down at it and nodded.

"It's beautiful. What was her name?"

"Cassie."

"I'm sorry you lost her."

"Long time ago, Kitten."

"I'm still sorry. Obviously, something like that'd stay with you a lifetime."

He gave a little shrug, "I can't say she would've been it for me for life, that I'd have married her, we were just kids and she was my first serious girlfriend, but I'm sorry everyone lost her. She had a lot of friends, a heart of gold."

I caressed the tattoo with my fingertips, "I'm also sorry I was a crazy bitch."

He shook his head, "Don't. You've said sorry already. We don't need to keep lookin' in the rearview. And I get it. I do. I just wanted to tell you my story in my own time. Not fuckin' pleased Spence was shootin' his mouth off again."

"Have you seen him?"

"Lucky for him, no."

"It wasn't him shooting his mouth off again … on a different day. It was from the same night. It's just stuff he said to Joe, Pippa's boyfriend, after you dangled him from the roof. Joe told Pippa and Jenna and Jenna was worried about me and it just took her a few days to tell me because I was so wrapped up in all that was happening I wasn't returning her calls. She didn't mean anything bad. She was having my back..."

"I see that," he said darkly, "But Spence and me will still be havin' a chat." He said 'chat' sourly.

I winced, "Are you in the habit of dangling your brother from rooftops?"

He glared at me so I waved my hand.

"Forget I asked. Um, how did you know I was here?"

"Saw you pull in. I'd just stepped into the bar for a drink but saw your car from the corner of my eye when someone came in, then where you headed, toward the wrong trailer. Knew you'd think I was with Trina. No way in the world I'd go from that scene we just had straight to fucking someone, Ella."

"I'm glad you stopped me from leaving to set me straight. I'm glad I'm here. I like your place..."

"We're not having sex," he informed me and he looked angry.

I was a little surprised. He laid down beside me, not touching me, but keeping his eyes on mine.

"Everything being as amped as its been? I've been spitting nails since yesterday. I don't want that cloud over this, our first time together. I'm ready to crash. It's been a long 2 days."

"Oh. Okay," my voice was small.

"But you stay. I want to wake up beside you. Tomorrow's a new day. That okay with you?"

I nodded and hesitantly curled up against him, resting my head on the pillow beside him. He pulled me closer and I put my head on his chest. He let out a big breath. It sounded like it was relieved.

I could feel his heart beating and I was staring down at gorgeous abs and those seriously sexy hip bones with a tiny trail of dark hair from his navel that led to his jeans. Without putting any thought into it I found my index finger tracing that line.

I felt his body jiggling with laughter. I lifted my head off his chest and our eyes met. His were amused. Finally, the angry dragon-fire was gone.

I was seriously *seriously* horny. I mean, how could I not be? I was in this bed with him and after all that? I wanted to lose myself in him.

"Was gonna ask you to kill the light, I'm wiped, but something on your mind, Kitten?" he teased.

I pulled my finger back from his treasure trail and balled my hands into fists. I shrugged, my face heating up.

"I'll just go get ready for bed," I was about to move but he tipped my chin up toward his mouth and kissed me. He tasted good. No, he tasted amazing. And before I knew it, his hand was on my boob, over my t-shirt, his thumb grazing my nipple.

I looked him in the eye again.

He looked at me and jerked his chin up, urging me to share what was on my mind.

"You sure you're too mad for sex?" I asked.

He gave me a little smile but didn't reply.

"You said you want me to fly my freak flag?" I inquired.

His smile grew a bit wider.

"Can we just play?" I asked, "If you're still pissed..." He didn't seem like he was pissed any longer but I forged ahead anyway, "I could just try to get you un-pissed."

He looked a bit surprised and then he rolled to his side and leaned over beside me, on his elbow.

"Play?" He looked intrigued.

"I could...take care of you," I suggested, "You don't have to do a thing for me, except maybe kiss me?"

His eyebrow went up.

"And maybe you could keep that promise you made me."

He looked confused, "What promise?"

My face went red.

I chewed my lip, "To give me a spanking if I pulled a stunt like Saturday. Which I did. Not on purpose but I did. And you did whack my butt out there but the feeling is already starting to wear off and you said it'd be a long time before I wouldn't feel—-"

Laughter burst out of him before I could go on and then his look switched to sexually charged and he sat up, grabbed me, and flipped me over his knee, my butt under his palm. He squeezed my bottom and groaned.

Oh yeah. Yes, yes, yes! I guess levity was a good choice to get him un-pissed.

"Nope," he changed his mind and then he flipped me back onto the bed, climbed up until his back was flush against the padded headboard and patted the spot beside him. I eagerly crawled up to him, loving the way he manhandled me.

"I was only kidding," I defended.

"No you weren't. Lay on your back across my lap instead."

"On my back across your lap?"

"Like this." He positioned me horizontally across his lap, my lower back over his crotch, and then he stuffed a pillow under my head. He then unzipped my jeans and pulled them down over my hips.

"Kick 'em off," he ordered. I did, leaving myself in just a pair of pink hipster panties and my t-shirt.

"Why—-" I started.

"This way I can watch your face when I slap this naughty ass," he said. At those words, my cookie spasmed.

He hooked an arm under my knees and lifted my legs up in the air and then transferred them to his other arm, which hooked around. He used his now free hand to pull my panties upwards until they rested at just below my knees. He grabbed them with the hand that was holding up my legs and kept them there by using my underwear to hold me in that position.

I felt my face heat up as his free hand travelled down to caress my ass. Deacon's fingers then slid through the moisture between my legs.

"You're soaked," he told me something I already knew and he looked very happy about it.

I nodded, speechless.

"You like to be spanked?" he asked, his voice so husky it got my juices flowing even more.

I shrugged, "I've never been spanked. But I've fantasized about it. And since you said you'd do it, I haven't been able to stop thinking about it. When you did it outside? That was hot."

His gaze darkened and his tongue traced his full bottom lip and then his hand left me and then he whacked my bottom. Not super hard but hard enough to feel it. His eyes were fiery hot and hadn't yet left my face. But then he leaned over further, still holding my legs up high, using my underwear like a handle, and his mouth was an inch from mine. "You like that?"

I nodded and swallowed. Oh, I liked it alright. I liked it a fuck of a lot.

His fingers dipped in again and pumped them inside of me,

"Tighten around my fingers, Kitten," he ordered and I complied, tightening my inner walls as hard as I could.

"I can't wait to feel that around my cock," he told me and I felt a rush of heat and tingles between my legs.

"And I would've felt it yesterday if you hadn't been such a bad bad girl," he admonished and then he whacked my ass again. I gasped. This was sexy.

He pulled on my knees and leaned over so that he could get a better look at me.

"You've got a pretty pussy," he told me, "I like that you keep it shaved. I get to see all of you."

"I get Brazilians. Pippa does them and—-"

And then he whacked it. He whacked my pussy. Holy crap. The sensations were electric. I was so wet I'd leave a wet mark on his jeans.

"Very fucking hot," he said, "Prettiest pussy I've ever seen, Kitten."

I whimpered, bereft of the ability to do anything else.

His fingers dove back in and I let out a moan. He added his thumb and got it right to my clit.

"Found it," he said and said and winked. I let out a big breath.

"You wanna come?" he asked me.

I nodded eagerly.

"But do you deserve to come?" he asked and his pierced eyebrow rose in that sexy way again.

I shook my head, "Nope," my heart was racing, "No I don't deserve to... to..." Holy shit. This was getting better by the minute. I swallowed hard, "Come."

"That's right. Bad girl." He let go of my legs and they fell and then he flipped me over on his lap so that my belly was now on his lap, feeling his very prominent erection against it, my ass bared, and he whacked it, this time a little bit harder. I jolted.

"But I'm gonna get you there, baby. I'm gonna make you come hard. Even when you're naughty. Being my girl? You're gonna get to come a lot. Lookin' forward to hearing about more of your fantasies. Up on your knees."

Then his fingers dove in and circled my opening again. I shuddered and I'm pretty sure my eyes rolled right into the back of my head.

"Knees. Now," he ordered and there was something so supremely hot about being bossed around like this. I complied.

"You like bossy in here?" he asked.

"Mm hm."

"Good, baby, I like that we'll roll like that, like it a fuckuva lot." He sounded very very pleased. He pressed against my back entrance and I went stiff and tensed my butt cheeks, trying to stop the invasion. But the position I was in made that difficult. His finger, or maybe it was his thumb, kept prodding there for a second and dipped just a little bit inside.

"Anybody been in here, Ella?" he asked, looking at me back there. I was so exposed. I sort of liked it.

"No," I breathed.

"Good." His fingers went back to my clit and he started working it and then I think his thumb was there again. The back door invasion went from feeling weird to feeling strangely erotic.

I could feel his erection against my stomach and it felt rock hard and beautiful. I started rocking against it and got my arm underneath and grabbed him over his jeans.

"Not yet," he grabbed my wrist, "Clasp both hands together over your head." He pinned my hands above me and held them in one hand while his other hand moved back to the target.

He started going faster, deeper with his fingers, and I felt like I was on the cusp of going off the edge into sweet blissful oblivion.

His hand left and then he whacked my ass again, "Your ass is fucking sexy, you know that?"

"Ah."

I was so turned on. I had goosebumps everywhere.

"You're so beautiful, Ella."

"*You're* beautiful, Deacon. Let me do something for you…"

"Not yet. You first. You gonna come for me, baby?" he said and kept at me.

I got closer, I was almost there, but then he stopped and smacked my ass again and I grunted, "Ugh. Fuck, Deacon. Please."

"Yeah. Beg for it, Ella."

"Please. Make me come," I said please but it sounded more like an order.

He let out a devious little chuckle, "Ask nice."

"Please, baby?" I whined.

"Mmmm, yeah, you can come. Such a good little Kitten, fuck."

He started circling faster on my clit and then his other hand went under me and tweaked a nipple and I grabbed the blankets and fisted them and started to hit a peak. I cried out. He plunged his fingers into me over and over while I bucked and trembled, sprawled across his lap.

He flipped me onto my back and then he was hovering over me, kissing me. I fumbled with his belt and got it undone and got my hand into his pants and when I found him, holy crap. I assumed by his height that he was very likely well-endowed but holy moly.

I needed that inside me. I wanted to climb it and go for a seriously wild ride.

"Fuck me, Deacon, Please. I don't wanna wait."

"No, Ella. Just touch me."

I moaned in dismay.

"Tomorrow, okay, baby? Wake you up with my cock. It'll be too fast if I do it now. Need time with you. Right now, I just need to come. You got me so fuckin' worked up."

I whimpered, wanting it now, but then that want was replaced with excitement; excitement about getting to help Deacon come. "Can I … go down on you?"

He made a growly sound, his eyes so heated they were making me burn up inside, and I took that as a yes so I shimmied his jeans and black boxer briefs down.

When his pelvis was completely unclothed I was seriously stricken. Fucking beautiful hip bones with a gorgeous defined V that led to Deacon's cock. It was massive and thick and looked like it was rock solid. My eyes widened at the sight of it.

"Whoooa," I sort of stuttered. My eyes were boinging from my head.

He chuckled and folded his hands behind his head but then his teeth sank into his lower lip and his carnal look helped me gather my scattered senses.

I was now on top of him, running my hands up his torso until my fingers threaded into his hair and I kissed him softly on the mouth and then slid my hands back down his torso until I got both hands around it. I looked up at his face and gave him a goofy smile. He laughed a little but then gave me a heated look so I suspected that meant, "Get down to business," so that's what I did.

I started moving my hands up and down. He closed his eyes and I saw his Adam's apple bob.

I got to my belly between his legs and got my mouth over the tip of him. I swirled my tongue around it and he made a happy mmm sound. And then I got *really* into it. I couldn't deep throat him; I gagged when I tried and he ran his fingers through my hair sweetly when that happened.

But despite not being able to take the whole thing, I was very enthusiastic using my mouth and my tongue and my hands. God, his cock was almost as beautiful as he was.

Have you ever seen a perfect cock? I had. In my Tumblr porn collection. But now I'd seen one in real life, too. I'd seen nice cocks. I'd even seen some above average ones. I'd seen both decent and less impressive cocks with guys I'd had sex with, and at male strip joints. But until then I hadn't seen one *this* nice up close and personal that was anywhere near as memorable as Deacon. It was more than perfect because it wasn't just his cock. It was the hips, his thighs, the feel of his skin, his warmth.

But how the heck would this ever fit inside me? I guess I'd worry about that the following morning. For now, I'd do my best to make him come and come hard.

I made eye contact as much as possible because I knew he was watching intently and he looked so damn sexy watching me, his teeth biting into his bottom lip, his eyes heated in that molten lava way again. He would close his eyes, getting into it, but then open them to take in the sight of me going down on him.

I ran my hands up and down his abs and then cupped his balls and went as deep as I could go, applying suction while trying not to bite.

"Ella," he groaned, throwing his head back. The corded muscles in his neck were straining and I was thoroughly pleased I was having that effect on him. But my jaw was hurting and my mouth needed a rest so I let him go, moved up, and whipped my t-shirt and bra off and got his cock between my breasts, held them together and moved up and down slowly, my rear end up in the air.

"Fuck, yeah, baby," he encouraged and then he growled after a minute and then I was flipped onto my back. He got completely out of his jeans and then climbed up, his knees under my armpits and slid his cock between my boobs as he pinched my nipples.

I leaned forward, lifting my shoulders off the bed, pressing my chin toward my chest, until I could reach his tip with my mouth, and then I started twirling my tongue around the crown of him while squeezing my boobs together. It didn't take long for him to lose control. He started thrusting forward over and over, harder and harder, until I could feel a bit of bruising on my breastbone. But he was close so I could endure that little bit of discomfort for the reward of giving him an orgasm.

He let out a masculine-sounding groan as hot liquid flowed over my cleavage, into the dip of my throat.

"Ella," he moaned and I ran my hand up the back of his leg until it rested on his butt. He was all out in goosebumps. He stilled, caught his breath, and then leaned over and under the bed and pulled up a clean folded bath towel and pressed it to my chest. His lips were against mine and his tongue dipped in, his hands fisting my hair.

"Awesome, baby," he breathed and then kissed my forehead. He collapsed onto his back beside me and looked like he was trying to catch his breath. He pulled me close and kissed me right on the mouth again.

Jay wouldn't kiss me after a blowjob, even if he hadn't come in my mouth, if my mouth had gotten anywhere near his dick, he'd turn his head. I called him out on it once, when we'd been staying in a motel overnight, and he told me it'd be gay if he did that. I was so pissed off that I used *his* toothbrush afterwards to brush my teeth, keeping that my little secret. *Take that!*

I loved that Deacon even gave me the tongue right after I'd had him in my mouth.

He got out of the bed went to the washroom.

I sat up and wiped my throat off some more and then reached under and found more towels stacked under there on a shelf so grabbed one and got up as he came back in. I went into the bathroom and got into the shower. Afterwards, I put on a clean tank top and boy black short panties that I'd brought with me to sleep in. They were plain-looking but Lycra and I thought they did great things for my butt.

When I came back out he was in the bed, lights off.

He pulled back the blankets and I climbed in.

He enveloped me close against him.

"Hi," I greeted.

"Mmm," he pulled me close and kissed my lips softly. I snuggled in.

"I brought your beer in. Didn't know if you wanted it so brought you a water, too."

"Thanks," I wrapped my arms around him. He was hard and smooth all over and he smelled amazing. I soaked it in for a few minutes. I soaked in that he'd given me another chance. I soaked in all that he'd done for me in bed. I marinated in the fact that he'd promised to keep me safe despite the intensity of the situation his MC was in. I thought about him, all he'd been through with women.

"Thank you, Deacon."

"For?"

"For liking me. For giving me another chance."

"Thank you, Kitten." He squeezed.

"For getting you un-pissed? Did I get you un-pissed?"

"For wanting that chance, for being brave enough to do this with me. Yeah, I'm intense. We're starting out at a volatile time so you gotta just breathe through it and know I'll keep you safe. I'll make it worth it."

"Okay," I said and snuggled in tighter, deciding I'd work hard to make it worth it for him, too. He wasn't getting a crazy bitch with me. He was going to get someone who had his back, who appreciated him and wanted to give him joy instead of pain. I wanted this so much, "I'll make it worth it, too. Your days of dealing with crazy bitches are over. Sweet dreams, Deacon. You got an alarm clock?"

He gave me a squeeze. "I'll set my phone. What time you gotta be up?"

"I need to be at work at 9:30."

"Okay, I'll set it for 7."

"Uh, it doesn't have to be that early. Not like my work is far away. I can go get my phone from out there in my bag."

"Naw, I'll just set mine. And yeah it does," he yawned, "We're gonna need playtime in the morning before work. Guess what part of me is gonna wake you?"

"Ohhhh." I giggled.

"Ohhh yeah," he agreed and gave me a squeeze.

It was barely eleven o'clock but I hadn't slept much the night before and all boneless from the orgasm and all the beauty of that evening, all comfy in his embrace after a nice hot shower, I was out like a light.

I WOKE UP TO SUNSHINE. There was a skylight over us and the sun was warming my face, shining, and birds were singing. I glanced at the shelves behind Deacon's bed. They held a couple Stephen King books, a dish with some change, a pack of gum, and a watch in it, and his phone. I lifted it to check the time. It was only 5:40. He was sound asleep beside me. He was on his side, his back to me. I peeked under the blanket. He was naked. I felt tingly all over.

I reached down and ran my hand over his bum and then nuzzled into his back, reached around, and found him semi-hard. He groaned and rolled to his back and his eyes were instantly awake and alert. His cock hardened in my grasp. He smiled at me; which felt like a gift, and my heart squeezed. What a beautiful sight to wake up to. I couldn't imagine ever taking that face for granted if I ever got lucky enough to see it smiling every single morning. Not just because he was beautiful but also because I figured that smile meant I was doing something right.

"Good morning," I greeted on a downward stroke.

"What 'cha doin'?" he asked.

"Saying good morning to Little Deacon." I squeezed.

"Little Deacon?" he quirked up a brow.

I wrinkled my nose with a shrug, "I'll have to think up a better nickname. I'll get back to you on that once he and I are better acquainted."

He grabbed me by my armpits and pulled me on top of him and laid a hot and wet kiss on me while grabbing my ass and sliding my panties down. His length moved between my legs and rested hard against me. I was so turned on so instantly that I felt him slide as I coated him with my juices.

"I want you intimately acquainted with him. Often. You on the pill?" he asked, caressing my face and then he stretched to reach under his bed without letting go of me and I heard a crinkling sound and then he had a strip of condoms in his hand. He pulled one off.

I nodded.

"You been tested?" he asked.

I shook my head, "Not in almost a year."

"Anyone been inside bare since then?" he asked.

I shook my head.

"No one?" he asked.

"Not this year, no. Also not ever. I made them all use condoms," I whispered, "I've always been paranoid."

It was true; I'd never admitted to anyone I was seeing that I was on the pill. I had been so paranoid about the small chance of pregnancy and about STDs that I wanted to be double safe.

"No one's ever been bare in you?" he asked.

I shook my head.

"Never?" he confirmed.

"Never ever."

He smiled big, "I haven't been bare inside anyone in about eleven or twelve years but I want it with you."

I nodded.

"You want it, too?"

I nodded again, feeling almost mesmerized by him.

"I'll get tested before I go bare. Extra safe."

I chewed my lip. I wanted him inside me bare. I hadn't wanted that yet from anyone but seeing how pleased he was about that possibility, now I couldn't wait for it.

"I can't wait to feel the inside of you against my cock," he whispered against my mouth, "But we'll both get tested first. Be extra sure."

I nodded, "I'll make an appointment."

"Never felt this way so fast," he said.

I shook my head, "Me, either." My heart soared. Not only never so fast for me, never at *all*. I really liked that he was laying it all out there. I couldn't believe I'd just blurted that I was on the pill. I was letting my guard down with him. Big time.

"Condoms suck," he said, "But even though they do, it'll be beautiful inside you even with that between us. As soon as possible, I want nothing in my way. See if your doc'll see me, too?"

"Okay." I chewed my bottom lip as I watched his strong hands, corded forearms, as he rolled it on and it was seriously sexy to watch him handle himself. I decided I'd really really like to sometime watch him jerk off. I'd also like to go down on him while he held it and fed it to me, being dominant. One hand on it, the other hand holding my chin up.

Mm yum.

He leaned over me and spread my legs and then was in position. He leaned down and tongued my nipple and groaned and I opened my legs wider and threaded my fingers into his hair.

His thumb started to circle my clit and I tried to maneuver him inside.

"Gotta get you ready for me," he whispered, circling some more.

"I'm ready, already."

"You're ready for me?" he whispered as he slid his finger through the wetness.

"So very ready," I whispered back.

He got his beautiful cock right against my entrance and at that sensation, I knew he was too big for it not to be a little uncomfortable, even as ready as I was. He was bigger than I'd ever had. Longer, thicker. God, I couldn't wait.

"I can't wait to be bare, inside you, where nobody but me has been."

"Mmm, oh," I opened my mouth and then his lips were on mine, swallowing my sounds. His circling on my clit picked up pace and I started rocking, and then he leaned back and looked me in the eyes and then started to sink slowly inside.

I winced, my eyes widened, and I let out a long stuttered breath. The feeling of fullness was extreme. Intense. But so so good. And his eyes on me while he advanced, so fucking hot. He worked my clit a little bit, trying to get me geared up for more. When he finally bottomed out I was panting and squeezing his shoulders.

"You okay?" he asked.

I swallowed back the bite of discomfort and nodded a little, "Gimme a sec."

I clamped down a little on him and he let out a masculine groan that turned my bones to water.

"Oh yeah, Ella. You feel so good. You good for me to move?"

"Mm hm," I encouraged and started rocking a little. My body adjusted and it started to feel good. Really really good. I wrapped my legs around his backside and dug my heels in and he picked up pace, taking my mouth with his, and then his circling fingers went faster and he whispered, "Sooo fucking good," right against my mouth and then I climaxed, loudly. Abruptly, without warning. Did I mention loudly? His right hand moved up my body, up my torso, and then he put his thumb right in my mouth.

"Suck, see how nice you taste," he demanded and I complied, feeling like another orgasm was coming because... holy hotness! He dipped his thumb back into the cleft of me and then brought it to his own mouth and sucked. He did all this while his hips kept moving, moving beautifully. My beautiful biker could multitask during sex.

I whimpered and then he started powering harder and faster and harder still. And then he flipped me onto my belly, yanked my hips up, and drove back inside from behind and the depth? Yowza.

I was so full of him; I'd never been so full of anyone. He slowed pace, going deep and then started to go faster, holding my hips, then kissing my shoulder and then he powered forward, rotated his hips, and a groan came out of him that I felt. I felt it deep in my soul.

God. He'd just ruined me for anyone else ever. Completely ruined me.

I came again, so hard that tears welled up in my eyes. He pulled out and flopped onto his back, simultaneously pulling me close so it didn't feel at all like he'd pulled away. I buried my face in his throat, put my hand on his warm, smooth chest. I felt his heart racing. Racing for me. I started to silently weep. Sex had never had feeling like this before. This was what I'd been wanting, craving, what I suspected it *could* be.

His hands were in my hair and used it to pull me back, to look in my eyes.

"You okay? I hurt you?" He looked so concerned.

I put my lips to his, "No. That was beautiful. I knew it could be beautiful but didn't know just how beautiful. You've just ruined me for anyone else, ever. My god..."

He wiped a tear away with his thumb and gave me the gift of his beautiful smile.

"Oh shit", I said. I couldn't believe I just blurted that out.

"What?" he asked.

"I can't believe I just blurted that out. I'm such a dummy."

"No, baby. Don't be sorry about that. It was beautiful. And that was just the beginning," he told me, "I've got a feeling we're gonna make a lot of beauty together. I like that you didn't guard how much you liked that. Don't ever hide who you are or what you feel, okay? Please?"

Joy bubbled up in me. I snuggled in and fell back to sleep tangled up with him. It felt like a whole other night of sleep when the alarm woke us. I felt like I was on top of the world.

Right after his alarm went off he kissed me and left the bed and I heard him fiddling in the kitchen and then he turned on the radio in the other room.

A news and weather report wrapped up and then John Mayer's Your Body is a Wonderland came on.

As I was about to get up to get another shower, sitting on the edge of the bed, legs dangling, he was back and he gently pushed me back into the bed and then began exploring my body as if empowered by the song and it was gentle and sweet at the beginning when he kissed my ankle and worked his way up, tonguing a loud orgasm out of me and then at the end when he gloved up and thrust powerfully into me until we cried out together, me straddling him, taking him so deep and man... it was beautiful. As I caught my breath I caught the aroma of fresh coffee.

Afterwards, after my shower, I could still feel him. I didn't feel his handprints on my ass (although I'd never forget that) but I knew I'd feel the ghost of Deacon's cock inside my cookie for a good long while.

After my shower he got one. His shower was too small for us to get one together and I didn't know how even he fit in there comfortably alone because it was a tight squeeze for me, even. I found mugs of coffee poured for us on the counter. I packed up my things and made the bed and we sat outside to have coffee at the picnic table. It was a gorgeous morning. It was early September, the end of summer, almost time for the leaves to change. Usually the end of summer made me melancholy. But, I was in a fantastic mood. I was looking forward to looking forward.

I hadn't fucked up irreparably. I had a beautiful night with him, several orgasms, I got to make him come three times, and I was excited about him, about us.

"What time you work to?" he asked me, pulling on a grey ribbed muscle shirt while sitting at the picnic table, wearing jeans, his feet bare.

"Probably around 3:30. He asked me to do a midnight shift this Friday night, which would totally screw the weekend but I forgot to answer his text," I made a gag face.

"Say no."

"I have one shift this week. It's gonna sting."

"You worried about bills?"

"I don't have too many but I help out my parents wherever I can. I just got paid so I'm okay this week. I've got enough to pay my car insurance and the water bill I promised to pay but next pay is gonna suck."

"You need cash, tell me," he said.

Like that was gonna happen. I smiled non-committally.

"I mean it," he leaned forward and grabbed my hand, "I've got money in the bank, did two healthy flips in a row just after investing with my Dad so the money hasn't even been touched. If you need cash, just say."

"Healthy flips?" I asked, trying to tamp down emotion.

"I flipped some houses back home the last few years on the side. Fixed 'em up and sold them at a profit. Own shares in the businesses with Dad, get a cut of the proceeds from the MC, we all do. I'm doing well."

That explained the fancy rock star trailer. I was about to ask how the MC made money but sort of didn't wanna know right now.

"Thanks, I'll be good. I'm gonna job hunt tomorrow in case he only has me on schedule for one shift again next week. He's giving all the shifts to his wife. I doubt he's even paying her. Business ain't great. What about the Roadhouse? Your dad—-"

"Nope. Not happening. And if I find out you're suffering because you didn't speak up about needin' cash, I'll be pissed. So if you need it, talk to me. What're you doing tonight?"

"If you're afraid about me working for the roadhouse that if we split it'll be ugly I can promise that if it feels even an eensy bit ugly I'll just leave. I wouldn't want to work in a toxic environment. So it's not awkward, you know..."

"You planning on breakin' up with me already?" he asked.

"No way, Jose. But if that's not what you're worried about, then what..."

"Having a pile of drunk bikers staring at your rack, your ass? No. Fuck no. That's why I'm sayin' no."

"Deacon, come on..." I laughed. A bit ridiculous. Sheesh.

"Come here," he said.

He was sitting across from me at the picnic table so I got up and rounded it. He flipped around so his back was to the table, grabbed me by the hips, and looked up at me.

"No, Ella. Most of those guys are my brothers, if not by blood then by choice, but the way things are with the club just startin' out here, with the type of business we are, catering to the needs of other MC's, buildin' relationships with men I don't yet know all that well, I'd need to tattoo 'Property of Deacon Valentine' on your forehead and I'd much rather tattoo that on your ass. On an ass only I get to see that tat on. Putting you there on display would be asking to make some enemies and we don't need more of that at this juncture." He moved both hands to my ass and brought me closer and kept them there. My hands landed on his hard, muscled chest.

"So what if I wanted to get a job as a waitress somewhere else? Like another bar?"

He shrugged, "If you'd already been doin' it when we got started, yeah. But you're with me now you don't go off and go working slinging booze for the competition, eye candy for their customers, eye candy for Roadhouse customers who'll drink somewhere else so that they can stare at your ass all night. No."

I shook my head but laughed, "That's nuts."

"It's a guy thing. A biker thing. A Deacon thing. Deal with it."

"You're pretty lucky you just got me super agreeable in there, Buster. Otherwise I'd be a lot more argumentative right now."

"Buster?" he raised his brows.

I poked him in the chest, "Yeah, Buster."

"Good to know how to keep you agreeable," he smirked and squeezed my ass with both hands.

I heard leaves rustling and voices. Spencer and Rider were coming down the wooden stairs that led to the trailer from the parking lot. Deacon didn't move his hands off my ass. I tried to move away but he kept me there. I saw a muscle working in his jaw as he laid eyes on Spence.

"Got coffee and milk, man?" Rider asked, "Mornin' Ella."

"Yeah," Deacon jerked his thumb toward the trailer and then I saw his eyes, eyes that went harder, stay on Spencer.

"We ran out," Rider grumbled, heading inside.

"Get me one, too," Spencer called. Spencer's eyes weren't on Deacon. They were on me. They moved from my face, which was turned in his direction although my body wasn't, to my ass, which was pretty much hidden by Deacon's hands.

"Let me sit," I whispered.

Deacon spun me and used his grasp on my hips to pull me onto his lap, calling in to Rider, "Bought me some milk and one for the shop. Take one when you go open up."

"Ya man," Rider called back out.

"Hey," I greeted Spencer.

"Hey, Ella. You guys had a good night, I heard."

I smiled.

Spencer snickered, knowingly, like he knew a private joke.

"What?" Deacon asked, glaring at him.

"I *heard*. Heard you guys. Came down to talk to ya bro, late last night, buuut.... heard you two at it. Came back down early this mornin' for milk and heard you again. Got yourself a moaner, hey man? Congrats. I know how you like the moaners."

Deacon looked absolutely pissed. "You wanna eat your meals through a straw?" He glared at Spencer.

Spencer looked smug. What an asshole. He hadn't looked at Deacon through any of that. He'd been watching me instead.

Instead of blushing, I piped up, "Yes, congrats *are* in order. You should know, I wasn't ever a moaner before you. You got some skills there, Tiger." And then I squeezed Deacon's thigh and planted a kiss on his clenching jaw.

His eyes moved to my face, filled with light, and he put his hand to my face and kissed me hot and heavy.

As he moved in for the kiss from the corner of my eye I saw Spencer's triumphant smirk melt into a glare aimed at the picnic table.

Rider came out as our lips separated and he winked at me. He'd heard the whole thing and seemed to be holding back from laughing out loud. He passed Spencer a coffee mug, "C'mon, Spence. See ya, Ella. See you in the shop, bro," Rider said. He grabbed the carton of milk tucked under his arm and waved with it.

I waved and took another sip of my coffee and checked my cell phone for the time.

"I'll be havin' words with him," Deacon grumbled and then cleared his expression, "So what're you doing tonight?" he asked me with a kiss to the side of my head as his brothers climbed the stairs.

"I have nothing planned," I said.

"Good. Come over. I'll meet you here at 6:00. We'll go grab some food. Pack another bag. Stay with me again tonight," he said.

I got to my feet and took another sip from my mug, "Sounds great. I'll just go rinse this and grab my stuff. Better get to work."

He followed me inside and after my mug was rinsed and put into the dishwasher he spun me around and took my face into both hands, "Be safe today. Watch out for the Jackals and steer clear of the fuckwad. And tell them no for workin' this weekend."

"Okay. Jay texted me yesterday trying to meet up for coffee again. I just ignored him."

"Where does he work?"

"He works from home for an IT company. He commutes to the office in Watertown only once or twice a week."

"Where does he live?"

"Uh..."

"Where?" he ordered.

"Deacon..."

"Forget it; I'll find him myself. Get going."

He swatted me on the butt and passed me my purse and slung my knapsack over his shoulder, "Walk you to your car."

"Bossy," I mumbled.

"Damn right. Do I have a good reason?" he challenged.

"Yeah," I huffed petulantly.

"Then let me handle him."

"Fine," I waved my hand, "He's all yours. Just don't get in trouble for dangling him from a rooftop."

He rolled his eyes as if the notion of him getting in trouble was preposterous. "Don't you worry about that."

I told Deacon where Jay lived after we got to my car.

7

AFTER A SLOW AND UNEVENTFUL shift and not knowing about the following week's schedule yet, I went home to pack a new bag and do some online banking.

Mom was doing a class, Beau was at a play date and Dad was busy in his garage welding something with four guys I didn't know who were dressed in full Dominion Brotherhood biker gear watching him do it, but he waved at me. So did all the bikers.

There was barely enough room for The Shitbox in the driveway what with all the motorcycles and cars parked. Jenna's car was parked in her parent's driveway so I suspected I'd have a visitor over shortly.

Not quite ten minutes after I was in the door, Jenna was in my room with me, putting a can of Pepsi on my dresser and opening one for herself. She'd waltzed in, as she always did, (I knocked on Jenna's parent's house door, which was expected by them, her parents would've had heart failure if I'd just waltzed in and made myself at home, but Jenna hadn't knocked on mine since we were small) and she flopped onto my bed.

"Hey you," she greeted.

"Hey you," I returned as I rifled through my underwear drawer to find a sexy black pair with a caged back with a big bow. I'd bought them when I was single and had considered, a few times, surprising Carson, the guy I was with (it only lasted about a month) before Jay, but had never actually had the nerve to wear them. Now they'd be for Deacon. Deacon was a t&a man and I suspected they'd be appreciated.

"I tried to call you last night," she said, with more than a hint of accusation.

"Don't touch it," I pointed at her. She had her hand on my cell phone and I'd changed my ringtone to something normal and didn't want her switching it back. "I was with Deacon."

Score! Found the underwear. I tossed them into my bag and opened my Pepsi.

"I know. I'm glad. I talked to Rider about his brother and he told me some stuff. About how Deacon got fucked over repeatedly so he's cautious about relationships and ... I'm gathering that you got that info from Deacon already, since you spent the night with him." Her face looked solemn and yet relieved. I could tell she felt the same as me after hearing the truth about Deacon from Rider.

"Yeah, I blew him off and hid and then when cornered I threw what I'd heard in his face and called it quits and then he schooled me on the facts and then walked away from me. I had to grovel."

She winced, "That's some heavy shit he went through. Sorry, Elle."

"Don't be sorry for sharing facts. You were having my back. I'd have done the same. He told me that there was stuff, that I'd hear things, and I agreed to discuss them with him but then I jumped the gun. I just didn't think there could be reasonable reasons for that, you know?"

She was nodding.

I continued, "And with everything else? Getting held at knifepoint, the shit I've heard about Jay, and now dating a guy who's going to war against the MC my uncle..." I stopped ranting and realized I might be saying too much, "Forget that last part."

Jenna waved her hand, "I already know. Rider told me to stay away from those guys and said we had to keep quiet about it. Said he figured you'd tell me anyway so he wanted to get in front of it. So last night? You groveled and all's good?"

I dropped on the bed beside her.

"He's amazing, Jen. I'm falling hard."

"His brother is amazing, too."

I rolled onto my belly and got close to her face.

"Are you falling?"

"Little bit..." she said and I could tell it was more than a little bit.

"Look at us! Dating brothers. Biker brothers. Can you believe this?"

She giggled. "Did you... *do* it?" she whispered.

I nodded big, "Yes and oh my god! It was phenomenal. Is his brother phenomenal too?"

"Oh my god. Yes. The best I've ever had. Not to mention the biggest."

"Me too."

We giggled really loud and uncontrollably and kicked our feet and then hugged.

"Oh my God, Jenna. I'm in so much trouble. So much."

"What do you mean?"

"I'm so totally cock whipped it's not even funny! Deacon just, like, puts me in this cock fog..." My eyes glazed over.

I don't know how long later -—Jenna was snapping her fingers in front of my face. While in that daze she probably changed my ringtone back to that fucking song.

"Earth to Ella, come in, Ella."

"See what I mean? I just think about it and I go all..." I stared at the tip of my nose to make myself go cross-eyed and she giggled.

"It's a good thing. Good you got some decent tail for once."

I nodded in agreement, "But I've gotta dash, babes. I'm going to his place. Spending the night again."

"Ooh. I haven't seen where they live yet. What's it like?"

"I haven't seen where Deke, Rider, and Spence are. They live above the Roadhouse. Deacon has a trailer out in the back."

"A trailer?" She made a face and let her tongue loll.

"Nuh-uh, nope, Jenna. When I say trailer, it's like a rock star pad. All new and cherry wood and granite and modern. And it's spotless. Like, what biker lives in a spotless rock star trailer? It even has a dishwasher."

"Your biker?" she threw out there.

"My biker," I sighed dreamily.

She sat up, "Well, if you were ever gonna hook up with a biker, this sounds like *the* biker, the only kinda biker you'd have. Girl time soon, okay? And double dates soon, too."

"Absolutely."

She hugged me, "You seem happy."

"I'm scared shitless. This is so far out of my normal comfort zone, Jenna. But I am falling hard and fast."

"Rider says he's had a lot of pain. A lot of it. But he is tough and loyal and smart. Rider says you couldn't ask for a better guy to have in your corner."

"That's really good to hear. Rider seems like a good guy."

"He does, doesn't he? It feels almost too perfect. He's gorgeous and sweet and funny and smart and amazing in bed. I'm so fucking scared, Elle."

I winced but then shook off my skepticism, straightened up and said, "Trust it. Maybe it doesn't have to be so hard."

She got up and then straightened up and said, "Rider also said Deacon can be the scariest mo-fo he's ever seen. No slouch."

"He's definitely intense," I said, thinking I needed a new word beyond intense. That word had me thinking about almost fucking up.

"Okay, so before you go, beyond your love life and my love life I have business that brings me here. We've got four Fall weddings coming up for the salon. Me and Pip are booked solid for hair and make-up, nails, waxing. Any way you can possibly help out those Saturdays? Not this one but next Saturday and I'll mark the others all down for you. For pay. I need someone coming with us, helping with the make-up and hair. I know you're not trained technically but you're great at make-up and I need extra hands to help pass me things, carry gear, clean make-up brushes, and stuff. I can get you flat ironing, setting curls, whatever. Basically be our bitch, but mostly mine. What do you think?"

"I think I'm game. I'm your bitch half the time anyway, might as well get paid. I'm getting shit hours at work and so I need the money."

"Cool. Hey… then in that case, what about being my part-time receptionist? Like, not full-time; just, say, Fridays and Saturdays for now? Those are our two busiest days of the week and it's so mental I can't answer the phone and greet customers or I get backed up. I need help with reception and shampooing, sweeping up hair, etcetera. Would that work? 'Cuz it'd help us huge. We have to close down a few Saturdays due to the weddings I'm doing so it'd help me huge if you could be with me on Fridays because that day just got a hella lot busier. I have one Sunday wedding coming up at the end of September, too."

"Yeah. Sounds good. Unless I can find something full time. That work? I'll try to give notice but unless the perfect job I can't say no to comes along and has to mean a quick jump for the Fridays but I won't let you down for the weddings. That okay?"

"Done. And maybe you'll love it enough to stay with me. We'll see. Business is good. And I can pay you $2 above minimum wage an hour for now and when we do weddings on the weekends the tips get split evenly among me, you, and Pip so you'll get a nice chunk of change." She went to my desk and grabbed a Sharpie and started jotting notes on my calendar on the days she had weddings. "And anything you upsell at the front desk when people cash out you get 10% commission on. Hair products, make-up, hair tools. Sound good? It can add up."

"Amazeballs!" I said. Things were definitely looking up, "Wait. Give me a flat iron at cost and take it off my first pay? Seriously, if I show curly-haired people the befores and afters on that iron I'll sell a fortune worth."

She put the cap back on the Sharpie. "Bitch, I'll *give* you one. Signing bonus."

"Wahoo!"

Jenna left and I finished getting ready for Deacon's place. I spotted Mom's gaggle of pupils wandering out with yoga mats so I headed to her studio. She was rolling up her mat.

"Hey, Ella sweetie," she greeted.

"Hi Momma, I'm spending the night at Deacon's. I transferred you the water bill money."

"Oh, thank you darling. Have a good time."

I hugged her.

I found Beau in the kitchen squirting whipped cream onto hot dogs at the table.

"Beau, that's not exactly a healthy dinner you've got there, bud. Who made those for you?"

"Mom did. And I hate them, Lella. They don't taste like regular haw-dogs. I don't know if they're expired or what. Mom says No but blech. I'm only finishin' 'cuz she said I can't have a special brownie until I have a whole one." He took a big bite and screwed up his little face but kept chewing.

I glanced in the recycling bin by the door and saw the cardboard from a package of veggie dogs. I snickered and gave him a kiss on his still greenish but slightly less green head, "See you tomorrow, bud. Going out."

He waved at me and picked up the whipped cream can again.

"Tinkerbelly!" Dad called as I headed to my car. He left his group of Man Cave buddies and approached me.

"Hey Daddy."

"Where ya been, what ya doin', where ya goin'?" He had a big smile on his face. He already knew. Clearly.

"I'm heading to Deacon's. Staying over. See ya tomorrow."

He smiled bigger at my confirmation. "Good you've worked things out, punkin."

I smiled, "Taking a step outta my comfort zone. I almost screwed it up, Dad. I'm grateful he gave me another chance."

He smiled, "He's got a brain cell in his head he'll give you as many chances as you need. You're worth it."

I got all vaklempt. "He said that. He said no limit to the chances he'd give me if my heart was in the right place."

Dad got vaklempt and kissed my forehead and then pulled his lips tight as he headed back to the garage. Obviously dad approved of my beautiful biker boyfriend.

My beautiful biker boyfriend. He hee. I felt giddy.

WHEN I GOT TO DEACON'S trailer, the door was open. The smell of food hit my nose and the sight of Deacon doing something at the sink melted me. Why? I don't know. But it did. I rapped on the trailer beside the screen door.

"Get in here," he ordered, after glancing over his shoulder at me.

I entered, walked toward him, putting down my bag on the way. He was bare chested, barefoot, and his hair was wet and loose. The faded jeans he wore were so faded they were nearly white and they were button-fly, the top button undone. He was shucking corn. The entire picture was super-duper sexy.

He dropped the cob on the counter and grabbed me by the bottom and pulled me tight against him. I nuzzled in to his bare sexy chest, and then he tipped my chin up and his lips were on mine. His lips were cold and he tasted like chocolate and smelled like he'd just had a shower.

"Chocolatey kisses, yum," I told him.

"Just drank chocolate milk," he said and kissed me again. "You don't knock on that door. Never need to stand on ceremony with me. In fact, I'll cut you a key."

"Mkay." I got up on tiptoes and arched my neck back, wanting him to kiss me again. He took the hint. It was hot outside and in here was cool. Deacon's body was smooth and cool and his cold chocolatey lips were delicious.

"It smells awesome in here," I said. He hefted me up onto the countertop, opened the fridge and grabbed a bottle of wine. It was a strawberry zinfandel. It wasn't wine so much as a wine beverage but it was my kinda wine.

"My favorite!" I clapped my hands.

"I know," he smirked and poured me a glass. The wineglass was huge and tinted pink but it was glass, not plastic.

"This is a cool glass," I said, "And how'd you know?"

"Bought it today for you," he said, "Seemed like it'd be your kinda thing and didn't want you to have to drink your wine out of a coffee mug."

"It is totally my kinda thing. Good call. What smells so good?"

There were potatoes ready to be boiled, sitting in a pot of water on the stove and he dropped the corn cob into a pot of water with another cob.

"Pork tenderloin in the oven. With honey mustard."

"I can't believe you're cooking for me?" Beautiful biker who cooks? Um, score!

"Evidently," he said, "We'll go out tomorrow. Tonight I decided to keep you all to myself."

"You shoulda told me. I would've brought dessert."

"Oh, but you did..." he said matter-of-factly and wiggled his eyebrows. I blushed and grinned.

"But I also took care of that," he added.

"Yeah?" I asked, "How'd you know I liked strawberry zinfandel and honey mustard pork tenderloin? You call my mother or something?"

He put the wine back in the fridge. I noted that the fridge was now filled and not just with beer.

"Something like that," Deacon said.

"Omigod. *She* called *you*?" I was mortified.

"I went to the store for a few things but ran into your mother there. She told me you love the cheesecake from that Italian bakery. So I got one. She also told me pork tenderloin was on sale and then told me you liked it with honey mustard on top. I took the hint. She had a binder with a honey mustard coupon in it. I can't believe I used a goddamn coupon." He shook his head in memory, "She was standin' there with me at the checkout so it wasn't like I had a choice."

"She did?" I beamed and then frowned, "Let me guess. She talked you into stocking your kitchen for me."

He chuckled and I knew that was the case.

"What makes you say that?"

"Because yesterday I saw your fridge contents consisted of a few condiments, milk, and beer. There wasn't a morsel of food in there unless peanut M&Ms count as food."

"They do," he informed me.

"I saw when you grabbed the wine. Now your fridge is stocked."

He smiled, "Need to feed my girl."

I shook my head, "But she shouldn't have—-"

"Don't worry about it, Kitten. I'm an alright to cook. I've lived on my own a while and I get sick of junk so I learned. I saw your Ma at the health food store where I get my protein powder. She and I got to chattin' and then I followed her to the grocery store next door and she picked everything out and told me how you like it. I stocked us up with some breakfast and sandwich stuff, too. I like that I can keep you here a while, feed you without us having to leave to go find food. You're gonna need fuel for what I have planned for us." He winked and continued, "I walked her to her car after the bakery, sending her home with brownies for your little bro."

"Brownies from that bakery are Beau's favorite. You just bought the right to date me for five years." That explained why Beau did all he could to choke down that veggie dog.

Deacon laughed, lifted his beer off the counter, and led me to the sofa where we curled up together and where I proceeded to fill him in on my day and my chat with Jenna. He was pleased for me to have some work coming up with Jenna. He was also pleased that I told them at the cab office that I wouldn't be working on the weekend. I told him I'd probably get spanked with no hours the following week but waved it off.

He lifted his finger up in a one second gesture and then stood up and pulled out his wallet and then yanked a stack of bills out and grabbed my purse and then dug in to my wallet and put the money in there.

"What are you doing?"

"Just makin' sure you're alright," he answered, "And no body spanks you but me."

"I'm fine. I just got paid."

(But mmm spankings...)

"Drink your wine, Kitten."

"A, I'm fine. B, don't go into my purse."

"Don't go into your purse?"

"It's rude to go into a woman's purse."

He leaned over and kissed me, "What're you hiding in there?"

"Whether I am or am not hiding anything, it's just not cool. It's sacred. You don't need to find my birth control pills, tampons, or my secret chocolate stash."

He kissed me, "You got any peanut M&M's in there?"

"I'm serious," I pulled back," And I'm trying to talk to you."

"Yeah, well I'm trying to distract you till you stop bitching about me putting money in your purse. It'll make me feel better to know you've got that buffer for now."

"So, how was your day?" I asked, with a sigh, deciding I'd put it back in his wallet when he wasn't looking.

"Average," he answered, "but it's better now that you're here."

"And what happened with Jay today?" I asked.

"He didn't answer the door. Saw his ma lookin' out the window, though, peekin' from behind the drapes. Waited. Finally, they must've figured I wasn't leaving so he came to the door but had her standin' there with him like a pussy. Like I wouldn't do shit with his mother there. Though, if she wasn't there, I'd have told him what I told him after giving him a broken jaw. Told him this was the last time I was tellin' him he was through harassing you. That you two were finished and that you wanted him to stop calling and texting to meet up with him. Said you had nothing left to say. His mother shouted him down for it. Fuckin' funny, actually. She yanked him in the house by his ear, apologizing to me for the trouble and reading him the riot act for fuckin' up with you. She told me his loss was my gain and sent her well wishes for you."

I cracked up laughing, "Mrs. Smyth loved me. Wait. How is it an average day when you spend it on terrorizing your new girlfriend's ex and then grocery shop with her mother in the same day? Your life must be kinda crazy for that to be considered average."

He snickered and shrugged but didn't disagree with me.

I took a sip of my wine and leaned over and kissed him and then climbed on his lap, facing him, and put my hands on his chest while we kissed.

Giddiness bubbled up in me at the thought that I could climb him like a tree just like I wanted to that first time I saw him in the gas station. I started grinding against his crotch and he tugged my hair back just a little bit roughly, catching my mouth with his. One of his hands went up the back of my top and he snapped my bra open. A split second after he undid my bra, I heard banging on the screen door.

"Fuck," he groaned and then did my bra back up, fast, like a pro.

I backed off him and he went to the door. As I turned, I saw Spence, Bronto, and another guy in a Dom vest that I didn't know, all at the door. The inside door was open, just the screen door blocking us and as it was mostly transparent, they'd obviously gotten a look at what we'd been up to. All looked serious, despite our compromising situation.

"Better be a reason why you're here instead of texting me," he grumbled as he stepped outside.

"Did man, three times. Came in a group in case something was up down here." That was Spencer and he was all business. The asshole seemed to be under wraps, for the moment. "Finally found out where Scoot got to last night. He was run off the road on his way back from just outside Ipswich. Jackals took his hog, his cut, his boots. Bloodied his face. Took the boots to his ribs. Ribs broke, cut on his shoulder needed to be sewn. Somethin' else had to be sewn, besides, if you get my drift. Meeting in ten minutes in the clubhouse to discuss the rest. Dad already said here on, no one rides alone outside city limits. He wants you to think about movin' your trailer. Says you're vulnerable back here. I agree."

"I'll be there in five. Bronto, Jesse, stay and look after Ella."

"That's why we're here," Bronto answered and looked inside and made eye contact with a small smile at me, "Ella duty."

I took a big sip of my wine. Deacon came back in, went to his room and came out pulling a t-shirt on and then he grabbed his cell phone from the counter. His eyes were on me and he looked angry.

"I shouldn't be long. Half an hour maybe. Guys'll hang outside. Can you turn everything down to low? My cell's dead but I'll charge it during the meeting for if you need me." He moved to the wall beside the door where a few coat hooks were filled with coats and hoodies. He grabbed his Dom vest and put it on and then sat on the top step that led to his bedroom and pulled some socks and then his boots on.

"If I have to be longer than half an hour you go ahead and eat."

"No, babe, I'll wait. I'll finish it up and we can just have it when you're back," I told him.

"Alright, baby." He kissed me on the lips, his hands tangled in my hair, giving me tingles, and then he moved back outside. I checked everything on the stove, Deacon had even inserted a meat thermometer in the pork tenderloin, and then I put on a pot of coffee and poured three cups and then delivered two outside to Bronto and to Jesse, who I was introduced to.

Jesse looked like a younger Dave Navarro. Maybe 25, and hot. Dark longish black straight hair that fell over his dark eyes, a bit of a goatee. Inked all over his arms and chest, which was bare, nipple piercings. He was only in jeans and his leather prospect vest. His neck was even tattooed.

"You guys want a sandwich?" I asked after a few minutes of shooting the breeze with Bronto.

"Deacon wants you inside," Jesse said, looking annoyed. He looked like a serious badass.

Bronto gave me an apologetic look, "Sorry, Ella. We're supposed to be protectin' ya. Jess has a point. Easier to do that if you're inside and we focus."

"No worries," I shot them both a smile. Only Bronto returned it. Jesse seemed on high alert, eyes scanning the perimeter and then he walked behind the trailer. I gathered up the milk and sugar and spoon and went back inside.

I played a game on my phone for a while, finished up dinner, loaded the dishwasher, and put the two plates into the oven on warm, and then after about another hour I covered the plates with foil and moved them in the fridge, and then I fell asleep reading on my phone's Kindle app on the sofa.

MY EYES OPENED AS MY hair was tucked behind my ear. Deacon was sitting on the edge of the sofa where I'd evidently passed out.

"Hi," I said, "What time is it?"

"4:30."

I sat up, "Wow. Everything okay? How's Scott?"

"He'll be okay. The fuckers who ran him off the road? They won't be. Sorry our night got ruined, baby. Didn't know I'd be that long."

"That's okay, it's not your fault. You're okay?"

"I'm good. Come to bed." He tugged my hand and I got up and staggered to follow him.

He flicked the lamp on and then pulled my top up over my head and then took his own shirt off. I unbuttoned my jeans and dropped them and climbed onto the bottom of the bed in my bra and panties. I crawled up and as I did, large warm hands settled on my hips, stopping me.

"Holy fuck," Deacon rumbled.

"Hm?" I asked, half asleep, glancing over my shoulder mid-crawl.

He palmed my rear.

Oh yeah, the caged back undies.

I'd changed into those while he was gone doing the MC meeting and whatever else he'd been doing.

"What are these?" His voice was gruff.

"They're for you," I was suddenly quite awake. I had halted on my knees. I put my palms flat on the bed and arched so that my butt stuck up further.

"For me?" He sounded pleased. He let go of me and I heard two things: a condom wrapper and Deacon's zipper. I stayed put.

"Yeah. Bought them a while time ago but this is their debut." I wiggled my butt.

"Mm." He pulled on my bra strap and I got back up straight as he snapped the bra open. It fell forward landing in front of me.

"I got us a doctor's appointment tomorrow at 10:30. Can you get away from the garage for a bit?"

"Yeah. Takin' the day off. Gotta move the fifth wheel and spendin' the day with you." His mouth was on the back of my neck and he was pressed up against the back of me. His hand slid up my belly and then he cupped one of my breasts.

I dropped my head back against the hard wall of muscles behind me and then he had the ridge of my ear between his teeth. My whole body broke out in goosebumps.

He released me and then put his palm to the middle of my back, "Back down. Keep this sexy ass up."

I put my cheek down to the mattress.

He put his palms flat on my ass and moved them slightly, touching me what felt like reverently. I looked over my shoulder at the mirrored closet and could see him and the way he was, it was definitely reverence on his face as he stared at my backside, caged in with just a few thin strips of ribbons but so very exposed, a black satin bow, just below the dimples on my lower back.

I closed my eyes, absorbing the feel of his hands on me and deciding I needed to go lingerie shopping if this was going to be the result.

I didn't feel like cutesy little Ella right now. I felt sexy. It felt great.

One hand left and then he was pulling the gusset of the panties aside and guiding his cock into me. An inch in, he shifted on his knees and must've felt resistance so he used his index and pinky fingers to spread me open and put his middle two fingers to my clit.

"Found it," he whispered and chuckled.

I giggle-shivered, "You are definitely very very good at finding it."

"I should say I'm sorry sex was so shit for ya before, Kitten, but I'm really not."

I laughed.

"I like that all your orgasms are mine."

"Almost," I corrected.

"Almost?"

"I'm pretty good at finding it, too, ya know" I admitted.

He chuckled, "I look forward to watching a whole lotta that."

"But I really really like that I no longer have to be responsible for all of my orgasms," I whispered.

"And I really really like that you can talk to me about being able to give yourself one," he told me and then he picked up the pace and I couldn't keep talking. I was incapable of anything but whimpering.

It was hard, fast, and yet it was still spectacular. I fell asleep while he was in the bathroom dealing with the condom.

WE WENT TO THE DOCTOR'S office on his motorcycle. I'd woken him up with a blowjob. I'd felt bad about waking him up at 9:30 after he'd been up most of the night but the appointment was made and I didn't want to put that off. I figured that a blowjob would make up for having to be woken after just a few hours of sleep and figured the payoff of bareback riding would also be worth it.

He was very happy to be woken that way. He said good morning, kissing me deeply afterwards (even though I swallowed) and then he gave me one of his big smiles. He wanted to return the favor but we were running late so I told him to save it.

But Deacon got a little bit annoyed with me at the doctor's office. He'd scowled at me in the hallway when the receptionist put us in separate rooms because my doctor, Dr. Lola Lowe, was a female and thirty-three. Yes, she had a porn star-type name. She also had a porn-star-like look to her. Lola was also all kinds of sexy.

I read his annoyance all over his face as we passed her in the hall when she said, "Hello there Ella, and the new man in Ella's life. Louise, put Mr. Deacon Valentine in room one, and our Ella in room two. I'll do Deacon first." Then she winked at me.

"That's the doctor?" he asked, as Louise was opening the door to exam room one. He did not look happy.

"Yeah. Dr. Lowe is great," I told him.

I could read it on his face. A female. And hot. And he had to talk to her about an STD test. I waited a long time for her to come into the exam room I was in.

She shut the door and gave me a pointed look.

"Ella," she greeted, "I'd ask how you're doing but I already know the answer." Her face went into an O and she started fanning herself with my file.

I laughed, "Never better. Although I'll be even better than never better when we get the all clear for bare back."

She busted up laughing. She was awesome. She had only been my doctor for a year. Our family doctor retired and she took over his office space. She was single, and fun and had even gone for drinks with me, Jenna, Pippa, and a few of our other friends once, a few weeks ago. We were due for another girls' night. She was a hoot, just about as wild as Jenna.

We weren't on daily texting terms or anything like that but she did text a few times for local info, and she was a girlfriend enough in the sense that I'd invite her to my wedding shower. I could see her becoming a regular part of my posse, really. She'd fit right in even with being ten years older than me.

Whoa. Wedding shower? Getting ahead of myself much?

She gave me a form, told me she'd also given one to Deacon, and we could head to the lab in the basement of the same building. She'd have the results back in a week to ten days. She also gave me six months' worth of free birth control pills.

He was in the waiting room, glaring at me, sexy arms folded across his chest, when I came out. We went down to the lab and did the whole blood draw, urine test thing, and then we decided to head to the diner for breakfast afterwards.

"Shoulda warned me about your doc, Ella," he admonished as he fastened my helmet.

I smiled, "You have a problem with a female doctor? That's very prehistorically chauvinistic, Deacon."

He kissed me on the lips, "Don't wanna talk about my sexual history with a woman I'm not fucking."

I raised my brows, "A woman you're not fucking? Why? Because you can't fuck her and want to?"

He laughed, "Who says I'd wanna fuck her?" He climbed on.

"But, let me get this straight. You're okay to talk with a male doc, though? Because there's no chance of fucking him?"

"Watch that sass, Kitten."

"No, I wanna know. Why wouldn't you wanna fuck her? Cuz she's *that* hot, I'd do her..." I climbed on.

He did a double take, bit down on his lower lip, and shook his head at me with a disapproving look but I just *knew* he was picturing exactly that. He said he had a thing for girls with all I had goin' on. Well, Lola had what I had goin' on except she was a redheaded version. She was busty, a little on the short side, spiral curled redheaded doctor. But she looked like a porn star in a scene dressed *as* a doctor.

Eesh. What was I thinking bringing Deacon to her?

"You looking for a bare ass spankin' right here in the street?" He raised his eyebrow."

"I'm kidding," I said, but I was actually tingling, "But seriously. She is hot and female but she's also my doctor. She's a good doctor. You didn't say, *'Make me an appointment with a doc with a penis'* You said, 'See if your doc'll see me.' So I did." I used a deep voice mocking him.

He shook his head and started up the bike, effectively silencing me.

Before we'd gone to the doctor's, I'd asked him about Scooter and all he'd said was that the same as the night before. Scoot'd be fine and that the Jackals who did that to him would not be. He didn't seem to want to give me any further detail so I didn't ask questions.

Clearly, things were starting to heat up with the Jackal / Dom feud. When we got to the diner, he told me he'd be towing his trailer out of the woods behind the parking lot before night fell that evening. He said he'd been eyeing a piece of property and wanted to show me. He was thinking of putting an offer in.

"Where are you going to put it in the meantime?" I asked.

"Got a room above the bar in the clubhouse but I'm not crazy about that idea. Spent the first two nights there after we got here and that was enough for me. Bought my trailer on day 3 and set it up same day. The clubhouse is in rough shape and there are bikers everywhere." He shrugged, "Dad'll buy a place eventually, I guess, but for now it's just a flop house, not a home. Need my own place, anything with them'd just be temporary."

"You could always sneak into my bedroom, which you are quite adept at..." I joked, as I stuffed a bite of syrupy waffle into my mouth.

His eyes lit up and he opened his mouth to speak but before he could, Laura popped back over to refill our coffee cups and at that moment, I heard the door chimes jingle as it was opened and saw Jay Smyth step in. His eyes landed on us and widened at me with sort of a pleading look. Kind of desperate, maybe?

I heard a rumbling sound and as I realized it was Deacon growling, yes, growling, Deacon pushed up to standing so fast that our dishes rattled and his chair fell over. His eyes were on Jay and they were full of angry fire.

Jay's eyes went big and he backed out of the restaurant out onto the street. We saw him collide with a person outside and then he ran in the other direction. Ran!

The diner was pretty busy, filled with people, but at that moment I think you'd have heard a pin drop!

"Holy Moses," Laura muttered and gave me big eyes before moving away from our table. She could say that again!

Deacon righted his chair and then sat back down.

I gawked.

"He's been told if he sees you he needs to walk the other way," Deacon told me, still pissed, "Not a good thing that he's so obsessed with you that he'd look at you like that with me sittin' right here. Fuck."

I was sort of speechless. But what could I say? Nothing that I could think of so I went back to my waffles. We ate the rest of our meal in silence, the air thick. And then we went back to his trailer and had a nap. A nap with Deacon spooning me.

It. Was. Awesome. And it was good because he woke up in a great mood, waking me with kisses. He drove us, in my car, about five minutes outside of town to the piece of land he wanted to show me. I guessed he didn't take his bike because of what'd happened with Scooter the night before and his dad saying people shouldn't ride bikes alone out of town right now. I didn't ask questions when he said, "We're takin' your car, babe. I'll drive."

He gave me shit about my attitude when I said "You wanna drive The Shitbox, it's all yours."

"That car is a classic. I don't get how you keep calling it a Shitbox. What gives?"

I shrugged, "It's an old guy magnet."

His pierced eyebrow shot up.

"I know you like it too, but seriously. The color, the size, the noise it makes, and the thing is a gas pig. I'd like a little car. But Dad gave it to me all proud so I didn't wanna break his heart. He has no clue I hate it. It's just not me."

He shook his head at me like I was out of my mind.

THE PROPERTY WAS GORGEOUS. It was tucked away while only being a five-minute drive from the Valentine block. It was private, and was filled with mature trees including a few fruit trees. There was a stream on the property and it had a dilapidated-looking cabin so there was already hydro, a well, and a septic tank so he was considering putting the trailer beside the ramshackle cabin and then building a place later on.

"I'll show you some house plans, see what you think," he'd said.

The asking price was reasonable. I told him I loved it. He called the realtor from his cell before we left to tell him to put an offer in at 20% below asking, saying that he'd go as high as 15% below asking if they counter-offered.

We heated up the previous night's dinner back at his place and after we'd finished I was loading the dishwasher when Deacon's phone dinged.

"Your Dad texted I could put the trailer at your place, Kitten. He and my Dad must've discussed the probs with the Jackals. He said I could store it there, no problem, even if I wanted to stay in it that'd be cool with him."

"Um...oh. Uh, cool," I hesitantly said. My heart tripped over itself. Of course it was cool with me but Dad should've asked me before asking Deacon.

"The Jackals know you're mine and know where you live. I don't think that's wise."

"Oh," I deflated.

"But that said, I don't like the idea of any of you there unprotected so if it's alright with you, I'm gonna ask him if I can stay there with you in your room until this shit settles down."

"Uh..."

Whoa.

"I don't want you vulnerable." He pulled me into his arms and held me close.

"But, um..."

My parents wouldn't care. Some parents would. Not mine. Especially not my Dad with how much he approved of Deacon. But did I want that this fast? This was warp speed fast, him moving into my bedroom.

"If I buy that land out there and Jackals find out, we're vulnerable out there. I won't put you in that spot. Dad and his VP, whenever he fuckin' gets here, have to shop around for a more fortifiable clubhouse and I gotta haul this outta here. Can you give me a hand putting some shit away so I can do that? You ponder while I do that. If you don't want me at your place I'll stay with dad and my brothers but Ella, I'd rather be with you, keeping you safe, your family safe, and sleeping beside you."

He wasn't playing fair. How could I say no? I pulled my lips tight and stared at him.

He gave me a smile. A fucking cocky smile. He knew exactly what he was doing.

"You're being extremely manipulative, Buster." I told him.

His smile got bigger, "I'll be manipulating your sweet body every chance I get, you let me stay in your room. What do you say? Bed buddies?" he chuckled and I narrowed my eyes at him.

"Joking!" he held his hands up in defense. I'd told him the night we met that I didn't want to be his bed buddy.

I shook my head and huffed, "Okay, fine."

"You don't look pleased," he observed.

"This is kind of extremely fast, Deacon. Doesn't look that that'll stop you though. Does it matter that I'm not?"

"Not if I can sleep at night because you're safe beside me." He dialed on his phone and then put it to his ear, "Rob," he said to my Dad and then he wandered outside to have his conversation with my father about sleeping in my room with me. I didn't eavesdrop. I started putting things away that were out and loose-like, doing it vigorously, trying to process what I was feeling at that moment. I thought we'd talk it out, have a conversation, but he'd just taken my snarky "Okay fine" and ran with it.

He was back a minute later with a couple guys who then helped get everything ready for the trailer to be moved.

8

A few hours later his fifth wheel was all closed up, sitting in the parking lot in front of the roadhouse, directly under a parking lot light, and I was driving my car with a big hockey bag filled with his clothes as well as a smaller bag filled with his laundry, in my trunk, with the cheesecake we hadn't eaten yet (he'd donated the rest of what was in his fridge to the clubhouse), and following him on his motorcycle. We pulled into my driveway.

My mind was sort of whirling. But I hadn't had much time to get my head around all of this, hadn't gotten a chance to get more than mildly annoyed about the whole thing. Rider, Bronto, Jesse, and another biker they called Little John (who was as big as Bronto but older, maybe in his 40's) were there when he hauled the trailer out of the woods so we hadn't had a quiet moment together.

By the time I got out, my parents were greeting him at the door with smiles on their faces. Mom's hand was on Deacon's arm and Beau was there, jumping and down, excitedly telling Deacon about some new Skylanders action figure he'd just gotten, a belated birthday gift from one of dad's buddies who had dropped by.

I felt sourness rise. Deacon called Dad and obviously dad agreed. Without calling or texting me to confirm anything.

As I got to the door I heard Mom say, "We'll have to have a key made for you."

"I'll take care of that, Momma," I muttered without making eye contact with anyone.

"Okay, sweetie. Come in, you two. It's gonna rain."

Deacon grabbed my hand and we all walked into the kitchen where Mom started putting on a pot of coffee. I unboxed the cheesecake and put it on the table and started slicing it, not looking at any of them, focusing on my task instead of my urge to start yelling.

"Wanna play Skylanders, Deacon?" Beau asked.

"Yeah, little man. Maybe in a half hour, yeah? I'll have coffee with your parents and then I'll come find you."

"I'm gonna kick yer ass," Beau threatened, his face beaming with mischief.

"Beau!" I exclaimed, "That's a cuss word."

"It's not. It's an animal word. A donkey is an ass. It's proper English to say ass since it's a proper animal name."

"Well..." I paused for a second, struggling for a retort, "Don't use that word," I said, "It's not proper when you're not talking about the actual donkey. Deacon doesn't have a donkey and if he did, you wouldn't kick a poor little donkey, would you?"

"Dad says donkeys are nasty little fuckers so I might."

"The F word is even worse! Cuss words do not sound nice coming from a kid," I said.

You'd think my mother would be doing this but she'd always had a free range parenting philosophy with me and Beau, only I was always much more reserved, cautious about things. Beau took full advantage of Mom's encouragement to let him explore and discover. She rarely reprimanded him, rarely reprimanded any of us. It's a wonder I was so straight and behaved. Like I'd said...Marilyn Munster.

"I've heard you say ass too. I've heard you cuss lots, Lella. Even F-words."

"I'm no longer a kid. And I try not to cuss in front of you, Beau. It's a bad habit, so not sure when you've heard me swear but..."

"I sometimes listen to you on the phone and when Jenna is here. And I hear you cussing all a the time."

"Shush, boy," Dad jumped in, "If you've got the 'nads to eavesdrop you keep the intelligence you gather to yourself."

"Till I need to use it for blackmail, right?" Beau asked.

"Oh my God," I groaned.

Dad put his index finger to his nose.

"Dad!" I practically screeched.

Dad, Beau, and Mom were all laughing. Deacon had a little smirk.

"I'm kidding, Lella. I wouldn't blackmail you. You're the bestest sister in the whole wild world." He threw his arms around me and squeezed.

I ruffled his hair.

"But I do listen sometimes," he added.

"I'll have to be more careful, then."

"What *is* a cock frog, anyway?"

Cock frog? Wait...oh no.

"A what, son?" Dad asked.

"Lella told Jenna that Deacon puts her in a cockfrog."

"Somebody kill me," I pleaded to the ceiling, my face beet red.

Deacon's body started shaking with silent laughter. My mother giggled outright. I glared at her thinking *Thanks for the help, Momma.*

"How 'bout you go get practicing that game, Beau?" Dad suggested.

"But, what is it?"

"Tell ya when you're older, son. Trade secret. Few men know about it but I do and clearly Deacon does. Grow up and put your woman there and you'll get whatever you want."

"Dad!" I shouted.

"Robert!" That was my mother and she went from gentle and sweet to growling

Momma bear. Finally!

"'bout time you weighed in," I hissed at her. She giggled.

Deacon laughed out loud. So did Dad.

Beau shrugged, reached into the pantry for a bag of potato chips, which was typical, since he refused to try cheesecake, thinking that there was no place for cheese inside a cake. He refused to taste it so we'd stopped pushing.

"Come play when you're ready. I'll just be practicin'" Beau told him, "so's I can kick yer donkey."

"Will do, little man," Deacon said.

"Oh, yeah, and thanks for the brownies."

"You're welcome."

I shook my head and inspected my nails. No way could I look any of them in the eye right now. Especially Deacon.

"So," Dad said, forking into cheesecake, "You're welcome here as long as Elizabelle wants you here. I've filled Bertie in and we both agree."

"Oh, Elizabelle *does* have a say, then?" I muttered under my breath; everyone heard me.

Deacon tagged my hand and pulled me close and kissed my forehead and then said, "Thanks, Rob. Appreciated. If it's too much, let me know and we'll figure somethin' out. I'm putting an offer in on a piece of property and figure we'll be out there most of the time when that happens. Once this latest threat is assessed we'll know more."

"Nonsense. Plenty of room. And oh yeah? Where?" Dad asked.

I was stuck on his statement about *us* being 'out there most of the time when that happens'.

I felt like a spectator, like I'd been railroaded, and that was what I was fixated on. I didn't mind that Deacon wanted to be with me most of the time. I quite liked that idea and I'm sure I'd have liked it more right then if all this wasn't happening because I didn't like was how this was playing out. It was playing out like I didn't have a voice. I didn't like it. At all.

I got up and started getting mugs out. The coffee pot wasn't yet ¾ filled. I fussed with getting sugar and milk and a spoon and then stared at the pot, watching it as it continued to fill way too slowly as Deacon told Dad about his fifth wheel trailer and said that we'd stay in (we!) while he built us (us!) a house out there since the existing structure needed to be scrapped.

Mom and Dad both sat with dumb smiles on their faces, listening to Deacon. Their smiles said the sun was shining down on him. Mom's eyes landed on me and she gave me a quizzical look.

"Why don't you sit down, Ella? Have some cake."

I shook my head, "Just gonna get coffee."

"Starin' at it won't make it brew any faster, doll." Dad pointed out the obvious.

"It's your favorite," Mom was still going on about cheesecake.

"Be right back. Little girls room calling me." I headed toward the powder room near the kitchen, hearing dad mutter, "She's riled, bud. I think she's about to erupt."

Um, ya think?

I blew out a big breath staring in the mirror. My face and throat were blotchy, which often happened when I was fuming about something.

I took much longer than necessary to use the facilities, wash my hands, and stare at myself in the mirror. I knew Deacon was dealing with stuff but I just felt railroaded and I didn't like it.

When I was back in the kitchen, just Dad and Deacon were there, talking quietly over their coffees and they looked serious. Dad cleared his uber-serious expression when I entered and smiled, "Ellie honey!"

"What's up, Dad?"

He shook his head, "Just getting an update, baby doll. Sit. Your Mom java'd us up. Here's yours." He motioned to the empty seat beside Deacon.

Deacon's eyes were on me. Serious. Assessing.

I sat down and he put his hand on my thigh. I gave him a tight smile and put my hand on his but I was a bit stiff.

Dad must've read something in the mood so he stood, "Poppin' out to smoke one. You indulge, Deacon?"

"Occasionally but I'll pass," Deacon said, "Oughta get in with Beau and play a game like I promised. I'll put my bag in Ella's room first, though. Babe?" He stood and reached for my hand.

I got up and took his hand and followed him outside. He grabbed his bags from the car and then we went up the outside stairs and he used his key to open the door.

Once inside, he dropped the bag and reached for me.

"You're pissed at me," he said.

"Very observant," I replied, stepping back.

"Care to tell me why?" he asked and stepped forward again, catching me by the hips and pulling me against him.

"I'm feeling railroaded. I don't appreciate you and my father conspiring. It's supposed to be you and me in this relationship."

"It is you and me, baby. Just need you safe," he told me.

I read more in his expression than I could pinpoint, "Is there stuff you haven't told me?"

He sifted a hand through my hair and then held my face with both hands, "There's a whole long backstory with the Jackals. Shit goes back years but what's happened in the past year and a half has been dark shit. Got a bad feeling, Kitten. Jackals are dirty. Filthy fucking dirty. Some shit went down just before we got here with them and other shit's about to hit the fan. I just got this sick feeling about it and I don't want anybody hurting you. I need to be close to you. You get that?"

I could see why he was protective, but I didn't like how all this had happened so fast. It felt like things were out of my control.

"There's good reason why we want these guys out of commission, babe. Good reason why other MCs beyond my brothers are all in on this plan. And they have a history of targeting the women of their enemies. They're spreadin' lies and plotting revenge and if I'm not here, I won't sleep. Your uncle and cousin are pissed that you're with me and that Rob is working with us. I'll be here with you every night anyway and I don't need to piss off your father by disrespecting his intelligence with sneakin' around. He saw me leave here that second night. This way is better. It's his house, I'm showing him respect. This isn't me and him conspiring. This is the men who care about you keeping you safe. My Dad and brothers'll know where to find me if they need me. You'll be safe beside me and I'll be here if they decide to pull anything." He reached into the side pocket of his bag and pulled out a handgun. I jolted.

"I'm packin' heat. I'll keep it in your nightstand. It has a safety on. Keep your door locked when we're not up here so your little bro doesn't come across it. I'll grab a lockbox from the clubhouse." He reached and opened my nightstand drawer and I gasped. He looked weirdly at me as he put his gun in there beside the black satin drawstring pouch that held my purple Lelo.

The tension completely left his face as he lifted it. I jolted. He opened it and peered inside, saying, "This what I think it is?"

I folded my arms across my chest and didn't answer but my face was burning.

He cinched it closed and put it back, moving closer to me, "Can't wait to watch you play with that," he said, "Watch you play 'till you put me in a complete pussy-frog…" His voice cracked on the word frog and he burst out laughing.

"So humiliating," I muttered in complete humiliation, put my palms to my flaming cheeks and took a deep breath and then folded my arms tighter.

Deacon laughed a big loud laugh and then pulled me against him. "C'mon. It's funny."

"Yeah, ha ha," I retorted sarcastically into his chest but then couldn't help but crack a smile. I wrapped my arms around his back and leaned against him.

"Haven't laughed as much as you've made me laugh in the past few days in years, baby. This is nice," he gave me a kiss and then added, "real nice," in a husky drawl.

I blinked at him, feeling like my insides were melting.

"Your parents are cool people. I like them a lot, Kitten. I'm gonna go play with your little brother for half an hour, then how 'bout we go to the Roadhouse for a drink? I think your girl's gonna be there with my brother. You two can catch up while I check on a few things. Sound good?"

"Maybe I'll stay back and make room for your stuff."

"We can do that later."

I shook my head. He walked me backwards into the wall and then he was kissing me, holding my face in his hands, "Just need you safe, Ella. Gotta take care of my girl."

"Okay," I whispered between lip touches, "I get that and I truly appreciate that you want to take care of me, babe, but go for a drink without me. I really just need some me-time. A bubble bath. I'll make room for your stuff. Change the bed."

"Ok, baby," he gave me a squeeze, "I'll let you stew but I won't be long. Half hour with your brother, an hour or two tops with my brothers. Alright?"

I nodded.

He kissed my forehead softly and left his lips there while his hands traveled up and down my back. My heart squeezed.

He left me to stew but although I was already kind of getting over it, I needed to vent.

༄

"WHY ARE YOU SO MAD?" Jenna demanded as if I was *actually* being unreasonable.

I was on the phone with her, I'd just spewed for five or maybe twenty minutes straight all my verbal diarrhea about all that was happening, and she didn't seem to get it. It wasn't like I was still angry, really, but I needed to vent. I needed a little validation, too.

"Did you hear anything I said?" I asked, aghast.

"I heard it all."

I recapped, "To recap, we've been dating like 4 days, including the day that I sort of broke up with him, and he has moved in with me. My father is conspiring to marry me off. He and my Dad discussed him staying here. Without me being in that conversation! He went about that with barely a word of approval from me. Point against him. Dad didn't send him back to me. Point against Dad. Actually two points against Dad because Dad instigated this by inviting him to park his trailer in our driveway in the first place, without asking me about it. Mom has shown no backbone through any of this. Three points against Mom. She giggles when I humiliate myself. You know I don't like people making decisions for me. Add to all that the fact that Beau spilled to Deacon about me talking about him putting me in a cock fog. He did this in front of my parents and Deacon. Deacon! And now I'm making room for Deacon's clothes in my closet. It has been exactly a week since I first laid eyes on him and decided he was the most beautiful man I ever laid eyes on and I repeat, his clothes are going in...my...closet! I have zero upper hand, not that I'm the kind of girl that needs it, but this is a bit much, don't you think? He even talked to my parents about building a house for us. US, he said. Us!"

"So, from everything you've told me, Deacon has gone full steam ahead with your relationship."

"Double warp speed," I corrected, "Is Rider like this?"

"No. And gotta say, I'm a little jealous. Ten points against you, Elle."

I held the phone, speechless.

Jenna continued, "Everything I've heard points to him being protective. Let him protect you. He's giving you orgasms. He's not annoying you. He wants to be with you as much as he can. You like everything about him so far?"

"Everything. Except these controlling alpha male ways. He's amazing so far. But I haven't even practiced my signature with his name yet. I had this whole plan to write it out five hundred thousand times before I picked the perfect one and I haven't even had time to write it out once, Jenna. Not even once!"

"Ella!" she kind of yelled.

"What?"

"Breathe!"

A moment passed and she asked,

"Are you breathing"

"I think so."

"Good. Then roll with it, chickie. Sounds like he has the best of intentions. I gotta go. Rider's gonna be here in five minutes. We're goin' to the roadhouse for a drink and then he's spending the night. I only have one eye made up so far so I gotta dash."

"Okay, have fun." I didn't bother to tell her that Deacon had invited me to come. She'd pester me about joining them and I really just needed me-time.

"Love ya!"

"Love ya," I returned. I hung up and looked around and decided maybe it'd be a good idea to smoke a joint. I wasn't going to. But if any time was a time when I needed to chill with a bit of herb, this was the time.

Instead, I cleared space in the closet to hang up some of Deacon's jeans and button-down shirts but I ran out of hangers and rod space so I piled several pairs of jeans, some track pants, hoodies, and t-shirts on a few of the built-in shelves beside the closet that previously held some photo frames and books. I'd cleared two drawers, one for his t-shirts and another for socks and underwear.

I put his shaving bag in my bathroom and then I changed the sheets, taking off Betty Boop summer bedding and putting on my thicker for fall and winter bed-in-a-bag that was teal blue and chocolate brown leaves with sheets that had the opposite pattern. It was pretty. And not as feminine. My six pillows and four throw pillows should be enough pillows for us.

Shit. Condoms. What about condoms? I didn't see any in Deacon's bag. I peeked into his shaving bag and there weren't any in there either. He had only brought some clothes and his shaving bag so no condoms from whatever stash he had under his bed, if there were even any left.

Maybe I should text Deacon to buy condoms. But if I did, that'd make him think I'm thinking about sex and if I'm thinking about sex then I'm not serious in my snit about the way he railroaded me.

And he needed to know I was serious. I got his point, I did, but he needed to know that this wasn't acceptable behavior in usual circumstances.

And then once I made that point known… then I'd have sex with him.

I HEARD A KNOCK ON the door and then Dad and Mom were in my space.

"You upset with us, baby doll?" Dad asked.

"A little. I would've appreciated you talking to me before inviting Deacon to stay here. But I'm kind of pissed at him, too. Before I could blink he was moving in here, calling you himself and me standing there like a ditzy blonde."

"Stuff happenin' with his club is heavy shit. Makes me happy he has a mind to your safety during all this. And that's where he's coming from right now, sugar dumplin', if you knew the half of what those Jackals were up to in this town and elsewhere…. shit. I'm real glad there are men out there workin' to put a stop to that shit." Dad's cell phone rang from his flannel shirt pocket so he answered it and went down the stairs as he dd.

I looked to my mother, "I'm in a new relationship and things happening in the early days set the tone for the relationship, though, don't they? If I let him make all the decisions…"

"It's not about that, honey," Mom said, "It's about knowing what's important. Find the balance between being who you are and letting him be who he needs to be. Don't sweat the small stuff in a relationship. Sweat the big stuff. Don't lose yourself but don't push so hard to assert yourself that you make him feel like he can't be who he is. Balance."

I allowed that to penetrate for a beat but decided that'd only work if Deacon did the same. It couldn't be all me standing on one foot.

"Is giving him what he needs, being nearby to protect you, going to take anything away from you? Do you not want him here?" she asked.

"No, Momma. He's amazing. I'm crazy about him. I didn't like that he called dad up. It should've been me. I also didn't like that this started by Dad inviting him to stay here in his trailer. That's what sparked it so really, it's Dad who—-"

"Sorry baby doll," Dad was back, "You're right. I jumped the gun. I apologize. I'll have a mind to that in the future. I just like that he can keep you safe through all of this shit."

I chewed my lower lip, making eye contact, and then gave dad a nod. He looked sincere.

"You need anything else to make him comfortable?" Mom asked.

"I think we're good," I answered, "I made room for his clothes. Bed's done. I'd ask if you two were really okay with him being in here with me but clearly you don't mind."

"You're an adult, sweetie," Mom said, "This isn't our sixteen-year-old daughter moving her boyfriend in. You're a young woman. You'll be out of the nest sooner than we'd like. I don't know how you grew up so fast. Soon Deacon'll build you a beautiful house in the country and you'll just visit for Rummoli." She started to choke up.

"Mom, I've been dating him a couple days. Not ready for wedding dress shopping, jeez."

She smiled big, knowing, "Sometimes you know that fast. You just know. I have a good feeling. Never had this feeling with anyone you've dated in the past and you know I'm a little bit psychic. Anywho…we're not going to hold you back. And with all that's happened lately with your uncle, we are happy to have the Dominion Brotherhood looking out for us."

"What's happened?" I asked, trying not to picture Deacon building me a beautiful house in the country, although I kind of, at the same time, wanted to let my mind drift there.

Dad shook his head, "Will's been shootin' his mouth off. Makin' threats."

"What kind of threats?" I asked.

"Just know that as little as I thought of my brother before, I think less of him now. He's all but dead to me." Dad said this with finality and with a coolness in his eyes that I'd never ever seen before.

Dad didn't want to talk about it, that much was clear. He left the room, saying goodnight and kissing me on the temple and then Mom hugged me. "Just take one day at a time, honey. Communicate with him but keep in mind all he's got on his plate. You're rational, you're pragmatic, you're very together. Be you."

I tried to smile. "The bath and my bubbles are calling me," I told her, and we said our goodnights and I went in and drew a bath and soaked for eons in my big antique claw foot soaker tub until my fingers and toes were verging on pruny.

As I toweled off, I heard noise in the bedroom.

I got dressed in a pair of black with white polka dot pjs, which I'd brought to the bathroom with me. They consisted of super-short sleeping shorts with a drawstring and a matching spaghetti strap baby doll tank, that was polka dot around the neck and straps but otherwise mostly black and near sheer from just below my breasts. I put my hair up in a high ponytail, washed my face, moisturized from head to toe, and brushed and flossed my teeth, and when I stepped out, Deacon was sitting on the edge of the bed, dressed in his leather cut, jeans, tee, and motorcycle boots, his hair in a ponytail. The room was dim; I'd just left the twinkle lights that were woven through my headboard on. It looked soft and romantic in the bedroom, actually. Maybe I'd done that subconsciously.

He was thumbing away on his phone. I closed the bathroom door. He looked up at me and dropped his phone. Fumbled and dropped it. He was staring at me. He was staring at me like I'd just walked out in the sexiest lingerie and high-heeled furry mule slippers or something. My pjs were a bit on the skimpy side, I guess. I thought they were cute more than sexy but his face said he liked what he saw, which was quite a bit of skin.

"Hi," I greeted and pointed, "I gave you those two drawers for socks, underwear, and t-shirts. The right side of the closet is your stuff but I ran out of hangers so there's stuff on the shelves, too. It's bit cramped but it'll do."

He moistened his lips and got to his feet and started moving toward me.

"And your bathroom stuff is in the eee," I squealed as he abruptly picked me up into his arms like I was a bride, "bathroom," I finished, circling his neck with my arms.

"You smell like berries," he said, nuzzling behind my ear.

"My bubble bath," I breathed, goosebumps rising.

"Still mad at me?" he asked and then he licked the ridge of my ear.

"Nooo, but... we have to talk. Get a few things straight."

"Can we do that after I spread your legs and suck on your clit for a while?" He sucked my earlobe in.

"Omigod."

"That a yes?"

I gawked, speechless.

He put me on the bed and said, "Two minutes," then went down the inside stairs to the door to the linen closet and pushed the slide lock over to lock it. He climbed back up and disappeared into the bathroom, saying, "Getting a super-quick shower." I heard the water turn on before I could tell him the shower was broken.

His head popped out and before he spoke, I told him, "Shower's broken. Sorry. You can have a bath? Or use the shower on the second floor. Bathroom is right at the bottom of the stairs. The door lock's broken but you don't have to worry. He sleeps like the dead."

He kicked his boots off, threw his cut off, and grabbed behind his neck to grasp and pull his t-shirt off, "Fuck it, had a shower this morning. I can wait. I'll fix your shower tomorrow. It'll take five minutes and a $2 part."

Yep, not a shock. Good ole Dad had that repair on his list the last two years.

Deacon then unbuckled his belt and then his jeans came off and hit my floor.

I was about to point at my cute Paris themed laundry hamper, so he'd know I didn't appreciate clothes on my floor, when he was suddenly on me and then I remembered his trailer was spotless so maybe he wouldn't be a messy roommate, and then I didn't think anything else because his mouth was on me, he was on his knees, hovering over me, and then his tongue was caressing my bottom lip, coaxing it open.

He spent all of three seconds kissing me before his lips started their descent down to my breasts. My top was up and off me and then his mouth was on my right breast, his hand on my left.

"These tits, fuck, these tits are beautiful," he said against a nipple and then his tongue flicked over it.

I inhaled a big breath, absorbing the sensations. And then the sensations changed as he bit down gently on my nipple.

"Oh god," I moaned and he did it again. I squirmed with need.

His fingers hooked at my shorts and then they were sliding off and I wasn't wearing any undies under them so in a heartbeat, he was at the heart of me, finding me slippery with wet, and pushing a finger deep inside, while another two fingers twisted my clit ever so slightly.

I whispered, "Bullseye" and then I shivered from my head right to my pinky toes as the sensations went deep, swirling inside me, making me feel like my entire body was that bullseye. His mouth got there and he sucked as his tongue darted inside. His fingers dove under me and separated my bum cheeks and fingertips pressed against my back entrance. I arched my back and he lifted me right up in the air, his tongue somehow magically moving deeper still.

"Deacon," I pleaded, for what, I didn't know. The sensations he made me feel ... my God.

A second later I heard something. His mouth moved away but touched my inner thigh as I heard a drawer open. And then I felt the vibrations rev up.

Oh wow. My Lelo? Holy shit!

"Deacon," I shuddered, as the tip of my Lelo touched my opening, and he thrust it inside and then twisted it around and pointed up, making it hit my g-spot. His tongue flicked at and lapped at my clit and then he must've pressed the button a bunch of times because it revved up, almost like a motorcycle, and went to full blast. In about 7.7 seconds, I came. Hard. *Seriously hard*. My legs shook, my back was arched, and my mouth was wide open. And it vibrated through me like an earthquake.

I had a fistful of his hair in one hand, the other hand holding the headboard, and my legs were up in the air, ringing. I went limp as he pulled the vibrator out.

"Did we forget to bring the c-condoms?" I inquired, breathless.

"We're covered," he said," Raided my brother's stash before I left the clubhouse." And I heard the crinkle of a condom wrapper. I then felt something warm touch me down there and he was sliding inside.

"Oh yeah," he moaned.

"Yeah," I agreed, legs and arms clamping around him.

"You feel so good."

"You, too." Post-orgasm emotions burst out of me, "I am so crazy about you." I blurted, "Seriously, Deacon. You are so..." I couldn't finish, couldn't put my thoughts into words. I ran my hand up his face, "I am so happy I get to be with you. And not just 'cuz you're amazing at this but because you're just ... amazing."

His eyes were warm, his mouth was smiling, "Good, 'cuz you're stuck with me. Don't look at me like I'm crazy."

"I'm not."

"Not yet, I'm saying don't do it though, cuz of what I'm about to say. I'm telling you right now, I am fucking done. You're it. You're the one. No way I let anyone hurt you. Ever. I don't want to wake up without you beside me. Safe, in danger, either way. You get me?"

I was speechless. My Gran talked about her and Grampa saying they were 'it'. True love. Forever love.

God, was I *it* for Deacon?

He started to really move and I reveled in the feel of him. I sniffed and he looked into my eyes and then kissed me softly as a few tears were falling from my eyes. I hoped that those said it all. He finished beautifully, groaning my name and burying his face in my neck.

We cuddled for a while and then I said, "Did you have any of that cheesecake?"

"Nope, wasn't hungry." he said.

"I'm gonna go get some. Want some?"

"Naw, I'm wiped," he replied and yawned.

I got my pjs back on and zipped downstairs into the dark and quiet house, and fetched one of the two pieces that were in the fridge, covered in plastic wrap.

I brought it upstairs and got into bed and started eating it. It was my favorite dessert but eating it there, in the dark, watching Deacon sleep, his head on my pillow, his bare chest on display, it was better than ever.

I finished my piece, brushed my teeth again, and then climbed in and curled up to him. His arm pulled me tight against his body and we fell asleep cuddled close, me with a smile on my face, listening to the pitter patter of rain outside, feeling a nice cool breeze along with the aroma of fresh rain sweep through my room.

I WOKE UP HEARING MY name, hearing knocking, while feeling Deacon move in the pitch dark. He was leaning over me, opening my nightstand drawer and pulling the gun. I jolted underneath him. I heard my name again. But it wasn't Deacon calling me. It was coming from outside.

Deacon moved to the fire escape door, holding the gun behind his back and he peered part-way under the blinds.

"Ella!" I heard a whisper-shout, from outside the door. The window beside the door was open, it'd been hot in my room so I'd opened it when I'd put Deacon's stuff away.

Was that Jay? Omigod, stupid stupid Jay. He'd never come up to my room before but he knew the fire escape led to it. What a stupid idiot. Didn't he see Deacon's motorcycle outside?

"That's Jay," I told Deacon and then things happened really fast. Deacon flipped the lock and ripped the door open, gun still in his hand.

"For fuck sakes," Jay moaned and then I heard the distinct noise of tumbling. I scrambled to find a pair of flip flops. I heard shouting of "Fucking told you" and I heard a "What the fuck" which came from Dad.

I scrambled down the stairs which were wet with rain, Deacon and Jay were at the bottom, the butt of his handgun was poking out of the back of Deacon's boxer briefs and he had Jay up against the house down at the bottom of the stairs. My Dad and Mom were outside the breezeway, Mom in her robe, looking freaked out, and Dad was standing off to the side, in a t-shirt and plaid sleeping pants; Dad was holding a rifle.

"You step foot on this property again, Smyth, I'll press charges," Dad said.

"Get this ape off me," Jay grunted, but Dad didn't move.

I stopped mid-flight.

"You need to stop, Jay," I called.

"Back upstairs, Kitten," Deacon said, gently.

"I just want to talk to you!" Jay pleaded through a split lip.

"At three in the morning?" Dad threw in accusingly.

Jay kept talking. "And he pulls a gun on me? What're you doin' with this guy, Ella?"

"Deacon, please let go of him," I said.

Deacon ignored me.

"Babe," I said, "I'll talk to him right here, right now. Get this over with and then we can get on with our lives. He obviously isn't gonna give up until he and I talk."

Deacon's tone was one of warning, "He is gonna give up because you're off limits to him."

Deacon looked over his shoulder at me and let go of Jay. I got to a few steps below the bottom step and got a better look. Jay's face was a mess. Deacon's hand looked bloody.

Deacon was standing between us and he didn't move. I got to the second to last step and tried to squeeze around him but he blocked me.

"Deacon..." I said and he didn't budge.

"Forget it," Jay muttered and started to walk off.

"She's moved on, Smyth. Give it up. You're humiliating yourself," Dad called.

"You don't fuckin' come back here. You don't get near her," Deacon warned him.

Jay muttered something under his breath and made his way across the street to where his car was parked. Deacon was absolutely seething.

"Anyone want tea?" Mom asked.

"No thanks," I replied. Deacon watched Jay pull away.

"Naw, sweet cheeks. Go back to bed," Dad muttered and wandered toward the garage and opened it. Deacon's bike sat inside. No wonder Jay approached my door. He didn't know Deacon was here.

"Goin' back to bed," Deacon said and he and Dad exchanged looks that made me shiver, looks that probably communicated that they had to do something about this guy.

Deacon made his way back up the stairs, catching my hand on the way. I squeezed and let go. "One sec. I'll be up in a minute. I'm getting us waters."

I went into the garage and opened the fridge and pulled four bottles of water out. Dad was loading his pipe.

"You shook up?" he asked.

"I'm okay," I said and headed back toward the stairs.

"Really pleased my girl has a guy like that," Dad said.

"A guy who runs out into the night in underwear brandishing a gun to stop my ex from speaking to me?" I asked, feeling both rattled and exhausted.

"Something like that," Dad snickered, got up and kissed my temple, "That Smyth ain't right, Elizabelle. Be smart."

I trudged back up the outside stairs into my room. Deacon was in the bathroom, door open, washing his hands, standing on a towel in his bare feet. I put two bottles of water in my mini fridge and put the other two bottles on my nightstand. I opened the drawer and saw his gun back in there beside my Lelo. I shoved the Lelo to the very back and closed the drawer. Wouldn't want to mix those two up. Sheesh. Either way would be bad. Laughter bubbled up and I shook my head at my ridiculous train of thought. Shooting my cookie or pointing my vibrator at an intruder.

I kicked off my flip flops and got back into bed and moved to the other side of the bed, deciding he could have the spot beside the gun.

He got to the bed, opened a bottle of water and downed it. He got under the blankets.

"Something's gotta be done about him, baby," he said, ignoring my stupid goofy smile, which was perma-stuck from my odd Lelo thoughts.

"Did you hurt your hand?" I grabbed it and examined it. Looked fine.

"He tumbled down the stairs, went head over heels a few times and then when he hit the ground my fist hit him in the mouth but I'm good, it was his blood, not mine."

"He tripped down the stairs?"

"With the help of my foot in his chest."

"Oh shit."

"He was trespassing. Banging on your door at three in the morning. Me and my boys'll be paying that fucker a visit in an alley, Ella. That's it. I don't usually let it get this far but I've been holdin' back since we're new but I'm telling you now, Ella, I'm finished fuckin' around where he's concerned. He's getting the boots taken to him. I've tried warning him and being a nice guy but it hasn't worked. We get in a situation like that again and I tell you to get back or whatever, do me a favor and actually listen to me. Yeah?"

I bit my lip and didn't say anything. He pulled me to him and tipped my chin up and looked into my eyes. His eyes were hard, serious. I let out a long sigh. Deacon's expression softened and he tangled his fingers in my hair, pulling my head to his chest, and then after a long time of laying there, I finally fell back to sleep.

HIS CHEEK WAS PROPPED on his hand, he was on his side, watching me sleep. It was morning but it felt really early. I smiled at his beautiful face and ran my hand up his arm to his cheek, which was sandpaper-rough with whiskers.

"Good morning," I said.

"Waking up next to you, yeah, Kitten, it is." His mouth descended toward mine and I hoped I didn't have awful morning breath. But before his lips touched mine, Gangnam Style started blaring. I glared over my shoulder at my desk, about to move toward it to grab my phone, where it was charging, but my phone wasn't lit up. The racket was coming from Deacon's phone, which was still on the floor at the foot of the bed where he'd dropped it last night. It was ringing that stupid stupid ringtone.

"How'd she get that on your phone?"

I scrambled to the bottom of the bed, reached for it, and then passed it to him. It said Edge calling, which meant Jenna changed his default ring. I was gonna kill her.

Deacon snickered, "She told me at the bar last night she wanted to put her number in."

"She's outta control, really pushing her luck with this song. It isn't funny anymore."

He swiped at it and then answered it.

"Yeah man... No... Oh fuck. How is she? ... With who? Okay, shit. I'll be on the road in under an hour.... Yep. I'll tell him."

He put the phone down and thrust his fingers into his hair. He looked rattled.

"What's wrong?"

"That was an MC brother down in The Falls. My sister was in an accident."

"Oh no! How bad?"

"They took her from the scene in an air ambulance. She was on the back of a Dom brother's bike and even a fender bender can be bad with a bike. Gotta get down there. Mom's in hysterics, shit's not good, no one knows how bad it is yet."

"Want me to come?"

He looked surprised.

He cut me off with his mouth to mine. He was kissing me and breathing me deep. He was a little shaky.

"I'll just be there for you, if you want?" I asked.

He leaned back and looked at me, chewing the inside of his cheek.

"My mother's kind of a bitch. No, not kinda. Straight up. You're not gonna like her. She makes any and all drama all about her."

"I'll deal."

"Lotta MC brothers'll be there. It might not be a good scene, especially if I find out one of them is the reason Jojo's hurt."

"I'll handle it. Whatever it is. I just wanna be there for you, Deacon. Unless it's too much for you to worry about me. I'm not looking to be any sort of—-"

"No. Come. I need you. If it's bad, I'll really need you."

"You sure? I don't want to get in the way."

"Baby, come. Thank you." He kissed me hard and fast and then reached into the closet for some jeans.

My heart warmed at the same time it prickled with fear. I hoped his sister would be okay.

He hit buttons on his phone with one hand while he rifled through the closet and drawers and started tossing jeans, t-shirts, socks, and underwear toward the bed. I grabbed a small suitcase from under my bed. "I'll do this. Go ahead and do what you need to do to get ready. I'll pack for a couple days for us."

He gave me half a smile and his warm hand landed on the back of my neck where he gave me an affectionate squeeze then stepped out onto the fire escape and I heard him say,

"Dad."

I winced.

"Jojo was on the back of Lick's bike and he wiped out. She's been taken to the hospital. Helicopter lifted her off the highway. Edge called me. I'm getting ready to start heading there now. Don't know how bad it is, don't know how Lick's doin' either, haven't called Ride or Spence yet. Me and Ella are ridin' out now… I don't know. Maybe I'll take the pickup. Then if it's all minor I can tow the toy hauler with some of my shit back when we come back. Okay. See you in a few."

I went into the bathroom, used the facilities, washed my face, and started to throw together some stuff for our suitcase.

He was back a moment later and pulled on a pair of jeans while saying, "I'm riding to drop my bike at the garage and get the pickup. Dad's coming with us. Be back in fifteen minutes."

"I'll be ready," I told him and he kissed me quick and then was in a pair of boots, carrying his t-shirt, phone, and keys and leaving via the fire escape.

I PACKED FOR US, ENOUGH for a few days, and put Deacon's gun in our bag, then jogged down the stairs. My Mom was up and making coffee. I filled her in and then texted Jenna and texted my boss Lloyd at the cab office. I hadn't seen the latest schedule yet but wanted him to know I'd be out of town a few days. I texted Jenna to tell her I couldn't do reception at the salon that day and Saturday. She didn't have a wedding booked until the following weekend. I just told her Deacon had a family emergency and I had to go to Sioux Falls, said I'd keep her posted. I didn't know if Rider knew yet what was happening so didn't want to give Jenna specifics beforehand.

I grabbed my purse and the suitcase and headed downstairs. When I met Deacon in the driveway, I had three travel mugs of coffee with me and the suitcase. When they pulled in, Deacon and Deke jumped out.

"Thanks for being ready," Deacon kissed me as he lifted the suitcase. Deke grabbed two of the coffees from the step, I grabbed the other one and my purse. Deke got into the back seat of the truck, giving me the front passenger seat.

"Thanks for the coffee," Deke said and was about to sip the black cup, passing me the pink one.

"Blue one is yours. Black one Deacon's, pink's mine. I figured you'd have no time to stop."

"You know how I take it?" Deke switched the blue cup with me and I put it in the cup holder closest to Deacon.

"Yep," I replied, "Watched at the garage. Little bit of milk. Lotta lotta sugar."

His eyes twinkled but I could see the strain and worry on his face.

"Any more news?" I asked Deacon.

"Had to talk to my mother. She said Jojo has a head injury, they're operating on her wrist, broken, and she got pretty bad road rash. Don't know yet how bad the head injury is."

"The driver?"

"Pronounced dead at the scene," Deacon said softly.

"Oh no." My heart dropped.

The silence in the cab of the truck was palpable.

"Someone from your club?" I asked.

"Yeah, Luke Hanson; Lick, we called him," Deacon replied, pulling out of my driveway, "He had just earned his patch a few months ago. We don't have any other facts yet."

"I am so so sorry," I said.

Deacon put his hand on my thigh and squeezed, but stared ahead.

I put my hand on his.

"Turn the radio on, son?" Deke requested in a gruff voice but I glanced back and he also looked angry. We got lost in the music for a while.

Deke chain-smoked, trying to blow it out the window but it was getting to me, a bit. He apologized for smoking so much but I waved it off, knowing it was his nerves.

At the half way mark, around 90 minutes in, we stopped for a bathroom break and to fill up the tank at a gas station. I ran in and when I came out, Deacon was still inside, getting us some bagels and coffees so I headed back to the truck. I heard Deke on the phone arguing, standing behind the pickup truck. I wasn't trying to eavesdrop but all the windows were rolled down so I could hear him loud and clear from inside the truck.

"Damnit, Shell, I just wanted an update on Joelle. You know, *my* daughter. Sorry if that's inconvenient. Fuck, woman, you never fail to give me a goddamn headache. We'll be there in about an hour...Oh yeah? Well give updates to Rudy so I don't have to fuckin' talk to you then."

Deke dialed another number and lit another cigarette, "Spence. She's out of surgery. Stable. We'll be at the hospital in just about an hour. Yep, makin' good time, your brother's flyin'. I'll call you soon after. Yep... Tell Ride? Right-o."

He gave me a tight smile, "My ex doesn't like talkin' to me on the phone."

"Sorry about all this, Deke. It sounds good that she's stable, though."

He nodded, "Things are fubar'd there, she don't like talkin' to me, period. Wait'll you see how thrilled she'll be to see me in the flesh." He let out a big breath and rolled his eyes. "Deacon fill you in?"

"He only said it was an ugly split. Didn't give me any specifics."

"Ugly is an understatement, little lady. Could barely stand one another the past few years. Shit, barely liked her when I knocked her up, but figured I was doin' the right thing and married her when I stepped up once I knew Deacon was mine. First look at that boy and it couldn't be mistaken; he was mine. Spent 28 years tied to a woman who didn't love anyone but herself. We must've split a dozen times over the years. I was tryin' to scrape her off after a coupla months of hooking up. It was casual, she was a sweet butt but had her sights set on me. But things weren't good; they weren't ever good for long. Then she flushed her pills and got pregnant with Rider to try to keep me tied to her.

Tried to save things, I 'spose but it only got worse. When Spence was knee high, she started using drugs, heavy ones. Left me with three little boys but I was good. I had lotsa help and thought it was good we were all quit of her. She turned back up very pregnant a coupla months later. Tried to fix things for the kids. Jojo was the light of all our lives. Somehow we lucked out and she was fine even though she was born in withdrawals. Shell wasn't a great mother. Lotta women in the club pitched in and made it better for my boys and their sister. Anyway, things hadn't been great in the marriage and then about a year and a half ago we had a rip roarin' fight after she crossed a line she couldn't come back from and I told her I was done. For good. She knew I was serious. Kids were grown. Joelle'd just turned 18 and Shell then tried to retaliate by tellin' me she wasn't mine. Said she was my brother's. Fucked my brother Joe. Repeatedly. Didn't believe her at first but she went as far as a DNA test which fucked the whole family up for a while and that's when I knew that Shell had believed, Joelle's whole life, that she wasn't mine."

My eyes widened, "Your brother's?"

"Not blood brother, MC brother," he clarified," and it's debatable which'd be worse. Did that DNA test and Joelle is mine. Guess it was wishful thinking for Shell. Even if it said she wasn't, she'd still be. You know? Raised that girl, light of my life. Shell even named her to hurt me, combination of her name Michelle and Joe, holding that back for 18 years, waiting to use it to annihilate me, probably hopin' Joelle wasn't mine, definitely believin' she wasn't the whole time. Went down a dark road with all that shit. That's when I drove my car drunk and wrapped it around a tree, lost my license." His voice went gruff, "Fuckin' woman knows how to push my buttons every goddamn time."

Deacon was coming out of the restaurant now with a bag in his hand and a cardboard tray of coffees.

"So, we have trouble bein' in the same room together and I'm sorry but you'll see some ugliness at that hospital today," Deke said as Deacon got back into the driver's side.

"I try to be civil but she does her best to make that hard," Deke finished and accepted the tray of coffees and handed them out. Deacon's eyes briefly hit his father and then they landed on my face. He clenched his jaw and passed out wrapped toasted bagels.

"Just had the pleasure of havin' a conversation with your mother. Joelle's through surgery. They say she's stable. I updated your brothers," Deke said.

Deacon nodded and let out a breath.

I put my hand on his thigh and squeezed. He let out a sigh and started up the truck. I turned on the radio and unwrapped my bagel. Deacon was definitely broody the last hour of the drive. Deke was quiet.

I braced myself. And it was a good thing, because I was about to meet Deacon's mother, Michelle Valentine, a.k.a the woman I would begin to think of as Hurricane Shelly.

9

Deacon's mother was outside the hospital smoking a cigarette, standing with two big bikers. She was the epitome of a fiftyish year old biker babe. She had lots of long dyed blonde hair, dressed a bit like an 80's glam hair band groupie, but she was definitely beautiful. Big green eyes and a great figure but a bit of a smoker's mouth and she wore a lot of make-up and right now there was a lot of black smudged makeup under her eyes; she'd been doing plenty of crying. She put her cigarette out on the ground, crushing it with her heel, and practically ran and threw herself into Deacon's arms. He let go of my hand to catch her.

She put her hands on his cheeks, "My baby!"

"Mom," Deacon gritted his teeth and stared at the two bikers in front of her, "Guys."

Deke hugged both guys with one handed back slaps. His mother didn't move out of the way so as the men approached Deacon, he tried to let go of her but she was crying into his leather so he kept hold of her with one arm and shook hands with both guys, "Brother," they each greeted him. They were in Dom cuts and jeans. One was older, greying tidy beard, chest-length silver and pepper hair (mostly silver), with a kindness in his silver eyes. The other was younger, around Deacon's age, maybe a bit older, almost as tall as Deacon, and had a bit of scruff and messy short dark hair with the sides shaved.

Everyone looked stressed.

"Any change?"

"She's not awake yet, baby," Deacon's mother said, "Her brain started swelling. They gotta keep her asleep to work on gettin' the swelling in her head to go d-down. It started to go up and they've put her into a coma." She choked up and Deacon let go of her and put his hands in his pockets. I sucked on my bottom lip, feeling the worry coming off him.

"Mom, this is my girlfriend, Ella. Ella, Michelle Valentine -—Shelly. This is Edge and that's his dad, Rudy."

Shelly glanced up as if she hadn't seen that I was even there before that second. She wiped at her eyes and gave me what I could only guess was an assessing look.

I had my hair up in a top knot, a pair of boyfriend jeans rolled to above my ankles, and I was wearing a long and drapey pink V-neck t-shirt. I had sunglasses on my head and no make-up on, pink flip flops. This had been an early morning call and long road trip so it wouldn't have been my preferred 'meeting-the-mom' outfit. She spared a glance at me like she found me lacking and didn't say anything. She looked back to Deacon and frowned.

Before I had a chance to ponder that, Rudy moved over and embraced me in a bear hug, lifting me right off the ground, "Good to meet ya, Ella. Ain't you a sweet little thing?" He gave me a warm smile and put me back on my feet. He was pretty solid and strong for being around sixty or so.

Edge moved over and shook my hand and put his free hand on top of it as well, "Really good to meet you." Then he smiled at Deacon, huge.

Deacon looked at his feet but his lips turned up just a little.

"Thanks, nice to meet all of you. Very sorry it's under these circumstances."

"Hello Stella," she said almost icily and then looked back to Deacon, "Where are your brothers?" She lit a cigarette.

"It's Ella. And Ride and Spence're holdin' the fort back home," Deke interjected.

"They didn't come?" She was aghast. She grabbed Deacon again and started sobbing into his jacket, "Do they h-hate me that much that they won't come for Jojo?"

"Ma, we have businesses to run," Deacon said impatiently, "They'll come tonight. We just came first. Not everything is about you."

"Shell..." Deke started.

She looked at Deke like something she'd scraped off her shoe and he shook his head and didn't finish whatever it was he'd started to say.

"Let's go see her." Deacon tried to pry her off him again and she finally let go, dropped a cigarette on the ground, ignoring the ashtray affixed to the wall of the smoking shelter, and took his hand.

"We can't get in to see her yet but let's go ask them for an update. I've been tryin' to get answers but no one will tell me nothin.'"

The older biker, Rudy, looked to Deke, "They just said, not ten minutes ago, there's no news and asking every five minutes isn't gonna make a diff—-"

Shelly glared at Rudy and he stopped speaking but shot Deke a look that I figured said he was losing patience.

Shelly pulled Deacon with her into the hospital and the rest of us followed.

Deke put his arm around me and gave me a little smile and a squeeze and walked me in.

We got into an elevator and went up to the third floor and Shelly pointed to a door that had a sign marked as Family Waiting Room, "Boys, you and Emma can wait in there while we get an update."

"Ella," Deacon corrected with a glare.

Deacon had talked about the girl who was in jail being called Emma. That was a low blow if it was intentional.

She waved her hand nonchalantly, as if it made no never mind. She pulled Deacon to the large nurse's desk and Deke followed.

"Want some shitty coffee, Ella?" Edge asked.

"Love some," I said. There was a bathroom, coffee station, and a few sofas in the room, which had windows that looked out into the hall and the nurse's station.

He fished change out of his pocket and put it into the machine.

I glanced out at the nurse's station and Shelly was waving her arms erratically and her face was red. Deke looked frustrated, not with the nurse that looked like she was trying to not lose her cool Shelly's behavior, but with his ex-wife who was having a conniption.

Deacon shook his head and walked in to where we were. I was stirring powdered whitener and sugar into my cup. I motioned to the coffee machine and raised my brows in question. He shook his head and strode to me and took me into his arms. I got up on my tiptoes and put my hands around his neck. "You okay?" I asked softly.

"Yeah. The nurse said nothing we didn't already know 'cuz there's nothin' else *to* know. They're trying to get swelling in her brain down. She's had surgery on her wrist, has had to have metal pins put in. She's got bad road rash. That's all they can tell us. They said they're watching but they are cautiously optimistic. It's good news, mostly. It's not enough for my mother, though. She's just over-the-top, high strung as usual. She always operates up here as it is." He held his hand up high.

"Get your fucking paws off me!" The door was opening and Deke was ushering Shelly into the waiting room.

"Settle down, woman. They're gonna call security on you if you don't fuckin' stop the nonsense."

She started to ugly cry, "That's my baby in there! And Lick's dead. He lost his goddamn head in that wreck and that is gonna wreck my Jojo. Fucking ran them off the road because of the club's feud with them and I hold the both of you responsible."

She poked him in the chest and glared at Rudy, "My baby could've lost her head, too, and she still might not make it. Or what if she makes it and she ain't our Jojo no more?"

"Shut it, Ma," Deacon said at almost the exact same time as Rudy said, "Lower your goddamn voice."

It was at that moment I noticed he had a president's patch on his leather vest, which was partially shielded by his long hair.

"You don't chill out woman, you'll wait at home," Deke added.

She stormed out saying, "You don't get to order me around no more, Deke. My baby might not ever be the same. And if that happens, you know who is responsible. You vigilantes, that's who."

"Oh yeah? How 'bout the person who started all this shit? Does that person hold any responsibility?" Deke challenged.

"Fuck you. I'm goin' for a cigarette," she hissed.

Deacon jerked his chin at Edge and Edge got up, looking less than thrilled. "You shadow her, alright bro?"

"Yup," Edge said.

"Apologies, brother," Deke muttered. Edge gave us a tight smile and followed Shelly.

"Chat?" Rudy said pointedly.

Deacon replied, "Go ahead. Ella's fine."

Rudy patted Deacon's shoulder, "Good, good. We don't know yet it's Jackals but a coupla boys are checkin' it out. It's lookin' that way but no good for Shell to be shootin' her mouth off like that until we've got solid evidence." Rudy looked at me and smiled.

I sipped my coffee, knowing he'd added that for my benefit. I knew better than to act the way she was acting. Most women, whether they were experienced biker broads or not, had to know.

DEACON WAS BESIDE ME, texting with Spence, Rider was driving them to the hospital and they were under an hour away.

I met close to a dozen other bikers in Dom vests ranging from their early 20's to, I'd guess, their 60's who were in and out, saying Hello, talking to Deke and Rudy in hushed whispers. A few women came in as well, giving Shelly a wide berth but saying hi to Deke and Deacon and getting introduced to me.

Everyone was super friendly, some seemed surprised when Deacon introduced me as his girlfriend. Actually, he didn't say girlfriend after the introduction to his mother, he said, 'mine' as in 'This is Ella, she's mine.'

It gave me tingles, though. The way he said it was protective, and kind of, maybe, with pride.

The mood in that waiting area was solemn, talking about Luke's family, who were local but not bikers, making funeral arrangements. Rudy told another older biker with a Secretary patch on his cut (I couldn't recall his name) to reach out and offer financial help to them as well as to offer their clubhouse for after the funeral, stating that the club's women would put on a spread.

In the early evening, Rider and Spencer showed up. At that time, the waiting room was just a few bikers, Shelly, and us.

Rider accepted a hug from his mother, but it was stiff. Spencer glared at her as if to warn her against touching him and it was extremely tense in that room. As they moved through the room getting hugs and back slaps from the guys, both Valentine boys came to me and gave me hugs.

"Hey Ella," Rider had whispered and kissed my cheek.

Then I was engulfed in Spence's arms and he hugged me a long time and whispered, "Thanks for being here for him," and it seemed genuine. I hugged him back big and rubbed his back. He didn't seem like he was going to let me go but then he whispered really low, "Sorry I've been such a dick." And then he kissed the side of my head and released me.

Deacon was watching Spence as Spence let me go and their eyes locked. At first I thought that Deacon was about to get possessive but I saw a damaged but still-there brotherly bond, as odd as that sounds. I knew Deacon heard what Spencer whispered to me and maybe that went a long way toward pulling together.

Both of them were worried about their sister and maybe Spence gave me the hug that he would've given to his mother if things were different.

Deacon moved to Spence and they hugged briefly and I felt my heart squeeze. Deacon then pulled me close and kissed my temple. I put my arm around his waist and snuggled into his chest. Shelly's eyes were on us and she was shooting daggers at me.

I'd felt kind of useless and tried, a few times, to offer her a drink. Once, she ignored me altogether and the second time she said *No Thanks Lucy*. Deacon missed that one but Spencer hissed at her, "You bitch," under his breath. She shrugged innocently. But the woman was filled with venom.

Who was Lucy?

I looked to Spence. At this moment, Deacon was on the other side of the room in a huddle with his dad and Rudy.

Spencer looked at me, "Don't let her get to you. She means nothing to D."

"Do I dare ask who Lucy is?"

"D's ex. The one who moved to France."

"Oh."

"She did that on purpose. Ignore her."

Club members or their wives or girlfriends kept turning up with things. Trays of coffees, bags filled with burgers, a couple pizzas showed up, and no less than four big boxes of donuts.

The doctor had spoken to us at around 9:00, a point where a lot of bikers were in that waiting room, and said that we should go get some sleep, that Joelle was doing reasonably well, that the swelling hadn't yet gone down but also hadn't further increased and that was a good sign. Visiting hours had come and gone and it was getting late so people started talking about heading out. Deke and Rudy were staying. Deke pushed Deacon, Rider, and Spence to go and get some rest.

Rudy, said he'd call over to sort guest room keys at the clubhouse. Deacon told him no, we wouldn't be staying at the club. People made faces but no one pushed. Someone offered their guest room at their home but Deacon said we'd stay at a motel that was close to the hospital and his tone invited no backtalk. Rider and Spence decided to stay there, too, and Shelly heard this.

"You boys either go to the club or you come home. Don't stay in no fucking motel." She screeched.

"Mom, leave it," Rider said.

"Ride…" Shelly started and big tears streamed down her face, "We have to come together as a family. For Jojo. You and Spence can stay in the basement in your old room. Deacon and Lucy can stay in Jojo's room."

"Ella, Mom. Fuck," Deacon bit off, "Are you fucking kidding me right now?"

Rider let out an exasperated sound.

"Got shit on my mind, as you know! Sorry. She looks like Lucy." She didn't look sorry. She shot another ugly look at me.

Deacon looked about ready to explode at that comment.

"We're here, mom. Let that be enough for tonight. We'll stay at the Red Rock. It's close," Rider said to his mother.

Shelly sniffed and stared, her chin trembling. And then she kissed Rider's cheek, hugged Deacon (he put one arm lightly around her but didn't give her much back), and then she stepped toward Spencer and he took a step back. She touched his arm and her chin trembled harder. He pulled his arm away. I felt bad for her. Obviously she'd alienated her sons.

I gave her what I hoped was a kind smile but she shot daggers at me again. I caught all three Valentine boys exchange looks. They'd noticed how she looked at me and I got the impression they didn't like it.

She left the family waiting room and was back at the nurse's station and waving her arms erratically. That poor nurse.

"Let's go," Deacon said to me. Deke hugged me and his boys, saying he'd be sleeping on a sofa in the waiting room and would keep us all posted.

Back at the motel, which was a small drive-up no frills sort of place, we said goodnight to Deacon's brothers, whose room was three rooms away, and when Deacon dropped the bag on our bed he asked, "Hungry?"

"No, I'm good. Are you?"

He shook his head, "Tried to eat pizza at the hospital and it didn't wanna go down. Fuckin' missed that pizza. Been dreamin' of it since we moved. Usually my favorite."

I approached him and he held me close.

"Things are tense with your mom and dad. I'm sure that made it even worse."

"Things are tense with her and everyone," he said.

"Yeah, I'm sorry, honey."

He shrugged, "It's how it always is. She's the most self-centered woman I know. Any drama becomes about her. And she wants all her boys to be a comfort during a time when we're all hurtin'. She's tryin' to use this to weasel her way back into the fold with us but it won't be that simple. The way she was with you, full of jealousy, shows me she's using this to her advantage."

"She's scared, I'm sure, and she probably isn't thinking straight enough to be manipulative."

"You don't know her enough to defend her."

"Sorry, that was out of line. I just can't imagine she would—-"

"She would."

I winced.

"You can't imagine 'cuz you're not like her. 'Cuz your mother's not like her. Someone like you is very different from someone like her. Take the other night, when Scoot was hurt, you had a mind to how I was dealin', didn't worry 'bout how it affected you. My ma woulda bitched she sat the whole night waiting instead of asking her man if he was doing okay. She'd have texted him a dozen times demanding to know where he was. You didn't utter a word of complaint. And you didn't hassle me. You knew I had shit to deal with so you left me to do it but where there for me when the night was done. Today, you dropped everything to sit in a truck for hours with puff the fuckin' dragon and then sat here in a waiting room all day, dealing with ma's drama, her dirty looks, fuckin' up your name. Calling you my ex's name. You kept offering to do things, get things, being here for me, for Dad. You were even there for my brothers when they got here and Spence has been a fucking jerk to you yet you were still sweet. You weren't trying to be the center of attention. My mother is all about Shelly."

I gave his hand a squeeze.

"I know my Dad filled you in a little about her drama. Don't know how much he told you but my earliest memories are of them scrapping. She gets physical even. Don't know how many times in my life I've seen her smack his face. I've seen her throw cups of hot coffee at him. I've seen him somehow keep his control and never strike back. Most men would've lost their shit with her long before he finally ended things for good. And he's a much happier person since they split. She's as toxic as ever but he's finally free and seein' how much happier and carefree he is now makes me hate her all the more for causing him all that pain."

"I'm sure you don't hate..."

"Naw, Kitten. I do. I hate that bitch. You can't imagine the bullshit we endured growin' up with her. Verbal abuse, neglect. She's a bitch. Half the time she wasn't around and those were the happiest times for our family. Honest to God."

I didn't argue but despite how the day had gone, he had treated her with care, maybe not the usual warmth you'd expect between a mother and son in those types of circumstances, but he certainly hadn't been mean to her.

"Gotta get a shower, babe," he said.

"Okay, I'm gonna just get something to drink from the vending machines. Pepsi?"

He kissed me, "Coke."

"Coke? Please tell me you know that Pepsi's way better," I teased.

He gave me a look, "I'm gonna have to rethink this."

"Rethink what?"

"My notion that you're perfect. Because, babe, Pepsi is far inferior."

It was nice to see a bit of humor after such a rough 24, no 48 hours if you counted what'd happened to Scooter the night before.

"What if they have no Coke, only Pepsi?"

"Then I'll take a non-cola. Any non-cola, anything, just no Pepsi."

I rolled my eyes and laughed.

"You got a Coke fridge in your room," he pointed out.

"If you notice, I put red tape over the e. Technically, that makes it a Cok fridge, not a Coke fridge."

He laughed and his body shook with that laughter as reached for and then held me. But then he let go and his expression darkened and I could see his thoughts drifted back to his sister.

"Is it looking like it was intentional?" I asked.

"My gut tells me it was. And if that's the case, it means we go from battling to straight out war."

Yikes.

"Don't think about that tonight. Getting that shower."

"Okay. I'll go get Pepsis."

"No Pepsi, Coke." He said in a pretty darn good John Belushi from that old SNL skit impression. I gave him a smile and he kissed the tip of my nose and went into the bathroom.

I rifled through my purse for change, didn't find any, so took a ten-dollar bill from my wallet (which, at quick count, had $500 more in it than what I'd had there before he tucked that wad of cash in it. Why on earth did Deacon shove that much money in my wallet?) and went to the vending machine. There wasn't a change machine so I walked down toward the main office on the other end of the parking lot to see if they could break that ten for me.

That was when I suddenly felt what I can only describe as an odd and ominous heat at my back and a hand appeared in my vision as fingers wrapped around my mouth. An arm hooked around my chest and I was being dragged backwards. I kicked and flailed, but before I could get away I heard multiple car doors opening, then multiple sets of feet and then felt grips around my ankles. I was thrown in a cargo van and everything went from dark to pitch black as tape was slapped, hard, against my mouth and then something fabric dropped over my head.

There was tape across my mouth. I was in a van. There was a heavy weight on me as they held me down. Oh. My. God!

"Get her hands tied behind her back," I heard a gruff male voice bark out. I kept trying to struggle but it felt like I was in a crowd with several sets of hands on me.

"Feet, tie her feet."

"Bitch sacked me. Tie her fuckin' feet!"

My God. What the heck was happening here?

I heard a bang, like a gunshot. I heard another bang.

"Fuck, it's one of the Doms. He's shootin' at us."

I heard tires squealing and I was tumbling around until I landed against a person who grabbed me and kept me still.

Please don't let it be the Wyld Jackals. Please don't let it be the Wyld Jackals.

SOMEONE MUST'VE BEEN on a phone. I heard, "Yeah, got one of the Valentine boys' women in the van. Valentine, yeah...." He sounded sickeningly pleased. Bile rose in my throat.

"Gonna do her right here...."

Do me?

"What? I dunno which brother this piece belongs to. The short-haired brother shot at us but no real damage to Dice's van. Yep. She's tied and hooded. Little blonde. Stacked. Can't fuckin' wait to blow my load on those." He started laughing sort of maniacally and my blood ran cold but then he stopped laughing. "Yeah? No shit? Fuck. Fuck man, you serious? Okay. Well, I didn't fuckin' know! See ya in ten minutes. No, we won't."

Then I heard, "What is it?"

"Outside. Gotta talk."

I heard doors slam and I tried to struggle but my hands and feet were tied very tight. I heard traffic but could hear their voices outside the van.

"Fuck. Change of plans. We gotta drop her off to Sarge."

Then someone else, "They tell us to unleash all holy hell on The Doms and then we get nothin' but flak. First Deuce and Logan get shit for takin' down Hanson because of who Hanson's piece is, said that was too bold for move one, now we're gettin' shit because of this. Sarge said don't touch her but won't say why. If you don't want all holy hell don't say it. Am I right?"

"Shh. Shut the fuck up, man, in case she can hear."

"She can't hear us."

"Let's just get this bitch there and go, then. I got shit to do," Someone else said.

"I need to wet my dick. Fuck, this sucks. Shoulda did her before we called. They said we could fuckin' do this, what the fuck?"

"Shut yer face."

After that, I heard the doors again and then heard nothing other than the noises of a vehicle running. And I was afraid that my heart was beating so fast that it'd explode.

But when the vehicle came to a stop, the doors opened, and I heard muttered sounds as I was thrown over a shoulder.

I was put down on something soft and the fabric was pulled off my head. My mouth was still taped and my hands and feet were tied, hands behind my back. It looked like I was in an unfinished basement and I was in a room with four men, three of them in Wyld Jackals cuts.

Fuck.

A tall and lanky tattooed dark haired clean shaven guy, maybe in his middle or late thirties, tipped my chin up. He had a Sgt. Patch on his leather.

"I'm taking the tape off but no screaming; got me?"

I nodded.

"I mean it."

I nodded again.

"You scream, I backhand you and tape your mouth back up."

I shook my head.

He ripped the tape off and I hissed with the pain.

"What's your name, honey?" he asked.

"Ella."

"You an old lady of a Dom?"

I nodded.

"Which one?"

"Deacon."

"Fuck. You fucking morons," he said to the others, "This is definitely Wild Will's niece."

Expressions dropped.

"What the fuck is Wild Will's niece doing with a Dom?" One said.

"Maybe this is a good thing, Sarge." Another said, "Will'd want her away from him. He can lock her up until she sees the light."

He leaned over, "You belong with one of us, baby." He was gross. I tried not to show any reaction but I probably didn't succeed at hiding my look of disgust.

"Back off, Dice. Call Will," Sarge said, "Then pass it to me. You're fuckin' lucky you called me before you touched her. Ella, today is your lucky day. You can thank your lucky stars you're family to the Jackals."

I was not about to argue that fact, even though it wasn't true and furthermore I didn't want it to be true.

Another guy, both dirty-blond and dirty-looking, about my age dialed on cell phone and passed the phone to the Sarge guy after saying, "Will, Sarge wants you."

"Will, yeah. Your niece is the basement. Someone got it in their head it'd be a good idea to grab a Dom old lady and strike back for Kailey and these bozos didn't know it was your niece... No, down here, she was with Deke's oldest. They must all be here due to ... you know, what happened on 42 last night. They haven't touched her. No, for sure they didn't. Naw, we haven't shared that intel widely. Right. We'll have to.... I'll keep her safe, man."

Sarge hung it up.

"Fork is on his way. He's about an hour out on a run and he'll take you home."

"Can I call Deacon? He's got enough on his plate worrying about his sister."

Sarge looked at me a moment and then nodded, "I'll call him. What's the number?"

"I don't know." I needed to memorize his number.

"We got her from the Red Rock."

Sarge fiddled with the smartphone a minute and then put the phone to his ear. "This is Sarge from the Wyld Jackals. You know who we are?

Yeah? Good...need some info. You got a Deacon Valentine staying there? Any other Valentines? Give me that one." He waited a moment and then said, "I'll leave a voicemail." Another beat of silence, then, "Rider, tell your brother his girl is safe. It was an error in judgement. She'll be delivered to her uncle back in Ipswich. No one's laid a finger on her. This courtesy won't extend to an old lady of yours, should we locate her. You know why."

"I need to get to Deacon," I said when he hung up, knowing that Deacon did not need this with all he was already coping with. I also did not like what he'd said to Rider, at all. I needed to tell him to get Jenna safe. Who knew when they'd check their hotel room's voicemail, if at all.

"I'll leave that to Fork. If he and his old man let you back near the Doms you tell Deacon what happened out on forty-two wasn't about the princess. It was only about Hanson."

"Okay," I said.

"I'll get you something to drink and then I'm lockin' you down here till Fork gets here. Don't give us any trouble, y'hear?"

"No trouble."

Even if I wanted to give him trouble, my hands and feet were tied. I needed to get to play it smart, get out of here, and get to Deacon and then get to Jenna as soon as possible.

He and the dirty blond left me down there. I was on a dirty old sofa that maybe used to be white in an unfinished basement that was littered with boxes and milk crates of tools, rolls of carpet, different sized pieces of drywall. It was as if someone brought stuff in to finish the space but never did. Everything had dust on it and the air was cloying with a smoky and musty odor. He was back a moment later with two bottles of water and an unopened bag of chips, which he put beside me.

"You need the bathroom?"

I shook my head.

"Let me know now if you do. I won't be back 'til Fork gets here and we don't wanna hear you hollerin' or anything."

He undid my hands and feet, "No trouble." He warned and his expression went so sinister for a moment that I knew he wanted me to know that niece of a Jackal or not, I'd be stupid to try anything.

I sat there and drank a bottle of water and after what felt like forever, I heard arguing upstairs. I couldn't make out the voices but then Chris was coming down the stairs with Sarge and the dirty blond guy. And Chris looked pissed off.

I glared at him but I was a little bit relieved that I'd be getting out of here, hopefully back to Deacon as soon as humanly possible as I couldn't imagine how he was feeling right now, his sister in a coma and I just vanish.

"Lizzie."

"Chris-toff."

"Gotta hood ya till we're off the property, Let's go."

"You're joking, right?"

"Nope. Not so long as you're sleepin' with the enemy."

He came toward me with a dark pillowcase and threw it over my head and then hefted me up in his arms.

"I hate you," I told him.

He laughed and we were on the move. I was put into a car, a seatbelt put on me, and then the car started up. A minute later Chris said, "You can take it off."

I did and glared at him. It didn't seem to have any effect whatsoever.

"Can you take me back to the Red Rock motel?"

"Nope."

"The hospital down the street from it then?"

"Nope, taking you to my Dad's."

"Chris..."

"If you think I'm dropping you off to those soulless bastards, you're wrong. And I'm taking the three-hour ride home to talk you out of stayin' with that fucker. Dad can call Uncle Rob to come get you from our place."

"Chris, please..."

"Shut it. I need a minute to chill out before I start talkin' sense into you. You don't know how close you came tonight to being very fucking sorry for hooking up with a Valentine."

"Deacon is going to be freaking out. He's already freaking out because of his sister."

"Ella, these guys are—-"

"Don't. I don't wanna hear it. I'm with Deacon and you and me… we hardly know each other, Chris. We're relatives. We haven't hung out together in ten years and the 13 years we did, you were nothing but a bully, making my life a misery. You tormented me. Cut one of my pigtails off when I was four. Locked me in that scary basement in the dark for two hours. The list goes on. And on. I am with Deacon and I know your clubs are warring but I'm not interested."

"They're on a mission to destroy us, Ella. You haven't a clue how lucky you are that you are who you are and that they figured that out P.D.Q."

I don't think he'd ever called me Ella before tonight.

"Maybe you guys deserve to be destroyed. Your club killed someone tonight and might have either killed or at the very least changed a girl's life. A lot of people are upset."

"Deke Valentine killed our VP, gunned him down in cold blood, because his wife was steppin' out on him. She lied about who it was with, it wasn't even a Jackal, it was a fuckin' Dom, and that escalated what was already a bunch of tension that started this war and now it's out of control. Your man and his MC brothers are responsible for Jackal several deaths, including an innocent 21-year-old brand new prospect who got caught in that crossfire. Four Sioux Falls Doms, two of which just moved to start up the Aberdeen charter gang raped a Jackal's old lady a few weeks ago. The list goes on, Ella. This really what you wanna tie yourself to?"

I didn't say anything.

"I know we aren't close, 'cuz, but seriously. What the fuck are you, of all people, doing datin' a biker? You're above this."

I was a little bit shocked.

He shook his head and lit a cigarette and took a deep haul off it.

"Chris, don't drive me home. Let me out here. I'll just find my way to Deacon." I unrolled my window.

"Ella, fuck!" he was pissed.

"Let me out of this motherfucking car!" I screamed at him and tried to open the door.

He swerved onto the side of the road, "Don't be stupid and jump from a fuckin' moving car! I'll tie you up and throw you in the trunk before I let you do something that stupid."

"As far I can tell, they're the good guys and you guys are the bad guys. Looking at the Jackals track record I have no reason to believe that your MC are the good guys."

He glared at me.

"Christian, so help me!" I hollered at him, "I'll scream my head off all the way home and I'll make your life a living hell if you don't take me to Deacon right fucking now!"

He stared at me a second and then threw his hands up in the air and said, "I'll drop you at the hospital. Fuck." He punched the dash of the car and then got back on the road.

"Thank you," I whispered.

"You always were a stubborn little bitch. I'll catch shit from my old man, who wanted you brought to our place so he could use you as an olive branch to Uncle Rob, but I'll deal. Fuck. Don't get yourself gang-raped or killed getting caught in the crossfire, Ella, you do it'll be your fault. This is all on you now."

I folded my hands across my chest and stared straight ahead as he pulled a U-turn.

"HIS SISTER OKAY?" HE asked as we pulled in to a parking spot on a main street. We weren't at the hospital but I could see the glowing *H* down the road a little.

"I don't know yet. She was stable as of a few hours ago. They have her in an induced coma due to brain swelling."

He shook his head. "Let you out here so I'm not spotted. If you're gonna be fuckin' stupid and you keep seein' this guy, at least be careful. You see the light and need help, you call me. What's your number?"

I rolled my eyes. "Maybe choosing Deacon is the smartest thing I've ever done."

"Give me your number or I'm not letting you out of this car."

I muttered the numbers and he programmed his phone.

"We're putting word out to all Jackals you're off limits. Tell Valentine that but tell him to be vigilant in keepin' you safe, anyway. Tell him Jojo wasn't the target tonight, either. At all. No one knew she'd be with Hanson. And see if you can stop your dad from his association with their club. It's gonna land him in jail."

"In jail?"

"Or dead. Yeah. He's being a fuckin' mule. Moving heroin and coke for them."

"He what?"

"I'm sayin' nothing else but your Dad is in over his head with these guys. They're puttin' him at risk and pissing off Jackals at the same time. Hospital is over there. Go. Before I change my mind. I need my fuckin' head checked."

I got out of the car and slammed the door.

"You got no damn shoes on. Shit."

"That drug store is open 24 hours. Maybe they've got something." I said, pointing.

"Get back in, I'll take you there."

He drove to a parking spot in front of the store and we went in together. They didn't have much to choose from but he bought me a pair of Maryjane knock-off Crocs and I thanked him. We parted ways without another word. He sat and watched me from his car as I walked toward the hospital parking lot and then he peeled away in his car.

When I got near the entrance, I saw two Dominion Brotherhood patches at the smoking shelter and hurried there. The men turned around and looked at me. I thought I recognized one from earlier in the day but couldn't remember his name.

"Hi, Um, I-I'm Deacon's girlfriend and I—-"

"Ella! Thank Christ," the familiar one said, obviously knowing who I was or recognizing me.

"Yeah. Um, can I—-" I was about to ask to use his phone but he put his arm around me.

"Fuck, good to see you, c'mon. You okay?"

"Yeah, I'm okay."

They ushered me back toward the doors. The one I didn't know was on the phone. "D. Got your girl here at the hospital. She's whole. Just showed up, yeah. Takin' her up to your Dad. We're walkin' her up there now and she looks in one piece."

He passed the phone to me.

"Hi?"

"Kitten."

"I'm okay."

Dead air.

"Deacon?"

"You're okay?" His voice sounded funny.

"Yes. I'm okay. Honest."

He let out a breathy growly sound.

"Dad'll get you to me," he grunted.

"Uh, ok."

He hung up. I passed the biker back the phone and when I got into the family waiting room back on the third floor after the longest elevator ride known to man because these two bikers looked like they were going to lose their cool for some reason (both with their hard eyes on me), I was engulfed into a hug by Deke. The room had three other bikers. Two of them were making calls and from what I'd gathered, they were calling off searches.

"You okay, little lady?" His eyes roved over me, assessing.

"I'm okay."

"Hey sweetheart," Rider stepped in and gave me a hug. He did the same thing with his eyes.

"Jenna. Jenna's in danger. They said something. They might hurt Jenna, I don't... I don't know, they left you a voicemail message at the hotel."

He pulled his phone from his pocket, "Be back." He slipped out of the room into the hall.

I heard Deke order everyone to 'clear out' and then he put a hand on my shoulder.

"Ride'll take you to Deacon," Deke said, "He's been tearing up the streets lookin' for you. Spence is out there lookin' too. Several of our guys are out doin' that," he said as the room cleared.

He passed me an unopened but slightly lukewarm bottle of water. I downed the whole thing and then went to the bathroom. I looked a little disheveled, tired, but that was it. When I got back out into the waiting room, Rider and Deke were close, talking low.

"Did Spence shoot at them? He's okay, right? They said the short-haired one shot at them but I heard two shots," I asked.

"He's fine. They didn't shoot back. He saw them draggin' you off while he was out havin' a smoke and he ran in, grabbed his piece, and tried to shoot out their tires. What happened?" Rider was talking gently, looking me up and down, again, maybe for signs of injury.

"Jenna?"

"Bronto is gonna stay with her until we get back. Don't worry."

I was hyperventilating.

"What happened?" Rider put his arm around me and sat me down on a sofa.

"Someone grabbed me on the way to the motel office to break a ten for the vending machine. They were Wyld Jackals. They threw me in a van that belonged to someone named Dice. They took me to some house, an unfinished basement. The guy was called Sarge. They found out who I was and called my Uncle Willie, who sent Chris to get me. He wanted to take me home but I threw a fit until he dropped me back off here. He said that I should tell Deacon all of what happened on highway 42 was about Hanson, not Jojo."

Deke glared at the floor and his lip curled and then he and Rider locked eyes for a second.

"What else?" Rider asked.

"Nothing else," I replied.

"Nothing?" Deke gave me a hard cold look.

I was a little confused.

He waited.

I shook my head.

"Anyone touch you?"

"No."

"Threaten to?"

"No."

"Honest?" That was Rider.

"Honest. I overheard them talking and I got the impression they were gonna... maybe do something to me but then they found out who I was."

He let out a breath.

"Sexual?"

I nodded. "As soon as they found out what the guys who took me did, they took me to that Sarge guy and he called Uncle Willie right away."

"And your cousin?" Deke asked, putting a hand on Rider's shoulder, as if to give him support. It was kind of weird.

"What'd your cousin say about us?"

I stared at him a moment and chewed my lip. Chris seemed genuine but I didn't trust it.

"Ella," Deke was looking at me with a severe expression, "I need to know what's been said. I know you've been through a lot tonight but please, darlin'. We need to know if anyone else is at risk tonight. What'd Fork say?"

"He said he was gonna talk sense in to me about seeing a Dom. He said they are pretty sure you killed their VP because you thought your wife was sleeping with him. He says she lied about that. And that made tensions worse. They said a prospect who was practically a kid got killed in the crossfire and that four Doms gang-raped a Jackal's old lady. They said you guys have my dad running drugs and that he's at risk."

The tension levels in the room ratcheted up significantly. Deke left the room, just left us there.

I took a big breath and rubbed my eyes. If I wasn't Willie's niece, those guys would've raped me as retaliation. I knew it but was trying to push it out of my head. And was it true about my Dad running drugs for them? Not pot, dad always sold pot, but heavy drugs. No one denied it.

"Ella, you don't listen to any of what they say, alright?" Rider told me, "Things are very fucking complicated with this feud. And I'm telling you right now, don't let this shit tear you and Deacon apart." He put both hands on my shoulders, "Okay?"

I could do nothing but stare at him. Was he saying that Deacon might be responsible for things that would make me want to end things? Rider looked stressed. He looked like he just read my mind and was admonishing himself.

He ran his hands through his hair, "No Dom raped a Jackal old lady. It didn't fuckin' happen. That cunt made it up. C'mon, let's go."

I winced.

We walked past Deke and a few others guys in the smoking area.

Deke gave me a quick hug, "See you tomorrow. Glad you're okay. Those responsible'll pay for that."

"Try to get some rest," I suggested and he looked at me closely, shaking his head, like I was a conundrum.

"Yes ma'am." He kissed my forehead.

Rider drove me the short drive back to the motel in his old school Dodge Charger and if it'd been normal circumstances I would've commented on how his ride was way cooler than mine. But I didn't say a word about the car. We got back to the hotel and we sat in his room, me watching TV and him furiously texting for about ten minutes and then he got up and opened the door an inch and sat back on the bed. A beat later the door opened and Deacon was closing the distance between us, then he was on me, yanking me up in the air and I was plastered to his body.

He was livid. His body was shaking. He leaned back and looked me in the eyes, "They'll fucking pay for this." His eyes shot to his brother and they were silently communicating something and the testosterone in the room was at what must've been lethal levels.

"I'm okay. No one hurt me."

"They'll still pay, Ella. Do you hear me?" His eyes searched me and the fury was rolling off him. The look on his face was primal, like a warrior getting ready to go to battle. He put his hands on my face and then rested his forehead against mine. I closed my eyes and even though I couldn't see it, I could feel it——the tension.

"Two seconds, bro." Rider requested and Deacon looked at him like he didn't want to let go of me.

"Okay?" Deacon asked me.

I nodded, "I'm fine. I just want a shower."

He planted a hard kiss on my lips, holding my hair, which was a curly mess, having lost the elastic in it somewhere along the way. "C'mon to our room." He let out a big breath and the three of us walked down to our room. He let me in, looked around, I guess making sure no one was in there, and then then stepped out of the room with Rider.

I went into the bathroom, shed my clothes, got into the shower and tried to wash the night away. I was numb. And tired. And my brain was going a billion miles a minute. I just wanted to shut it off.

When I got out, Deacon was sitting on the edge of the bed, his head in his hands, his elbows on his knees. The TV was on but the light was off. He looked up at me.

"Baby," his voice was choked.

I sat beside him. He pulled me tight against him and we laid back on the pillows.

"Longest three hours of my fuckin' life," he said.

"Babe," I snuggled in to him.

"Of my life," he repeated and held me tight. "Spence came in shoutin' while I was still in the shower. He opened the door with your fuckin' keycard, which he found beside your goddamn shoes lying there on the pavement. Fuck."

"I'm okay. It was scary but I'm okay. Rider filled you in?" I asked.

"Yeah. I'm so sorry, baby. If I had any idea…"

"You don't have to be sorry. You didn't do anything wrong."

"Thank God your uncle is a Jackal. If it weren't for that, I don't wanna think about…. How fucked is it that I'm relieved about you being related to a fucking Jackal? I didn't even know if while you were gone it'd make a difference but thank fuck it did. Was out of my goddamn mind hoping they figured out who you were before they touched you and that somehow it'd win over their need for revenge."

"Did Rider tell you Chris said they weren't targeting your sister. Only Hanson?"

"Yeah. When I find out which Jackals did that…"

"I know who did it, Deacon."

"What?"

"I heard them say who ran them off the road."

"Tell me in the morning. Or I won't sleep. I'll go hunt them down. I need to sleep."

Should I be keeping that to myself to stop Deacon from targeting those people? Some girls might've. But I didn't want secrets in this relationship. I didn't want anything to put us at risk. I hoped he would give the information to the police, do the right thing. I knew that wasn't exactly in the biker creed but maybe I could talk him into letting the police do their job here.

"I'm sure you've got questions and I haven't filled you in on the ugly history but baby, I wanna hold you, make love to you, fall asleep knowin' I'll wake up beside you after thinking the worst tonight. Talk more tomorrow. Ask your questions then. Yeah? That okay?"

"That's okay." I was way too exhausted and way too numb to even form questions tonight.

He looked at me, assessing my face.

"That shit didn't happen. Bitch lied and now they want retribution."

I stared blankly at him.

"Longest fucking three hours of my life." His palm rested on my cheek and he kissed the tip of my nose.

We didn't make love because it only took me about a minute to fall asleep. He held me tight the whole night.

10

We woke up to a phone ringing a normal ring tone. It wasn't my phone. I guess Deacon had deleted Jenna's ringtone.

Jenna. I needed to call Jenna and make sure she was okay. He rolled away from me to answer it and I listened to him talking to his Dad. It sounded like good news.

It was great news. His sister had been woken and preliminary tests were all good. She was groggy but had woken up a few times and so far, she seemed like herself.

We got up and I showered while he made calls and then I updated Mom and Jenna with texts (but left out the part about being kidnapped). Jenna wrote back saying she had a biker shadow bodyguard but typed with emoticons and LOL's so I guess whatever she'd been told, it must've been sugar-coated.

I also replied to a text from Lloyd at the cab office who had texted the night before to ask me to work midnights Sunday night, Monday night, and Tuesday night. I told him I couldn't, that midnight shifts were not possible for me right now and said I was still out of town on an emergency. My phone rang as Deacon and I were pulling into the hospital parking lot. Lloyd.

"Ella, I need you to work those shifts. I also need you to answer your texts quickly so that when I need you I know whether I can count on you or not."

"Lloyd, I can't do midnights. I had to get another part time job after you cut my hours and it's days so it'll mess me up to go back and forth. I texted you that I'm now working Fridays and Saturdays. And I need to be there for my boyfriend right now. His sister is in the hospital after a bad accident and we're in Sioux Falls for a few days."

"Ella, if I can't count on you, I'm sorry to say this but I'll have to replace you. I need a team of people I can count on."

I was pissed. Pissed. I lost it.

"Seriously? Have at it, then, because I have worked for you for two years and you've counted on me, leaned on me endlessly. Constantly changed my hours and I've been nothing but flexible. I've always gone above and beyond, working late, coming in early, canceling plans at the last minute when you needed me and not only have you taken my hours down, which I understand, but you're out of line, Lloyd. I have a family emergency and I need to be present for that. If you can't give me this then you do not deserve to have the continued support I give your company."

He was quiet.

"I have to go. If you want to fire me, send me my last pay in the mail. If you want me working, text me in a couple days and we can talk about shifts that'll work for me. Bye." I hung up.

Deacon pulled into the hospital parking lot, "Good job, babe. Fuck them."

"And I don't answer my texts fast enough, apparently. Sorry Lloyd, I was tied and gagged with a pillowcase over my head in a van because they wanted to gang rape me or I'd have answered your text sooner. Fuck."

I put my head in my hands and then I felt the emotion of the past 24 hours overwhelm me and a sob bubbled up. He released my seatbelt and pulled me into his lap and put his arms around me. The steering wheel was digging into my back a bit but I still melted into him, hiccupping with the sobs. I felt the seat move as he reclined a bit to give us more room.

I think it was all just on top of me. I hadn't even given myself a chance to dig out of the emotional avalanche yet. I'd been kidnapped and could quite possibly have gotten gang-raped last night and heard all sorts of garbage that I hadn't quite processed. Everything had swirled around and I'd pushed it all away. Jenna could've been in danger, might still be in danger, Jackals waiting for Bronto to mess up and let his guard down for two seconds. And my Dad, running drugs?

In Deacon's arms right then, I felt sheltered and protected. He was big and strong and his embrace right then was so comforting.

I had questions. I had lots of questions but his sister was the priority. Everything else could wait. I allowed myself to just feel the comfort.

As if he'd read my mind he said, "Things are fucked up, baby. I'm so sorry you had to deal with all that last night. It's getting ugly with the Jackals and it's gonna get uglier before it's over. But I won't let anyone harm a fuckin' curl on this beautiful head, you hear me?"

I sniffled. "Today we got good news. Let's focus on your sister. Sorry for being a crybaby."

I reached for my purse so I could grab a Kleenex to dab my eyes and he grabbed me and kissed me. "Kitten," he muttered and said it with so much emotion. I put my hands on his cheeks.

"Yesterday was a shitty day. Let's have a good day today," I said.

His eyes searched my face and he shook his head as if astonished by me. I let the feelings that evoked wash over me as we made our way toward the door. We found Spencer and Shelly in the smoking shelter and Spencer was yelling at his mother.

He saw us, pointed at her as he finished whatever he'd said and put his cigarette out in the ashtray and then breezed by us, giving Deacon an exasperated look, "Mornin' Ella," he grumbled and then kept going.

"Hi." I don't even know if he heard me.

Shelly's eyes were on me.

"Hi, Shelly," I greeted.

"Hello," she answered coldly and then looked to Deacon, "Jojo's awake. Doctors say looks like she'll be okay, but Deacon your brother…Spencer is all over me. You gotta talk to him. And your fucking father—-"

"Mom," Deacon cut her off, "Now ain't the time. I'm going up to see my sister."

"But can you—-"

"We'll talk later. Let's just focus on this good thing for one minute before the next drama, yeah?"

He pulled on my hand to go inside and I heard Shelly scoff.

"Should she be by herself?" I asked.

Deacon frowned, as if confused.

"After what happened last night, maybe someone should stay with your Mom. I mean…Deacon?"

What if they kidnapped her? Shelly looked at me curiously.

"She'll be fine," Deacon muttered and tugged my hand.

"Don't you worry," Shelly told Deacon, her voice dripping with sarcasm, "I'll be fine; no need to put yourself out."

"Are you fucking kidding me?" Deacon spun around to face her and bit off, "You know that they won't target you since you're givin' it regular to Mantis. Fuck. Gimme a fuckin' break. You do know that they took Ella last night?"

"I heard," she muttered with an eye roll.

"Oh, ya did, did ya?" Deacon sneered, "And you didn't even ask her if she was alright? Didn't express a shred of concern. The whole time those fuckin' goofs had her all she did was worry about me, worry about how stressed out our family was gonna be when we already had Jojo to worry about. Ella could've been fuckin' gang raped last night. And you fuckin' know it."

"I don't need this shit," Shelly threw her cigarette on the ground and stepped on it, again ignoring the ashtray affixed to the wall. "I been up worryin' about your sister, dealing with your fucking father, getting the cold shoulder from you and read the riot act from Spency. Only Ride has given me the time of day."

"But it's all deserved, ma, except for Ride bein' cool with you. C'mon Ella, let's go. Don't worry about her, she's like a cockroach. There'd be a nuclear blast and she'd emerge from the fuckin' ashes. Just no limits to who she'd trample to get to the fall-out shelter."

"Deacon Oliver..."

He evidently got whole-named in his family when he was in the dog house, too.

I had to jog to keep up with his long strides. We got into the elevator and when the door shut and we were alone I breathed, "How did you know I was worried about you when they had me?"

"Fork called me."

"You talked to Chris last night?"

He nodded. "Dunno how he got my number but called me after he dropped you off. Wanted me to know where you were and what I had in you. How fuckin' lucky I was and warned me not to fuck you over. I told him I already knew and that it wasn't gonna ever go wrong."

Whoa. Chris actually gave a shit enough about me to do that? What the what? The elevator dinged. We were on the third floor.

I must've been staring, dumbfounded.

"Later, okay, baby?" He grabbed my hand and led me to the family room, which was filled to the brim with bikers. I was introduced to more people, got hugs from every one of them, and was fawned over by a bunch of biker women who ranged from not much older than me to older than Shelly.

"So good to meet ya, honey, I'm Delia," an older attractive redhead said, "I'm Rudy's old lady and I'm just so sorry about what happened to you last night. Didn't get a chance to meet you yesterday. Me and some of the women were here just before you and Deacon got here." She pulled me into a huddle with three other women and kissed me on the cheek.

Deacon was talking to his father in hushed tones and Rider and Spence were there, too.

"Ella," Deacon stepped in, about to say something to me but Delia grabbed him and gave him a big kiss right on the mouth and then wiped the lipstick off, "How are you, baby?"

"Fine Aunt Delia, fine. Can you look after Ella while I go see Jojo? Don't let Shelly spread her poison, yeah?"

"Absolutely," Delia replied with obvious understanding.

"You don't leave this room, okay, Kitten?" Deacon kissed me, "Aunt Delia is like a mother to me. You'll love her. That's Trudy, Jet, and Connie. They'll tell ya who they belong to, I'm goin' to see Jojo. Dad said she's doin' good."

"That's great," I kissed his jaw.

The other ladies told me their men's names. Jet said she was with Edge, she was a pretty brunette with gorgeous jet-black hair in her 20's. Trudy and Connie were older, around Shelly's age, and they told me who they belonged to but I didn't recognize the names: Bud who was really named Lou and Duckie, who they didn't elaborate on his actual name.

Delia was the oldest but she was pretty and youthful at the same time, one of those women who would always turn men's heads. She fawned over me like she was Deacon's mother. I guessed she was one of the women who Deke had said stepped up as a mother-figure for his kids.

"It is so good to see him with someone like you, honey. We heard amazing things about you from Deke, Spencer, and Rider."

"Thank you. We're very new but I really really like him."

"As you should," the one named Connie said, "He *is* a catch! So much like his Daddy." Connie stared at Deke over by the coffee machine and smiled and waved at him. He returned her smile and his eyes were on me as he came over.

"How you doin' Betty?" He gave me a big hug and kissed my forehead.

"I'm good. I'm very glad Jojo is doing well. Said lotsa prayers yesterday for her."

He gave me a smile, so much like Deacon's smiles, "Yeah. She's gonna be okay."

"Did you sleep? Have you eaten?" I asked. He looked kind of rough.

He laughed, "Not much. But I'll sleep good tonight. Right after I drink about a gallon of whiskey."

"We're organizin' a family party at the clubhouse," Delia told him, "not to worry."

Shelly stepped back into the room and the expressions on all four women's faces dropped. In fact, the vibe of the whole room seemed to change.

Shelly rolled her eyes, "Shoulda fuckin' known."

Deke turned his back on us to speak to Spencer.

"Deacon's got better taste in women than his old man, that's for damn sure," Delia muttered.

"What a relief," Trudy muttered.

"Truth," Deke said over his shoulder and I was a little bit mortified.

Shelly went to Rider and started speaking softly to him and then took him by the arm and led him out into the hallway.

The coffees Deacon and I brought were handed out and a short time later, someone did another coffee run and I got another decent cup of coffee from Starbucks and listened to the 'old ladies' shoot the breeze. They were talking about details for that evening's party and for Lick's funeral.

"If we're still here, I'm happy to help," I said, "I can cook, be on the clean-up crew, whatever. Or if we go but come back, I'll help. Whatever you need."

All of them beamed big smiles at me and gave one another looks of what looked like approval.

The crowd thinned out and then Deacon was back and I couldn't read the look in his eyes. Was it relief? Was it worry? Was it just pure raw emotion? He came right to me and pulled me full contact against him. I put my arms around his lower back and looked up at him. "You okay?"

He nodded and just buried his face into my neck, then sat down, pulling me on his lap, and kept me close.

I kissed his forehead and kept my arms around him. He was so big and strong but he was drawing strength from me, it seemed.

Everyone but Deke, Spencer, and Rider cleared out, including Shelly, but she was watching us through the window from the hallway.

"She looks so fucking small in that bed," Rider mumbled.

Deacon loosened his grip on me and looked to his brothers with a fierce look on his face. It was kind of scary.

"They need to pay," Spence said through gritted teeth.

"We'll discuss it later," Deke's eyes moved from Spence to me.

"They're going to pay for Jojo *and* for Ella," Rider's eyes were harder than I'd ever seen them. He looked at Deacon and shook his head.

Deacon's eyes narrowed, "Yeah. They are. Ella knows who it was. She heard them talkin' when they had her."

"Who was it?" Spence demanded.

I looked at Deacon.

"Who, babe?" Deacon urged.

"Deuce and Logan. Or Dice. I heard both names."

Spence snarled, "Deuce. Dice is someone else."

Deke grabbed his cut from a chair and shrugged it on.

"Clubhouse," Deke said, "You and Ella stay there tonight so she's 100% safe while we take care of business."

Deacon made a face at his dad but nodded and rose, grabbed my hand, and we all left the hospital, breezing by Shelly in the hallway. She was looking at her phone but I figured it was all for show. I couldn't give that too much thought, though, because I felt a bit freaked. What the heck did "take care of business" mean?

As we got outside, the boys were talking about checking out of our motel and then meeting at the clubhouse amid getting goodbye hugs by a dozen or so bikers of all ages, shapes, and sizes outside in the smoking area, when my phone rang. I didn't recognize the number.

"Hello?"

"Elizabelle?"

"Yes?"

"Girl, this is your uncle."

"Oh. Um, hi Uncle Willie."

Conversation around me halted. Deacon ushered me to the pickup truck and I got inside. Deke, Spence, and Rider stood in front of the passenger window, waiting, watching, listening. Windows were rolled down so everyone was listening, including the several bikers standing off to the side of the truck.

"Last night won't happen again. It shouldn't have happened but no one knew you were my niece."

"Um, alright." What could I say?

"Don't want you to be scared. Need a favor, though."

"A favor. What sort of a favor?"

"You ask your man to meet with Chris. They can iron out some details of an agreement that'll draw some battle lines so shit like this doesn't happen again. I'll text you his number and you give that to him."

"Okay, I'll pass on that message." I wasn't about to say that Chris already had Deacon's number but decided against revealing that in case Chris didn't want that known.

"No one'll lay a hand on you, girl. Alright? I was very fuckin' not pleased when I got that news last night."

"Okay. So Jenna's not in danger? She's Deacon's brother's girlfriend."

Deacon's eyes were glued to me and he looked wired. Rider's eyes went wide.

"Depends on which brother," Uncle Willie stated.

"Um...what difference does it make if she's with Rider or Spencer?"

"It makes a difference."

I looked at Rider with horror on my face.

"Fuck," Rider gritted.

"I can't promise but I'll try," Uncle Willie said.

"She's like a sister to me. I know we haven't seen each other much in the last decade but you've known her since she was five."

"I don't know if you know who you're in bed with, sugar, but..."

"Please don't," I cut him off, "I don't want to offend you, Uncle Willie, but I really don't want to be in the middle of this. What difference does it make whether she's with Rider or Spencer?"

Rider started pacing. Spencer was staring at his boots.

I looked to Deke and Deacon and their eyes were on me.

"Elizabelle, come over when you're back home. Come to my place and we'll have a hot chocolate and clear the air. There's things you don't know and I don't know your man but I know of him, and I know I don't want the Valentine brand of vengeance raining down on our women because of you bein' taken last night. Not sure why the fuck you weren't protected. Doesn't say a lot about him that he let that happen."

"What do you mean he let that happen?"

"You shouldn't have been out there in the midst of this. Shoulda been at their club, behind those gates—-"

I cut him off, "And Deacon would not target a woman for vengeance. Please tell your guys to back off the women, too. All of them, regardless of who they're with."

"Don't be so sure you know what they would and wouldn't do," Uncle Willie advised.

"Anyway, we're uh...busy with Deacon's sister being hurt, you know, since some of your guys did that so, uh..."

"I'll text Chris's number. Pass it to your man."

"Fine," I snapped.

"Tell your Daddy I'm sorry I shot my mouth off. Didn't mean what I said."

"Alright."

"Love ya honey. Miss your sweetness. Hope we can see one another real soon."

I didn't know what the heck to say to that.

Even if I knew he was a bit of a jerk in public, drinking too much, loud and scrappy, he'd always been nice to me as a little kid. Before his wife left him. When I used to sit with Jonathan while he made us hot chocolate with milk instead of water, lots of whipped cream, he always told me jokes, told me I had the best giggle he'd ever heard. I saw him backhand Chris once for making me cry. It'd been harsh and made Chris even meaner the next time Uncle Willie wasn't looking. But he'd tried to defend me. But all that creepiness about him leering at me when I went into puberty? Was this all for show? I didn't know what to make of it. I needed to talk to Dad.

"Okay, please see what you can do about Jenna."

"I'll try."

That wasn't very reassuring. I put the phone into my purse.

"Chris's number's coming. They want a meeting to draw battle lines. He seems to think you're going to go after their women in retaliation for last night."

Bikers in the parking lot were all ears, as were the Valentine men.

Rider looked wired, "What'd he say about me?"

"Nothing. He can't promise about Jenna but said he'd try. He wants Deacon to meet with Chris but why wouldn't he agree to not target Jenna depending on who she's with?"

No one answered me.

"Rider?" I pushed but I knew. I fucking knew that they blamed Rider for what they were claiming. I felt sick.

"Let's get to the motel and then we'll talk," Deacon said.

Rider and Deacon exchanged fierce looks. Spence lit a cigarette and was punching numbers into his phone as he walked away and put it to his ear kind of growling,

"Brother, Jet with you?"

WE WERE BACK IN THE motel room, cuddled up on the bed. As soon as we got in, he pulled me into his arms, didn't even turn on the light, and collapsed on the bed with me and kept me tight to him. It'd been a few minutes of just silence and darkness. After being in the darkness of that van with a hood on my head last night I wasn't crazy about the darkness but

Deacon's presence helped. I guess I was gonna have to make the first move in this conversation.

"Is my Dad running drugs for your club?" I blurted.

Deacon stiffened.

"Chris said Dad'll end up in jail or dead." I reached for the lamp and fumbled until I got it on. I looked at his face.

Deacon twirled one of my curls and looked like he was measuring his words.

"Forget it, you just answered me," I sniffed and tried to move away. He tightened his hold on me.

"There's a lot happening. A lot of it has to do with taking the Jackals down more than club earnings. There's a lot goin' on. Your Dad's helping. He is one of many who are helpin' us take these fuckers down. He started doing parcel deliveries for us, cabbies often do. No questions. Now that you're mine and he knows about our plans with the Jackals, he's chosen to get more involved."

I shook my head.

"It's between him and dad."

I huffed but didn't say anything. The fact that he'd referenced club earnings told me that his club was clearly playing with fire on a regular basis.

After a minute I finally asked, "What's the story with this Kailey person?"

"She lied. No Dom laid a finger on her that she didn't want." Deacon didn't hesitate before saying this.

"What does *that* mean?"

"It means she wanted to be gang banged. Begged them to take her hard and dirty. She took four Dom brothers at once but it was consensual. She lied afterwards, ran to the Jackals and spouted a bunch of bullshit."

I was in shock.

"Were you part of that?"

"No."

"No? Even if it was consensual?"

"Absolutely not. After what happened to Cassie? Never in a million years would I go there, Kitten."

I could believe that.

"Ride *did* go there. Lick and Edge and…"

"Scooter," I guessed.

He nodded. Obviously it was Scooter, Scooter had been beaten up badly a few nights before.

"He have a girlfriend?"

"No."

"Lucky."

"Not *that* lucky."

"What?"

"Two Jackals took turns ass raping him on the side of the road while two others held him down after they took his bike, boots, his cut."

"Oh fuck," I felt bile rise in my throat again trying to push away that I would've been gang raped in that filthy van last night, a pillowcase over my head.

"Scott is a solid guy. He'd rather take that than have his woman deal with that nightmare. She wanted it. No Jackal or Dom'd take on a piece of club fuckmeat as an old lady after that and she wanted to elevate her status and didn't care which club it was with. No Dom would've given her the time of day for more than a quick fuck. Rumor is that she approached Black Reapers who we are tight with, and Danny, their VP turned her down, so knowing that there's a feud, she used it and approached the Jackals. She's now an old lady with a low-level Jackal. And now we've gotta protect Jojo, and Jet."

I felt a little bit sick. Club fuckmeat? I couldn't begin to wrap my head around this right now. I couldn't let myself think about Jenna being "a little bit" in love with him. And poor Jojo, losing her secret boyfriend because of gang rape claims.

"Don't forget Jenna. You guys have to protect her, too."

He nodded with a look of exasperation, "Yeah. Of course."

"Did Hanson, Lick, did he do that while he was dating your sister?"

"Lookin' that way," Deacon's jaw clenched.

"Jet said she and Edge have been together four years."

"Yeah."

I knew the MC world wasn't necessarily as dark and dramatic as the TV show Sons of Anarchy. I also wasn't expecting unicorns and rainbows. But what kind of a dark and depraved world was I getting myself into here?

"Not all bikers are one woman men," he said, "And that doesn't just apply to bikers, Kitten. It also doesn't just apply to men. Plenty of women cheat, too."

"Oh fuck," I got up. I was sickened.

"I already told you that when I'm exclusive with someone, I don't fuck around. Since we are exclusive, that's all you need to worry about."

"And Rider?"

"None of my business what Rider does. None of yours, either."

"Yeah, well if he's dating Jenna, it's my business."

"No, Kitten; it ain't. I don't know that those two are anywhere near what you and me are. Not everyone moves as fast as we did."

"Why *did* we move so fast, Deacon?"

"When I know I want something, I don't fuck around. Would you rather dance around? Wonder whether we're going somewhere or would you rather know where I stand?"

He kind of had a point. But I suspected it was more than that, too. I was guessing that the danger made things move fast, too. By staking his claim, or whatever, he could move in and protect me. I'd obviously shown that I needed protection, what with the armed robbery and whatever Jay had said that tweaked Deacon in the diner.

"Ella, it's irrelevant anyway. What happened with Kailey was before he even met Jenna. So, that's his to share, not yours."

"The hell it isn't..."

"Ella," he caught me and pinned me to the bed, "Don't stick your oar in."

"Let me go. Gonna start packing our shit."

"In a sec. Listen to me. You let Rider deal with Rider's business."

"She—-"

"Stuck her nose in with you and me to protect you when she heard shit about me, I know, but look how well that went. It almost ended you and me. You don't want to get in the middle of this. Let them work it out."

I glared at him.

"We'd better get to the clubhouse. Before we go, I need to clue you in to a few things about the culture there. I know you aren't completely green about the life, baby, that you've known bikers but you haven't spent time with a club, right?"

"Right."

"This is an old school club; it's the mother charter. Ours is new so culture is still to be established. There'll be overlaps that exist in all MCs, of course, but at the Dominion Brotherhood MC, these family parties are one thing. Club life outside of family parties is another. Some charters are more family-oriented than others. You and I are staying there tonight because I need you safe while I see to business and so things'll be tame what with a family party happenin', a lot of brothers head home after these instead of partying late at the club but that said, they may not be 100% what I'd want you, as my girl, to be around. Lotta guys'll be staying that are free and single but if you see any brother fuckin' around on his old lady, you keep quiet and ignore it. Any club pussy that's around will show you respect as mine but if any of them try to fuck with you, you let a brother know, point them out. I'm talking about anyone tellin' tales about me, I'm talking about any of them even lookin' at you sideways. I'd rather you stay in the room there after I head out to take care of business, meet with Fork, so you're not exposed to anything after that family party but I wanted to get this out now in case anything happens."

I shook my head in shock.

"I'm being upfront with you here. I'd prefer you try to avoid that. The charter we're building is gonna be much more family-oriented. Club parties will be 75% family parties if my dad has his way instead of the 20% they are here. Make sense?"

I was absolutely livid. I glared at him.

"You are fucking kidding me, right?"

He looked confused, "About what part?"

"What part? What part? All of it! Club pussy? Club fuckmeat? The fuck?"

"Ella, listen..."

"No. Stop. I don't wanna hear any more of this. Go do what you have to do tonight. I won't leave the room. I don't wanna see none of that shit. Not any of it so don't worry."

"Ella…"

"I can't talk to you about any of this right now. I have to process all this. Dad moving drugs, Rider and those guys and Jenna, all of this. Let's just pack and go to your club or whatever."

I had a beautiful biker boyfriend who carried a gun, who'd turned my completely safe and predictable life upside down and inside out in about a week. I had an uncle and cousin embroiled in some mysterious feud with my boyfriend's MC. I had a father running heavy narcotics for my beautiful biker boyfriend's MC in order to enact some sort of revenge, maybe, on my dad's brother, and I had a best friend who was obliviously in danger of getting gang raped as retribution for something her new biker boyfriend did. And I'd narrowly escaped being gang-raped myself last night after being kidnapped. What a fucking detour from boring and responsible-ville, indeed.

He stared at me.

I gave him big eyes and threw my hands up in the air and got out of bed, ready to grab our stuff and start throwing it together, but he grabbed me and put me back onto my back and pinned me.

Fuck, did I seriously say I liked how he manhandled me? Because right now…

"I'm part of this life, it's in me, but it's not all I am."

I swallowed and pulled my lips tight.

"Tell me you know that."

I nodded.

"You do?"

"I know that. I wouldn't be here if I didn't."

He stared a minute. Time stood still as he searched my face. He moved in like he was gonna kiss me but maybe my expression didn't invite that so he backed up.

He let me go.

I rolled away from him and got out of the bed and angrily and loudly packed up.

On our way to the front office, we saw Rider and Spence sitting in Rider's muscle car near that office.

They both got out of their car, about to approach us. I let go of Deacon's hand and stormed the few steps that separated us and my index finger poked Rider right in the chest, "You tell her. Or I fuckin' will."

Deacon grabbed me by the waist and pulled me back, clipping, "Ella!"

Rider's expression dropped.

"I mean it!" I snapped at Rider, trying to pull away from Deacon.

Rider looked shocked. He got back into the car. Spence didn't say a word; he got back in and Rider pulled away.

Deacon pulled me by the hand into the front office and I stood beside him as he checked us out. I don't know what look he had on his face, I didn't look at it. I just stood there, staring straight ahead, seething.

Both of us were broody on the drive to the clubhouse.

IT WAS IN AN INDUSTRIAL area that flanked a nice residential neighborhood. We got to a big iron gate that was attached to a concrete wall. Beyond it, a large building sat. Nothing outwardly pointed to any Dom logo. A simple sign out front said Dominion Moving & Storage.

Before we got to the gate, he stopped the truck and released my seatbelt and pulled me into his lap. He got me nose to nose. I was breathless, not sure how to feel about that move amid all this turmoil and emotion.

"The club fuckin' adores you so far. Bikers and old ladies alike. I'm getting all kinds of pats on the back for choosing you. You've impressed every single one of them and I can't even begin to tell you how much gratitude I have for you and how you've been here for me through this. My dad and my brothers are also crazy about you. Don't let bein' pissed right now change their mind about you with all this goin' on. Always be you, you're pissed at what's happening, worried about Jenna, I get that, but please put it aside for this here today, a day when we have celebrating to do for my sister. When they're all also celebrating because we got you back in one piece. Okay, Kitten?"

His hands held my face and his tiger eyes were filled with warmth. His lips were almost touching mine and I was overwhelmed with emotion.

"I'll never steer you wrong," he said, "Won't let nobody hurt you. Nothin' bad'll happen to Jenna. Promise. You with me?"

I choked on a sob and nodded. He wiped a tear from my cheek with his thumb and then brought my hand to his mouth and kissed it.

"Fallin', baby," he told me and put his mouth to mine, "Falling so hard."

"You are?" I breathed, blinking at him.

"Oh yeah," he confirmed.

"Me, too," I said, "Plummeting."

"I'll catch you. No splat," he promised, making me think of that night at the bar when I was hammered, talking about my heart going splat.

His eyes twinkled and his thumbs caressed my cheeks. His lips moved in to mine while he brought my face closer and then his lips were against mine, tasting, teasing, and then his hands glided down my arms to my hips.

The spell was broken when the gate squeakily swung open and two bikers I didn't know were standing there, grinning at us, taking in the vision of me in Deacon's lap, us making out hot and heavy.

Deacon's lips touched mine softly again and then, not letting me off his lap, he slowly drove through the gates and pulled into a parking spot.

Rider and Spence were getting out of Rider's car. Both sets of eyes were on us, as were many other sets of eyes. Inside the gates there was a big parking lot filled with motorcycles and a few cars and trucks. There was a big grassy area with probably a half dozen picnic tables and three big fire pits, and all this was in front of a large single story warehouse with a big pergola attached to the side of it as well as an older but big-looking swing set, slide, trampoline with a big net around it and a tall dome-shaped monkey bars apparatus.

I could see a loading dock with several big and smaller trucks on the side of the building but this *did* look like a family place and people were aiming smiles our way as we got inside, too. We had our bags in hand when we stepped into the building. We were in a big and open area. It looked like a bar slash cafeteria and there were plenty of people mulling around. Being inside a warehouse this area had exposed rafters and the noise really carried. Music played with a bit of an echoing and people, including little kids, ran around. Long tables were filled with bowls of chips and covered salads, looking like a big potluck meal. Two big barbeques were being wheeled outside through a set of bay doors off to the side that led to the pergola area.

Delia came up to us, "Show her around and then I get her in the kitchen. Okay?" She passed Deacon a keychain with a tag with a number on it.

"Yeah," Deacon kissed her cheek and she kissed my cheek and then scurried toward Rider and Spencer, who were behind us, with sets of keys in her hands for them.

Rudy was approaching us, "There'll be another party when Joelle gets released. This group is always lookin' for a reason for a party. You two'll have to come back down for that."

I smiled.

"Gonna give her a tour," Deacon said and put his arm around me and led me out of the room down a hallway, pointing to where Delia had disappeared to, "Kitchen area."

We headed down a hallway and this area was more finished, with drop ceilings.

"Coupla offices and meeting rooms. One big boardroom at the end of the hall that we call the chapel for church. Club meetings." The hall branched off, "Down there are club member rooms for local members. All local charter members have their own room. Some stay a little but have their own houses, some live here. We've given ours up since we've moved to Aberdeen but there are a few guest rooms. We'll take one of those. Some of the women already got one ready for us. This is a big place, easy to get lost, but the rooms are numbered. Some areas are unfinished, some for storage. Some are party zones. Two hundred zone, members. Four hundred zone, guest rooms, some storage. One hundred, club member and family zones, five hundred, storage and off limits. There are some grow rooms in there."

"Grow rooms? For pot, you mean?"

He nodded. We went down another hall and he pushed the key Delia had given him into a door and opened it. Inside was a simple bedroom with a double bed that had some drawers underneath and a folding chair beside the bed that had a stack of clean and folded towels plus some small hotel sized toiletries in a basket. There was a small flat screen TV affixed to the wall with a mounted shelf underneath that had a DVD player.

"This one has an ensuite, not all of them do so you won't have to leave after I head out tonight. The kitchen has a couple fridges in it. Stocked with coke, beer, whatever, food. Maybe even Pepsi."

I nodded.

"Ella?"

"Hm?"

"We okay? For now? I know you're holding a lot of anger right now but..."

"No. Stop. Today is about good news. Tonight you go meet my cousin and talk. I only hope they aren't gonna pull a fast one. I don't know how these guys operate, Deacon, so please be careful."

"I do. I know exactly how they operate so don't worry. I *will* be careful." He caressed my face.

"I have to find my way in this new place I find myself in. We can talk about it later, when we get home. I can deal with all this. I promised you when I offered to come here with you that I could deal with everything and I will."

"Fuck, I'm so goddamn lucky I found you," he said against my lips. I just stared at him.

He pulled me tight to him and kissed the top of my head.

"But all that said, when do you think we can head home?" I asked.

"Most likely tomorrow or the day after. I'll do this meeting and see where things're at. See Jojo once more before we go, too. I'd like you to meet her."

"Okay."

"Okay, now let's go show our faces at this party before I decide I need to fuck you because Kitten, I know this is serious shit but that sass you've had goin' all day on has been making me fuckin' hard."

I was a little thrown by that comment and unsure of how to respond so I didn't. But I looked down at his crotch and he wasn't lying.

He burst out laughing at me for looking and I blushed and smiled shyly as he pulled me tight against him and kissed the top of my head.

"Fuck, I love how much you make me laugh. And you're fuckin' foxy when you let out that little kitten roar. Those little kitten claws are cute," He slapped my butt and then shoved the keys in my front pocket and I stuffed my cell into my back pocket and then we went out to join the party, my face flushed pink with something between embarrassment, and arousal.

11

The Dominion Brotherhood MC evidently loved parties. They ate, drank, and partied hard as a family. They were celebrating that Jojo was okay and Deacon wasn't lying; they were also happy about me getting away unscathed.

No one seemed to hold my Jackal affiliation against me. Everyone seemed to love Deacon and the group was generous with food, booze, and affection.

I helped with getting food ready in the kitchen and met all sorts of women and bikers and kids. Almost everyone was nice and welcoming.

I saw a few catty gazes from biker broads but that would be the case in any environment. Why were so many women so competitive? The world would be a better place if everyone was more down-to-earth and less worried about being the prettiest or the one with the best clothes, etc. Thankfully, the vast majority of these people were welcoming and had what looked like genuine smiles.

At first, Rider stayed out of my way but he was celebrating, too. I saw his eyes on me a few times and finally, he exchanged looks and a few quick words with Deacon and approached me and led me with a hand to the small of my back away from the group. We got to a hallway when he said, "I am keeping her safe, Ella."

"Okay," I was guarded because I knew that a 'but' was coming.

I was right.

"But she doesn't need to know what went down with Kailey. It's none of her business."

"Rider—-"

He lifted a hand, "Ella, she's a nice girl. We're havin' a laugh. She's not my old lady."

I winced and it was audible. Jenna was in love with him. Already. Shit.

Rider must've read my expression.

"I won't let anything happen to her. I put her under protection last night for you. Jackals wouldn't even know she exists other than being your friend but after your conversation with Wild Will, she's definitely on radar. I just wanted to get that straight."

"So it was me who put Jenna in danger is what you're saying?"

He took a big breath but didn't answer.

"Rider, maybe you better get things straight with Jenna when we get back to Aberdeen, because I think she thinks you guys are going somewhere."

He chewed his cheek, looking perplexed.

"Yep, alright," I said and started to head back to Deacon but Rider put a hand on my shoulder, halting me.

"What?" I demanded.

"You pissed at me?"

"No, Rider. It's not your fault that she's more into you than you are into her. I just didn't know that was the case. And now I'm not only worried about my best friend's safety, which apparently is my fault, but I'm also very worried about her heart getting broken."

"We've hooked up a few times. That's all. She's been playing it cool with me. I didn't know she..." he shrugged, "I didn't know it was more than casual for her."

He had a point. I had barely even talked to Jenna about him, I'd been so wrapped up in my drama. My assumption that they were at a similar place to me and Deacon was just that, an assumption.

"And I didn't rape that girl, Ella. I've never raped anyone. Never would."

"I believe you." And I did. And I didn't say anything else about the rape allegations because what else was there *to* say?

"Quite honestly, I don't know how serious Jenna thinks things are, Rider, because I've been very wrapped up with Deacon this past week but the few times we've talked I do get the impression she's falling for you and ecstatically happy so... I don't know..."

He frowned and then kissed the top of my head and put his arm around my neck and led me back to Deacon without saying anything further.

Deacon looked at me, assessed my face, but Jet and another biker's woman, Leah, a pretty blonde, came over and said, "Ella, we're stealing you!"

They pulled me over to a table with a bunch of other women where there were a whole lot of shot glasses lined up. Shot glasses that, many of which, were in a rainbow of colors.

"Uh oh," I giggled.

Jet held out a hand like one of Barker's Beauties, "Jell-O shots, pudding shots, and orgasm shooters. The Dominion Sisterhood Holy Trinity Trifecta."

We had a captive audience. Deacon, his dad and brothers, and around a dozen other bikers were suddenly behind me, at least half a dozen women at the table with Jet.

"Your initiation, should you accept entry into the Sisterhood, is to drink two of each, within two hours."

"Uh..." I chuckled nervously.

I looked over my shoulder at Deacon. He had an expectant grin on his face, that eyebrow up in the air, looking like he was wondering if I'd rise to the challenge.

"Don't you tell them you can't throw 'em back, Betty Boop," Deke called, "'Cuz the folks at Deke's Roadhouse already know different."

"Challenge accepted," I announced and a round of applause sounded. Spencer blew a whistle with his thumb and middle finger.

I threw four shots back immediately, consecutively. And by the end of the two hours, I not only threw back the six I had been challenged with, I threw back two extra pudding shots afterwards. They had chocolate and Bailey's in them; they were fucking delicious. And I was fucking sloshed.

"OH MY GOOD GOD THIS is the best thing I've ever eaten in my life!" I told Deacon as I gorged myself on the barbequed pulled pork sandwich he made for me.

"Rudy knows his way around a smoker," Deacon said.

"Is my face all saucy?"

We were sitting by a fire pot. All three were going and there were quite a few people still around, partying.

I'd been giggling with a bunch of girls and having a hoot, doing any line dance we could think of. I also led the train for Girls Just Wanna Have Fun, which we'd done twice, right in a row. People with kids had started leaving an hour earlier so the girl crowd had thinned and at least my drunk antics weren't being witnessed by young and impressionable minds.

Deacon got up to get me some more napkins. Through all the fun, he'd simply watched me, often smiling. He had conversations with people, seemed to be enjoying himself, but I'd seen him with one beer and saw him take a few puffs off a joint someone passed him, but that was a few hours ago and now he was drinking water. Mostly, the women seemed to be a whole lot more in the party mood than the men.

I looked around and spotted Spencer, making out with a girl I didn't recall seeing before then. He had her pressed against the wall beside the pergola, both of her legs wrapped around his waist and they were going at it hot and heavy.

"Things're gonna start getting rowdier. You tired?" Deacon was back, putting napkins on my lap and then he crouched in front of my lawn chair. He'd seen where I was watching.

"Nope. Is that why you fed me? So I'd go pass out and you can go do big bad biker schtuff?"

He smiled and gave me a chuck under the chin, "You're a smart cookie, aren't 'cha?"

"Ha!" I swallowed down the last bite and grabbed the stack of napkins from my lap, "I'm often the designated driver in my group of friends and I am an expert at corralling drunks and in getting them to shut the fuck up and go to bed already. Food is usually a part of that. And yes. My cookie is pretty smart. And she likes you. She really really likes you." I winked.

"You're cute, Kitten, but you're losing a little bit of your usual sex appeal. Can't take you seriously with all that barbeque sauce on your chin." He wiped my chin with one of the napkins that I had in my fist.

I started to laugh and almost fell over. Deacon steadied my chair before it toppled.

My ass buzzed. I regained my balance and reached into my pocket and pulled out my phone.

It was a text from an unknown number.

"Hey, Ella. Tell DV the meet is @ 1:45. Address coming. – CF."

And then another text came through with the address. Almost immediately, my phone rang with an unknown number.

The music was loud so I moved away from where we were, "Hello?"

"Tell him don't come."

"Chris?"

"Yeah. Tell your man not to show up."

"What?"

"Got me?"

"I got you but I'm confused."

"I did what I was told, sent you a text with the time and address. But tell him don't come, don't send any of his boys. Hear me?"

"I hear you."

"Tell him and tell him not to say this came from me."

"Okay, Chris. But..."

"Bye Lizzie. Stay safe." He hung up.

I made my way back to Deacon, whose eyes were on me.

"It said 1:45 AM and an address but he just called me and told me to tell you not to come, not to send any of your boys either."

"He's warning of a trap," Deacon said.

"Eek. Why would he tell us then?"

"He either has a clue that his club is fuckin' wrong. Or he's got another motive." He shrugged.

"I always thought he was a douchebag. Maybe he's not."

Deacon took a swig from his water, "Don't know him. Only know what I've heard and yeah, Fork sounds like a complete douchebag."

"Weird," I muttered and put my phone back in my pocket. I was feeling the phase two effects of the booze after eating, as was expected. I yawned.

"Ready for bed, baby?"

"Mm hm. I think so. But what're you gonna do?"

"Don't worry. It's all good."

"Are you gonna do something about their trap and reverse it?"

"No. That might be the actual trap."

That made sense. "You're smart, Tiger." I leaned forward and puckered my lips, "Kiss me."

He did, but just quick, "Be right back. Gotta speak to dad a sec, then I'll tuck you in."

"Mkay."

I pondered it all for a minute while he went and talked to his dad at the next firepot. A girl about my age, who I hadn't seen before then, was climbing into Deke's lap. He didn't argue. He leaned in and kissed her neck while Deacon was talking to him.

Alrighty then… so the family party was beginning to transition to a regular 'ole biker party.

The music got louder and You Shook Me All Night Long by AC/DC came on and Jet and Leah leapt from their chairs and pointed at me. I leapt from my chair and pointed at them. "I fuckin' love this song!"

I dashed over to the girls, who were at the next firepot all standing up with their fists pumping, singing together and joined in, temporarily forgetting the drama and singing along. Someone passed me a red Solo cup and I took a sip and it was rum and Coke. Spence.

"Heyyy!" I high fived him. He laughed and ruffled my hair and then walked over to his dad and Deacon.

Deacon was by his Dad, still, smiling at me, his arms folded across his chest.

When the song was over, the boys were breaking up the girl circle and taking us in different directions. Leah and her man, who was a large beautiful bald and bearded bi-racial biker named Axel, were going home but Jet was staying here, too. Deacon told me he was putting me to bed and Jet and Edge headed down one hall and me and Deacon headed down another.

"Oh!" I said excitedly, "We haven't had drunk sex yet," as we made our way down the hall.

"I'm aware," he agreed.

"I can't wait for drunk sex with you," I told him.

"Tell me about it," he smiled, "It ain't gonna be tonight, though, unfortunately."

"Awe" I pouted, "'Cuz I still got barbeque sauce on my face?"

"Nope," he chucked, "You're good. And that wouldn't stop me."

"'Cuz you gotta go?"

"Uh huh."

"I've decided to rename Little Deacon," I told him.

"Oh yeah?"

"Yeah. I call my girl part my cookie. I've decided that Little Deacon should be Cookie Monster. How long you gonna be?"

"No idea," he looked amused.

"How's about I feed your cookie monster a quickie cookie before you go?"

He picked me up and threw me over his shoulder and started running down the hall. I lost it in fits of laughter.

"BUT YOU'RE NOT DRUNK," I informed him as I bounced onto the bed in our room.

"No, we'll save that for when I can let my guard down. I only do that when things are completely calm." He was undoing his belt, "My guard isn't down if I'm worried about your safety."

"I have a very important question for you," I asked and his face went serious and his hands halted on his belt.

I took a big breath and then asked, "Do you last or are you a minute man when you're drunk?"

"When I'm drunk I can go all night, baby. Guaranteed, you won't be walking the next day."

What a sexy smile on his face.

Yowza.

"Yay!" I said.

He dropped his pants.

"You could be a cock model," I muttered and he chuckled.

"We should cast it to make the perfect dildo. We'd make a fortune."

"You're cute," he told me and started to stalk closer.

"Oh no. Lemme go pee first." I needed to take my birth control pill, too.

I rolled off the bed and landed on the floor on my ass.

He helped me up.

"I just gotta pee. Don't go nowhere. And don't let Cookie Monster go anywhere either," I giggled and dragged our suitcase to the bathroom with me.

I swallowed my pill with a mouthful of tap water and then the last thing I remembered was that I seemed to be peeing for forever.

THAT WAS THE LAST THING I remembered until I woke up in mostly dark, the light from the bathroom helping me figure out where I was. I was alone and I felt spinny. Oh, shoot...I was definitely gonna puke.

Wait, maybe not. Maybe if I just closed my eyes and stayed very very still the acid that kept coming up would go back down and stay down.

Maybe?

Please?

Nope. I was definitely going to barf.

I got to my feet. I was still fully dressed, except for my shoes. I barely made it to the toilet before I was hurling shooters and pulled pork into the bowl. Yuck. In my drunken state, I clearly hadn't chewed much when I wolfed down that sandwich. Blech.

I looked at my phone when I got out; it was on a folding chair beside the bed. 3:32 am.

I nabbed it and flopped on the bed, blowing out a big breath. And then I texted Jenna:

"Pulled pork pudding shooter puke. Say that five times fast. Ha."

"Hey Jenna, I'm drunk texting you after puking pork pulled and shooters that were made with pudding. #Gross #AmIRiteOrWhat"

"Jen, Deacon is so awesome. I love him so mush."

"I do. I definite love him. I'm gonna tell him. Can u belief? Just over a week and I'm gonna say the L-word to the first guy ever."

"Evarrrrrrrrrrrr"

"Where r u?????????? Jenna furrrrr. Jenny ben benny bananarama fo fanna?"

What happened to Bananarama anyway?
I started singing that Venus song,
She's got it. Yeah baby she's got it...
She wasn't answering my texts.

"LOL. Good night. I hop ur awak3 and just ignoring these texts thinking shes so noying' cuz now you KNOw MY PAIN!"

I was gonna change into pjs but found a flannel shirt of Deacon's in our bag and it was so soft. So so soft. So I put that on with a pair of pj shorts but his shirt was so long on me it probably looked like I was wearing it without any pants.

I laid down on the bed. And the room started to slowly twirl.
Ugh.
I needed Advil and Gatorade. Double doses. One dose for now and a dose on standby for the morning. I wondered if they had any of that in the kitchen. I played out the route in my head. It was straight down the hall and to the left and then the right. Or was that a right and then a left?

I got into the hall and I was definitely swaying a little bit. Ugh. So drunk. So so drunk. I let loose so that I could let go of the shit in my head, the worries I had. I wanted to follow the tone of the day, celebrate. And celebrate I did. I was gonna be sooooo hungover in the morning. So so hungover.

I got to the kitchen without a hitch and punched the air in victory.

"I've got it. Yeah baby I've got it. I'm your Venus, I'm your fire..."

It was empty and clean of all the mess from earlier but the light was on. I looked in each of the four fridges and there was no Gatorade. I found a half a dozen jugs of Sunny D in one fridge so I took one with me to the kitchen cupboards. I opened and closed them, in search of Advil.

"Hey," I heard a voice. It was a pretty 20-something girl in a skanky lemon-colored spandex dress and super high heels. She had loads of blonde hair almost to her waist.

"Hey," I greeted, "Those shoes fucking rock." I was feeling a little bit less woozy but evidently not feeling less drunk.

They were super-high, yellow like her dress, and had laces that criss-crossed all the way up to her thighs.

"Thanks. What 'cha need? I know my way around this kitchen."

"I... Advil. I'm so fucking sloshed," I laughed, "I wish there were Gatorade but I only found Sunny D. I puked and know I'm gonna be real sorry if I don't get hydrated and get some Advil into me."

"Sure," she strutted over and opened a cupboard,

"Bingo," I said. It had Advil, Tylenol, boxes of Zantac, cough syrup, and a plethora of other over the counter medicines.

"I think I saw a massive can of powdered Gatorade. One sec." She started digging through a lower cupboard. She had the most round and perfect butt. I wasn't into chicks but man, her butt was ... wow.

"I'm Gianna," she said.

"Ella," I told her, "And no word of a lie, you have, like, the best ass I have ever seen. I'm not into women but I had to tell ya."

She giggled, "Thanks. So, uh, who are you here for?" she asked me.

"Deacon," I answered and rolled up my sleeves, Deacon's sleeves. They were way way long.

"Oooh," she giggled, pulling out a big can of blue PowerAde, "Deacon's here? The one hit wonder with the monster cock... lucky girl. Enjoy."

I frowned.

She smiled as she stood up and shrugged, straightening her dress, "We're an incestuous bunch. We all joke that the girl who lands him a second time'll go down in the history books as a legend. Your rack is rockin' and these bikers like their boobs, don't ya know. Deacon's never interested in seconds. Sadly. Don't take it personal. I highly recommend his brother, Spencer. He fucks like the Energizer bunny on crack. Serious staying power. He'll come back for more and more and more. And he's as hung as Deacon. But sadly they moved out of town. Aberdeen, I think. I wonder if he's here, too. You'll be back with someone else, no doubt. Just watch out for Rider, their middle brother, unless you like it rough. Which I do. Ride and Edge both like it rough. I'm here waiting for Edge. He texted and told me to get over here. He should be here soon."

She opened a fridge and passed me two bottles of water. I put the Sunny D down.

I felt anger bubbling in my gut and rising. She looked at me as I took the two bottles of water and the PowerAde can and I could see she read my expression and realized her mistake. It was all over her face. *My* face must've been an opened book.

"I've already had Deacon more than once. In fact, I took him off the market. Guess I *am* a legend."

Her mortification was all over her face.

"And I partied tonight with Edge's girlfriend, Jet, who I know is also staying here tonight because of a security issue so maybe you should go find a single biker to take that rough ride with. But not Rider. You go near him before he ends things with my bestie and I'll claw your eyes out. And furthermore..."

Before I was able to finish I heard a deep voice bark out, "Gia. Out. Get home." That was Edge.

"Sorry, just got here, didn't know any—-"

"Go," he barked and glanced at me. I shot him daggers with my eyes. He pulled his phone from his pocket and dialed a number and stepped out of the kitchen.

Fucking cheating dirt bag.

She shot me an apologetic look and ran on her fantastic high heels out of there.

I tucked the can of PowerAde under my arm and put the bottle of Advil into the shirt pocket and decided to get back to our room as soon as possible. Before any further enlightenment. I had a bottle of water in each hand and off I went.

But I must've went the wrong way. I found myself in an unfamiliar hallway. The rug was different, I think. I needed to double back. I heard music. I knew I was seriously the wrong way. I should get my phone and text Deacon. I reached for my back pocket. Shit. I didn't have back pockets. The can of PowerAde dropped from the crook of my arm where I'd been holding it.

I stopped and looked at a door. It said 202. What was our room number again? I reached into my front pocket for the key. Shit again. I still had no pockets because I was wearing cotton sleeping shorts. Shit, shit, shit.

I sat on the floor against door # 202 and pulled my knees up to my chest. My head started to pound. I opened a water and fetched the bottle of Advil from the shirt pocket and took two and then put my forehead on my knee.

The music got louder as the door across the hall opened wide and two scantily clad girls spilled out, giggling. A kind of scary but yet sort of hunky blond Viking-looking tattooed biker in just a pair of Calvin Klein boxer briefs was behind them. He smacked both their asses and said, "Off you go."

He leaned against the doorframe and looked down at me.

"Hey, Ella." I didn't remember his name. I'd met a lot of bikers the past few days.

"Hiya." I saluted.

"What's happening?"

"I'm lost," I told him, "I can't find my phone or my room key. I don't know where I'm supposed to be. And I'm getting a preview of tomorrow's hangover early."

"Alright, babe. I'll sort ya out." He reached for my hand.

I let him help me up, "I feel woozy. Need my PowerAde and my water."

He passed my bottles and the can from the floor and lifted me up, "I got you," He walked down the hall, carrying me. I was sooooo frigging woozy.

"Not gonna puke on me, are ya?"

"Nope. Already did. In the toilet. I think I'm empty."

He turned a doorknob and then we were in a room filled with people.

"What the fuck?" I heard.

I spotted Deacon.

"Babyyy..." I reached for him with both arms. The biker passed me off, "Found her in my hallway, lost. Against door 202."

"What? You fuckin' with me?"

"Naw man, honest..."

"I'll fuckin' kill you."

"No Deacon, he saved me. I was lost. It's okay. I'm sorry. I woke up and needed Advil and Gatorade." I looked to the other biker, "Sorry, he's a little bit protective."

The other biker started laughing, a big belly laugh, and I heard other laughter. We had an audience. We were in a doorway of a big boardroom looking room and there were bodies everywhere, tobacco and pot smoke in the air. Deacon's face had thankfully morphed into looking amused.

"Is this church?" I asked.

"Yeah, babe," Deacon muttered.

I started playing with his hair. "Sorry. I know there's no girls allowed in your biker *church*." I put air quotes around the word church, "even if that's slightly chauvinistic and don't you know it's the 21st century, but any hoo... I went to find Advil and Gatorade. Learn now that when I'm drunk if I don't have it on my nightstand it's trouble. It's gonna mean wandering. Okay, Tiger?"

Deacon's lips were twitching with amusement.

"Roger that, babe. Can you walk or you need me to carry you?"

"I probably could but I'd like you to carry me. It's very alpha. I like that. Are we gonna have drunk sex now? I don't remember having it earlier, although I'm sure you were wonderful. As you always are."

"That's 'cuz you passed out sittin' on the toilet, Kitten. So I didn't get the chance." We were having this conversation while making our way out of that room and there was lots of laughing.

"Back in 5, guys."

Apparently when I was around him drunk no one else existed, which meant I had even less of a filter than normal drunk Ella.

"Well, we can do it now, if you want? But hopefully it'll take more than five minutes."

More laughing.

"Weird you wound up against 202, babe. That was my room before we moved."

"No shit?"

"No shit." He took us down another hall and then unlocked the door and put me on the bed.

"Ohhhh, you had the key. Wait. I decided I don't want drunk sex," I informed him, climbing under the covers.

"No?" he undid his belt and looked down at his own crotch and then notched that bar belled eyebrow at me.

"Nope. And too bad for you because I was gonna talk dirty. I was gonna let you do very dirty things to me."

"Well you already left me hanging tonight once. Why not again?"

"Yeah, well... that's right."

"You sure? You look fucking edible wearing my shirt. I really fuckin' like that. Didn't like seein' my brother strolling with you in his arms, him in his fuckin' underwear but at least you were wearin' my shirt."

"It's soft."

"So?"

"So what?" I asked.

"You sure you don't want drunk fucking?"

"I'm sure. I think."

"Ya think?"

"I'm trying to not want drunk sex. You're very very beautiful so my resolve is fading. And when you say the word fuck it's very sexy."

"Why you tryin' to hang onto that resolve?"

"Cuz a) I puked. And b) I met Gianna in the kitchen," I informed him.

His tongue poked out from his cheek and then he shook his head, "Knew we shouldn't have stayed here." He did his belt back up.

"She was very nice. She has, like, the most ass-tastic ass I've ever seen. And she just schooled me on the fact that since you and your monster-sized cock wouldn't be back for seconds I should consider Spencer after tonight, since he's kinda built in the downstairs department like you. Apparently.

Not that I asked. And she was here for Edge. Edge, who is with Jet, who I really really like."

"Fuck sakes."

"and Jet's here! So what? Does Edge fuck Gianna in one room and then crawl in with Jet?"

"Not our business, Ella."

"Pfffffff. Club whores and bang gangs. Gang bangs. Whatever. He's a dirt bag." I got the blankets right up to my chin, "No drunk sex for you."

"What did *I* do?"

"I don't know." I yawned.

I heard him laugh and then felt him pull me close, "You have the best ass, Ella. Hands down. No ass more ass-tastic than yours."

"That's bullshit. But thanks for saying it. Mm yum," I mumbled against his yummy chest and then I must have passed out.

12

The Advil must have helped. And the fact that I'd puked. I never got any of that PowerAde into me before passing out but I wasn't feeling too bad when I woke up. Deacon wasn't there, though, and I checked my phone and it was 1:30 PM. There was a

LOL. Call me when your hangover is over.

text from Jenna and a text from Deacon that said to text him when I woke up and he'd come get me.

I found a bottle of red Gatorade and a can of Pepsi on the chair beside the bed beside an extra-large bottle of Advil liqui-gels, which were fast acting. My hero. I drank up and took two of the pills just in case the hangover was a little delayed and got a shower.

The skanky girl in the kitchen? The 20-something year old girl on Deke's lap? Doms lived by their own code, outside the confines of ordinary society. Obviously. Many of them didn't care about fidelity or the law. Some went out of their way to spit in the face of fidelity and law.

I was in uncharted waters but I wasn't completely oblivious. I'd been exposed to biker culture enough to know that MCs were family that you chose for yourself and that there was fierce loyalty with a philosophy of living life to the fullest.

The conversation with Gianna last night? It wasn't something I would choose for myself but how could I be mad at him for it? Yeah, he'd been with her but that was before. He'd told me he hadn't been exclusive in three years but he hadn't proclaimed that he'd been celibate during those three years, either. And by all accounts, it looked like he really was *with* me, serious about me. Plus, he warned me to stay in the room and I went wandering. I should've known better.

Last night one of the older biker ladies told me she knew Deacon all his life and that day she'd seen him smile more than he had in years.

"I wanna thank you for that. It's clear it's you. He lights up whenever he looks at you," she'd said and this was well into my drink-fest so I got a little teary-eyed.

I thought back to all he'd been through with women. And maybe I didn't even know it all. He had a rough home life with his mother, that was clear, and he lived in a world that probably straddled the line between good and evil on a regular basis.

I was worried about all of what was happening, but something about Deacon's protectiveness definitely settled me in my heart.

>I texted him,
>**"I'm alive."**
>**"Want to come out for breakfast or want some brought in?"**
>he replied.
>**"I'll come out."**
>**"Be there in a min."**

I LOOKED AT DEACON and saw that he was watching me. It was like he could see through me. We were sitting outside at a picnic table with a bunch of other people, eating pancakes, bacon and scrambled eggs, which had been set up on a table in a bunch of chafing dishes.

Jet sat beside me and glared at me, "You don't look hungover."

I shrugged, "I'm kind of not. Somehow I dodged that bullet."

"Ugh. I thought I liked you. But I think I changed my mind." She put her arms to the table and then her head down on her arms.

Edge was behind her, squeezing her shoulders, "Food, sweets?"

"Ugh," she replied.

"Bacon sandwich and a red eye," he said, "I'll get it." He kissed her on the top of her head and then his eyes landed on me.

I looked the other way, feeling my face get red. Deacon put his hand on my thigh and squeezed. He wasn't looking at me. But I could read both Deacon and Edge like a book right then.

I shook my head and shoved another piece of bacon into my mouth.

I heard laughter and glanced over my shoulder and it was a group of five of the Dom women walking together toward the food table, arms linked as if they were sisters. They were in their 40's or maybe even their 50's and they looked tight, close.

This club environment was definitely family-driven. These people pulled together. I liked the idea of being part of that, even with all the other dark and dangerous stuff thrown in. But most of all, Deacon had such worth to me. And this was his life. This was where he came from.

When he'd come in to get me, I was getting my teeth brushed.

"How you feeling, babe?" he'd asked.

"Better than I expected," I'd said, spitting, wiping my mouth, then slipping into my pink flip flops. I was wearing skinny jeans and a green and black flannel shirt with a black glittery Betty Boop tank top underneath. He kissed me and while he did, he started doing up my buttons.

I broke from the kiss and looked down, "Uh, I am quite capable of that."

"Were you gonna do it?"

"Um, I don't know. This room doesn't have a window so I guess I'd decide that once I saw what it was like outside."

"This tank is cute, baby, but it's too cute so it'll draw eyes to your tits." He cupped both of my boobs and gave them a squeeze, "Even more than eyes are already drawn to these beauties."

I raised my eyebrows at him and then he resumed the buttoning and got the top button done up.

I then undid half the buttons and pointed at him, "Unless you plan to start wearing a man-burka because believe me, women are constantly going to look at you no matter what you wear, don't you dare."

His eyes went molten for a second and then his lips quirked up into a grin and he walked forward, forcing me to walk backwards, until I fell on the bed and then he came down on top of me but not with his full weight. He hovered over me, "You hungry? Want bacon & eggs? Or you wanna fuck?"

"How 'bout food first and then we see how that goes?" I asked, ignoring the urge to spread my legs. I needed food.

"But you think it's sexy when I say fuck. Fuck." He kissed me, "Fuck, I wanna fuck you."

My tummy growled, "My stomach just answered for me. I'm hungry."

He got off me, "You okay about that shit last night?"

I waved my hand, "As long as that behavior is in your past, I can deal."

"It's in my rearview and I am so fuckin' crazy about you it's but a speck in that mirror. I can't imagine living like that again."

I smiled at him and kissed him, "If you start to feel the urge to live like that again, please just cut me loose first. I don't wanna ever be a chump."

Poor Jet.

He frowned, "I'll never feel that urge. And I'd never do that to you. Never fuckin' ever."

I tried to lighten things up, "Good. Then bacon and eggs and then what's next on our agenda for today?"

"Lots of people stayed here last night so there's a big spread. We eat, visit with people a bit, then we go see Jojo. Tonight we've got some club business to take care of after dinner. Rudy and Delia are making dinner at their place, we're invited. We'll swing by my ma's to grab my fat boy and some of my other shit and then tomorrow we head home. Sound good to you?"

"Roger that," I'd said and we'd headed out to have brunch.

JOELLE VALENTINE WAS gorgeous. She loads of had dark curly hair, big blue-green eyes, gorgeous lips and high cheekbones; she was built like a Victoria's Secret model. She was sitting up in the hospital bed, eating some Jell-O, her left arm in a sling. She had a sad look on her pale face, she looked lost in thought, but then she saw us and her eyes lit up.

"Are you Ella?" She was so freaking pretty it wasn't funny. And she had inner beauty, too. It was shining through, radiantly, in that smile.

"I'm glad to meet you. Sorry I couldn't meet you under better circumstances."

She smiled bigger, "I have been hearing lots about you. So glad to meet you before you guys go."

"I'm here, too..." Deacon muttered, amused.

She let out a big laugh and she was even more beautiful. He leaned over and kissed her on the forehead and then ruffled her hair.

I was a little bit shocked that she was all smiles. After all, her boyfriend had died.

We didn't stay long at all. Deacon told her we were going back tomorrow and that he'd try to see her again before we left. Five minutes into the visit, two girls that were Jojo's age came in and were fawning all over her. Deacon stepped into the hall for a minute so I was standing back while they talked to her and told her how happy they were that she was okay.

Deacon stepped back in, "Gotta hit the road, Jojo. See you before we go." He kissed her cheek and then took my hand. A tall blonde friend of Jojo's gave me some serious stink eye.

Yeah, I'd bet that Jojo's friends had crushes on all of her big brothers.

"Really good to meet you, Jojo," I said and squeezed her hand on her uninjured arm.

"I'll come down and visit you guys as soon as I am better. Mom's doin' my head in," she said with an eye roll, but then added, "Thank you for putting that smile on his face." She winked at me.

We left the room and while waiting for the elevator I said,

"She's taking Lick's death well?"

"She doesn't know."

"No?"

Oh no.

He shook his head, "She doesn't remember the accident. All she knows is she was on the back of his bike and they wiped out. She asked if he was admitted and Dad said he wasn't but before he got a chance to tell her she acted relieved and then started talking nonsensical small talk shit. She's probably so wrapped up in keeping their thing a secret that she's made that a priority. He's gonna tell her today."

"Oh God, that poor girl."

Deacon clenched his jaw and that was when the elevator opened and we came face-to-face with his mother.

"Deacon. Uh..." she looked at me like she was trying to remember my name.

"Ella!" Deacon snapped right in her face and she jolted back and then stepped aside and got out of the elevator.

"I'm goin' by the house to get my Harley," He told her.

"Want me to—-"

"No." He pushed the button and it closed.

We drove for quite a while and he was quiet. I stayed quiet, too, knowing he was probably pissed off at his mother but also pissed off about what kind of pain his sister would endure when she found out that her guy was gone and not only that he was gone but *why*.

I didn't know what he thought of Luke "Lick" Hanson before, but the fact that Lick's actions with that Kailey girl put Jojo in the hospital must've been weighing heavily on Deacon.

We had gone pretty far out of town, I guessed we might be a half an hour away from the city, when he pulled the car over at the side of a back road.

I looked around, confused.

"Where's your Mom's house?"

"Back in the falls. Wanted to have a little time with you, away from all the shit. Let's leave our phones in the truck. Take a walk."

He got out of the truck and rounded it and then opened my door. Then he reached into the bed of the truck into the storage box and pulled out a folded up red and black checkered fleece blanket.

He took my hand and we walked, for a good long while, along an old trail until we were pretty deep into a forest and then there was no trail left. We kept going until the denseness cleared and then we were by a lookout point that overlooked a valley. There was a dug-out where people obviously had camp fires. There was a wooden bench. The big old oak tree had all sorts of initials carved into it.

"This is cool," These were the first words I'd said since we got out of the truck. I'd gathered from the mood and heaviness in the air that the walk was a 'clearing my head' kind of walk and I just followed along.

"It'll be even better in a few weeks. Leaves have barely started to change."

He spread the blanket on the ground, laid back, leaning on an elbow and patted the spot beside him. I got to my knees and then climbed to where he was and cuddled up against him.

A breeze picked up but it was nice, relaxing. We stared out at the valley.

"Used to party here when I was in my teens. I can see it's still a popular spot."

"It's a great spot. How are you doing?" I asked him.

He gave me a weird squinty look. "How am I doing?"

"You're dealing with a lot right now. Are you okay?"

He stared at me, looking perplexed.

"Sorry. If you don't wanna talk about it..."

He cut me off by kissing me. He started to devour my lips hungrily, like he couldn't get close enough to me.

He abruptly broke free, looked around, then took off his leather Dom vest and put it on the ground. He took off his flannel, leaving him in a black tank, and balled it up, "Lay back," He put it under my head. He started to undo my flannel shirt.

"You fucking amaze me," he said against my throat, "All this shit goin' down and you're worried about how I'm doing. Fuck."

I was taken aback. Of course I was. His sister was in the hospital. A motorcycle club member had died. And they were in a dirty ugly feud with a rival MC and were worried about what kind of axe might fall next.

"I'm worried about you. Worried all this shit is gonna scare you away. But I won't let you go." He looked in my eyes, "I can't."

"I'm not going anywhere," I told him.

"Fuckin' right you're not."

He closed his eyes and looked like he was in pain for a second but before I could process it, he startled me because suddenly his mouth and hands were on me.

His lips moved over my face, my jaw, my throat, then my tank went up above my boobs and he yanked the cups of my bra down. I heard the fabric strain. He started kissing my boobs.

"Should we really?"

"Why not?"

"So much goin' round in our heads right now. And we're out here, outside. I don't know if—-"

He cut me off, "Stress relief. Best there is." He undid my jeans and shimmied them off.

His fingers dove into my underwear and right inside me. My head rolled back.

"We should've brought a condom," I mumbled.

"I brought two," he said and shoved his hand into his front pocket.

I giggled, "Yay. Okay, so outdoor sex like teenagers, it is. Only way better, 'cuz you know what you're doing." I ran my palms up his muscled back.

"Two nights now you've passed out on me and the last two mornings have been fucked so I'm in withdrawals, Kitten. I'm craving you something fierce."

"Mmm, me too. Let's scratch that itch."

He wrapped up and then he flipped us so that he was on the ground and I was on him.

"Ride me, baby," he whispered against my lips.

I did. He bit my nipple through my tank top. My bra was now sitting bunched up above my breasts but my tank top wasn't coming off. I didn't want to be 100% exposed out here.

"Ah!" That sent sparks all through me. He did it again and I grinded harder.

"God you're beautiful," I told him and wove my fingers into his hair and brought his mouth to mine.

I felt him smile against my mouth, "Not as beautiful as you," he said.

"Nope, you're way beutifuller." I giggled.

"You're beautifullest," he said and grabbed my hips tighter and helped me move.

"That's not a word," I breathed.

"But beautifuller is?"

"Mm hmm; fuck me harder my beautifuller biker."

"I can do that my beautifullest kitten," he said and then he flipped me back to my back and then he slammed into me and powered into me over and over and over. It was definitely beautiful and it was also deep, and I couldn't believe it but I actually had an orgasm without him touching my clit. It was deep inside me. The earth moved.

When I started to shake really hard he looked into my eyes and watched me unravel. He picked up the pace even more and then he shuddered as he came.

I wrapped my arms tight around him as he breathed heavily for a minute, getting up on his knees but burying his face in my chest.

He leaned back, pulled the condom off, tied it, and put it into his pocket. Then when I thought he was gonna get up, he grabbed my ankles and spread my legs and then his head descended and his mouth was right on the bullseye. He tongued my clit and dove his fingers into me until I came hard, which didn't take long since I was already super sensitized down there.

"THIS WAS A REALLY GOOD idea for stress relief," I said, snuggling.

"It definitely was," he agreed and played with my hair and then pulled it all back into a fist and pulled down to guide my mouth to his. He balled his jacked under his head and threw his flannel shirt over my backside and we cuddled for a while, enjoying the scenery and the quiet. He lazily rubbed my hip and my bottom while we enjoyed a caressing gentle breeze. Too soon, he broke the spell of serenity around us by saying, "We should head back to the truck. Get to the house and get my shit before she's home."

"Okay," I said, grabbing my jeans, sad that the bubble was about to burst.

WE DIDN'T GO INSIDE of Deacon's childhood home, which was a big ranch style bungalow with a three car garage. We backed into the back yard where a toy hauler trailer was parked and then pulled it out to the driveway. He went into the garage and he brought his three bikes out and put them into a toy hauler trailer with a bunch of tools and a couple of boxes from the mostly empty garage. Being a family with mostly boys and all bikers, I'd bet that the garage was packed with stuff before Deke and Shelly split. Now it was mostly empty. Deacon locked the garage and attached the trailer to the pickup and we drove back to the clubhouse.

As we were parking, he got a text and he turned the truck off and read it. With an angry face he walked me straight inside, ignoring the half a dozen or so people sitting outside. I tried to smile and say Hi to all of them as we passed.

He deposited me back in our room and asked me to stay there.

"What's wrong?"

"Let me figure that out. Be back. Stay here, no matter what. Alright? Very important."

"Okay."

I sat on the bed and texted Mom and Jenna updates, telling them that we would be likely leaving the next day, Monday, to come back.

He left me in there for forty minutes and then we headed to Rudy and Delia's for dinner. He was in a bad mood.

"Everything okay?" I asked.

His grip tightened on the steering wheel but he nodded. I gave him his headspace.

"You wanna know, I'll tell you but can I just say you don't really wanna know this right now? Can we talk after this dinner?"

"Okay," I whispered and his right hand let go of the steering wheel and he grabbed my hand and held onto it. I let out a big breath and didn't ask any questions. I'd ask later.

He glanced at me, "Do you know how fuckin' awesome you are?"

I gave him a smile but I don't know how big. I felt really uneasy.

"Fuck," he shook his head in disbelief and then he let go of my hand and cupped the back of my head and pulled me closer so he could kiss my head without taking his eyes off the road.

His touch was settling to me somehow and I tried to just push it all aside so that I could be present during this dinner, be with people who mattered to him and actually be present for it instead of being in my head, worried. Because it felt like there definitely *was* something to be worried about.

DELIA MADE DELICIOUS cabbage rolls and salad as well as four different types of vegetables to have on the side and then served a triple layer angel food cake with ice cream for dessert. The ice cream was this amazing flavor that I'd never had before with berries and white chocolate and dark chocolate. It was delicious.

"What flavor is this?" I asked Delia.

"Blackjack berry something, I forget, I'll check the label before I go," she said, "I'd say it's almost better than sex. Nothing as good as sex but this comes close, doesn't it?"

I almost choked. Rudy gave her an eyebrow wiggle. Deacon seemed like he was lost in thought, not even in the conversation at that moment.

It was just the four of us. Delia had been a bit miffed, saying that Edge and Jet had been expected but had called and backed out at the last minute. I had a feeling it had a lot to do with me and the things that I knew. Either Edge didn't want me getting near Jet, for fear I'd out him or maybe he just didn't want all the awkwardness. Whatever the case, I was kind of grateful.

Delia and Rudy weren't his biological parents. They'd talked about how they'd taken him in as a teenager, they didn't share the whole story but said they'd saved him from the street.

Deacon was quiet but Rudy and Delia were both talkative. Delia tried to talk them into leaving me with her for the night while they did their thing but Rudy insisted the clubhouse was safer. Deacon got up to use the washroom and she offered to come hang out with me there but Rudy made a face and said, "No. Clubhouse is closed down to any women but Ella tonight." The face he made? Yeah, it was looking like this was due to me.

"It's what?" Delia seemed shocked.

Rudy shook his head and said, "Never you mind."

She pulled her lips tight, like she'd done it to stop herself from asking other questions, which I could tell she really wanted to do.

Deacon was on his way back into the room when Rudy's phone made a sound. He glanced at it and then said, getting up, "Deacon and me need a minute."

Deacon gave me a quick peck on the mouth and then moved out of the room with Rudy.

"I'll wash the dishes," I said and got to my feet.

She was giving me an assessing look.

"Something happened last night at the clubhouse while you were there." It was a statement, not a question.

I pulled my lips tight.

"You don't have to say what; I know that what happens there ain't supposed to leave the premises. I just can't believe they're locking it down for the night. Those boys'll be losing their minds not having access to their sweet butts on site. Place'll probably be empty."

I gathered the very pretty Old Country Roses china dessert plates into a stack in her lovely dining room with the big cherry wood dining suite, family pictures all over the walls, and she got to her feet and picked up the coffee pot and gathered all of the coffee stuff onto a tray and then I followed her into the kitchen and we loaded the dishwasher together.

"One day, you'll be in my shoes, likely. Your man could even wind up the leader of this motley crew and you'll learn that you have to turn a blind eye to some things that makes these boys who they are, that makes them the kind of men who'll do anything for us but that they need a bit of letting off steam once in a while. There are types who never stray. I can't say I know for sure what kind your man'll be but some of these guys, they don't do what they do to hurt their women, they just do it because life is rough, and sometimes they wanna let that steam off at the clubhouse, their safe zone, so that they don't bring their anger or their frustrations home to their wives or girlfriends. It's part of this life and for some women, it's worth it."

"Well, I don't dispute that Deacon is worth a lot but I've decided that I won't settle for anything less than fidelity. And I think he knows it's a deal breaker. Last night there was just a girl who he used to be with and...this lock down or whatever isn't because I told him I wouldn't stay there. Maybe he's just trying to be extra cautious. Or maybe it's not even about me."

"Really wouldn't surprise me if he weren't a one-woman man, knowing that boy his whole life. And this club loves your man. A good portion of the members wouldn't ever dream of shutting things down simply due to one old lady being present but they think a lot of Deacon, he'll be a chapter prez for sure, one day, maybe even run the whole club and he clearly thinks a lot of you. Our boy Edge, Jet knows who he is. And she's made her peace with the fact that he needs to blow off steam sometimes so that she gets what she gets from him. He's a good boy. Loves her. Has a lot of demons from before we took him in. He works that pain out in his own way."

I wasn't going to argue with her logic. I also wasn't going to ask her about her own relationship because to me her little speech meant that she probably overlooked Rudy's wandering eye. Who was I to say what was and what wasn't okay in someone else's relationship? I only knew what I would and wouldn't put up with in my own. Although, fidelity notwithstanding, I had a feeling that there was a lot I'd put up with for Deacon.

Deacon had said his father never strayed from his mom even though she might not have deserved his faithfulness. I was relieved that Deacon believed in being faithful.

Delia's cell phone was on the kitchen counter and it made a noise. She lifted it while I put the cream back into the fridge. Delia made a grunt sound, then said, "Oh no."

I didn't know her well enough to ask what was wrong but she looked at me and told me anyway.

"Jet texted to tell me she's left him."

I gulped.

"What?"

"She says she can't tell me why but she says she wanted me to know that she needs a minute. She's goin' away for a few days, doesn't want him to know where she is, and doesn't think she wants to come back. What the fuck happened last night?"

I opened my mouth but no sound came out.

She dialed a number.

Did Jet find out that he'd had that girl there? Oh no; were they gonna think I tattletaled?

Deke, Deacon, Spencer, and also Edge were coming into the kitchen. I had no idea whether or not Edge knew that Jet had left. Maybe he did; maybe that was why he made an excuse about dinner.

"Ma," he said to Delia as he leaned over and kissed Delia's cheek. He had a hard look on his face.

"Call me, honey, right away." She said into the phone and then disconnected and put the phone down.

"Who's hungry? Lots of food left."

"Hey Ella," Edge greeted.

"Hi," I said but my voice was raspy.

Deacon came to me. "We should head out."

"Okay. Um, thank you for dinner. It was delicious."

Rudy smiled at me and Delia let go of Edge and hugged me. I looked at his face. He wasn't looking at me but also wasn't intentionally avoiding me, from what I could tell, so I didn't know how to read the situation.

"Can't wait to see you again, Ella, honey. Don't know that we'll see you before you two head out so have a safe trip home. Will you be back for the funeral? We should know tomorrow when that'll be."

She started making plates up for Edge, Spencer, and Deke who all sat down at the kitchen table.

"Not sure if Ella can make it. She's got work," Deacon said and then Rudy was hugging me and then passing me to Edge, who also hugged me. I got a hand squeeze from Deke and a kiss on the cheek from Spencer.

These were a huggie bunch. I didn't read any odd vibes from Edge so either he didn't think I had been talking to Jet or he didn't even know she'd left him.

I grabbed my purse and Delia and Rudy saw us to the door. Edge stayed in the kitchen.

Once we were in the truck, I said,

"Um, did you know that Jet left Edge?"

Deacon nodded, "Yeah. That was the drama before we headed here. Someone sent her an anonymous email at work. Somehow she knows the lie about Kailey. Did Jet call Delia?"

"She texted. Um, what kind of email?"

"Jackals can't get to her to get revenge in person, he's had her covered by 24/7 security, so they sent her an email. We don't know what it said but she knows. Now she's given the prospect on her the slip and taken off."

"Oh that poor girl."

"Fuck."

"Does she actually believe he raped Kailey? Or is she just upset that he cheated on her?"

"Dunno. Not my relationship. Got shit to do late tonight so I've gotta leave you alone at the clubhouse again. Sorry Kitten. But we'll head home first thing in the morning."

"Okay. What about this funeral?"

"Don't think we'll come."

"No?"

"Not sure I wanna be at the funeral for the guy that nearly got my little sister killed. MC brother or not. But I might use the garage or you needin' to work as an excuse."

I was a little surprised and was weighing whether to tell him that he might want to be there for his sister, if not for Luke "Lick" Hanson, but he looked like he had a lot on his mind so I was quiet the rest of the ride back to the clubhouse until I got into the gates of the compound and my phone starting blaring out Gangnam Style.

I answered and said, "Hey Jen, Can I call you back in like five minutes? I'm just getting out of the car."

"Kay," she was crying.

"What's wrong?"

"I got... I got this video text and... and..."

Oh no.

"What was in the video?"

Deacon turned the truck off.

"I... I...I just sent it to you. But maybe I shouldn't have. It's really horrible, Ella."

Oh shit.

"Rider, he... he..." she choked on a sob.

"Jenna, it isn't true."

"Ella, it is. The video shows it. Wait. How do you even know what I'm talking about? What the fuck?" She was in hysterics.

I got out of the truck and kept talking, following Deacon inside. He was on his phone and I heard him say Rider's name.

"It's all unfolding here. I heard this rumor. And it's not true. They're saying that it was just a scene. A consensual fake rape scene and it was before he met you."

"And you didn't fucking call me?"

"Jenna, listen, there's a lot to talk about here. Things are unfolding. It has to do with the accident with their sister and the guy she was secretly seeing and that's why you're under protection and..."

Deacon grabbed my phone from my hand and put it to his ear, "Jenna, Deacon here. Where are you? Bronto said you took off and he needs to keep you safe. There's shit that you don't know."

Deacon held the phone.

"Hello? Jenna? Hello?" He glanced at my screen.

"She fuckin' hung up."

I'd only been vaguely aware of people around the inside of the clubhouse as this unfolded on our way to the room. Once we were inside, I noticed Deacon was calling her back on my phone and holding the other phone in his hand.

"She's not answering." He tossed my phone on the bed and I saw that there was a text there. I lifted it. It was a video. No words with it.

I stared at the screen but didn't touch the little triangle to make the video play.

"Yep, call me back." He put his own phone down and moved to me. He held his hand open and I put the phone into his palm.

He pushed play and backed away from me. I could hear the sound even though I couldn't see what he was watching.

I heard a scream and the sounds of skin slapping skin, and then I heard a male voice, "Yeah, you fuckin' whore, we're gonna fuck all your holes until they bleed."

Deacon hit the screen to make the video stop. His face was sour. No, it was beyond sour. He looked like he was either about to smash something or vomit.

He picked his phone back up and dialed,

"Dad. Church. Senior members. We were set up. That dirty cunt didn't just take info to the Jackals, the whole thing was staged. They filmed it. Yeah. Sent it to Jenna. I'm guessing Jet got the same video. Nope. Tryin' to locate 'em both. I'm already here. I'll see you there. You got a lift? Right."

Oh shit.

He hung up and sat beside me and put his head in his hands, "They fuckin' set us up."

"You're kidding."

He got up and was pacing.

"She had to have baited them. Baited Edge, Scoot, Lick, and Ride. I need to fuckin' hit something."

"Do you think they're gonna take it to the cops?" I asked.

He shook his head, "Not likely but I dunno." He ran his fingers through his hair and started fishing around my makeup bag and found a black elastic wound around the end of my brush. He took it and tied his hair back.

"C'mon, let's go to the kitchen and grab you a drink and get you back in here so I can go talk to my Dad."

"I'm okay, not thirsty."

"I don't know how long I'll be and I want you in here, not out there." He reached for my hand.

"Delia said no one else would be here tonight. No women. So if I need to hit the kitchen I won't likely run into any of your..."

Deacon rolled his eyes, "I'll be right back. Stay here."

He left the room.

I started texting Jenna.

"Can you call me? We need to talk."

I avoided the previous text, which was a window that showed me what I didn't want to see, what I didn't need to hit that 'play' triangle to see.

Four men and a girl bent over a bed.

I called her. She didn't answer.

And then I waited.

A minute later he was back.

"What're you doin?" he looked annoyed and snatched the phone out of my hand.

"I'm texting her. Trying to call her."

"You didn't delete it?"

"No."

"You don't fuckin' watch this."

"Do you think I wanna watch that?" I glared at him and my temper was rising.

He shook his head, "You're right. Sorry. I just didn't wanna fuckin' see that and I had no choice. Stopped at 3 seconds and the thing goes on for four fucking minutes." He threw the phone on the bed. He'd brought a 20 oz. bottle of Pepsi, a red Solo cup, and a 1-gallon bottle of water. He put them on the chair beside the bed.

"I gotta get back. Gotta take your phone."

"Oh, uh, would you rather I just forward this to you and delete it? I'm gonna be in here with nothing to do and if Jenna calls..."

"Fine. Here." He took the phone, "Texting it to Dad."

He pushed buttons and then passed me the phone,

"I deleted it."

"Ok."

Good. I didn't want that garbage on my phone.

He leaned over and kissed me hard, grabbing my hair a little roughly, "Be back soon. Stay in here. Just makes me feel better."

"Okay."

He kissed me again and put his lips to my forehead and held them there a second and then he released me and he was gone.

I picked the phone up off the bed and texted her.

"Deacon's gone. I'm alone if you wanna call."

Ten minutes later I wrote,

"I'm sorry if you're mad but I have had a lot going on and didn't know how to handle this rumor, certainly not by phone. I also know that it wasn't forced on that girl. I was talking it through with Rider about him talking to you about it. I can't say much on here because it's sensitive but it seems this is part of the rival between the two MCs and the bad guys are trying to make the good guys look like the bad guys. They've hurt people in retaliation for the feud and they're trying to use this to break up relationships since they can't enact the physical retribution because you are guarded. Know what I'm saying? You need to stay safe in case they try that. They tried to hurt me. Do the same as the girl in the vid. Only for REAL! They found out who my uncle is and that stopped them. There's a lot you don't know. We are coming home tomorrow I think and you and I can talk then but for

now, please don't hide from bronto because he's keeping you safe in case they want to try to hurt YOU. Know what I'm saying?"

Less than a minute later my phone rang the Gangnam Style ring and I was never so happy to hear that song.

"Jenna!"

"They tried to hurt you?"

"Thank God you called me."

"What happened to you?" her voice was small.

"They nabbed me and were gonna gang rape me. They sodomized Scooter on the side of the road because he doesn't have a girlfriend to get back at for Kailey, the girl in the video. But she *let* those guys gang bang her. She wanted it. It was a sex game. But then she started dating a Jackal and lied. They did that to Scooter, ran Lick and Jojo off the road. Lick's one of those 4 guys and now he's dead. The only reason they probably didn't steal Jojo and do that to her is because she and Lick were in a secret relationship so they didn't know who she was. Jet, the girlfriend of another guy in the video, she got an email at work today because she's been under guard and now you. Jenna, there's so much shit swirling around it's like a damn hurricane."

She sniffled, "I'm not asking about any of that shit. Don't care about any of it; I care about you. They didn't hurt you?"

"No. They hooded me and tied me up but then they found out who my uncle is and Chris came and got me and dropped me back off with Deacon."

She let out a big breath.

"Bronto was assigned to keep you safe in case those guys came after you but Jenna, it's my fault..."

"Your fault?"

"My fault they know about you. I started to plead with Uncle Willie who said he'd put word out that no one was to touch me, that he should put that word out about you, too, and that's what put you on their radar."

"It's not your fault that these dirty fucking bikers are scumbags, Ella. I'm coming down there and getting you and getting you the fuck out of there. What's the address?"

"No idea. I'm at the Sioux Falls Clubhouse but you don't need to come get me. Deacon..."

"You need to fucking end things with that biker, Elle. This shit is whacked. First all that shit we found out about him and then all this?"

"You know that wasn't his fault. You don't even know all of it."

"What I do know is that nothing but bad has happened since you met him."

"I'll be home tomorrow. We can talk then. For tonight, let Bronto look after you. Rider and you can talk."

"No fucking way any Dom is getting near me again. Bronto has been staying at my apartment, hanging out at the shop during the day. It stops now."

"Where are you?"

"Your room."

"You're in my room?" I asked, "Have you spoken to my parents?"

Deacon was coming in as I was saying this. He backed out of the room and shut the door before he'd fully come in.

"Do my parents know any of this?"

"Your Mom and Beau aren't here. Your dad is in the garage with Jase and Uncle Lou. They saw me and said you weren't here and I just waved and said I was borrowing a belt. Hey."

"Huh?"

"What? No, I'm not. What are you doing?" Jenna asked.

"What?"

"No. I'm not going with any of those motherfuckers. I'm talking to Ella. Why?"

She wasn't talking to me.

"Jenna who's there?" I asked.

"Your dad is here and he's calling someone and saying I'm here and he's gonna keep me here until they get here. What the fuck, Elle?"

I got to my feet and opened the door. Deacon was in the hallway on the phone.

"What's happening?" I asked him.

"Right, bye." He hung up the phone, "Your Dad's keeping her there until Bronto and Jesse get there."

"Why?"

"Jenna?" the line was dead, "Deacon! She hung up. What on earth?"

"She can't be running the streets or running her mouth."

"Deacon..."

"What did you say to her?"

"I gave her the super condensed version."

"Fuck."

My voice went up a few octaves and I was yelling, "She already saw the video, she needed context for her to know that your brother and those guys didn't rape that girl. She was freaking out."

"Okay, Kitten. Chill."

I took a breath. My heart was racing.

Jenna wasn't going to be happy but at least she was safe.

"I'll go grab you a laptop so you can watch a movie or something while you wait for me. Back in two minutes. Don't tell anyone else what's going on."

"I'm not stupid," I snapped.

His eyebrows rose and I felt a pang of something. Fear? I don't know. The look on his face...

He leaned over and put both fists to the mattress, one on either side of my thighs, his nose was only an inch from mine.

"You want your ass smacked?"

I leaned back and narrowed my eyes, looking down my nose at him.

He smiled a super sexy smile.

I felt a gush of damp hit my panties. This was *so* not the time for that.

"Don't try to get my motor running when shit is hitting the fan," I muttered.

"Don't be sexy sassy then." He kissed me and then he was gone.

I sat there in a fricking fog.

He was back a minute later and he plugged in a notebook computer for me and logged me into a Netflix account.

"Be careful if you go out there," I ordered.

"I will. Stay here. I'm gonna text you a brother's name and number who'll be in charge of getting you anything you need if I have to leave the building." He kissed me again and left the room.

My phone rang. It was Dad.

"Dad?"

"Tinkerbella. What's cookin'?"

"Uh..."

"You alright, baby doll?"

"Yeah, I'm... okay."

"I don't know all of what's goin' on there but heard a coupla things. Deacon's looking after you?"

"Yeah."

"For sure?"

"Yeah, Dad. I'm good. I'm safe."

Dad let out a big breath.

"What about you, Dad? You playing things smart?"

Silence.

He knew I knew something.

Finally, he said, "Don't you worry 'bout your old Dad. I'm covered."

"Alright. I sure hope so, Dad."

"Gotta run, Belly. Don't worry. Jenny-penny's good. She's with the two prospects and they'll keep her safe. When ya back home?"

"Tomorrow, I think."

"Good. See you then. We'll talk."

"Love you, Dad." I wanted to cry.

"Love you, too, baby doll."

My nerves were shot to shit. I wanted to cry.

Jenna was a wreck. Dad was doing risky things. God knew what Deacon was going to get up to now that the Jackals had shared that video, making it very obvious that this war between the two clubs was being taken to the next level. They'd killed Lick, hospitalized Jojo, hurt Scooter really badly, and now destroyed Edge & Jet's relationship and sent Jenna's feelings for Rider into a flaming pit, rendering them a pile of ash.

I knew her. She wasn't one to give a guy a second chance. If she said she was done with him, she was done. But I guess a consolation was that she could be the one that ended things in her mind instead of having her heart broken. Actually, I didn't know what was worse. Her ending it with him thinking he was a rapist or him breaking her heart because he didn't want anything serious. Either way meant pain for my best friend.

I went into the adjoining bathroom and washed my face with cold water and then surfed through the Netflix menu for twenty minutes, not interested in a single program.

My brain was going a zillion miles a minute with everything that was happening.

Deacon sent me a text:

"Leaving for a bit. Need anything, call or text Brady. 555-2453. He's the brother who carried you to me last night."

"Ok <3"

I tried to text Jenna.
"What's happening? Are you okay?"
I didn't get an answer.

I tossed and turned while watching a chunk of Season 1 of Star Trek Voyager on Netflix, the laptop propped on the chair beside the bed. Eventually, I fell asleep.

I woke up to the sound of Deacon getting undressed. It was dark.

I felt the bed move and he was beside me.

"Hi."

"You watch Star Trek, babe?"

"Yeah."

"Just this one or them all?"

"Them all. Except the original. Only saw a few. Most of it was cheesy."

"Don't say bad words."

"Hee hee."

"Which captain you like the best?"

"They all have their merits. But Captain Janeway is definitely my favorite."

"'Cuz she's a chick."

"Probably. What about you?" I yawned.

"Picard."

"Hm. Not bad." I snuggled into him.

His skin was cold.

"You're warm," he told me, snuggling close. He was naked. I was wearing his flannel shirt again. It was really comfy.

"You're freezing."

"Warm me up."

"Okay, but give me an update." I snuggled in.

"Jet, M.I.A. We looked for her but Edge called it off after getting a text from one of her friends in Portland who said she's there but told him to give her a day or two to chill out. We figure she's safer at her friend's place in Oregon than here. Jenna, safe. She threw a fit when Bronto and Jesse got to your place to get her. They've taken her to our family cottage. It's half way between here and there."

"Why?"

"Ride's orders. He's on his way there now."

"What else?"

"What else what?"

"What other updates?"

"What do you mean?"

"Where have you been all this time?"

"You wanna know this?"

"I asked, didn't I?"

He slapped my butt.

"Sassy girl," and then he had my earlobe in between his teeth.

"Deacon."

"I don't think you wanna know."

"Were you out trying to get revenge?"

"Not trying. Getting."

"What does that mean?"

"You don't wanna know."

"What if I do?"

"Kitten."

His hand slipped between my legs.

"Are you trying to take my mind off my questions?"

"Naw, I'm trying to make you moan for me."

"Lying."

"Both?" he tried.

I clamped my legs shut to let him know I wanted my question answered.

His mouth got to my ear and he whispered, "We got our hands on Deuce and Logan. One of them ain't breathin'. The other one, barely. I got my hands on Dice, the guy that grabbed you. He's not doin' real well, either. Shit is really gonna hit the fan now."

"Oh boy. Maybe I shouldn't have asked."

"Yup. Told ya. Now spread your legs for me, Ella."

"I…"

"Shhh, need you, baby. I need you right now and then I need to sleep a few hours so we can get the fuck outta here," He kissed me quiet.

I warmed him up.

And then he set *me* on fire with his touch.

And then we both fell asleep after some pretty spectacular sex. Yeah, it was weird that I'd let that happen after finding out he was out there being violent but it felt like he needed me and touched me like he wanted to get lost in me and never again be found.

Deacon set the alarm for six o'clock, which would give me about three more hours of sleep. He said we were heading home early, getting out of Sioux Falls before the shit hit the fan even more as well as so that the businesses could be opened.

I was looking forward to getting home. Little did I know; things were about veer into even crazier territory.

13

We were almost home. It was me, Deacon, Deke, and Spencer in Deacon's pickup truck. Rider had left in the middle of the night to go to Jenna. Spence slept all the way home and Deke smoked a lot and texted a lot.

I found the Rider news a little bit odd and I was more than a little curious about what was happening now between those two. Guess I'd have to wait to find out.

The ride home was fairly uneventful and extremely quiet, other than the music that played on the radio. Jojo was doing well and would likely be released in a day or two. They needed to take care of business with the garage, dealership, and the bar. The garage and the dealership had been shut down for the weekend and staff had been managing things at the bar but Deke was anxious to get back. It was now Monday morning.

Deacon dropped them off at their block and then drove me home.

The garage was wide open and there were Dad and Mom, sitting in there on lawn chairs drinking their coffee. We had a nice porch with a swing that would be even nicer if someone took the time to sand off the peeling paint and slap a new coat of paint on it but everyone always wound up in the Man Cave.

We approached and Mom pulled me into a hug with a big smile on her face, "Missed you, sweetie pie. Deacon, how's your sister doing?"

"She's much better, thank you. I gotta get to the garage but wanted to just help Ella up with our bags."

"Right, we'll catch up later."

Dad gave me a hug, "Hey Belly Button. Deacon."

He shook Deacon's hand and gave him a back slap and he wandered back in through his breezeway to the kitchen with his and Mom's empty cups to get refills.

We followed so that I didn't have to dig out the keys and went upstairs to my room. I dropped my purse and Deacon dropped our suitcase and then I dropped to the bed on my back and he flopped beside me. I rolled into him.

"Gotta get to work," he said but he looked in no hurry.

"Alright." I scrubbed his scruffy cheek with my nails and kissed him.

"Your bed's pretty fuckin' comfy," he said through a yawn.

"Yeah."

"Probably mostly 'cuz you're in it."

I played with his hair, which was in a low man bun but a few thick curly pieces had come loose.

"Stay here till I get back. I'm gonna work out prospect detail so someone hangs with you. I dunno if Jesse and Bronto are back yet."

"Huh?"

"You need to go somewhere?"

"Well, I don't know. I hadn't thought that far."

"Can you hang here till I get back? Give me some peace of mind while I take care of a few things? I don't want you out alone."

"Um, I guess so, okay."

He kissed me and got up and left by the fire escape door.

I unpacked our suitcase and was about to head down the stairs with my laundry basket but then my phone started to ring.

I didn't know the number.

"Hello?"

"Ella?" Jenna. She was crying.

"What's going on?"

"Where are you, Elle?"

"We just got home. Where are you?"

"This asshole biker has me at a cabin and he took my phone and I just found where he hid his. I need you to find out where this place is and come fuckin' get me. I'm not spending a minute longer than I have to here with him." She sniffled.

"Rider has you there?"

"Yeah."

"Why is he keeping you there?"

"He doesn't like that I broke it off. He's trying to convince... oh fucking shit."

"Nuh, uh, uh..." I heard him admonishing her, and then the line went dead.

What on earth?

I stared at the phone a second and then a text came through.

"She's fine, Ella. It's just me. Rider."

Easy for him to say. She didn't sound fine. What the heck?

I texted Deacon,

"What's happening with Rider and Jenna?"

Ten minutes later Deacon replied:

"Don't know. I'll try to find out."

MY PHONE RANG AT 10:10. It was Pippa calling me.

"Pip?"

"Hey babes. Know where Jenna is? She's not at the shop. She didn't come home last night."

"You haven't talked to her?"

"Nope. You?"

"Yeah, she's with Rider."

"Oh. She has an appointment here, waiting. She's late."

"Uh, she's out of town."

"She what?"

"Yeah. It was... unexpected. Do you think you could call in Debbie to see if she can help out today?"

Debbie was the lady that used to own Jenna's salon and who still rented a chair there part-time.

"I could try. I can't believe she didn't tell me she was going."

"I don't think it was intentional. Things are a bit wonky right now. If uh, Debbie can't help maybe cancel her appointments today, maybe. Say an emergency came up."

"Is there an actual emergency?" Pippa asked.

"Kind of. I think. I'm not really sure. There's some drama with the MC. I can't really get into it."

"Okay. Well... keep me posted? Or have her call me? She's okay, right?"

"I think... I mean, yeah. She's fine." Pippa didn't need to stress out by knowing what we were dealing with. And Rider seemed like a good guy. I had to believe she was okay by what he'd said.

"Okay. Sounds like we need a girlie night with some drinks."

"Do we ever!" I said.

"Whoa. For you to say that? Sheesh. Okay, I'll call Deb. Bye."

"Bye."

I texted Rider.

> "Are you bringing her back today? Pippa called about the salon. There are appointments, etc."

Pippa texted me,

> "Debbie said she can take Jenna's appointments today. And tomorrow if needed."

"Ok. Thanks, Pippa. Pls tell her yes."
Rider replied a while later,
"Probably not."
I replied to him:

> "Tell her I told Pippa to call Debbie and now Debbie is at the salon taking care of things, not to worry."

"Thx Ella."
What the heck was going on there, anyway?
Deacon texted me a few minutes later,

> "Don't worry about your girl. He's got her and it'll all be good."

I wrote back:

"Ok… whatever that all means…."

He didn't answer after that so I figured that was all the detail I was gonna get for now.

I GOT OUR LAUNDRY GOING and my room dusted and vacuumed and then I worked my way down, got the second floor vacuumed, got all the stairs, done, and then I had to take a break half way through the main floor because the vacuum cleaner was overheating and making a burning smell.

When I turned the vacuum off I heard someone knocking on the front door.

I opened it. Jay was standing there. Jay. *Shit*. Double shit. I should've looked first.

"Um, hi. What are you doing here?"

Where was Dad? Dad normally spotted anyone at the house and I'm sure he would've circumvented Jay coming to the door.

"Can I talk to you?" He looked angry. No, he looked like he was trying to hide angry. Unease prickled up the back of my neck.

"Uh…"

"We spent months together. I told you I loved you and you broke my fucking heart by dumping me and then you moved on immediately. Don't you owe me at least a private conversation?"

"It wasn't immediately. It was over a month. But talk," I shrugged.

He took a step closer. I stared.

"Gonna let me in?"

"Um, I'll come out." I stepped out onto the front porch. I sat on our old peeling wooden swing that was suspended from the ceiling of the covered porch. I motioned for him to sit, "We can talk here."

"Somewhere private would be better," he said and I shook my head, a little bit baffled.

"We have plenty of privacy here," I assured.

"Not for this." He sat too close to me. I instinctively leaned away but he wrapped an arm around my shoulder and yanked me closer while he whispered in my ear. "Even though you're fucking someone else, we can still help one another out."

"Wh-what?" I pulled away and got up from the swing.

He stayed there and got a smug look on his face. He looked around, seeing no one was nearby, and then said, "Your new boyfriend has been real physical with me a few times. I'm thinking I've got grounds for assault charges. I'm also thinking that you can make that go away."

"What?"

He got up and yanked my wrist and pulled me toward the door. He got it open and in a flash I was against the door on the inside and he was against me. He had his pelvis directly against me. He was hard.

Oh shit. I felt repulsion crawl up my spine.

He got to my ear and said, "You can be on my speed dial for when I get an itch. An itch that you're real good at scratchin.'"

"I don't fucking think so." I tried to bring my knee up to nail him in the balls but he twisted and dodged me while he slammed me against the front door at the same time.

He was six feet tall. He wasn't super muscular but he definitely had more strength than me.

"Why would you calling the cops bother me? I've been dating him a week," I tried, "Besides, you've been verging on stalker territory with me. How do you know I won't file a restraining order, make your life difficult, too?"

He smirked, "Because beyond that, I've also got some inside information about a local cookie artisan, you might know him; he sells cannabis cookies along with pot on its own. If that doesn't get him arrested, then certainly Child Protective Services might be interested in that and all the dope smoking going on around here with a small kid living here."

"You're a fucking asshole," I hissed, "I can't believe you!"

"I wanted you back. You moved on and didn't give me and all I gave our relationship a backward glance. Instead you acted like a slut and started fuckin' some biker. You wanna be biker pussy, go ahead. I already know how cock starved you are so I'll give you a piece of this." He grabbed his crotch, "I'll keep taking my piece of you until I've gotten my fill. I'm gonna be taking what I'm missing most about you until I've had enough. And I don't see that happening any time soon."

I shoved him back with both hands. He only went back about a foot but that was enough for me to reach behind my back and get the doorknob. I went to open the door and he slammed it shut with his hand above my head. He pushed me back against the door and got right up to my ear, "I want you. I want you tonight. Eleven o'clock. Meet me at the Holiday Inn on 7th. I'll leave a message at the desk with the room number. Then we'll talk about things."

"Fuck you."

"You're not there or you tell your biker boyfriend about this, you'll be sorry. I've got even more ammo than what I've just laid out for you. And even if I make you sorry, trust me Ella, I'll have your hungry sweet twat again." He grabbed my face roughly and shoved his tongue in my mouth and grabbed my breast roughly. I stomped on his foot and broke away from him.

"You don't even know what to do with a hungry twat so don't bother."

Fucking gross pig.

He grunted but then gave me a slithery look of promise, "I'll look forward to making you scream my name, sweetie." And then he winked and opened the door and walked out. He looked around the corner down the driveway and then walked the other way down the street.

I watched, heart rapidly thumping, until I saw him get into his car in front of the house on the other side of Jenna's parents place.

Deacon was *so* right about him. Fuck.

I looked out and saw Dad's truck was still here and Dad's garage was opened. Where the heck was Dad? I heard laughing. Uncle Lou? Dad was walking up the street with Uncle Lou, who lived about a block away. Maybe Dad had gone over there?

I ran upstairs to my room. My heart was thundering in my chest.

I grabbed my keys and my purse and then dashed down the fire escape stairs to my car.

"Belle. Where ya goin?" Dad asked from the garage.

"To see Deacon," I said, getting the door opened.

"You goin' right there? We don't want you really out and about with… you know."

"I'm goin' right there."

"Okay, doll. Get there safe. Text when you get there."

I got into my car and started it up and drove right to the garage. I was freaking out. No way was Jay Smyth going to do this to me. No fucking way.

I saw activity in the parking lots of the businesses. There were cars and bikes and people and the bay doors were open to the garage but Deacon wasn't out where I could see him. I ran inside and saw several bikers in that back coffee room standing in a circle.

Deacon, Spencer, Deke, Jesse, Scooter (his face a swirl of red, black, and blue with a whole lot of bruising) and four other guys in Dom cuts were in there and it looked like they were in a serious discussion.

Scooter spotted me first and said something to Deacon and Deacon took one look at me and then was moving toward me. He must've read my expression.

"What is it? What's wrong?"

I fell into his body, breaking into the sobs that had been held back until that minute. He caught me.

The vibe in the room went scary angry.

He picked me up. Picked me up! He took me outside and walked down toward the roadhouse with me in his arms.

"One sec, Kitten." He walked fast, still holding me, up the stairs at the side of the building into the clubhouse.

I didn't take much in other than a big and sort of messy rec room-like open living space, which he moved through, and then we were greeted by a very enthusiastic German shepherd. I'd forgotten about him, the dog that Deacon had picked up from the shelter before we'd met.

The shepherd yelped with excitement at seeing Deacon, and then I was sure he recognized me from the shelter as he started whimpering at us. His tail was thumping a mile a minute.

"Sit." Deacon ordered and the shepherd immediately sat but made one of those exasperated doggie sighs.

We were down a hall and in a bedroom which was sparse, just a stripped bare double bed and a dresser with nothing sitting on top.

He sat me on the bed and got to his knees on the floor in front of me, his hands on my knees, "Talk to me."

"Jay came to the house."

He stiffened. His eyes went angry.

"He tried to blackmail me into having sex with him. He said..."

Deacon rose to his feet and his facial expression was murderous.

"He touch you?" His fists were clenched at his sides.

"He shoved his tongue down my throat and groped my boob and slammed me against the door and yanked on my wrist and I..."

I looked down and my wrist was actually red-looking. I rubbed it.

"Stay here." He was out of the room and I heard him yell, "Get the fuck up here!" and then he was back, "You okay? You hurt?"

"No, I'm okay. He didn't really hurt me. I shoved him and got him off me. But he's demanding I meet him at the Holiday Inn at 11:00 tonight or he's having you charged with assault, reporting my Dad for his pot shit, and he's acting like he's got some other ace up his sleeve. He's threatened me, said not to tell you."

"He ain't doing shit. He won't be breathing past 11:01 when I show up at that fucking hotel instead of you and I put knife in his gut and yank it up to his throat."

My mouth dropped open.

He pulled me against him and held me a second.

"What's goin' on?" Spencer was the first one to get to us.

"Ella's ex. Tried to blackmail her for sex. Using charges against me and against Rob as collateral. Put his fucking hands on her, his tongue in her mouth."

Spencer's jaw tensed. The doorway filled with bikers.

"Be right back, baby."

"Got intel for ya I hadn't had a chance to share yet," I heard a deep voice say, "About that Smyth dude."

Deacon kissed me and left me in there behind a closed door.

It was early, it was still morning. I had hours to talk him out of it.

I heard sniffing at the door. The dog.

I got up and opened it and let him in and about ten minutes later Deacon found us curled up together on the bed. I was sitting in the corner of the bed, which was pushed against the wall, and the dog had his head in my lap. If he could've gotten completely on my lap I think he would have.

"Chakotay, down."

"His name is Chakotay?"

"Yeah, he belongs to Spence."

"Spence likes Star Trek Voyager, too?"

"All of us watch all of them. Even Jojo. She goes as Deanna Troy to every Cosplay event she can."

He sat down.

Chakotay was Captain Janeway's number two on Star Trek Voyager. What an awesome name for a dog.

"Jojo definitely has the hair to be Deanna Troy. And Chakotay is *the shit*."

"Agreed. Now about this shit…" Deacon said.

"So's this dog. He's Spence's dog?"

"Yeah."

"Oh." I was a little sad. I was going to suggest that if this was Deacon's dog, he could come to my room too.

"Why?" He was looking at me funny and started petting Chakotay's head.

"I was gonna say he could come with us to my room."

"You like dogs?"

I nodded, "You remember where you first saw me, right? I'm jonesing missing all the dogs and cats at the shelter."

"What's your favorite breed?" he asked me, stroking my hair and pulling me close.

"I like big dogs. I've always wanted a Saint Bernard."

He smiled, "That's a great dog."

"Loved all those Beethoven movies when I was little. Turner and Hooch, even if Hooch drooled all over the place; I wouldn't care."

The way he looked at me had me thinking about living in his Fifth Wheel with him, living on that property outside the city, a big fluffy Saint Bernard puppy with us. All the drama around us melted away for that split second as I stared into his eyes.

"This your room?" I asked, breaking the loaded silence.

He made a kind of disgusted face glancing around, "Yeah. Downside of using this as our clubhouse is that we can't batten the hatches like we can in the falls. Soon I'm hopin' this Jackal problem'll be history and it won't be as much of a concern but we're all in agreement that this place ain't fortifiable enough for us. Let's get back to your place. I'll explain a few things about your ex and how it'll go down tonight."

DEACON HAD TAKEN ME home on his motorcycle, leaving my car at the garage but parking it inside in one of the bays. Maybe he didn't want Jay to see that I'd gone there. I'd tried to say I'd bring it home but he'd simply taken me to his motorcycle and then we were on it. This was the old one he'd brought back from Sioux Falls. It was a nice bike. I didn't have the right frame of mind to fully appreciate it but in a few minutes we were home and I was back in my bedroom frantically trying to talk him out of going to the hotel.

He shook his head when I told him I didn't want him to go to jail for murdering my ex. He tried to calm me down but I was pretty determined to talk him out of murder until he lifted me and put me on the bed and pinned me to halt my freak out, "Jay Smyth ain't even likely to be there. Jackals will."

"Huh?"

"Jesse spotted Jay meeting with Key and Gordino this morning."

"Who are they?"

"The prez and VP of the Ipswich Jackals charter."

I frowned.

"Ambush," he said.

"They involved Jay?"

"Looks that way. Bet any money he did what he did knowing you'd tell me and knowing you won't show, I'll go instead to straighten him out so he won't even be there. Even sayin' 11:00 doesn't make sense. Why would he try to get you to sneak to meet me at a time when you'd be home in bed with me? I'll tell ya why, because that'll be quiet around that hotel so whatever the Jackals have planned will have minimal eye witnesses that time of night on a Monday."

"But he..."

"He wants you. I know this. He wants me out of the picture. Lotta Jackals don't like you're with me because of who your blood is. I can see them working with your ex. An ex that already has issue with me since I've publicly humiliated him and stopped him from getting into your room the other night. He probably figures they'll get me out of the picture so he can move back in on you."

I shivered, "He doesn't seem like he just wants me back. He was being cruel and cold to me. He seems like he wants to demean me."

Deacon's eyes narrowed and his jaw muscles were working as he seemed like he was trying to keep his cool.

"Ugh," I grunted and massaged my temples with my fingertips.

"Smyth know Fork is your cousin?"

"Yeah. We saw him in public a few times. I pointed him out once and they actually met once when Chris walked up to speak to me and I introduced them."

"Gonna get back. You don't leave this house. I'll be back."

"Wait. What'll you do?"

"We're still talking it out. I'm thinkin' we get Smyth before he gets to the hotel, if he's even planning on goin' there, and we leave the Jackals at the hotel and hit them on their way back to their clubhouse."

I thrust my hands into my hair. This was nuts!

"Jesse's got you. He's here until I get home. Gimme keys to the Impala."

I opened my mouth, about to speak, not sure what to say, but he kissed me and then he opened his hand. I passed him the keys and then he was gone. I walked out the fire escape door and stood on the deck and watched him talk to Jesse, who was on his motorcycle in our driveway, talking to Dad. Deacon talked to them both a minute, slapped them both on the shoulder and then he got on his motorcycle and gave me a chin jerk and then he was gone.

Jesse wandered toward the garage. I went down. He was sitting with Dad and Dad was rolling a joint.

I sat down and put my hands in my hair.

"You up to speed on things?" I asked Dad.

Dad nodded and passed me the joint, his eyebrows up.

Yeah, I could use something to chill me out. I smoked it, passing to Jesse after a few puffs and he passed it directly to dad without having any and then it came back to me and I finished it and then said, "Jesse, make yourself at home. I'm going for a nap."

Jesse's eyes were on me but he didn't reply. Man of few words, evidently.

"Sorry he got to you Elizabelle," Dad said, his voice a bit gruff, "I just went down the block for ten minutes. He must've been watchin'."

"It's okay, Dad."

"We'll take care of this shit," Dad vowed, his eyes serious as a heart attack.

"I know," I kissed his cheek and then, feeling the gooey feeling after smoking setting in, I made my way back upstairs and then I curled up and tried to read. It lasted all of five minutes before my Kindle fell on my face and I rolled over and fell asleep.

I slept until it got dark and woke to Deacon playing with my hair.

He'd turned the dial on the string of little white lights wound around on my headboard and in the soft glow of the room it occurred to me that he never looked better. And he always looked amazing to me.

He was sitting on the edge of my bed in a black t-shirt that stretched across his broad chest. His biceps looked mouthwatering. He was wearing a pair of black cargo pants.

"You're dressed like you're about to go burgle someone," I mumbled, "Wait, no. You kind of look like a hot commando."

I scooted into his lap and put my head against his chest. I was kind of in a ball. He laid down and got me close and kept playing with my hair.

It dawned on me why he was dressed like that. He smelled freshly showered. He'd come in and showered and changed so that he could get ready for whatever was gonna go down at the Holiday Inn that night.

"If I got to go commando on fuckers so that they don't fuck with me and what's mine, that's what I'm gonna do," he told me.

I stared at him.

"No one fucks with you. Not you, not your family. Alright?"

I nodded.

"You grab a shower downstairs?" I asked, playing with his hair. His hair was still damp.

"Nope, fixed your shower."

"You did? I slept through it?"

"Yep. Your parents went to take your grandmother out for dinner, took your little bro. You hungry?"

"Yeah." I missed my Gran. I hadn't seen her since the day I ran and hid at the library all day. It was only last week but felt like months ago. So much had happened.

"As you should be. Heard you smoked a big fatty and passed out." He was smiling, looking amused.

"Yep. I needed to just turn off my brain for a bit."

"Let's go get a bite to eat? I'm starved."

"Let me make myself presentable first."

He smiled and kissed me.

"We taking the car or the bike?" I asked.

"Bike. We're always gonna be on two wheels unless it's absolutely necessary to be on 4."

"Gotcha." I liked that.

I went into the bathroom and saw why he'd given me that smile and didn't tell me I already looked presentable. I seriously didn't. My ponytail was off to the side as if I was in an 80's Olivia Newton John music video and I had eye make-up smudged all raccoonish below my eyes.

He must really like me if he was being all sweet and physical despite me looking like a train wreck.

I washed my face, fixed my hair, and put some fresh make-up on and then I changed into a fresh pair of jeans and a thin hooded t-shirt with cool little pearl buttons all the way down the front and sat on the edge of my bed and pulled on the motorcycle boots that Deacon got me.

He was lying in my bed, eyes closed, his fingers woven together and behind his head.

I leaned over and kissed his beautiful lips. I found it hard to believe it had been less than 2 weeks since we'd met and I already had such strong feelings for him. Stronger than any guy I'd ever been with or crushed on. He was *it*. My ultimate crush but yet he was mine. Not someone I admired from afar. Not someone who I wished was mine. He *was* mine. He was beautiful but so much more than that. He lit my body on fire and he was protective. He looked at me with so much emotion that it melted me.

His eyes opened and warmed, maybe because of the way I was looking at him. His fingers tangled into my hair and he brought my mouth down to his.

"Wish we could've started out when there wasn't so much fuckin' drama going on," he said.

I blew out a big breath and was about to say something in agreement but then he knocked my socks off because he said,

"But startin' out this way instead, shows me what you're made of. You're amazing, you know that? I knew what I was fuckin' doing when I staked my claim with you."

Um, wow.

"And only you, babe," he was shaking with laughter

"Only me?"

"Only you could work that look. A shirt with pearls with motorcycle boots." He looked at my boots.

I smiled.

"Let's go eat," he said and was about to sit up.

"Wait," I ordered and straddled him. I took his jaw in both hands and planted a soft kiss on his lips, "You're worth it. All the drama, all the danger, it's all worth it because not only are you the prize at the end but I've got you all through it and I know in my soul you'll protect me. You make me feel safe and you make me feel alive."

He sat up, hooking an arm around my lower back to keep me straddling him. He grabbed my jaw with his free hand and then his lips were on mine. He kissed me with rough emotion. When he released my lips I saw his eyes were molten.

"Wanna skip going out for food and get naked?" I asked.

He smiled big and his fingers gripped me harder.

"Then we can stay here and talk after while I make us a sandwich?"

"Sounds good to me," he told me and then he stood up, my legs wound tight around his waist and he turned around to put me on my back on the bed.

"Condoms?" he inquired.

I whispered, "We have two left. They're in my nightstand."

He grabbed one and then pulled my boots off and began to undressed me, slowly, reverently. After my second sock was off, he kissed the arch of my foot, which tickled and made me squirm with desire at the same time. Holy wow. And then he planted a soft kiss on my ankle, and then his lips worked their way up, but completely bypassing my cookie and that whole zone but then when he got to my belly, pulling my t-shirt up and off my head, he kissed it sweetly and then said, "One day, after we've got a coupla years under our belt, I wanna make this big and round." He kissed it and then ran a palm over it.

I fucking melted.

He smiled, knowing he'd done that to me, "Maybe repeatedly."

I sat up and yanked his t-shirt over his head and I started to ravish his chest with my mouth as I tried to work his jeans undone. He undid my bra, pulled it off, and tossed it, and then I was pushing his jeans down with my feet, desperate for crotch to crotch contact.

"Dr. Lola should be calling any day but we might need another box. Or five boxes." I licked his nipple and looked up at him.

He bit into his bottom lip and his eyes heated as he rolled the condom onto himself, watching me while he did it.

"Can't wait till she calls," he told me.

"I can't wait either. Nobody but you will have been inside me bare and I'm so glad it's you."

"Nobody but me will ever be," he said and then he grabbed my hips with both hands and as if the idea of that supremely pleased him, he slammed straight into me and I gasped, going liquid.

Deacon fucked me hard and fast and I almost cried at the beauty of it when I got my happy ending with his fingers to my clit as he powered into me.

He went faster and faster as he grunted, "No one fucking touches you but me. No one." And he looked pissed. I knew he was thinking about Jay and I actually felt sorry for Jay for a split second because I knew right then by the look in Deacon's eyes that he was going to pulverize Jay later that night.

"No one," he grunted.

"No one," I agreed.

"He doesn't put his hands on you again, Ella."

I nodded and kissed his jaw.

He pulled me tight to him and I tucked my forehead into the nook of his collar bone.

A minute or two of silence passed and then he swatted my butt.

"What kinda sandwich you gonna make us?"

"Is that you saying I should get up and go make it?"

"Starvin', babe. Didn't eat a thing today and it's almost 8:00."

"Oh. I'm so comfy, though." I was nuzzled into his warmth.

"Seriously, Ella. I'm starved. Or I'll do it. Want me to make you a sandwich?"

"No; I can take care of my man." I sluggishly rolled away and got to my feet and started putting my clothes back on.

Back in my room twenty or so minutes later I'd whipped us up some meatball garlic bread submarines that I'd grilled on the panini maker with three kinds of cheese and marinara sauce on it along with my signature garlic butter concoction that everyone loved. They were packaged meatballs but it still tasted like it was cooked with love. I served it with a cold beer and two bites in he said, "Babe, this is fuckin' great. When you said sandwich I wasn't sure it'd put a dent in my appetite because I haven't eaten all day but this is hittin' the fuckin' spot!"

I smiled and dug into my sandwich thinking that this was the first time I'd made him something, other than finishing off the dinner that he'd tried to make me the night that Scooter got hurt.

"I have a plethora of delights in store for you..." I promised, "Most of them smothered in garlic and cheese." And then a glob of sauce fell out of my sandwich onto my teal and chocolate brown bedspread.

"Oh, man!" I groaned.

He smiled and took a big swig of his beer to wash down what was in his mouth and then he said, "I look forward to that."

I'd put on the TV but it was just background noise. We got up and stripped the comforter off and I took it downstairs to Shout it out.

When I got back upstairs he was finished his giant 12" panini. He was also on the phone. He ended the call as I was about to bring our plates to the kitchen, I'd only eaten half of mine, but he grabbed my plate and gave me a look and then proceeded to eat the other half of mine.

I sat down and scooted against the headboard and lifted my phone and started scrolling Facebook.

"What's his name gonna be?" Deacon asked me.

"Hm?" I asked.

I was scrolling but really, I was in deep thought about what Deacon had to deal with later that evening. I'd also been thinking back to the last few nights and times he'd been with his MC brothers instead of me, dealing with drama, making plans for revenge, etc. Did I even wanna know what sort of things he'd been doing?

"The Saint Bernard you want. What's his name gonna be?"

I smiled and immediately answered, "Tuvok." Tuvok was the Vulcan from Star Trek Voyager, the same show that Chakotay was from.

He burst out laughing, "Perfect."

He muted the TV and leaned over me, "Food was awesome, Kitten. I gotta get ready to head out."

"What's the plan?" I asked.

"You don't really wanna know all this, do you?"

I shook my head, "I guess not. No, tell me. This is about me directly so I want in the loop. Other stuff, you can tell me if you think I need to know. I don't want to be blindsided. How about we deal with things that way for now?"

"I can do that. Give you all the truth you want; told you that before. But I really don't think you want all of it. Anyhow, we're meeting up first. Got a text a few minutes ago. Jay Smyth hasn't left his house since dinner time. He went to the corner store, bought milk, and came back. We watch him first to see if he's heading to the hotel. If he tries to leave, we follow and stop him. He's had a Jackal prospect watching him but the guy hasn't clocked our guys so that prospect will be immobilized. Smyth is going somewhere where I can have a chat with him before the night is through. We have other plans for whatever Jackals are waiting at that Holiday Inn. What room number he give you?"

"He said I should get it from the desk when I get there."

"Fuck," Deacon bit off, "You can't come."

"I don't wanna come!" My eyes bugged out.

He picked up his phone and made a call, "Jess. You still hooking up with that stripper with the blonde curls?"

I stared.

He continued. "Need her to pose as Ella…. Right, well, have her wear the wig then. Tell her no heels. We need her for the Holiday Inn. 10:50 she needs to go to the desk, ask for the room number for Jay Smyth, text it to you, and then skedaddle. Right."

He put the phone down.

"So you're going?"

"Yep."

"Okay, before you go, what's happening with Jenna? Did you talk to your brother?"

He smirked.

"What?"

"Let's say that Ride is lookin' at your girl in a new light since she tried to scrape him off."

"What does that mean?"

"Ride ain't used to hearing the word No. I think he's kinda diggin' the chase. He's working to convince her not to scrape him off."

My eyes were boinging again, "By holding her at a cabin against her will?"

He shrugged, "We do what we have to do to get what we want."

"Pff." I was a little bit pissed, "Evidently. But I don't think that's the way he's gonna win Jenna around."

He kissed me, "From what I hear, she's already comin' around. Don't worry about her. Ride is gonna probably drop her off to you any time actually. He's meeting us to deal with this shit tonight."

I frowned at him. It'd be interesting to have a chat with Jenna, that was for sure.

"Got a message today, my offer was accepted on that land. Once his shit settles a bit, I'm gonna start building a house. You can go Tuvok shopping."

"Did you just try to buy my acceptance of your brother kidnapping my best friend off with promise of a puppy?"

"Did it work?"

"Fuck yeah," I said and then he burst out laughing and then kissed me. I laughed, too, and we made out for a few minutes and then his phone made another noise and he broke away.

After he texted whoever it was, he pulled his boots on and then he reached into my nightstand and pulled out a little black combination gun lock box that I hadn't noticed he'd put there. When I unpacked that day I hadn't seen his gun in our bag at all. He hit a few buttons and opened it and then shoved the gun and an ammo magazine into an inside pocket of his Dom cut.

I deflated.

"Please be careful," I pleaded.

"Always," he kissed me, shrugged on his leather Dom cut, and then grabbed his keys and left, saying, "Lock this door. I don't have any spare bodies tonight to watch you here but your Dad has been briefed and four of his buddies are in the garage right now keeping an eye on things."

My brows shot up and my mouth dropped open.

"My dad's stoner buddies are my bodyguards?"

"You dad handpicked them and has a few cabbie friends monitoring the city, posting at both ends of this street and elsewhere, keeping us posted on movements."

"Wow. That actually sounds organized."

"Yeah. I'd feel a whole lot better if we had a clubhouse that's lockable. That was the plan but things with the Jackals got jacked faster than we expected."

His phone rang. He answered it.

"Ride? Yeah. You dropping your girl off here? Oh yeah? Alright. Later."

He was smirking as he put his phone into his pocket.

"What?"

"Jenna isn't coming. He still has her locked down. Ride'll be meeting me here in five."

I made a face, "What's funny about that?"

"Let's just say Rider is seriously enjoying the chase."

I glared, "No. this isn't cool. I joked about buying me off with a puppy but seriously?"

"We'll talk later. She's fine, Kitten. Promise. My brother won't fuck her around. I gotta fly. That box password is 831 if you need to open it. There's a second loaded weapon in there."

"Okay."

"You know how to handle a loaded gun?"

"I do," I confirmed.

He gave me a smile and his eyes traveled up and down my body.

"Does that turn you on?" I asked with a bit of a huff.

"Everything about you turns me on," he kissed me and then headed for the door.

"Deacon?"

"What?"

"How can you be so calm? Joking about buying puppies and your brother keeping my best friend hostage and flirting with me when you're heading into an ambush tonight?"

"We're good. We're way fuckin' smarter than those idiots and this shit is what I thrive on. I'm cool."

"Thrive on? How can you thrive on this?"

"The thrill of taking my enemies down. Yeah babe. Fuck yeah."

I went bug-eyed.

"Don't want this shit, don't like seeing anyone I care about at risk but stopping an ambush? Being a step or two ahead of the enemy? Fuck yeah. Gotta fly. See you in a few hours. Don't wait up."

"As if I'm gonna sleep."

"It'll be a late one but I'll call or text you when the worst is over so you know I'm good and you can sleep." He ran his thumb over my cheekbone.

I was flabbergasted.

"You remember the number to that box?"

"831."

"Good girl. You know why that's the combo?"

I shook my head.

"That's the day I decided you were mine, that I had to have you. And if I had to lock *you* in a cabin with me and chain you to the bed to convince you, that's what I would've done." He winked at me and left via the fire escape door

I blinked a couple times. August 31st was the day that I saw him that first time at that gas station.

Swoon.

Wait, was he telling me Jenna was chained to Rider's bed?

IT WAS A LONG EVENING, trying to not worry about Deacon. And Jenna. And everything else.

First, I took a shower. In my own bathroom. It was fantastic to be able to do that. Deacon had put in a new big rain shower head and it was phenomenal.

And then I put on my big fluffy fleece robe that had been away for the summer. It was finally chilly enough to warrant wearing it. It was midnight blue with cyan blue polka dots on it. It was only to my waist so I had on a pair of Deacon's fluffy socks warm, straight out of the dryer as they'd come out with my comforter. They were huge and fluffy. Did I say fluffy? I was totally moving these to my own sock drawer. Or, I'd probably put them right on each time they came out of the dryer.

I was going to love having access to his wardrobe. All the soft flannel shirts and big fluffy socks I wanted. Not to mention big hoodies that I already had my eye on for around the campfire.

I'd kissed my sleeping little bro on my way downstairs; I hadn't seen the little monkey in days and I missed him. I was going to take him to the park the next day, if I could.

I wandered through the main floor and glanced out the window. Dad and a few of his buddies were in the garage. I could hear them laughing.

I knocked on Mom's bedroom door and she called out "Come in."

"Hey Momma."

She was in bed but on top of the blankets, dressed for bed in a long and flowery caftan, and she was reading while crocheting at the same time, her book balancing on her cocked knee, her finger moving a mile a minute as she read. She crocheted so fast she could do it without more than the occasional glance.

"Hello my Sunshine."

I climbed in and got under the blankets and put my head on her shoulder. She stroked my hair.

"How was dinner with Gran?"

Mom sighed, "It was a little rough."

"Oh? Why?"

"She seems … frazzled. Distracted. Easily frustrated. Forgetful. I think it's escalating." Mom looked upset. She and Gran had always been close and while we had an idea this was something we'd have to deal with, it didn't make it any easier.

"I'll try to see her tomorrow. If things aren't too drama-y."

Mom looked at me looking perplexed, "Drama-y?"

"Dad tell you any of what's going on with the Dominion Brotherhood and the Wyld Jackals?"

She shook her head, "No. of course I know something is happening but I don't wanna worry so I haven't asked any questions. I figured if there was something I needed to know, someone would tell me."

I fingered the pale pink round doily or whatever this was that she was working on.

"Is there something I need to know?" she asked.

Mom was a gentle almost angelic spirit. She often just let things go. She never really stuck her nose into my business and I never liked making her worry. Neither did Dad. It wasn't like we didn't think she could handle it, Dad just didn't like seeing worry in her eyes and I guess I'd sort of absorbed that habit over the years.

"Nothing you *must* know. But things are stressful at the moment with a feud between the two clubs and it's a bit dangerous."

"Deacon won't put you in danger," she said, rather than asked.

I looked her in the eye, "No. He won't."

"That young man is smitten with you, darling."

"I'm pretty smitten, too," I blushed.

"Good. I'm happy for you. So happy for you." She kissed the top of my head.

My phone made a noise so I fetched it from my robe pocket.
"R u coming at 11?"
that was Jay. Ugh.
"Only to talk you out of this ridiculousness."

"Where is the biker?"

Shit. Maybe I should've asked what to say before answering. I quickly texted Deacon,

"Jay is texting me asking where you are and whether I'm coming."

"Ella?" Jay again.

"He's out running errands. I'll have to be fast as he'll be here when he's done. But we already know that won't be a problem for you. Fast."

Was I playing with fire? I wanted to be convincing.
"Wow, you're really pissed at me."
"Do you blame me? Blackmail ain't pretty, Jay."

"Yes. I blame you. I loved you and you broke my heart. I'll take what I can get from you and if this is all it is, so be it. You wanna talk about getting to back where we were, I might be willing to listen."

He was certainly playing along.

"I didn't mean to hurt you. We just weren't compatible. You don't have to make me do this. Please don't make me do this."

I hoped that was convincing.
"You really coming??"
I guess I *was* being convincing.

But, was I foiling the plan? I had to stop the track of this conversation. I didn't want them to think that their plan was backfiring.

"Yes, coming. Since you insisted. But I can't talk now. See you then. Don't expect to get lucky. Expect to get talked out of this nonsense."

I hoped that was convincing.
I texted Deacon again,

"I told him I was coming but only to talk him out of blackmailing me. I hope that was the right thing. He was getting all bajigitty."

"He just left his house. I don't think he was gonna come but whatever you said maybe he chgd his mind. We'll get him. Jackals are already at hotel waiting. We have ppl @ the hotel too/ no worries baby."

"Ok. XO. Be safe."

"Always."

"Gonna go up to bed, Momma. Goodnight."
"Goodnight, honey. And try not to worry. Men are gonna do what they're gonna do and you worrying about it won't do nothing. It's about as productive as rocking in a rocking chair. You busy yourself but you accomplish pretty near nothing."

Sage advice.

Not so easy to follow, though. I worried until I'd watched four and a half episodes of Star Trek Voyager and then finally, FINALLY, he was texting.

It was almost 4:am and not only had I watched that much Star Trek but I'd polished off half a tub of ice cream and 3/4 of a can of BBQ Pringles.

Stress eating.

"If you're still up all is good. Be home in a few hours, though. Sleep, baby. XO"

"OK. XO" I wrote back.

But I couldn't fall asleep. I was awake until 6:15 when I heard a vehicle pull in.

I looked out and he got out of The Shitbox. Deacon went toward the garage instead of coming up the stairs so I waited. Maybe Dad and his buds were still up and in there. Ten minutes later he was in my room, having come in from the inside door. I heard him open my door and then shut and lock it. I sat up.

"Hey, Kitten," he whispered, "Sorry I woke you."

"Are you kidding? I haven't slept."

"Just grabbin' a quick shower and then I'll be in."

I heard the shower turn on and then I couldn't wait any longer so I went into the bathroom. He wasn't in the shower, he was shirtless, rinsing his hand, which was all bloody.

"Oh god, are you okay?"

"Not my blood, Kitten."

My eyes boinged.

"Whose?"

"That fuckwad ex of yours."

My eyes boinged bigger.

"Where is he. Is he..." I didn't know how to finish that question. I didn't want to finish that question. I stared at the blood going down the drain in my bathroom sink.

"He's been dropped off at the hospital. He'll live." I looked up to Deacon's face. The look on Deacon's face made me wonder if that was something he was happy about or not. He finished rinsing his hands and then started to shed his clothes. Cargo pants, underwear, and socks hit the floor.

"Wash my back?" he asked, looking tired. I wanted to ask questions so I just sort of stood there staring, trying to find the words.

Finally, he lost patience and grabbed my robe and undid it and then pushed it off my shoulders. He smiled at the shirt I was wearing as he it pulled off. It was one of his, a black Harley tank top that came down to my thighs. We got into the shower and I washed his back. He washed mine. And then we dried off and he took me to bed and held me, both of us naked. He kissed me and said, "We only got 1 left?"

"Mm hm," I said.

"Fuck, I'm tired. We'll use it in the morning." He nuzzled into me and goosebumps rose on my body. "Need something from you now, though. You too tired?"

His thumb caressed my nipple and then his hand slid between my legs. I reached for his cock and stroked it.

"Nope," I breathed as I opened my legs a little bit wider and tried to push my emotions away. This felt like it'd be the perfect anxiety relief.

We touched and kissed and I held back coming, waiting for him and I think he was holding back waiting for me.

"Come, baby," he whispered against my mouth, his hand working faster between my legs.

"Waiting for you."

He laughed. I started stroking harder, tighter.

"Come, baby, I'll come with you as soon as you do. I'm hangin' on, too."

I rocked into his hand and let the build crest over the top.

"Ahhh," I breathed out as I had a sweet orgasm and he groaned an instant later and then his mouth was on mine.

I fell asleep as the sun came up, wrapped up with him.

I WOKE UP TO A TEXT alert. I reached across Deacon for the nightstand and fumbled for my phone.

It was Pippa,

> "Is she still away? Deb's here."

I wrote back,

> "Hopefully she will be back tomorrow."
> "WTF, Ella?"

"I'll pop in and see you today. K?"

"K."

Deacon hadn't moved a muscle through my reaching over him. He was still fast asleep. I looked at his bare chest, one of his arms thrown over his head, the other hand on his belly. I put my phone down and nuzzled in close.

He wrapped his arm around me and kissed my forehead.

I slid my hand down and found Not-So-Little Deacon was half awake. I slid down and kissed "Little Deacon" good morning.

And then we used that last condom.

DEACON NEEDED ME TO drop him at the garage since he'd brought my car home last night. They'd had Jesse's stripper friend / decoy use it to go to the hotel the night before in case she was being watched. Deacon had told me that Jay had headed there after he hung up from talking to me and waited until he saw the decoy go inside. He apparently stopped at a hardware store on the way to the hotel and then he went to the hotel afterwards, aiming to talk to me and maybe take me somewhere else.

Deacon had said there was rope and duct tape in the trunk in a hardware store bag with a receipt dated that day. In his interrogation of Jay, jay had feigned innocence about that but my blood had run cold at that notion, remembering Deacon warning me that day that I almost lost him that I'd wind up in a pit in Jay's basement. Deacon told me that Jay was working with Uncle Willie, who'd approached him. Jay had apparently cracked under pressure; whatever Deacon had put on him.

"What pressure?" I'd asked.

He raised his eyebrow at me and I shook my head and said, "Never mind, I don't wanna know."

Deacon got up to get ready to head to the garage at about ten o'clock. He said they were way behind and he had to get in and work and meet with his MC brothers and didn't want me out alone.

"I wanted to take Beau to the park, visit my Gran. And I need to pop into Jenna's salon and talk to Pippa."

"I'll send a prospect back with you," he said.

"Which one?"

"Likely Jesse. He's being voted in next church. He's the one I trust the most out of the prospects to keep you safe."

I would've rathered Scooter or Bronto from a personality perspective. Jesse was extremely broody. Bronto was like a teddy bear. Scooter was a laugh.

"Oh."

He watched me a beat, "You want me to come with you for one of those things?"

"You're busy."

"Yeah, but which of those would you want me to do if I could do one. Beau or your gran. Obviously not tag along to the salon. Don't be liberal with whatever info you share with your friend."

"I'd love you to meet Gran. And don't worry."

"What time you seein' her?"

"I'll take Beau to the park around 3:30 or so, after school. I'll probably see my Gran around lunch time, maybe. I usually bring lunch when I go. For her and her friends."

"Okay, Kitten, let me get a few things done this morning and I'll try to meet you to see her. But let Jesse look after you."

I smiled, "She will love you. You got grandparents?"

"Yeah, on Dad's side. I'm close to them but only see 'em once or twice a year."

"Okay."

We got dressed and grabbed coffees to go. Beau was gone to school and Mom was teaching a class. We had to get someone new, who was blocking us in, to move their car and didn't know the drill but then we headed to the garage, where we were greeted with fire trucks and police cruisers.

"What the fuck?" Deacon pulled into the parking lot.

Fire fighters were hosing down the building. At least 75% of it was burnt.

14

The fire was out and the fire department was packing up to go and Jesse and Scooter, who were sitting on their motorcycles, told us that Deke and Rider had gone to the hospital, Spencer to a local vet with his dog, whose leg was broken.

Deacon called his dad, who answered and said everyone was okay and then we drove to the hospital to meet him. Everyone had evidently slept in what with the late night the night before and the bar hadn't been due to open yet so no one was in there, thankfully, because in addition to the fire set on the stairs, which Deacon figured was done with a trail of gas, some Molotov cocktails had been tossed through windows of the bar.

Only Deke, Spence, and Rider had been there, the other bikers staying in the clubhouse had already left.

Deacon's dad and brothers were fine but Rider was being checked out by doctors after having hurt himself climbing out a window and they'd wanted to check out Deke for smoke inhalation.

Because the staircase had been set on fire they had gotten out a window out the other end of the building.

Spence's dog had hurt his leg when Spencer and Rider worked together to try to get the dog out the window to the ground, and while Chakotay was being treated by a vet, he would be fine, according to Spencer, who'd updated Deke with a text while we sat with them in the ER. Spence was showing me more and more that he was actually a decent guy.

Deke was shaking his head at the fact that Spence had taken his dog to the vet in lieu of getting himself checked out, against paramedic advice.

"We had security watching. If we hadn't, my dad and brothers would've burnt to death," Deacon mumbled from the hospital ER waiting room after he got a quiet minute alone with them while I'd gone to the rest room. I didn't know what I'd missed but the mood between the three Valentine men was tense, and a little bit scary. As I'd sat down, a nurse came out and called Deke back.

Not long later, we were good to go.

As we got outside, Deacon said,

"It's gonna be strike after counterstrike here forward until this is done. We have to be vigilant." His eyes were on me. "You're not alone. Ever."

I swallowed hard and looked to Rider, "Where's Jenna?"

"Half way between here and Sioux Falls," he said.

"Why?"

"I'm keeping her safe. I'm gonna head back there tonight after work."

"She's got a business to run and—-"

"And she's not safe. Who cares if there's a business if she's too broken to run it?"

I winced.

"Sorry, Ella. Stressed," Rider rubbed his eyes with the heels of his hands, "She's not safe here. Jackals made another direct threat and she refuses to listen so she's somewhere I can keep her safe."

I looked at Deacon whose face gave me nothing.

"Another direct threat?"

No one said anything.

Finally, Deke broke the silence, "I'm meeting with a real estate agent. Gonna look at a potential property for the clubhouse. Was goin' anyway but now I'm really hoping it's the right fit. Gonna have a lot ahead of us getting the bar rebuilt. Need to get business hoppin' in the other areas so that we stay liquid."

Deke turned to me.

"Ella, you good with computers, office type shit?"

"Um, uh huh. Why?"

"Deacon said you've been taking business classes. Rider said you did Jenna's website up?"

"Yeah..."

"Trina just gave two weeks' notice. We need someone to run the office for the dealership."

I looked at Deacon.

He let out a big breath. He looked relieved.

"Um..." I was a little thrown.

"She'll train you before she goes. It's all still new so a lot of shit is still to be worked out. Dealership stuff and when it's back in one piece, the bar. Plus, the garage is run from the same desk. Ordering parts and supplies and then reception and sales paperwork for the dealership. Payroll. Need websites for all three businesses, too."

"I—-"

"Really could use your help, Boop. Pay's good. Benefits. Nine to five. Weekends off."

"Can I let you know?" I asked.

Deke's brow frowned but he nodded, "Sure darlin'."

"I'll get back to you as soon as I can."

"Right-o."

Dad pulled up.

"What are you doin' here?" I leaned over at the passenger window and asked.

"Givin' Deke a lift," Dad smiled at me.

"Oh, um, can I talk to you privately for two seconds?" I asked.

"Sure," Dad said and I got in and left Deke and Deacon for a minute as Dad pulled out and circled the parking lot.

"Can you and Mom put Deke and the boys up for a couple days? I know it'll be a full house but I figure they can stay in the playroom. I can go home and clear it and set up the sofa bed and those camping air mattresses we have."

"Sure, Belle. Was plannin' on making that offer anyway. That it?"

"Yeah, I mean, I guess. I'm not about to talk to you about moving around some dangerous cargo and putting yourself in danger or anything. I mean it'd be crazy for a 23-year-old to talk to her 47-year-old father about such things."

"Not something I tend to say to you too often, baby doll, but back off."

I glared, "Uh, are you joking right now?"

"Not a bit. Now, is that it?"

I shook my head but knew that look on his face. It was rare but he meant what he said when he said something using that face.

"Then that's it."

"Why didn't you ask me in front of the guys if we could make room?"

"Uh, because that's what you do. You talk to the people involved privately about such offers. You don't put someone on the spot. Father."

He chuckled, "You're a fucking hoot." He ruffled my hair and then I got out, shooting a glare over my shoulder at him.

"She's got claws out, Deacon. Tread carefully," Dad advised and Deacon's shoulders shook a little bit with silent laughter.

"I'm glad my claws amuse you," I said to Deacon with my best stink eye.

He yanked me against his body and kissed me hard, with tongue, right in front of my father.

I pulled back and glared at him. He gave me a big blinding smile.

I shook my frustration off and I looked to Deke and Rider, who were both watching the exchange looking highly amused.

"Where are you guys gonna stay tonight? Do you want our spare room? There's a pull out couch and we have a couple of spare air mattress. One of those big ones."

"Thanks, little lady," Deke said, "Just me and Spence tonight. Ride'll be commuting the next coupla days from near Sioux Falls."

"Quite a commute," I said.

"Yup." Rider agreed.

Scooter pulled up in Rider's Charger and got out so Rider could get in the driver's side.

I waved bye to them and then Deke got into Dad's truck.

"No kiss for your old dad?" Dad pouted at me.

"No," I snapped, "Affection might encourage your poor behavior."

Dad chuckled but the laugh didn't quite touch his eyes and that bothered me. It dawned on me then that this club was small and they had three prospects that I'd met so the fact was that Deke probably didn't need to pay my dad to drive him around. That told me how deep dad was into this stuff. Seriously deep.

Deke got in and they pulled out and we were still outside of the hospital and I regretted holding back that kiss. Things were dangerous and it felt ominous all around us right now.

"Everything alright?" Deacon asked and his hand landed on the back of my neck. He started to massage it.

I looked at his face. He looked warmly at me.

"Yeah, I just wanted to talk to him on the side about asking if we could make room for your Dad and brothers."

"That's it?" he pushed.

I shook my head and wrapped my arm around myself, "I'm just a bit freaked out about everything."

"I've got you," he said and pulled me close and put both arms around me. I snuggled in.

"What do you think about working with us?" Deacon asked me, his lips against the top of my head, his hand going up and down my back.

"I'm... not sure. What do *you* think?" I asked. I looked up at him.

"I think it'd be good. We need someone hard-working that we trust. That'd be you on both counts. You'd probably enjoy it. And you're in the building beside mine all day? That works for me." He gave me a smile.

I wasn't sure how I felt about that. I'd had my life completely taken over by Deacon in less than two weeks. We were living together, he had me under guard, and now I'd be working with him and his family?

"If you're worried about Jenna you can still help with those weddings, you'd just have to give up the receptionist gig. That was only gonna be part-time anyway."

I nodded and chewed on my thumbnail.

"Think about it. We pay Trina well. She'd make close to six figures if she hit all her bonuses had she stayed."

That was a heck of a lot better than the $2 above minimum wage Jenna was paying or the $1 above minimum wage I was making at the cab company.

"Why is she leaving?"

"She thought she and her old man'd try Aberdeen. She worked in the office at the moving company in the falls but she wants to move back. He can't find work and she moved here because of her sister livin' here and they had some fall out." He shrugged, "Whatever. Who cares? Point is that there's a job there and I bet you'd excel in it."

"I don't know..."

"You wanna work?"

"Yes. I wanna work. What does *that* mean?"

"Put away those kitten claws. I'm not bein' confrontational, I'm asking. If you wanna go to school, do something else, we can talk about that. I would be down with flippin' some houses here if you wanted to get your real estate license and then we do that together like that reality show on TV, you know that couple? We could pull down some serious cake. Or, you wanna go to school full time and explore some other avenue, I'm good to support us both while you do that. Not trying to push you into getting into the motorcycle biz if that's not your gig, Kitten. Just tryin' to have a conversation here. See what I can do to help."

"Support me while I go to school full-time?" I could barely believe my ears.

"Yeah," he shrugged.

"Deacon, how many days have we been together? We aren't even at the two-week mark yet."

He smiled and put his arms around me and backed me up against the wall, "So? You don't see a future with me?"

"I didn't say that. Your clubhouse and bar just burnt down."

"I'm aware."

"And everything is absolutely fucked right now. How about we take a day at a time?"

He was talking about building us a house, about puppies, making my belly round. My god. This wasn't fast. This wasn't even warp speed. I didn't know what the heck this was.

"How's this? Take the job for now. If it's not your thing, let us know and we'll advertise for someone else and you go do somethin' else?"

"Deacon."

He waited for me to continue. I was just staring. So he continued.

"This'd solve two problems. One, we fill the position. Two, you're a stone's throw away from me during the day without being on display in the bar. I see good things in my future of packed lunches if that sandwich last night was anything to go by …"

"I'm the sandwich queen…" I informed him with not a shred of humility, "I would rock your sandwich world."

He smiled, "That sounds good to me. Long as you don't expect me to chase it with Pepsi. Done deal?"

"Wait. I don't know…"

"Talk to Trina. Let's go there now. You can learn more about the job and think about it."

"How about we do that tomorrow. I'd like to have a day to just see Gran, see Pip, play with my little brother, and hang out with you after work. Is that an option? Can we be a normal couple tonight? Or do you have more revenge to carry out tonight?"

"Shhh," he warned and lowered his head and then kissed me.

"Sorry," I whispered against his mouth, "But do you or can we have a night in Boringville? Just one?"

"Unless they plan to strike hard, they'll probably sit back now and wait for our next move after the fire. Hopin' we'll get a day or two to breathe but no guarantees. And there's no way it'd be boring to spend the whole night with you. I can think of all sorts of non-boring shit we could get up to." His eyes were lit with lust.

I chewed my bottom lip and ran my hand up his chest.

But then from the corner of my eye, I saw Mrs. Smyth and then I saw Jay. They were leaving the hospital and heading toward a parked cab.

"Oh my god." Jay's arm was in a sling and his face was black and blue.

"Hello Ella," Mrs. Smyth called out, "Hello again," she said to Deacon with a smile and Jay froze on the spot.

Mrs. Smyth clearly had no idea that Deacon was responsible for that.

Jay sat in the cab, lowering his body slowly, leaving his legs outside the vehicle. Mrs. Smyth told the driver 'one second'.

She was a big woman who walked with a cane. She bustled over, "How are you Ella?"

"I'm...oh...kay..." I was a little floored. I let go of Deacon.

She gestured at Jay, "He got jumped after the bar. Troublemakers from out of town. Ridiculous. Broken ribs, broken jaw, two broken fingers, bruises everywhere."

"Oh my god," I said again, because what else could I say.

Jay grunted with pain as he slowly turned and got his feet into the car and he didn't look our way although I knew he was very aware of our presence.

He grunted at her, probably because he couldn't speak with his jaw wired shut.

It sounded like, "Murrrrrrrm."

His face was seriously swollen. He didn't make eye contact with me.

At all.

Yikes.

"Sorry, got to go." She said, "Hope you're doing well. See you around sometime." She bustled her way over to the cab. Jay stared straight ahead as she shut the door and then got into the front passenger seat.

I stood, speechless, while the cab pulled away. The cab driver waved at me. I knew him a little, from the office. I waved back.

And then I looked up at Deacon and he had been watching me.

He swallowed and raised his eyebrows expectantly. I think he was waiting for me to lose it, say something, do something, but I just blinked at him. It felt like the color and all my energy literally drained from my body and I blew out a breath and face planted into his chest.

"He won't put those fingers on you again. He even looks at you again he loses his eyes."

I shuddered.

He tipped my chin up, "He needed to be stopped."

I squeezed my eyes shut.

"He has been stopped. You won't even see that fuckwad again. Let's go see your gran now," he told me and planted a kiss on my lips.

I was not about to dwell on Jay Smyth right now. I didn't even want to think about Deacon beating him up that badly. I didn't know how to feel about violence like that.

Jay had worked with the Jackals to ambush Deacon, to get back at me, and the idea of him picking up duct tape and rope on the way to meet me when he headed to that hotel? I didn't even wanna think about it. So for now, I'd just put it aside. Maybe I'd just put it away for forever.

GRAN WAS SMITTEN WITH Deacon. And it did cheer me up. Actually, it might be more accurate to say that she had him in her sights. So did her best friend, Alma.

We walked into the TV room just before lunch, and I'd brought a couple of pizzas, because I was sure that others would poke their head our way for a slice. Deacon paid, despite my arguing with him about the fact that

500 of his dollars were still in my wallet. We walked in, hand-in-hand, Deacon balancing three extra-large pizzas on his hip, and approached her. She'd been sitting on one of the many sofas with her friend Alma and they were watching The Price is Right, shouting out prices at the screen.

"Ooh," Alma said, "Elizabelle. Who is your young man? Izzy, look at your granddaughter's young man!"

Deacon was wearing a pair of jeans and a chocolate brown Henley with his motorcycle boots. His hair was tied in a ponytail, no leather cut, and he had shades on. He'd taken the cut off before coming inside, but he had stopped at home to get clean-shaven before we drove here and he looked completely delicious.

Deacon removed his sunglasses and tucked one arm of them into his shirt opening. Gran looked up and her eyes lit up.

"Gran, Alma, this is Deacon."

"New boyfriend?" Alma asked.

"Yes," I replied with a smile.

"Good. The old one? Not near as good-looking as this one," said Alma, "And that's saying something 'cuz he was pretty dreamy."

(More like nightmare-y, cheap, and creepy. But whatever)

Gran gave him a once over, "He's tall." She had her hair coiled in a low bun with a sparkly gold cage holding it in. She was wearing a pink cashmere sweater set and a pair of taupe slacks, pink ballet-looking slippers, a dozen bangles on each wrist, and rings on every single finger. She loved her accessories, my gran.

"He is," I agreed.

"This is why I haven't seen you."

"Sorry, Gran."

"Don't be. I wouldn't come up for air for months."

Alma giggled and they bumped shoulders.

Deacon gave them a gorgeous smile and let go of my hand to shake Gran's.

"I'll take a hug instead of a handshake, young man. Put those pizzas down and give Gran some sugar."

I laughed. Deacon smiled big, passed me the stack of boxes and gran got up and when he hugged her she pointed her toe up in the air and then she goosed him.

He jolted with surprise. Goosed!

"Gran!" I gasped.

Alma leaned forward and slapped her knee with the hilarity, then got up shakily and said, "My turn."

"Okay, Alma but keep your hands where I can see them. He's mine."

Alma hugged Deacon for way too long and then said to me, "I'll fight ya for him."

We all laughed. Me and Jenna had regularly joked that when we got old we would wreak havoc at a nursing home just like Gran and Alma. They were a hoot.

Gran gave me a thumbs up and then walked out of the room into the hallway and came back with four elderly people who all shared pizza with us as well as entertained us with their stories, many of which I'd heard before but I sat and smiled and let them tell them to me, anyway.

I was well-known at the nursing home. I was often there a few times a week, hanging out with Gran and her friends. Many of them had few visitors and lots of love and stories to share. I'd occasionally brought pets from the shelter, too, which was double-duty because it gave these people something to shower with love and gave those lonely shelter cats and dogs some human contact.

I'd come empty handed today (other than the pizza and Deacon) and a few asked me about that. I had to explain to Deacon and he looked at me warmly when I did. In fact, throughout the visit I kept catching him watch me with this sweet look on his face. It gave me tingles.

After about an hour, Deacon told me he had to get to the garage. We agreed I'd stay and he said he'd have Jesse pick me up, made me promise not to leave until Jesse did.

I kissed him goodbye and then he kissed Gran on the cheek and shook hands with everyone else as he left.

Gran was beaming a big smile at me.

"You found it," she announced.

I smiled, knowing what she meant. She and I'd had conversations since I was a small child about finding true love. She'd fallen deep with my grampa, who I hadn't met, he'd died before I was born in a work accident, but she'd never sought out anyone else. She couldn't imagine her life without him. She'd told me that some people could find love over and over but others found it once and it was so perfect, so *'it'* that they'd never look elsewhere, even if they lost it. They'd had such good from *it* that they were topped up for life. She never sought out a replacement for grampa because he'd given her so much when he was here that even though he died when she was just in her early 40's she never had the urge to love another man.

She evidently thought Deacon was my 'it'.

I smiled and shrugged, "Maybe."

She nodded, "Definitely. I know it when I see it. I see it. The way he looked at you the whole time you two were here? It."

She seemed completely herself during our visit. She wasn't confused or frazzled and I'd sort of been expecting it.

We took a walk on the grounds of the nursing home and I texted Jesse to come get me and hung out on a bench out front with Gran and Alma until he arrived. I expected them to have comments about his motorcycle and all his tattoos but he turned up in my car and was actually wearing a shirt that day. He got out and looked around as I approached.

"No motorcycle? I thought you were gonna give my gran and her friends some biker eye candy." I winked.

He looked at me like I was insane.

"What?" I was self-consciously blushing.

"If you think Deacon would let me put you on the back of my bike you're insane. And next time better wait inside."

"Oh. Right. And why? Are you not a safe driver?"

He laughed. He'd been nothing but broody and serious every time I'd seen him and I'd thought he was good looking then but when he laughed and flashed a beautiful white smile it just about knocked my socks off.

"Babe, I knew you were new to the life, I didn't realize just how green you were. Good thing I'm not so I'll let you know that if any biker, any biker at all beyond your old man asks you to get on the back of their bike, you decline. That's akin to sittin' in another man's lap. You hear?"

"Really?"

"Really." He shook his head and laughed again and then opened the car door for me.

I waved at Gran and Alma and another lady, Beatrice, who'd come out and was watching us with avid curiosity.

They all waved at me.

JESSE DROVE ME TO THE salon. He followed me inside.

Deb and Pippa were standing there; the salon was empty. They both gave Jesse a once over. He sat and picked up a magazine. Pippa bit down on the knuckle of her index finger, giving me a look. I followed her to the back room and waved Deb in.

"Listen, I don't know what's happening with Jenna. She's okay but there are some pretty wonky circumstances around things with the Doms and the Jackals and long story but Deb, is there any way you might be able to help out a few more days until I know what's happening?"

Deb nodded, "I've got nothing on this week. I can't help beyond Friday, though. I actually booked next week off. We're goin' to Vegas for a girls' trip."

"The book is light," Pippa said, "But we have a wedding Saturday."

I winced, "I'll find out what's happening."

"No way Jenna would let the bride down. She's a good customer and…"

"I'll find out what's going on."

"You run into problems for that, I know someone," Deb said.

"Good. Thanks, Deb." That was a relief. I didn't know when Jenna would be back.

A bell sounded and Deb poked her head out and then headed out to help the customer.

Pippa and I were alone.

"What the fuck?" Pippa asked.

I grabbed her forearms, "It's like a biker soap opera. There's so much and I can't get into most of it but she and Rider… things got rocky and my understanding is that he's got her at a cabin trying to salvage things. And keep her safe. Shit is heating up with a biker feud and... I can't say much else right now. Sorry. But be safe, watchful, okay?"

"I saw Rider this morning at the coffee shop..." Pippa looked confused.

"Long story." I didn't want to scare her.

She gave her head a shake in confusion.

"When she gets back, we'll have a girls night. Let it all hang out." I promised.

Pippa's eyes lit up.

THE NEXT STOP WAS HOME and the place was empty. Mom had gone out somewhere, probably because I'd texted that I'd be picking up Beau from his bus stop and taking him to the park. After a little while, that was what I did, Jesse in tow. We hung out at the park, Jesse watching us from a nearby bench.

Me and Beau were upside down goofing around on the monkey bars, having a conversation about what he'd learned at school that day and the conversation took a turn to some first-grader drama because he and his best bud both liked the same girl, and had discussed the merits of fighting over her to see who could continue to like her and as I was working on talking him out of that, I heard the roar of motorcycle pipes. Not just *a* motorcycle. It rumbled like thunder.

I righted myself, sitting on top of the dome-shaped climber, and counted 14 motorcycles pulling in to the park, all of them wearing leather cuts with the rabid dog Wyld Jackal emblem on the back. I felt absolutely sick.

As they rolled on by, driving very close to the playground equipment on the grass and slowing and every single biker giving both me *and* Jesse a mean-looking stare-down, fear prickled. But they drove on by.

Jesse got up and said, "Let's go, you two. Park time is over."

I ushered Beau into The Shitbox and got into the driver's seat.

"Uh! Move over," Jesse ordered.

He'd driven us here, too and I hadn't said anything.

"Um, it's my car, Jesse."

"I'm in charge of keeping you safe and the best way for me to do that is be in control of keepin' you safe. Move over. Now."

Bossy and broody and hot. Did he go to the same biker school as Deacon?

I scooted over.

"Belt up, bud," I told Beau but he was already buckling his booster seat.

Jesse drove us home and did a walkthrough of the house before settling on the sofa and pulling his cell phone out. He was texting.

I got a text at that same time.

"Ella, this is your Uncle Will. Need to speak to your Dad but he's not answering."

"He's not home."

"I'm popping by."

"I'm on my way out actually but I'll tell him to call you."

"Jesse, my Uncle Willie says he's coming over here." As those words were out of my mouth I heard motorcycles pulling into the driveway.

I looked out the window and there were four Jackals in the driveway. Uncle Willie was walking toward the kitchen door.

"Fuck," I said.

Jesse got in front of me, dialed the phone and said, "Wild Will plus three. Make that three top fuckers. Kitchen door. Now." and opened the door. Fearlessly. Why weren't we hiding?

He stood in front of me and looked eye level with my Uncle Willie, who was standing there with three Jackals behind him, two older, one younger. Jesse crossed his arms.

"Um, Dad's not home and I don't know when he'll be back, so..."

"We'll wait. Step aside, son."

Uncle Willie side-stepped and Jesse moved but still blocked me.

The four Jackals sat at our kitchen table.

"Got any beer, sugar?" Uncle Willie asked.

I looked to Jesse. Jesse was texting. I stepped toward the fridge. Jesse moved as he texted, blocking me. He took beers from my hands and planted them on the table. His face was like stone.

Uncle Willie looked the same as always. He was heavier and a little bit shorter than Dad. He had short hair but a long beard and the full backs of his hands were tattooed as well as full sleeves of tattoos. He had a bit of a red puffy face, the kind of face that said he drank too much and maybe ate too much salt.

The other three were typical rough-looking bikers. One was a lot younger than the other two. The other two around my Dad's age. All sets of eyes were bouncing between me and Jesse.

"Why are you here?" I asked.

"Need a conversation with my brother and your man's father."

"Then why do you have three jackals with you?"

"Why do you got a Dom prospect coverin' you?"

I folded my arms.

He shrugged and took a sip of his beer.

"Why don't I call dad and see if he'll be here soon?"

"I already texted him from the driveway and told him I'm here. He's on the way. Believe me, he'll hurry." He snickered and the other three jackals also made amused sounds.

As the word *hurry* came out of his mouth the door flew open so hard it hit the wall and it was Deacon, flanked by Deke, Spencer, Little John, and Scooter. Deacon got between me and Jesse and then demanded, "Where's Beau?"

"In the living room."

Uncle Willie let out a chuckle. "Send him in. I haven't even met this nephew of mine yet."

"Take him upstairs," Deacon ordered over his shoulder at me.

I saw Dad's truck pulling in.

"Now, Kitten."

Mom wasn't with him. Thankfully. I moved out of the room.

"Beau, let's go upstairs to your room for a bit." He was on the living room floor playing his Wii.

"No," Deacon called out, hearing me, "Your room."

"Oh, we'll grab some Bionicle stuff and build models in my room, okay, bud?"

Deacon must have wanted me near the fire escape door, the extra gun, or both.

"But you suck at building models, Lella."

"I know," I agreed, "But let's go anyway."

We grabbed his box of his Bionicle stuff from his play room and headed to the third floor.

Not ten minutes later I heard the roar of motorcycles leaving. I looked out the window and saw that it was the Jackals that left.

I wanted to fly downstairs to find out what was happening but I didn't want to ditch Beau who was telling me all about some Pokemon game that he wanted. He was the kind of kid who knew when you were 'yeah yeah'ing' him and not paying real attention. He was smart as a whip, really.

Five minutes went by and then Deacon was coming up.

"Hey 'lil man, can you go play in your room for a while? Me and your sister need to talk."

"Mom home yet?"

"Not yet."

"Alright," Beau said, "Bad guys gone?"

"Yup," Deacon said.

See, Beau was perceptive.

"Alright. Good job," Beau said and lifted his palm for a high five. Deacon gave him one. Beau grabbed his box of models and headed down the stairs, "Lella said your dad and brother are staying. I'll go make room an just heave halfa my shit to one end."

"Beau! Cussing!"

"Sorry, Lella. It's just a word." He shut my door on his way.

Deacon looked at me, "Future badass biker right there, babe." He pulled me close and kissed the tip of my nose.

I nodded, "Yep. And I see it escalating what with all these new bikerly influences around him. So what's up? What was that all about?"

"Wild Will accompanied Key, Gordino, and Mantis. Said they wanted to schedule a meeting and call a temporary treaty. Picked here 'cuz they probably figured we wouldn't put bullets in them on sight at the home of my girlfriend and Will's brother. But they wanted our attention for sure."

"Key and Gordino are from here and Mantis is from Sioux Falls?"

"Yep."

Yowza.

"Is this thing gonna come to a head and maybe be over?" I asked.

"Not likely. Not yet anyway."

I frowned.

"They got attention by doing the drive by with you in the park, which was intentional. Jesse told me about that. And then your uncle texted your Dad that either he came by his own house to talk or he could pick his daughter and son up at the Jackal clubhouse and talk there."

"What? You're kidding me."

"Nope," Deacon looked livid, "But it's over for tonight. They have two funerals and we have the funeral in the Falls for Hanson so this visit it was agreed we'd schedule a meeting for next week, calling peace until then."

"Yeah? You sure they'll keep that peace?"

"Not sure, no, but they called it. They break it no club'll ever trust their word for a temporary cease-fire again."

I let out a breath. Breathing room. Thank the Lord.

"Dad wants me to see a place that could work for our new clubhouse tomorrow. He thinks it's a good location. I think they'll only need to stay here the rest of the week. You sure that's cool?"

I nodded, "Yeah, of course. I'll go set things up for them in the playroom."

"I'll help." He followed me and we helped Beau tidy up his toys and pulled the sofa bed out. I made it up and Deacon went and got a camping air bed from the garage (We had several. We frequently had people crash here after partying in the Man Cave).

IT WAS NIGHTTIME.

We'd had dinner outside with my parents and a gaggle of bikers and cab drivers and friends. Dad had grilled burgers and brats and I whipped up a salad. Deke was back. Spence had come with Chakotay, who apparently only had a sprain, not a break, but Beau had rolled him around the yard in his Little Tykes wagon for a bit, anyway, and the pooch looked like he was eating up the attention. And a few other Doms rolled in and out over the course of the evening along with a few of dad's cabbie buddies. Everyone ate, after Beau went to bed everyone else smoked dope (except me and Deacon and Mom), and drank beers and Jack Daniels' and it turned into a bit of an excuse for people to get smashed.

I ran up to my room to use the bathroom and I was about to head back down to the party but I found Deacon coming in from the fire escape door. He took my hand and led me to my cell phone sitting on my desk, charging. He locked the fire escape door and closed the blinds.

"What?"

"Listen to the voicemail that's there."

I felt a bit of panic spike but then he smiled at me.

I lifted my phone and dialed into my voicemail while he went down the inside stairs that separated us from Beau and now his dad and brother, too, and he shut and locked that door.

"Ella, this is Dr. Lowe. I'm calling to tell you all is good with your test results. I put a rush on them for you and you're good to go. I'll call your boyfriend next and while I can't tell you about any results but your own, I can say I'm sure you'll have a fun evening. By the way, I won't tell him this. I'll just talk to him about his own results so feel free to have a little fun before you have your fun. Bye!" Obviously that said it all.

I tried not to show my real reaction. Instead, I put the phone down and closed my eyes and chewed my bottom lip.

I felt Deacon go tense at my side.

I looked at him and did a fake wince. I glanced at him.

His expression dropped.

"I, um... have to tell you something," I said.

His eyebrows knitted for a second and then he swallowed and looked at me, waiting.

"I, uh...that was Dr. Lola."

"Yeah, Kitten. She called me too."

"And you're good to...uh...go?" I chewed my lip for effect.

He blew out a breath and nodded, "Yeah, I got the all clear."

"Oh." I turned my back to him and looked at the closed window blinds. I was having trouble not giving it away.

I felt his hands on my shoulders. He gave me a reassuring squeeze.

"Baby, look at me."

I turned around to face him.

"Deacon?"

"Yeah, Kitten?" He looked so concerned. I couldn't hide it any longer. I cracked a smile.

"Wanna fuck?" I asked, the word fuck coming out breathy.

His eyebrows shot up.

"You fuckin' around? Trying to scare me?"

I laughed and put my arms around his middle, "Couldn't resist. I'm good to go, too."

His eyes narrowed and then his hands were on my hips and suddenly I was sailing through the air as he lifted me and swung me around and then he was on the bed with me across his lap.

"You are getting' such a fucking spanking for that," He yanked my yoga Capri pants down to my thighs and then walloped my ass. Hard.

"Eeeeyow!" I protested.

And then I was on my bed on my stomach and he was behind me.

"I'm not only gonna spank this little ass, I'm gonna fuckin' bite it." He leaned over and nipped my bottom. I squealed and laughed and tried to scamper away. He flipped me over onto my back, I was still tangled up in my half down yoga pants and panties. His mouth came crashing down on mine and he said, in an adorable and perfect Cookie Monster impersonation,

"Me want cookie!"

I cackled with laughter as he yanked my shirt and bra off and was taking off his chocolate brown Henley, his eyes lit with amusement.

"Never laughed so much, baby."

My giggled slowed and I nodded.

"Have so much fun with you. Even when the rest of my world is upside down."

I kicked my pants the rest of the way off and opened my legs wide, he got between them on his knees, working his belt. He leaned over, an inch from my mouth. I parted my lips, anticipating a kiss.

"I love you," he whispered against my lips.

I blinked.

He gave me a squeeze.

"I love you, too," I said and my whole body broke out into goosebumps.

He reached down and guided himself to my entrance and my eyes welled up with tears.

He ran his thumb across my cheekbone sweetly and rotated his hips as he slid in, to the root, and I hooked my ankles together and let out an 'Ah!' as he picked up pace.

My hands glided up his chest, my thumbs grazing his nipples on the way, and then my fingers tangled into his hair.

It was gentle, slow, and deep for about a minute and then he pulled out, flipped me onto my stomach, and said, "Knees up." I got to my knees. He slapped my ass, "Fuck, you're sexy." And then he grabbed both hips and slammed into me, hard.

"Holy fuck fuck fuck fuck." I'd been supporting myself on my hands but they slid with his forward motion and I landed on my elbows.

One of his arms hooked around my middle, then slid up from my belly to my jaw and he cupped it tenderly but yet possessively while he continued to plow me from behind.

I fell onto my chest and he kept going. He let go of my face and laced fingers on that hand with mine and then his other hand slid down my body and got between me and the mattress to cup me between the legs and his fingers started working magic on that bullseye.

I came spectacularly hard. Open mouthed, face smushed into the pillow.

He groaned into the back of my neck when he came.

And then he rolled off and pulled the blankets aside on his side and pulled me over and under them with him. He fixed the blankets on top of us.

"I've never said that to any guy," I admitted, the fact that I'd said it and meant it so deeply washing over me like a warm shower.

"It has been said to me," I continued, "Four guys have said it but I've never felt it so I never said it back."

"You feel it with me." He smiled and kissed me and held me tight, "No one inside you bare but me. No one getting those words? Thank fuck. That's a beautiful gift, Kitten."

I guess *he'd* said it before. I think he saw my expression change a little because he said, "I'm sorry, babe; I *have* said it."

I was about to wave him off and say it was okay but I didn't get a chance. He kept talking,

"Said it to two girls."

"Don't, it's okay," I tried to stop him, my heart squeezing in my chest.

He put his index finger to my lips to shush me and kept talking.

"One, my first girlfriend and she died before I said it so she never got to hear it. I said it at her grave after she was gone, after I beat the shit out of her stepbrother, after I got out. Two, was the girl who left the country and broke my heart. But I said it under duress, hopin' to make her stay. She'd already said it to me and when I didn't say it back 'cuz I wasn't sure I think that's what made her retreat from me. I thought saying it could make her stay. It didn't. But that's a good thing because only with you have I put it out there first and I lay it all at your feet, babe, because I won't leave things unsaid anymore. I also won't say something I don't mean. Where I am now, all I've seen and done, it's never meant as much as it does with you. I see a future with you, one I'm so fuckin' happy about. You keep telling me I'm moving too fast and even when you aren't saying it I see it in your eyes but Ella, why wait for something I want? Why deny myself that when life is so unpredictable? I don't know if Lick loved my sister but all they had, whatever it was, was in secret, under wraps because of fear. Look where that fear got them? I won't fuckin' rob myself of whatever happy I can grab onto."

"Okay," I said, tears in my eyes. I decided I wasn't going to tell him he was moving too fast any more. It all still surprised me, little ole me snagging this beautiful (inside and out) man.

But, there, in that moment, seeing that his feelings were real, feeling how real they were with his arms around me and his lips on mine, his eyes that beautiful molten amber and brown and I decided I was going to stop being afraid of it. I was going to try to give myself permission to enjoy every second of it.

"When you walked into the roadhouse that first night every eye in that place was on you. You only had eyes for me. Whenever your eyes are on me, it's like I'm the only man in the world. I like that."

"I never had a chance to play hard to get," I told him, "The minute you were interested in me, I couldn't fathom it. All I could do was keep telling myself that I didn't want to pinch myself in case I was asleep because I didn't want to wake back up in Boring and Responsible-ville without you. I love you so much, Deacon."

He rolled, took me to my back and then we made love again.

15

I woke up early. I woke up refreshed. I woke up totally and completely *in love*. I wanted to think about it with all the carefree emotion I had but we were in the middle of some very tumultuous things.

I ran into Mom in the kitchen, literally. We collided as I walked in because she was rushing around, stressed because she wanted to accompany Gran to a doctor's appointment and was running behind. I told her I'd get Beau off to school and then I cooked a huge breakfast for the house full of bikers we had.

The smell of the bacon beckoned three of the four sleeping men to the kitchen. First Dad, then Deke, then Spencer. Deacon hadn't come down.

They all ate bacon, toast, and scrambled eggs heartily while drinking coffee and I went upstairs. He was still out like a light.

I climbed up on my knees into the bed beside him and kissed his chin, his mouth, and then his hands left the pillow they were holding onto and were on my ass, pulling me against his hardness.

"Morning," I said.

"Mornin'," he kissed me, "You smell like bacon, babe."

"It's a new perfume I'm tryin'. Like it?" I teased.

"Mmm," He kissed my neck and then tongued my earlobe and flipped me onto my back.

The phone rang and at the same time, someone was knocking on the bedroom door.

I jumped up and went to the door as he went to the desk for his phone, in his boxer briefs.

He answered the phone saying, "Rider."

Spencer was at the door. "Sorry, Ella. Need to talk to him."

I opened it wider and waved up the staircase. He climbed it. I followed.

Deacon had his back to us. I looked at Spencer and his expression was grave. A chill spiked in my gut.

"Yeah man. Alright. Okay," Deacon said into the phone and then he turned to me and Spencer and I guessed by the thickness in the air that Spence was coming to tell him what Rider had just told him.

"They got Jet," Deacon said.

"What?" Spence straightened up.

"She was found in front of the gates of the Sioux Falls clubhouse this morning. Murdered." His eyes were hard, cold, and sad all at the same time. I gasped and Deacon took me into his arms and held my head against his chest.

Spencer spoke, "Ben Costner was found dead last night in a dumpster here in Aberdeen."

"Fuck," Deacon bit off.

"Who is that?" I asked Spencer.

"The Sioux Falls Jackal Kailey was dating. It was just on the news. Bet any money they're gonna try to frame us. Bet any money they used him. He was low level and a piece of shit that Mantis suspected of skimming so how gung ho they were on revenge for that fucker all makes sense now. I'd bet Kailey is one of Mantis's pieces and it was all a game. Jackal fucks."

I pulled away from Deacon and sat down on the bed, hand over my mouth. I felt sick. Poor Jet. Poor Edge.

"Where's Dad?" Deacon asked.

"Garage outside."

Deacon kissed my forehead and followed Spencer downstairs.

I SAT THERE, NUMB.

My phone rang a few minutes later. It was an unknown number.

I stared for a minute, sickened, and then I thought about Jenna so I decided I had to answer in case it was her calling me from another person's cell phone again.

"Hello?"

"Where are you?"

"Chris?"

"Where are you?" he demanded.

"Like I'm gonna tell you. You and your fucking biker gang of sick fucking thugs—-"

"No, Ella. You're safe?"

What?

"Yeah." I frowned. God, I hoped so.

"Junior there?"

"Deacon?"

"Yeah. He with you? Put him on the phone."

"What?"

"It's urgent."

I walked down my stairs to the second floor, down the next staircase to the main floor, and found Deacon, Deke, Spencer, Scooter, Little John, and my Dad in the garage. I went that way because I was, frankly, scared of walking out the fire escape not knowing who might be outside.

I looked down the driveway and saw three more Dom brothers pulling in on their motorcycles. Jesse, another Dom that I'd seen but not never been introduced to, and Bronto. If Bronto was here, who was watching Jenna?

"Deacon. It's Chris." I passed him the phone. He'd been sitting in a lawn chair and the air was heavy in that garage as all this news was being relayed.

He got up and said, "In the house, baby. I'll come in when I'm done here." Then he ground out, "What the fuck do you want?" into my phone.

I woodenly went back inside. Dad followed me and when we got inside I choked out a sob and he hugged me. He walked me up to my room and sat with me until Deacon came up.

Dad looked upset and he wasn't saying anything. He just had his arm around me and kept squeezing, kissing my forehead.

When Deacon finally came in, he said, "Pack yourself a bag, baby? Pack clothes and shit for just you for a couple days."

"What's happening?" I asked.

"Tell ya on the way. Got a few calls to make. Rob, can we chat a minute?" Dad and Deacon went out the fire escape door and left me in my room. I watched out the window and my Dad looked like he was giving

Deacon shit for something. He was talking low, pointing at Deacon aggressively.

Deacon came back in.

"What was that?" I asked.

Deacon blew out a breath.

"Give me all the truth, Deacon. I need it." I said.

"Chris told me that your uncle is cookin' up a scheme to nab you and use you for ransom."

"He what?"

"Yeah."

"Oh my god."

"My Dad know?"

"Just told him. He's also not too happy about the Jet situation."

"Who would be? It's horrible. I can't even believe it. What happened there, does anyone know?"

Deacon took my hand and sat me down on the bed,

"They found her naked, in front of the gates. Covered in blood. Words written on her body. She'd been strangled to death. Your father knows that part and wanted to make sure I had things under control to keep you safe."

I stared at him.

"Raped?" I asked.

He nodded, his expression grave.

"The truce?"

"Bullshit."

"Oh god."

"It's their funeral. Pack that bag, Ella. I'm getting you out of town, getting you safe. You and your ma and Beau are all going away for a few days. We're lockin' all the loved ones down so we can clean up this fuckin' mess without worrying about these fuckers hurting any of you."

"I—Oh shit."

"I love you. I'll keep you safe."

"I can't believe all of this." I put my hands in my hair.

"Please, Kitten. Just let me do what I was built to do. I was built to keep you safe. Tell me you trust me with the job."

"I trust you, Deacon."

"Pack a bag, baby. Then pack a separate one for your Ma and Beau so you can all leave as soon as she's back. Your dad'll go get your brother from school. Hurry."

⁂

WE WERE AT AN RV PARK not far from Mt. Rushmore in Deacon's Fifth Wheel. He drove us out, Dad following, and then they left us there with two prospects who were staying in a tent trailer right beside us and two older retired Doms from their Rapid City chapter were there as well. One of the Dom brothers owned the park. The other was apparently Axel's (Leah's man) dad. Beau was thrilled with the adventure. Mom was quiet and reflective but seemed to be taking it in stride. Deacon had kissed me long and sweet, giving me the keys to his trailer, before he and Dad left in Dad's truck to head back.

I couldn't help it when he left, I was crying. I was scared something would happen to him.

"You okay?" he asked.

"I'm scared," I told him.

"I'll be back for you in a couple days, babe. Please believe me. Someday I want you to make babies with me. Be in my arms every single night being mine for as long as we breathe. I promise I'll stop anyone who even thinks of hurting you. I will never ever make you regret taking that road away from predictable with me."

"Okay," I sniffed, "Text me lots. Let me know you're okay."

"You, too. I might not be able to answer right away but I'll text and call as much as I can. I love you, Kitten."

"Love you, too, Tiger. Go get those bad guys."

⁂

THE WEATHER WAS STILL nice enough to enjoy being at an RV park and there was plenty to keep Beau busy, which kept me busy because I tried to occupy him. We swam, he looked for frogs. There were kids around, a big park, and plenty of trails to roam and explore.

Me and Mom talked a bit about Gran and how her doctor's appointment had gone. Gran was now going on medication to slow the progress of Alzheimer's Disease. Mom was hopeful. I was realistic but tried to put on a hopeful face for Mom.

Mom knew that things were dangerous with this Jackal/ Dom feud but that night I talked to her about it in more depth, after Beau had fallen asleep in Deacon's bed. Mom was going to sleep in there with him and I was going to sleep on the sofa.

I'd texted Pippa, who was gathering help for Saturday's wedding, just in case. I told her we were in a dire situation and to please be careful around town. I was vague but I think she got the message. At first she was pissed and swearing and getting really upset about not knowing what was happening with Jenna and now I was out of town and she was left holding the ball. She texted back a few hours later and said that Deb found some help and had hooked Pippa up with a referral.

It was a long night on that sofa, alone, not sleeping beside Deacon and wondering if all was okay or not. He'd said that Doms from other charters were helping out, that a big meeting was planned for as soon as they got back from getting us away from Aberdeen. I didn't know what was next but I prayed hard that night that Deacon wouldn't get hurt, that no one on our side would. That somehow, magically, this could end without further bloodshed.

Some of those prayers were not going to be answered.

THREE DAYS HAD PASSED. Deacon sent me Good morning, I love you and Goodnight, I love you texts each of those days and we'd exchanged a few other texts and quick phone calls but hadn't spoken much. I knew, from Stoagie, our host, the guy who owned the RV park, that everything was going okay. He'd told me that Deacon and Deke had been checking in regularly and that they'd had a lot of help from Doms and from some other MCs in North Dakota, South Dakota, and in Nebraska who'd also joined in on the fight.

I wondered what was happening with Jenna. I knew that she and Rider were apart but he still had her stashed somewhere safe and I had also found out that he'd stashed her somewhere with Jojo, who had been released from the hospital so whatever was happening, at least Jenna had company. When I mentioned it to Deacon he said that after Jet was found dead, they didn't want to take any chances. It had gotten around that Lick and Jojo had been involved. Lick's funeral had happened and Deacon had gone.

When he told me he'd gone not for Hanson but for his sister (without me ever having to even say to him that he should) I felt a pang of love in my heart, knowing he was the kind of man to put his emotions aside and be there for his sister on a day that had to be very very hard. Deacon had said that Jojo and Jenna were both there and that they'd bonded but that they'd been heavily guarded and sent somewhere safe again after that.

Deacon had also told me that Blow, the VP for his chapter had finally rolled in to Aberdeen. Blow was really named Sean O'Grady and was apparently a serious badass. Along with Blow, he'd brought four other Doms who would be relocating to Aberdeen with him. He also informed me that the club had decided to develop the vacant land behind the Valentine block into a clubhouse. It was going to be built to spec and Deacon told me to expect it to be similar, though smaller in scale, to what they'd had in Sioux Falls. Deke and his boys liked the idea of gates, closing things off. The industrial part of Aberdeen where things were situated also meant they'd be in a location away from residents, where noise would be better tolerated, too.

On the evening of day three apart from Deacon, I was sitting on a lawn chair outside Deacon's fifth wheel and Mom sat down and told me, after a long chat on the phone with dad, that Dad was buying the cab company from Lloyd.

She was smiling and happy when she broke this news, news that shocked me.

"How is he going to buy it, Mom? Where is the money coming from?"

"He's buying it with the Dominion Brotherhood as investors. Silent partners."

"Dad is a cab driver. What does he know about running a company? What does he know about turning a company that's struggling into a profitable company?"

"They've got plans to make it a taxi and courier business. Adding a few vehicles for the couriering part. And he's very enthused, Ella. I've never heard him so enthusiastic about anything other than music or marijuana."

I felt like cold water ran through my veins. Was this all part of whatever Dad was doing to help bring down the Jackals? Was this about heroine and whatever other dirty drugs were involved?

Mom read my expression.

"What?" she snipped.

I shook my head, "Nothing."

"Elizabelle?"

"Nothing. I, I just hope it's not too late for the taxi business. All the Uber stuff and how bad business has been, you know."

"Why are you lying to me?" she demanded. The rarely seen but serious Momma bear. Uh oh.

A long moment of silence stretched between us. Beau bounded up to us with another little boy he'd been chumming around with for the past day. The boy and his family were Canadians, traveling the continental USA by RV. Beau was doing 'school' with the little boy, whose parents homeschooled him and his four other siblings (yes, that many of them lived on an RV).

"We're getting pock-sicles," Beau announced with his adorable mispronunciation of Popsicles and then he and the little boy dashed inside.

A minute later they dashed back out and toward the other boy's RV, which was in sight of our site.

"Elizabelle..." she said.

"There's a lot going on with the Jackals. I don't like dad involved. I don't think it's gonna get any better and him being so closely involved now and with the cab company? It just doesn't sit well. It makes me very nervous."

"Your Dad is smart. He knows what he's doing," she dismissed it.

I stared at her but didn't say anything.

"I've waited a long time for him to have his own piece of something. You don't see how hard it has been for him. Floating from one thing to another, never feeling like he's found the right thing for him. I want him to have this. I know it ain't all taxi stuff but it's a short term risk for a longer term gain. He needs this. At his age? He needs something to go right."

She got up, straightened her skirt and went inside the RV.

I sat, quietly reflecting. Mom often knew what dad's schemes were and left him to them. Maybe she knew more about whatever he was up to with Deke than I gave her credit for. The sharp look in her eyes when she'd said that to me really got me thinking.

I'd never accuse my Mom of being oblivious. She wasn't stupid. But she and Dad had an odd relationship. I guess like she was a free-range parent she was also a free-range wife -—giving him whatever leeway he wanted and needed. I'd assumed up until now that she'd been fairly oblivious regarding all of this but maybe she wasn't.

She came back out with her yoga mat and set it up on the grass and started to stretch.

"You should practice with me," she suggested without looking at me, "You're all tense."

I walked down and got onto the grass beside her and followed her lead.

⁂

MY PHONE WAS RINGING. I answered it. It was Deacon.

"Kitten," he breathed.

"Hey baby," I cooed. I'd been asleep on the sofa bed in the RV. It was 2: am.

"I'll be there beside you before you wake up in the morning," he told me.

"Okay. Yay."

"I'm on my way now. See you in about four and a half hours. Your Dad's comin', followin' with my pickup. I'm riding. Me and you are gonna hop on the hog and go on a little trip. Your parents'll bring back the RV. Got lots to tell you."

"Good stuff, I hope?"

"Yeah, babe. Mostly. Love you. See you in a few hours."

"Mostly?"

"Gonna go, get back on the road so I can get to you, babe. Just gassing up."

"Okay. Love you. Ride safe."

16

I woke up to my hair being tucked behind my ears. It was still night.

"Why aren't you in our bed?" he whispered. He was sitting beside me on the edge of the sofa bed.

"Hi," I said sleepily and put my arms around him, "Man, that smells good."

"What?"

"Leather and wind. You." I inhaled deeply behind his ear. I smiled, remembering that faint scent and how badly I wanted to just bury my noise here on him the first night I stood behind him at the Circle J.

"The reality is even better than the fantasy," I added sleepily.

"Missed you," he kissed me on the mouth, "Need to sleep a couple hours and then we'll head out."

"Where?"

"Talk then, Kitten. I'm bushed." He crawled in beside me and I heard soft voices, my parents. And then I saw Dad getting something from the fridge.

"Hi Dad," I whispered.

"Tinkerbella," he whispered and blew me a kiss and then took the bottle of water back up the two steps to where Mom and Beau were sleeping.

"Just like you," Deacon whispered against my throat as he kissed it. I nuzzled in.

"Hm?"

"Giving up the bedroom for your ma and baby bro. That bed's just the same size as this one. Just shows me even more how sweet you are." He gave me a squeeze.

"It's still dark. It hasn't been four and a half hours," I mumbled.

"I got to you as fast as I could."

I nuzzled in and fell back asleep.

I WOKE UP AGAIN AND it was bright. There was a note on the counter as I passed it on my way to the washroom.

Ella, we went for lunch to give Dad & Deacon extra time to sleep. Be back soon.

-Mom & Beau

It was 11:00. I attempted to quietly put a pot of coffee on and grabbed clothes to take into the bathroom so I could catch a shower.

When I dressed and came out, Dad was outside smoking a cigarette, drinking coffee and Deacon was putting the sofa bed away. It was a very tight squeeze when it was opened up.

I approached him and got my good morning kiss. I made it a good one.

"God, I missed you," I told him and hopped up.

He caught me by the bottom and kept me wrapped around him, but loosely, and then whispered, his voice rough, "Your dad's outside, Kitten. We need to get the fuck outta here as soon as possible so I can take you someplace I can show you how much I fucking missed you."

"Your face!" I exclaimed.

Deacon had a bit of a shiner and a bruise on his jaw. I put my hand to it and he winced and jerked his head away from my touch.

"Are you okay?"

"I'm good," he kissed me, "Just a couple bruises. Taking a shower. Pack up? We're outta here when I'm done."

"Oh. Okay."

I got outside with my Dad and my coffee while Deacon showered.

"Hellooooo Dolly, how are you?" Dad asked.

"Oh god, I thought you forgot that one."

He snickered.

He often called me baby doll or Doll and called me Dolly once in front of my friends when I was about thirteen and hadn't quite grown into my ginormous boobs yet. That led to many of the boys at school calling me Dolly

Parton or Ella Parton and sometimes Dolly Fucker (their intentional mispronunciation of Forker) off and on throughout high school.

"Figured you'd be over it by now."

"Um, not quite sure I'll ever be over *that* trauma."

"Actually I didn't think about it; it just rolled out."

I kind of loved how I never knew what Dad would call me. He'd look at me and a pet name would just roll out.

"So, I understand congratulations are in order," I said, inspecting my nails instead of making eye contact.

He didn't answer me. He pursed his lips and I think he was trying to assess my face.

"You're being careful?" I made eye contact.

"I am," He replied but did averted his eyes.

"When do you take over the cab company?" I asked.

"Next week," he answered.

"Oh. Well, I guess I should hand you my notice then. I don't think I've been officially fired yet."

"Yeah, Deacon told me things were up in the air with Lloyd and all that. You don't wanna work there? Give you as many hours on the phones as you want. As we grow there might be more challengin' stuff to do, too. I'm gonna need help in the office."

"Deke offered me a job of office manager for the bike dealership. It sounds like a good opportunity. Maybe Mom can help you out. I can show her a few things on the computer. Deanna's really great, too. Single mom. She could use full time hours."

"Heard about that job offer you got, too. Smart decision to take it."

I nodded. I'd only decided at that moment that I'd definitely take the job.

"You're takin' the job, Kitten?" Deacon was coming out, bare chested, his hair wet, wearing a pair of jeans. He was putting on a t-shirt but I noticed a big white bandage on his side, extending close to his abs.

"Yeah," I said, "What happened to your side?"

He started thumbing at his phone, "I'll tell Dad you're taking it. Good news, babe."

"Deacon, your side? What happened?"

"Just a jab. I'm good."

"A jab? A jab as in, a knife jab?" I was aghast.

"Shh, talk later," Deacon said and glanced around. The RV park seemed to be mostly quiet but everyone camped in close proximity and there were a number of walkways and pathways around us and voices *did* carry.

I took a sip of my coffee, "Might as well go pack up since I'm not getting any answers."

I went inside, pushing away my feelings about him having been 'jabbed' and made the bed Dad, Mom, and Beau had slept in and gathered my things up. My phone had been charging on the kitchen island and I noticed a text from Pippa.

> **"Sending to you both J&E. Wedding yesterday was a hoot. Here are pics. The bride was thrilled with the results so no worries."** Hope you're both safe & getting SOME in scary bikerland. Xo. Love yas."

There were a few pictures of the bridal party and they all looked amazing.

I texted Mom and asked her to come back, told her we were riding out and I wanted to say Bye before we left.

DEACON AND I WERE RIDING out. I'd been running low on clothes and had planned to wash them that day. Deacon still had some clothes in the RV but didn't bother packing after he'd changed. He told me to leave most of my stuff with my parents to be brought back home and we'd stop and get more on the road. He stuffed the few things we could fit into his saddle bags, leaving a bit of room, saying we had to grab some supplies, that we were going to a hideaway for a few days. We were on his old Harley after saying bye to my parents and little brother (who declared he was buying a Harley just as cool as Deacon's as soon as he was old enough). Dad and Mom would bring both trucks and the RV back home.

After about twenty minutes on the road, we stopped a gas station and then headed into a little coffee shop and sat with coffees and muffins.

"Where are we going, anyway?" I asked.

"We've got Little John's brother's cabin for a few days before we head home. Wanted some time with you."

"Is everything settled at home?" I asked the million-dollar question and did it softly. The place was busy but I was still in the dark about what'd happened the last few days so didn't want to ask any obvious questions.

"I wouldn't call it settled but it's definitely better."

"Yeah?" I asked.

"Yeah. Their prez in the next town? Put in the ground. Second in command? In jail for crack and meth and a few weapons charges. Four other of their guys in jail and likely won't get bonded out before they go to trial. We've taken down most of that charter. Your uncle is in hiding."

"Who stabbed you?"

"Your uncle."

"Holy shit."

"It was just a jab," he shrugged.

"Any losses on our side?" I asked.

"Nope. Spence wiped out on his bike but he's alright. I got the jab, which really isn't bad at all. Another brother who just moved to our charter with Blow got shot in the belly but he'll live."

Holy crap.

"Are cops involved at all?" I asked.

"Yeah. Obviously in the falls with what happened to Jet. There's an investigation. At home we're working closely with someone on the force."

I stared for a second.

"Lotta people want the Jackals taken out. Like I said. We have help."

"What about my cousin Chris?"

"Don't know," Deacon said, "He hasn't surfaced since that call before we brought you here. Owe that guy. Big. Word is he's out of town on an errand. Maybe he's just laying low while we clean house."

I didn't know how to feel about that. I stared into space, trying to gather my thoughts for a minute.

He balled up our garbage, got up and reached for my hand and we headed outside.

When we were where no ears could possibly hear, he said, "At this stage, we have Mantis and therefore their entire club by the balls. He makes any moves he'll go to a federal penitentiary for the rest of his life for the pile of evidence we have ready and anything happens to any of us that trigger will get pulled so I don't think any moves'll be made for now. Until he figures out how to strike back. Or we take him out. Let's just chill for a couple days and then we'll head back. I've got a couple guys covering the garage who came down to help so business is ticking over alright while we're gone."

"How long is the drive?" I asked.

"About another hour and a half. Not far over the Nebraska border. There's a little town nearby. We'll hit it on the way for supplies to get us through tonight and then we'll go back for more in the morning."

LITTLE JOHN'S BROTHER'S cabin *was* little (unlike Little John, who was very much like Little John of Robin Hood and his merry men; that was to say: HUGE). It was a tiny pretty cabin with a lake in the back yard. The cabin itself wasn't much bigger than a granny flat. It was kind of more like a Bunkie with a big porch on it but it was in a great spot and it was a bit on the rustic side but still nicely furnished.

It had a double bed in a fairly tall loft, a little living area with a sofa and recliner, a small kitchenette with fridge and stove and a sink, a wood stove, and a bathroom and that was it.

"How on earth does Little John climb up to that loft?" I asked.

Deacon looked up at it and the ladder-like staircase that dropped down from it.

"He probably doesn't. His brother ain't a big guy. Betcha when he comes he sleeps here on the couch."

We explored out back and found a screened-in gazebo plus a staircase that led to a dock down to the waterfront. A canoe was upside down on shore beside two kayaks and there was a spot at the shore for a campfire.

We'd grabbed a little bit of groceries on our way there without much room to stow them so kept things simple and had only gotten sandwich supplies and something to drink. I also got a first aid kit with bandages for Deacon's wound, and I went back inside to put them away but as soon as I got in the door I was being lifted in the air and put on the sofa on my back.

"You okay?" He asked me.

"Yeah, Are you okay? You're the one with the injuries."

"I'm better now that I have you in my field of vision again. Felt sick being that far from you, Kitten. I knew Stoagie and his boys'd keep you safe but I was still uneasy."

"I felt sick with worry about you, too. And with good reason." I gestured to the shiner and gently laid my hand on his side.

"Do you need that changed?" I asked.

"In a bit. Need you first." He threw his shirt off and started to work my jeans buttons undone.

His cell phone rang, halting his progress. He grabbed it and answered.

"Hey Rob. What's up?"

He talked to my Dad a few minutes about something to do with his trailer hitch and I took that opportunity to put things away and tidy up as well as go up to the loft and make the bed. The bed had been stripped but there was clean bedding in a small chest of drawers up there. The cabin wasn't dirty but it was a little dusty.

When he was off the phone he came up to the loft and playfully tackled me to the bed.

He pulled my shirt up and off and ravished my chest with his mouth first and then my pants came off and his mouth was on me, down there. His mouth and hands were working me urgently, like he was starved for me. I hadn't had an orgasm in a couple days, clearly, with staying in the Fifth Wheel with Mom and Beau, and so it didn't take long at all for Deacon to get me there. With his beautiful mouth, his hands holding my thighs apart.

We finished spectacularly, me doing reverse cowgirl, staring out the tall windows, that could be seen from the loft, at the lake. The leaves were a myriad of pretty fall colors, the air was crisp, and here we were. Me and my beautiful biker in a cabin on a lake, making love.

The property he was buying would be similar to this with lots of trees so the ability to be pretty spectacular at this time of year and I knew I wanted lots of windows overlooking that nice stream that ran through the property.

"What 'cha thinking about?" He asked, kissing my forehead and nestling my body against his, I felt like I was a bit like a little puzzle piece that fit perfectly. I put my hand to his abs, trying to avoid the bandage.

"Thinking about house plans. That property? Can you build the house to overlook that stream and put lots of windows in so that when we make love we can have a view like this?"

He didn't answer so I lifted my head from his shoulder and looked up to meet his eyes. He had a twinkle in them.

"You read my mind, Kitten."

I kissed his jaw. We dozed off. Me, for just a half hour or so, him for about three hours. While he slept I kept busy doing not much of anything, which was just fine by me. I explored outside (but not too far), I filed my nails and tweezed my brows in the mirror in the bathroom with tools from my little travel manicure kit, and then I'd stretched out on the sofa and re-read some of an old favorite romance novel on the Kindle app that was on my iPhone.

I read for a while and finally, I heard him stirring and he came down the ladder/stairs. He lifted his phone as I got off my butt and started making sandwiches for us.

"Dead. Fuck."

"Your phone is always dying," I remarked, "And with that big crack on your screen I think it's past time for a new one."

He fished around in the saddlebags, "Don't have a charger. Fuck. Need to use your phone, babe. Gotta check in with my dad." I had my charger but I had an iPhone, he had an Android.

My phone was lying on the couch. "Go ahead."

He lifted it and hit a few buttons and then his eyebrows shot up.

"Fuck."

"Hm?" I'd been in the kitchen making sandwiches for us. I wiped my hands.

He was staring at my phone and I could see by the way his thumb moved that he was scrolling.

What was he looking at?

Oh no. Please no. Not my Tumblr app. Not my Tumblr app that was in the same folder as my fucking Kindle app, which I was *just* looking at. I moved closer. He was. Shit, he was looking at that.

I had all my book apps in a folder. I had Apple iBooks, Kobo, and Kindle in a subfolder on the last page of my iPhone and in there I'd snuck my Tumblr app, which had a remembered login. I hadn't even been in the app in the whole time Deacon and I had been together.

"Gimme that..." I tried to snatch it from his hand. He lifted his hand up in the air so I couldn't reach it and for a second his expression was teasing but then he took another look at my screen. And then he made a face. He made a face of what looked, to me, like disgust. He scrolled a bit more and then he dropped the phone on the sofa, giving it a flick like he wanted the filthy thing out of his hand, spun on his heel, and stepped outside without another word.

I stood there, my face hot, my heart rapidly smashing against my chest, and then I lifted my phone and could see a gangbang scene on the screen, playing out. My favorites list was filled with pages that posted all kinds of dirty things and yes, plenty of dirty things like *this*.

My head rolled back and I felt shame wash over me.

I closed the app and stood there, unsure of how to proceed.

I'd had all sorts of dirty fantasies. I liked dirty porn. I got off with my Lelo between my legs looking at really dirty porn on an almost daily basis for years before Deacon. I'd been a member of a secret book club on Facebook and we all liked smutty romance novels and that's where I'd heard about the dark side of Tumblr.

It felt safe. And anonymous. It felt daring and thrilling and not at all dangerous. It also felt secret. It was a dirty little secret. My dirty little secret.

Not that I had a spank bank, I'd joked about it with the girls when I was drunk and even set one up for Jenna as a joke with all the stuff I figured she'd get off on but my dirty Tumblr account profile was secret. It didn't have my name. I even had a fake email account attached to it that I didn't use for anything else because I followed a bunch of really *really* dirty pages.

Tumblr was an open-personal blogging site and it had millions of users who posted whatever they wanted to post. I had a non-dirty Tumblr account, too, but I hadn't used it since I was 16 and used it to post poetry and pictures of my celebrity crushes.

Sometimes when I was in a certain mood, I'd look at just those really dirty images to get myself off. Other times I'd stay in my general feed which had everything from BDSM and voyeurism to dirty gang bangs. There were gang bang pages and 'victim girl' pages, Dom/sub pages, and spanking fetish pages, and while general porn wasn't something that mortified me, some of those things in there were the kinds of kink I would never want anyone to know I sometimes looked at.

I never thought about them being real. I never thought about the real danger of that stuff and how it impacted real lives because to me, it was just a fantasy. Porn studios or amateur pornographers and kinky people put stuff up on their pages and other pervy people (men and women) followed them. Some of these pages had thousands and thousands of followers. I obviously wasn't the only person out there who got off on looking at this fantastical stuff. There probably were tens of thousands of websites online catering to a variety of different fetishes.

Now, with all that had happened after Rider, Scooter, Edge, and Lick had acted out one of those fantasies? Because of that, Jet was dead. Scooter had been sodomized. Me and Jenna and Jojo had been put somewhere safe after threats that were obviously serious if Jet was now dead.

And Deacon had been wrestling with demons of what had happened to Cassie, who had been gang raped before she had her face blown off.

I felt like a heel for having that stuff on my phone. I felt like an absolutely perverted sicko. What would he think of me now? Would he be repulsed by me for my sick fantasies?

I sat down and deleted the app from my iPhone. And then I put the phone down and closed my eyes and put my hands over my face.

After a while, maybe half an hour, I heard his footsteps as he came back inside.

He walked right by me to the kitchen area and I heard the fridge open and the fizz of the root beer bottle cap being twisted off. We hadn't been able to agree between Coke or Pepsi in the store, both of us refusing to drink the other, and didn't have room on the bike to bring both so we'd settled for Root beer.

I heard him pour a glass and then I heard him pour a second glass. He put two glasses on the coffee table in front of me and then I heard him fiddling at the counter and he sat beside me and put sandwiches on the table that I'd made but abandoned.

I stared at the sandwiches and drinks and didn't say a word. My face felt hot again.

"You wanna look at me," he asked.

"No," I answered, not looking up.

"Why?"

"I'm afraid to look at you right now."

"Look at me, babe."

I did and as soon as my eyes met his I started talking fast, "I'm sorry you had to see that. That's old. I haven't even been on there to look at that app in there since..." I trailed off.

He lifted his hand, "Don't apologize. I didn't mean to open it. But I hit it by accident when I picked up the phone."

"I'm so mortified," my voice cracked.

"Don't be mortified." he said softly, gently. His eyes didn't look cold or angry.

"It was like you opening my Pandora's box. Seeing my porn stash and judging me for my perversions."

"You think I'm judging that?"

"Aren't you?"

He didn't answer.

"How could you not?" I asked.

He moistened his mouth with his tongue and then took a sip of his drink.

"I don't think I could get turned on by that kind of thing after the past two weeks, Deacon. I would've deleted it all. I just haven't even looked at it since..."

He pulled me close and kissed my forehead, "Shh, it's okay."

I started to sob. Hard. He held me close and comforted me.

"Ella, baby, don't cry. It's okay."

"No it isn't. I made you re-live that again. And after all that's happened." I was sobbing uncontrollably, "I'm sorry. I saw how you reacted when Jenna sent me that video text and I should've deleted that shit off my phone right then and there. You must think I'm sick in the head. But I haven't looked since…"

"Kitten, I don't."

"Yeah right." I wiped my eyes and took a sip of my root beer, "I do. I think I must've been sick in the head. It was just pretend. Only now it doesn't feel that way with all that's happened and with all I know about your girlfriend that died."

"I've looked at that kind of porn before, too," He said and his voice sounded funny, "It's fake. Most of it. But I came across some that was real. It's how I found out what really happened to Cassie."

"Oh my god." My heart dropped and I pulled back from his arms. This just got worse.

"98% of men look at porn, especially since the internet," he said quietly, "And of the other 2% that swear they don't look at porn, 1.5% are liars, babe. Lotsa porn out there to suit any fetish at all. And I liked looking at the *frape* stuff. Fake rape. Just like you. Got off on the idea of it. Had a fantasy, an early one, of stealing a beautiful girl and tying her up in my room, keeping her for me only. Yeah. You're not alone in getting off on that kind of thing. Until one day I recognized the girl in one of those online videos as my dead girlfriend and saw it wasn't fake. It wasn't on that app. Just online on a porn site, one a lot like YouTube."

I reached for him.

"Gimme a sec," he pulled away and I could see in his eyes that he'd one to a dark place in his mind, a place that he maybe hadn't been to in a long time.

He ran his hands through his hair and let out a long breath.

"I saw it months after she died. I bought the lies until that point. And it took a long time to go to trial. He had a good lawyer, that meth head piece of shit. So, I'd moved on. I was sad but it'd been a few months. I wasn't seeing other girls yet but I looked at porn. Of course I did, I was a fuckin' horny teenager. Stumbled upon that video and recognized her. Thought I was trapped in hell when I found that, my dick in my hand, close to bustin' a nut, watching, then realizing who it was. Knowing immediately she wasn't into it as a game; shit was real. Started doing some digging. Told Dad. Told a few of his MC brothers and they helped me track down the fuckers that did that to her. Idiots videotaped it before her face got shot off. One of 'em was haunted and admitted the whole truth. Another of them shared it once to a buddy and it went viral in the porn world from there. God knows how many guys and girls looked at that and got off on it, feelin' like it was pretend. When I went to court to answer for nearly killing her stepbrother, I had to share that video as part of my defense. It got put into evidence and it made me sick because I knew others would see her. See what those fucks did to her and know that I'd watched it being a fuckhead teenager lookin' at dirty gang rape porn with a goddamn hard on. Karma, right?"

Tears streamed down my face.

Deacon's eyes looked so filled with pain, so bleak. It had been more than ten years since this happened but it looked like he was re-living that pain, like it'd just happened.

"The Jackals? They filmed what they did to Jet. Wore hoods. Raped her. Filmed it while one of them strangled her to death. Sent it to Edge. Sent it to me. To Rider. They know about Cassie. Wrote Cassie's name on her body with black marker. Wrote Jenna's name. Wrote your name. I didn't watch it. Knew not two seconds in what they'd sent to me. Edge is un-fuckin' done. And I know how he feels. I couldn't let them near you. When your cousin said that Will was gonna grab you and he told me he knew what they'd done and told me to watch out because I'd get a video, I fuckin' freaked. Been havin' dreams of you in Jet's place."

"I'm so so s-sorry."

"Need to take a ride. Clear my head." He got up, grabbed the empty saddle bags, his keys, and then he left.

He didn't kiss me goodbye before he went. He just went.

I TEXTED RIDER'S CELL.

"Hope all is good. Tell Jenna I miss her and love her if she hasn't got her phone Pippa got the wedding taken care of yesterday and all was well. I'm texting because deacon's phone is dead and we forgot his charger where we are so if you could text your dad and tell him deacon wanted to check in, that'd be appreciated. thx"

He answered me a minute later.

"Thanks, Ella. Jenna's fine. All is good. Dad's fine and I told him Deacon and you got where you were going ok. If anything is up we'll call your cell."

It was getting dark so I went up to the bed in the loft with my phone trying to read, clear my own head, but I wasn't sleeping.

I heard him come in, finally, which was a relief because I heard him lock the door, which I hadn't locked because he hadn't taken the key to the cabin with him when he left.

He got into bed and was beside me but not touching me.

"Kitten?" He finally called, his voice soft.

"Yeah?" I felt sick to my stomach. I felt like the earth was about to fall away from me. I felt like I wanted to reach for him, to give him comfort, but I was petrified that he'd recoil. I was afraid he was too disgusted right now to be able to stomach being touched.

I worried he wouldn't be able to help but think of me in the same way he thought of those girls like Kailey who'd asked for this kind of thing. *Club fuck meat.* Would he think I was no better now even if he didn't want to think of me that way because he knew I got off on that shit?

"Didn't mean to wake you."

"I wasn't sleeping."

"Sorry I took off. That wasn't cool, you being stuck out here. Not able to call me. Forgot my phone was dead; I won't do that again. I wouldn't have gone if I thought anyone knew you were here, though. Wanted you to know that. You weren't scared alone?"

It felt like there was a cold pit in the center of my chest.

"No. It's okay. You needed space."

"I'm beat. Gonna crash. Goodnight, baby."

He still wasn't touching me.

"Goodnight." My heart hurt.

I felt his warm lips touch my temple and then softly land on my lips and I choked on a sob.

The strangling emotion in my throat? It hurt so fucking much that I was the cause of him feeling all this pain tonight.

"Hey?" He pulled me tight to him. I felt relief sweep through my body at feeling his touch. He cradled me close. I nuzzled in.

"I'm so sorry to make you re-live that," I whispered, "So very sorry."

He squeezed, "Love you, baby. Let's sleep, okay? Tomorrow we move forward. Forget this shit. I'm kinda glad you know it all. I'm sorry I had to spew all that out but it feels like a weight is off me."

"Okay."

"Ella?"

"Uh huh?"

"Forget something?"

"What?"

"You still love me too, or?"

Shit, he'd said that and I hadn't said it back.

"Oh god yes. I love you, too. Sorry. I love you so much, Deacon."

"Okay. Go to sleep, baby." He kissed me again and turned me over onto my side so that I was a little spoon and he was the big spoon. His forearm wrapped around me and rested against my chest. I put my lips to his arm and fell asleep.

When I woke up, I was alone in bed. I climbed down, put the kettle on the stove, which he'd obviously already done as it was still a bit warm, and spotted some instant coffee on the counter beside a sugar bowl and a recycled margarine tub filled with what I'd deduced be powdered coffee whitener. I looked in the fridge, which was mostly empty other than our sandwiches, which I'd wrapped and put away because we never got to eat them, and our half empty bottle of root beer as well as a brand new bottle of Pepsi.

I smiled a little; he'd bought that for me last night when he was out. I'd been lying in the loft worrying I'd fucked up beyond repair and he went out and got me a bottle of Pepsi.

I saw his phone charging on the counter with a cheap-looking fuchsia cord so guess he'd hit a convenience store on his ride.

Instant coffee with powdered whitener was not my usual morning go-juice but it'd have to do. I was wearing a pair of jersey shorts and a tank top but it was a little nippy in the air and I caught a glimpse of Deacon in a hoodie down by the water so I reached into our bag and found a white Henley of his and I put it on and tied my hair up into a bun, grabbing a ponytail holder from my purse.

He was sitting there with a fishing rod. I stepped out with two mugs. He had an old school circa 1986 ghetto blaster and White Snake was playing. He had a tackle box and an empty coffee mug by his bare feet.

"Good morning," I greeted and he gave me a little smile.

I passed him the mug.

"Thanks, Kitten. How'd you sleep?"

"Okay. You?"

"Good. First good night's sleep in days. Now that I got my bed buddy back," he winked.

I smiled and took a sip of the coffee and actually, it wasn't too bad. We were in a private little spot on the water and even if it was crisp, it was also sunny and the leaves around us were starting to turn so it was kind of beautiful.

And I felt like I was closer to him that I'd been even the day before. We'd weathered a storm.

I shivered and rubbed my hands up and down my arms.

"Cold?" he asked.

I nodded and my teeth chattered a little.

He put the fishing rod down and patted his lap. I got out of my lawn chair and put the mug down and then climbed into his lap and snuggled into his chest. I fit on his lap like it was built specifically for me. He unzipped his hoodie and then wrapped it around me and re-zipped it so that I was right against his bare chest.

"My god. We both fit with room to spare."

"Little John's. Left it behind. Fits us both."

I smiled and looked at his face and was able to pull my hands up and put them on his jaw without unzipping the hoodie we were both in. I scrubbed his stubbled jaw line with my nails. He looked yummy. He was smiling. He looked happy.

Any feelings of uncertainty were starting to melt away.

He held my head to his chest, palm over the back of it, mouth buried in my hair at the crown, his other arm wrapped protectively around me and it felt like he wanted to hold me there, inside his clothes against the warmth of his bare skin forever. I wanted him to. There was no place in the world I'd rather be.

"How long are we staying here?" I asked.

"Till tomorrow. That alright?"

"Yeah."

"Don't wanna talk about the bad shit at home the rest of the time we're here. We'll talk next steps when we get back. That cool with you?"

"Yep." Definitely, I could use a break from drama.

"What do you wanna do today?" he asked.

"This seems pretty good."

He chuckled, "Then this is what we'll do. Maybe go out for food soon? We skipped dinner last night."

"Those sandwiches I made us are still in the fridge. Want one?"

"Yeah," he said and unzipped to let me free. I went inside and he walked down off the dock onto the sandy area near the shore line and started gathering wood and built us a little fire. Because the sandwiches had been in the fridge all night I decided to fry them up like they were grilled cheese sandwiches. So then we sat and ate our fried turkey and Swiss sandwiches and drank our instant coffee and just enjoyed the peace.

It was nice.

"Kitten, you definitely rock my sandwich world," he remarked.

"You rock my world in general," I told him and that earned me another beautiful smile.

WE HUNG OUT THE REST of the morning until midafternoon when we rode into the nearby town and went to a diner and got burgers and fries. We also found a little clothing store and he bought us jeans and t-shirts. Their selection wasn't that expansive so I said I'd just hand wash our underwear and socks that night and hang them to dry.

He looked at me like I was a little bit crazy.

"You're gonna wash my underwear by hand? And my socks?"

"Yeah."

"My underwear and my socks?"

"It's not a big deal. I'll just let them soak in the sink with mine, squirt some dish soap or shampoo in, and rinse them about a dozen times and then hang them up to dry."

"We'll hit another store. You're not doin' that."

"Huh?"

"No." He was a bit pissy about it. We left the store we were at, put our stuff in saddle bags, and then he drove to the other end of town to another little clothing store and we found socks and underwear there so he bought them. He wouldn't let me pay and I had a bit of a tantrum about it.

"What the heck is this $500 you put in my wallet for, then? Is it just for decoration?"

"No. It's for if you need anything."

"Well, we needed underwear. Why didn't you let me buy the underwear with it? You were acting in there like I was spending my money but it's your money. Here, let's just put it back in your wallet."

"No."

"No?" Now I felt more than a little pissy.

"No. If you need that and you're somewhere where I'm not, which probably won't happen any time soon because it'll be a while before I'm comfortable enough to have you out of my sight, then you spend it. We're together, I pull out my wallet. You don't."

"That's stupid."

"It's how it's gonna be."

"And prehistoric and chauvinistic."

"Oh well," he shrugged.

"Deacon. Seriously."

He grabbed me and kissed me hard, kissed me quiet, essentially, "Let me take care of you right now. I need to take care of you right now. It's stupid but just give me this, okay? I don't want you to stress about money."

"I'm not gonna stress about money, Deacon. You and your dad just hired me and are going to be paying me fairly well from what I understand. I live with my parents so I don't have huge bills. So I'm fine. Not stressed…"

"When you start working, then it's different."

"Oh. So, when I start earning again you'll let me put my hand in my wallet?"

"Maybe. We'll see."

"Listen, Buster…" I poked him in the chest and he kissed me quiet again. And then he said, "Get on the bike and wrap your arms around me."

"I'm giving you shit here."

"Give me shit back at the cabin instead. Then I can spank your sassy ass."

That shut me up. I got on the bike and waited eagerly to get back to the cabin.

The mood was light that day and I thoroughly enjoyed it, despite the spatting about money, which a little more like banter than spatting.

I'd told him I wanted to get marshmallows for a campfire and some beer and suggested we just take a pizza back with us so that we could just snack on it. That wasn't going to be fun to carry on the bike so instead we decided to just grab more sandwich stuff and I decided to make us pizza subs. I bought jarred sauce, submarine buns, salami and pepperoni, and a monster bag of shredded mozzarella and we bought a bottle of Coke (since we already had Pepsi), a little bottle of rum, and a six pack of beer. We filled the saddle bags and then went back and later that night, I cooked the subs under the broiler in the tiny oven in the cabin and rocked his sandwich world yet again.

I WAS ON MY SECOND rum and Pepsi Deacon was on his second beer. And I was a little bit tipsy.

He'd checked in with his dad and all was quiet back home. I'd texted my Mom and they'd gotten home safely, too.

It seemed we had a moment to breathe and I wanted to enjoy it.

We were starting to get past enjoying the 80's glam rock mixed tape in the ghetto blaster for the bazillionth time when Deacon finally got the antenna dialed in to a station that played rock.

What you Give by Tesla came on and I got a little vaklempt by the fire because it made me think of him.

We talked about our childhoods. He talked about how he and his brothers regularly beat the snot out of one another growing up. He started talking about scars and battle wounds on his body and named the stories where they'd come from and started talking about the same things about Rider and Spence. He laughed a bunch and I had a perma-smile seeing him happy and carefree.

"Your sister doesn't seem like a tom boy. I'm surprised though. Growing up in a house with three big brothers and all those extended big brothers from the MC?"

"Naw, she's definitely a girlie girl. Was always a little bit of a princess but sweet as pie. Not spoiled at all. Not in the usual princess spoiled sense. She can throw a fit too, believe you me."

"So, not to get too heavy but why are things so rocky between you and Spencer? I mean, you seemed okay this last week or so, once the drama hit, but before that? I kind of just don't get it."

"I blame Shelly. Our mother often tried to play us against one another. Spence was spoiled until Jojo came along. She'd pit us against one another with Dad sometimes. When Jojo came she cast Spence aside and showered her attention on her baby girl and Spence started acting out. Ride ignored him, went his own way a lot, but Spence wanted attention so he started lashing out. I had a short fuse and he could get a rise outta me so he'd often try his luck. Got to a point where it seemed he'd always go gunning for me whenever he was frustrated with life. I'm no psychiatrist or anything but he knew he'd get a fight when he wanted one and then when he was done I'd let him back in again. Often got tired of his shit but kept giving him a passes because of how fucked up our mother was and how I knew it affected him. She was always playin' games. Coming home drunk and fight-in' with Dad. Not coming home at all. Buying shit for herself with the grocery money instead of food knowing one of the club women would catch word we had no food in the house or that we were again home alone while she was out gettin' tanked or high and getting off and one of the other club women, like Delia, would just turn up with groceries instead. She'd pull stunts every single time dad was out on a run for more than a day. Anyway, enough about her. I got so many stories about her ugliness it'd make your lip curl in disgust. Don't wanna get too heavy here. But Spence, when he first hit his teens he was awkward as fuck. He was skinny, got bad acne, and was pissed off at the world. Couldn't get girls to look twice at him. Got bitter about me and Ride gettin' all sorts of action."

"Things evidently turned around for him." I remarked.

Deacon's eyebrow shot up and he gave me a look that suggested he didn't like that I'd noticed that Spence was good looking.

"What? All three of you are hot. Seriously good genes. Both your parents are movie star attractive. Your sister could be a supermodel."

Deacon smiled.

"I only have eyes for you, Tiger," I winked at him and took a big sip to finish rum and coke number three.

He took a big sip and finished beer number three.

"Gonna get shitfaced and entertain me tonight?" he asked.

"Naw, I think I'm finished with the booze for tonight," I said, despite the fact that the rum and cokes were going down very smooth that night.

"Oh. No drunk sex then?" He asked.

"How about tipsy sex? I'm a little tipsy."

"I'm not anywhere near tipsy."

"Then how about you do some shots?" I suggested.

"Naw, we'll save drunk sex for another time."

"How about we play a game then?" I suggested.

"A game?" He looked intrigued for about a nanosecond and then I don't know what kind of darkness crossed his mind but I said, "I want to be your fantasy."

Okay, maybe three rum and cokes had made me a little bit daring.

"Too soon?" I asked, feeling a bit of remorse.

"No. You're safe with me. No need to ever hold back. Okay?"

I looked at him, unsure.

"Promise me, baby. No holding back."

"Let my freak flag fly? You've already seen it and it turned your stomach."

"It didn't. Be you with me, Ella. Honest. You're safe."

"Okay. Last night as awful as that scene we endured was and as bad as I felt and as sorry as I am, when you talked about having some of those fantasies too? I'm just sitting here thinking it really sucks that all those bad guys made it so that we have to feel bad about our fantasies because they twisted fantasy into something ugly."

"You *are* my fantasy already, Ella."

"Then I want you feel like you can live out your fantasies with me. I want us to be able to lay our cards on the table and be honest about what we want." I said, pouring rum into my glass and taking a shot without Pepsi. I poured another two fingers in.

I leaned forward and passed him the glass with the rum in it.

"I am. I'm yours to do with as you wish. I completely 100% trust you and I completely 100 % want you to someday, maybe not today if you're not ready but some day, take me and pretend you've stolen me and tie me to your bed and feel 100% free to use me as you wish. Because you know what?"

He downed it and then put the glass down, "What?" he wasn't looking at me. I felt a pang of fear. Maybe this was a bad idea to even bring up. But in for a penny, in for a pound, especially when I was a bit tipsy, which was equivalent to putting my filter behind a firewall.

"I want that with you. I want us to someday be able to act out our fantasies because we don't feel like anything we could do together is wrong. That's what I want from a life with someone. To be free to completely be me. When you gave me the speech about how life would be for a girl who was with you I was so excited about the freedom to be me. Even if it means I wear pearls with motorcycle boots. I like that you're okay with that."

He got up and walked down to the water and came back with a bucket of water and doused the fire.

I watched him do it. A beat later, he reached for my hand and grabbed the handle of the ghetto blaster and we walked, at a very brisk pace back inside the cabin.

He got everything shut down and then slapped my butt and said, "Get up there. Strip down to your panties. No shirt, bra off. I'll be there in a minute."

My mouth dropped open.

"Now."

I giddily hurried to the bathroom, brushed my teeth, and then went up to the loft and laid on the bed and waited.

I heard noise downstairs. I heard fiddling around and peeked over the railing and saw he was rifling through the drawers in the kitchenette until he seemed to find what he was looking for. A spool of yellow twine. He held a couple of feet's worth out and then used a kitchen knife to cut. He then pulled out another length, matched it up, and sliced through the twine.

"Get back in bed," he called up.

"Are you in bossy alpha male mode?" I called down.

"Fuckin' right," he answered

"Yippee."

He glanced up at me, "Move your sexy little ass and get that shirt and bra off."

I scampered into the bed and did what I was told.

I heard him go into the bathroom and the water was turned on. And then the water went off.

I waited and then the lights downstairs went out and I heard him climb up.

He was close.

"Hi," I said.

He turned the loft light on.

"Shh. Be quiet. You're my prisoner, don't you know? No talking."

"What if I do talk? What's my punishment, Mr. big bad biker?"

"I'll spank you," he threatened. He lifted one of my wrists and I felt the rope go around.

"Oooh. What if I like spankings?"

"Then I won't spank you. Maybe I'll punish you by teasing you. Naughty little kitten that you are."

"How?"

"By tying you up and teasing you until you're begging to come. Only maybe I won't let you come. Maybe I'll just keep bringing you to the edge, make you beg me. Then I'll spank you and keep you on that brink until you think you can't take it anymore."

"Then what?" I was panting. He was now securing my second wrist to the headboard.

"Then I fuck you. I want to take you hard, fuck you so hard that I can't go any harder. I wanna give you all I've got, every fucking bit of it until I think you can't possibly take it that hard. But then I hear your sweet voice begging me for more."

"Oh my good god," I whispered.

He kissed me over my panties right at the cleft of me.

I moaned.

"Open your legs," he ordered.

He got naked.

"Be a good girl," he warned, "Be a good girl and you'll get a reward."

"Oh yeah? You got a lollipop for me, mister?" I asked all breathy.

"I sure do," he told me.

"Please can I lick your lollipop?" I asked.

"Fuck. Yeah, Kitten. Yeah you can." He moved up.

"This is your fantasy, Deacon. It's all yours except can I ask you for just one thing?"

"Anything," he said and I believed him. My heart warmed.

"Can you feed me your cock. Stand beside me and feed it to me, holding it while you feed it to me? Not this second. Just at some point. Surprise me when. I've been dreaming about this since the first night I saw you. I jilled myself to images of that the first night I saw you."

"Fuck, Ella."

"Gentle at first and then rough okay? Even if I gag. Tease me with it. Slap me with it. Then feed it to me. Okay?"

"Fuck," he groaned and his cock was standing at attention. Serious attention was being paid.

"Okay sorry. Back into character."

"What are you gonna do to me when you're more than tipsy and totally drunk and *not* passin' out. When you want to drunk fuck? You might fuckin' kill me."

"I like it dirty. I've never had it good dirty except in my fantasies until now. I never felt safe enough. I tried a couple times to voice a couple things but it didn't... it..." I stopped talking because his face changed.

"Sorry. Forget it. We shouldn't talk about that right now, like this. Me tied up and us both naked and ready. Sorry."

"Yeah. No. We shouldn't ever talk about you being with anyone else. Especially in the middle of a game that's supposed to be about me and you. Fuck sakes, Ella."

I winced, "Fuck," I said, "God my big mouth."

He got out of the bed and leaned over and I thought for a second he was gonna untie me and say forget the whole thing. But he didn't. He got right to my face and said "Yeah, that big mouth. Let's shut it up, shall we?" He lifted his big heavy cock up slowly into his big beautiful hand, god those hands, and he moved toward me.

"Open your mouth, you naughty little kitten and show your big growly Tiger you're sorry."

My eyes bugged out, my lips parted, and Deacon guided his cock to my lips.

"Lick it."

I obeyed.

"Kiss it."

I did.

"Open wider."

He tapped it against my cheek. I squirmed.

He smirked, 'You like that?"

I nodded.

He tapped it against my mouth. I opened my mouth bigger. He took a step back and I leaned up to try to get it. I couldn't. I was restricted by my hands being tied.

"Please, Mister. I'll suck it real good."

As if he didn't have a choice in the matter, he thrust his pelvis at me and I got 2/3 of his cock right in my mouth. I slurped and sucked him deep and he hit too far back and that made me gag. I choked. He pulled back, looked at me to maybe ascertain if I was okay, and then he did it again. I gagged again. I was soaking wet between my legs. I spread them wide and lifted my pelvis up, digging my heels into the mattress, as if I was trying to get my cookie closer to him. The tip of his cock was in my mouth, his hand around the base, and he switched to his left hand and his right hand slid down my torso right between my legs and his fingertips brushed by my clit and then slid through my wetness.

I groaned. His cock went deeper and then he pulled out and slapped it against my lips.

"Fuck, Ella, you are so fucking amazing."

"Am I a good girl? Do I suck it good?"

"Oh yeah," he walked down to the bottom of the bed and got between my knees and spread my legs wide and looked down.

"You're mine, aren't you?" he asked.

I nodded, "Yes. Yes, I am 100% yours."

"I can fuck you any way I want to," he said, looking at my pussy. Rubbing his thumb around and around my clit. I rocked against his thumb.

"Yes. Yes, you can. I'm tied up and I can't go anywhere. I'm here for as long as you want me."

"What if that's forever?" He asked.

"Then I'm the luckiest girl in the world."

His lips crashed down onto mine and then his cock slid into me. He tweaked my left nipple as he rotated his hips, hitting deep inside. I wanted to put my arms around him, to hold him to me, but that wasn't an option. I felt the sensations completely take over.

"This is so beautiful, Tiger. I could stay here forever."

"Mm. Yeah, baby. Me too. Could spend my life inside you like this." He bit my shoulder and his hand roughly went under my bottom and he ground me against him as he continued sliding in and out of me.

I moaned and wrapped my legs around him.

"You can take it when I fuck you hard?"

"Yeah, give it to me hard. As hard as you want to. As hard as you can."

"My sweet Ella. Fuck, forever baby. You and me."

"Yeah." He was going harder. A vein was popping in his forehead a little and his eyes were on fire.

"Gonna put babies in you," he groaned.

"Yeah."

"Make your belly big and round, grow my sons and daughters in you. Build you a house. Get you a dog. Make a life with you."

I nodded, sobbing, and coming. Coming hard.

He yanked back and then went from his cock inside me to directly into my mouth and he started fucking my face. Roughly. It was like he came unhinged, lost control. And it was beautiful. I tasted him and me. I tasted us. I choked as he came down my throat. He didn't stop until every drop streamed down my throat.

"Fuuuuuuck." He grunted as he finished and then he pulled away, untied my wrists and then wrapped me up in his arms.

He looked at my face and grabbed a t-shirt as it was the only thing probably in arm's reach and then wiped my eyes, which were all wet and maybe mascara streaked.

"Baby?" he asked.

I choked on a sob. I was crying.

"Oh fuck, Ella. No."

The alarm on his face. Oh no.

"No, Deacon, that was beautiful. I'm just emotional. Sometimes when we have a moment that's beautiful my emotion just leaks right out of my eyes." I held him tight and got myself under control.

"Oh shit. Fuck. I thought... I thought I went too far."

"No. I want you to be able to let go with me. I'm so glad you did."

"Fuck, I love you."

"I love you, too."

" Need a drink, anything?" he asked.

"No. I'm good."

"Seeing that this is what you crave, what gets your motor running? It confirms what I suspected."

"What's that?"

"That me coming to Aberdeen when I really wasn't sure at first, that it was meant to happen. Me being there to save your ass? It was fate. I saved you from that junkie robbing the circle J. I saved you from that douchebag. I don't give a fuck. That fucker had it twisted up when it came to you. If I hadn't been around, he'd have kept sniffing around until he got you back or it would've ended badly if you kept refusing. I know it."

I nodded, not wanting to think about Jay.

"And you, kitten? You save me. You save me from the lonely place my heart was shrouded with before I met you." He kissed my temple, "I was in pain after Cassie died. Fuckin' fed up with bullshit by the time psycho Emma cheated and then when Lucy left I was so fuckin' over it I never thought I'd go down this road again. I'd become too intense, as you called me. I tried to guard myself after that. But with you. I want you to know me. Me.

The minute I saw you I was absolutely consumed with the need to protect you. At all costs. My brother called me smothering because I have always been protective, with Emma, with Lucy, with other women I'd dated before I stopped going back for seconds and thirds. But my need to protect? It has never been this strong. Because you're the one."

"It." I told him.

"Hm?"

"I'm it for you. You're it for me."

"Yeah."

"My gran told me that my grampa died when she was 42. She was young and beautiful. You should see the pictures of her. I mean, she was a knockout. She looked like a movie star. After he died, she could've married again. She could have her pick of eligible men. But she said the love she had from him, it topped her up for life. She never wanted anyone else. And she didn't sit around and pine for him. She missed him, like crazy, but she lived a good life. She focused on my Mom. Did lots of charity work. Worked hard. Lived hard. She says some people can find love over and over again. Some people never find it. But some people find it. It. The one love that's all they think they'll ever need. I'm pretty sure I found it with you, Deacon."

"You did. You really fuckin' did. I promise you that. I'm not gonna burn out my flame though and leave you a young hot widow. I'm gonna make babies with you and we're gonna sit around one day with a whole lot of grandbabies, too. You'll make sandwiches that rock their world, or bake or something. You bake?"

"A little."

"Okay then you'll bake, too."

I giggled.

"And you'll spend your life giving our kids, me, our grandkids, Beau's kids, everyone around you a whole lot of love and joy. I know this about you. You give at that shelter, that old folks home, to your folks, to Beau, to me. As soon as the old ladies at the clubhouse met you, you won them over. Offering to help out. Asking my dad if he'd eaten, if he'd slept enough. That's the kind of woman with staying power with a biker, not because he leaches from her and takes from her but because they look after one another."

I looked up at his face, feeling joy well up within me.

"So you know you're an amazing catch?" he asked.

"I do! I'm also amazing in bed," I gloated.

"That, you are."

"I knew if I found someone amazing I could be good at this sex stuff, too."

He laughed. And then he got out of bed.

"Where are you goin'?" I asked.

"I'm getting us a Coke." He said.

"No Coke. Pepsi," I said in my best impression of John Belushi in that SNL skit.

He laughed at me and went down the steps and got me a Pepsi and him a Coke.

And then I giggled some more as we kept going to and fro from silly to sweet. We tasted each other's drinks and still vowed allegiance to our favorite, and then we fell asleep.

17

A week had gone by. We were home and things were quiet and fairly normal, if guarded. They weren't boring by any stretch of the imagination.

The day after we got home, Jenna also got home. And she was absolutely livid.

With the world.

Deacon mentioned to me that Rider had said they'd just gotten home but that he still had a prospect on Jenna at all times. And Jenna wasn't happy about it. He'd switched from Bronto to Scott because Jenna had worn Bronto out. Deacon told me Bronto was on the verge of a nervous breakdown, Jenna was giving him so much shit.

I also was not allowed to be alone yet. I was okay with this. The prospects were good guys. Jesse was super serious and broody but he occasionally made me laugh and I'd work hard to get a smile out of him because he was seriously hot when he did let you see it. Not that I had the hots for him or anything. No way would I ever jeopardize what Deacon and I had. Bronto and Scooter both joked with me and it felt like hanging out with a buddy for the most part.

The remaining Ipswich Jackals were being quiet but we had no idea where Uncle Willie was and I hadn't heard anything more about Chris. The Wyld Jackals around here seemed to be minding their own business. For now.

Things in Sioux Falls were also apparently quiet. Edge had gone underground, no one knew where he was. He and Deacon were tight so he'd answered Deacon's short three to five-word check-in texts with 'Yep' or "OK".

He'd disappeared after Jet's quiet funeral, which no one but Edge, Rudy, and Delia from the Dom MC attended because Edge wanted it that way. Her parents were apparently really conservative and really really unhappy about Edge and Jet's relationship prior to what'd happened. I could only imagine what the vibe was like after her violent death.

And no one yet knew exactly who was responsible for Jet's death and I suspected that's what Edge was working on. Deacon also suspected it was an order direct from Mantis. Deacon and his brothers had driven one morning up to Sioux Falls to talk to their mother about Mantis. I wasn't privy to the conversations they had about the discussion but Deacon had told me that she was involved with him and they wanted to either get information or get her to stop.

Apparently the intervention had not gone well, particularly since Rider had spirited Jojo away somewhere safe and left Shelly alone. Deke was talking about selling the house and that was also apparently not going over well. Jojo had decided to go to New York to stay with a best friend who was in school there. They had her in Aberdeen until things were deemed safe enough for her to go there.

Finding out Jenna was home the day after we got home, I got Deacon to drive me to Jenna's apartment. When I got to the door, it opened and Scooter greeted us.

He made a face.

"Hey Scott. How's things?" I asked.

He shook his head and opened the door wide. "She's hell on wheels," he muttered.

I walked through to find Jenna in her bedroom, slamming things.

Her gorgeous long dark wavy hair was moving with her jerky movements. Her blue eyes were ablaze.

She spun around and glared at me and was breathless.

"Hey," I started. She held her hand up to halt me, "I've gotta get to the salon. If you have anything to say to me, do it there while I open up. I need a minute to get dressed."

I stepped backwards a foot and she shut the door in my face.

She had been naked in front of me a million times. She was a total exhibitionist with me. We used to joke that if she'd grown up in my house instead of with her uber-conservative parents, she probably would've ended up a stripper. She was constantly stepping over my own personal bubble boundaries. For her to kick me out of her room was about way more than privacy.

Right now she obviously wanted space. We hadn't seen each other and she hadn't hugged me, barely looked at me, and instead asked me to give her privacy.

I turned around and saw Deacon standing there with Scooter. I felt my shoulders slump.

Deacon made a face and put an arm around me, "Let's go outside and wait for her to open."

"Where's Rider?" I asked Scooter.

"He left for the garage. He slept on her couch last night. I slept on the floor. She locked him out of the bedroom."

"So they aren't, uh, really together?" I asked.

"I think to him they are; to her they aren't."

I winced and looked at Deacon with concern.

He led me outside to the back parking lot behind Jenna's salon while Scooter waited for Jenna.

Rider was there, sitting on his motorcycle, texting or something.

I approached.

"What's happening?"

He looked at me curiously, "With what?"

"With Jenna." My reply was kind of laced with *Um duh!*

Deacon's hand came down on the back of my neck and it was warm and comforting but a little bit of a squeeze might have been to calm me down.

"She looks like a wreck!" I exclaimed after he stared at me blankly.

"I'm keeping her safe."

"And what about her heart? How's her heart, Ride?"

Jenna came down the back stairs, her eyes shooting ice daggers at him. It was as if I wasn't even standing there.

"I'm working on winning it," he said softly, looking at her.

She heard us.

"Don't bet on that," she said with a glare.

He gave her a look of promise, "Oh, I *am* betting on it. In fact, I'll bet my Harley." He gave a chin jerk and I looked over his shoulder and saw that it was aimed at Scott.

Rider and Scott exchanged looks and then Rider's eyes were back on Jenna. He put a pair of shades on, started up his bike, and pulled out of sight.

She stood there, looking defeated. But then she straightened up and walked around the building, through the alley, and I followed her to the front of the salon where she unlocked and opened the door.

Deacon kissed me goodbye, "Gotta get to the garage. Text when you're ready and I'll get you picked up." He got onto his bike, which was parked out front, and gave Scott a nod.

"Babysitting again, Scott?" I asked with a smile.

Scott opened the door and waved me inside with a grin.

I found Jenna in the utility room hitting the button on the Keurig.

"Coffee?" she asked.

"Yeah. And girl talk. What time is your first appointment?"

"Not for an hour," she said. She wasn't looking at me.

"Good." We needed girl talk time. Big time. I shut the door, leaving Scott outside the utility room and giving us some privacy.

We'd had girl talk time and updated one another on all our ordeals throughout the next hour. There were some tears. And I hadn't seen Jenna cry more than maybe two or three times since I'd known her and I'd known her 18 years and had seen her nearly every single day. I had to say, Rider sure had his work cut out for him.

It *was* a long story. A wild one. It could be made into a book! I only hoped it would have a happy ending for Jenna and for Rider.

IT WAS NOW A WEEK AFTER being back at home and everyone was still watching things closely. I was being brought to the dealership by Bronto, who was driving his car, a little red VW bug, which made me laugh because he was such a big guy getting into the little car and I was a little girl who had a really big car.

I'd gotten Deacon to drop me off at Jenna's salon where I got some waxing done by Pippa and picked up my new flat iron that I bought from Jenna. She wanted to give me one but since I wasn't going to do the reception gig I decided I'd just buy it.

I'd made some money, too, because I helped them with a wedding on the weekend and it had been fun to play dress up with helping all the bridesmaids and the beautiful bride feel even more beautiful. There were two more weddings I was helping with, because I'd committed to it, and then I was off the hook. But I didn't know if I wanted to be. It was a laugh. I'd told Jenna that she could use me if she needed to but she had help from the girl Lulu, that Debbie had hooked Pippa up with while we were all in our 'safe houses'. Lulu was a hoot and she was fitting well within our tribe. She was Dr. Lola's younger sister. Jenna was still not completely herself. Very reserved and withdrawn but I was hoping she'd come around. Rider was still showing up at her apartment nightly as if they were together and she still had around the clock security detail.

"This car is adorable. I want one. Trade you for a big ugly green Impala?" I tried.

Bronto laughed.

I hadn't driven my shit box of car in a while. I was being taxied around on the back of Deacon's bike, in his pickup truck, or in a car or truck of various club members who were appointed Ella-sitters.

I was going to the dealership for some more training with Trina, who was only going to be working two more days before heading back to Sioux Falls. She was being nice to me. I actually liked her. She was rough around the edges but she was a hard worker and had set things up nicely for the businesses so I wouldn't need to make all that many changes.

Bronto and me got stuck in traffic. There seemed to be a serious traffic jam, which was odd because it was around eleven o'clock in the morning, which wasn't usually a busy time in this part of the city. When it cleared out a bit I saw that it looked like there was a barricade of motorcycles only letting cars through one at a time.

What on earth?

Bronto got out of the car to look ahead and figure out what was happening up there and that was when it happened.

He looked at me and said, "Wyld Jackals."

I heard a loud bang and Bronto fell forward.

I gasped as he hit the ground. He'd been shot in the backside. He tried to scramble to his feet but a Wyld Jackal, one that had been in my kitchen. Gordino, maybe? Key? Wait. Key was dead. This must be Gordino, and he was getting into the driver's seat.

Another shot rang out and it hit Bronto in the arm and then the biker leaned into Bronto's little VW bug and smiled with an ugliness that made acid churn in my gut. He approached the car, eyes on me. I reached for the handle to my door and saw my Uncle Willie standing there, blocking me, a sickening smile on his face, a gun in his hand, pointed in Bronto's direction.

He got into the back seat and the barrel of the gun dug into the back of my neck,

"Hey sugar. Gordino clear. Let's go."

The biker who was driving pulled a U-turn, narrowly missing Bronto, who looked conscious, thank god, and spun around.

I tried to inconspicuously feel for my iPhone in my front pocket of my army utility jacket. *Good. It was there.* I placed my hand over it on the outside and left it there. In a minute I was going to try to turn the volume down so I could hopefully hang onto my phone without it ringing.

While being Ella-sat by Scott the other day, I'd gotten him to take me into the Best Buy and I'd bought Deacon an iPhone as a treat with money from a combination of my wedding money and the stash he'd put in my wallet. He'd rolled his eyes at me.

"Kitten, Coke and Android. Not iPhone and Pepsi."

"Psh!" I waved at him and then when I'd shown him a feature called Find Friends and we'd added one another so he agreed he'd keep the iPhone. I laughed and told him I'd start slipping him Pepsi and get him weaned off that awful Coke eventually.

"Don't push your luck," He'd warned and swatted my behind.

The Find Friends app had been fairly accurate the times I'd used it so far. I only hoped I could keep my phone so he could find me wherever they took me. I also hoped and prayed that my Uncle Willie hadn't decided that it'd be okay, despite my being his blood relative, to use me as a lesson to the Dominion Brotherhood in the same way that Jet had been used.

I was quiet as we left Aberdeen and started heading down the road toward Ipswich.

I thought back to a conversation I'd had with my Dad earlier in the week while I helped him make some sense of some of the paperwork in Lloyd's office.

"What did Uncle Willie threaten you with?" I'd asked.

"Don't wanna talk about this shit with you, Elizabelle," he'd muttered, rifling through papers.

"Dad, please. I need to know what I'm up against here. He's out there somewhere still. Have you filled Deke in at least?"

"Oh yeah, he knows. So does Deacon."

"Tell me, please. Or I'll have to ask Deacon and you don't want me and the future potential son-in-law of your dreams to have a fall out, do you?"

Dad slammed the filing cabinet drawer shut.

"He was stayin' here with us when you were a kid for a while, when your Aunt Jolene threw him out. Remember?"

"Yeah."

"He wound up throwin' her out and keeping the boys but for a few days he was here. Till I found out that a) she was splittin' with him because she found kiddie porn in his garage. And b) I didn't like the way he was lookin' at you. Your mom saw him watching you sleeping."

I'd cringed.

"Fuckin' Jackals are into all sorts of dirty shit. And my brother eluded to me getting you away from the Doms or he couldn't stop you from getting gang raped. Said he might even watch. And it'd be my fuckin' fault if that happened to you. These sons of bitches move all sorts of shit for the mafia including for the slave trade, are dirty fuckers *in* the skin trade. Stash and then move the women around so that they can be shipped to places like Bangkok and Mexico, other places besides. They work with mobsters out of NYC on all sorts of dirty shit. Got caught pissin' in the yard of a connected family out in Portland and even those guys're workin' with MC charters to help bring these fuckers down. The major players and dirty fuckers all have to be taken out and the few Jackal chapters left when all this is done will be patched over by whichever club is the one close by workin' on the clean-up. A lot of people are involved in this effort. I know you think I fucked up by getting involved in shit but I'm a good guy here, working on the side of the white hats, okay baby doll?"

"Okay," I'd said, sort of shocked at all of it.

I brought it up to Deacon in bed that night, when we were talking about our day.

He'd told me that the Wyld Jackals had pissed off every single decent MC in at least a six state radius. He told me Uncle Willie was doing a good job of staying off radar. He said it was suspected that he was hiding out in Saskatchewan with a few other higher level Jackals.

But evidently, if he'd been in Saskatchewan, he was back. And Gordino was no longer in jail and it seemed he and Uncle Willie were going to use me to make some sort of a point.

THEY TOOK ME TO A LITTLE run down house in the country. It wasn't far out of town, not even all the way to Ipswich. This wasn't the Jackals clubhouse. But this was clearly a biker hangout. I was inside a dirty bedroom, sitting on the edge of someone's unmade bed. The room stank like cigarettes and stale beer. I'd been ushered into the room and left by myself for a good half an hour before Uncle Willie came in. On my way in I'd seen three Jackals were outside and they were armed with guns. Soon after I was behind that closed door I'd heard a whole lot more motorcycles and voices.

"What's happening here, Uncle Willie?" I finally spoke when he'd put a can of Coke in in my hand and cracked open a beer for himself.

"Want this over, girl. Don't want no bullshit. Need to come to an agreement with them."

"Oh."

"Got a phone on you? Hand it over."

I took my phone out of my pocket and saw a missed call from Deacon on my lock screen. I handed it to him.

"How do I call him?"

I leaned over and showed him.

"Valentine. It's Will Forker. Your dad, Gord, me, and Mantis need to meet. I'll let you know where. It'll be tonight. No, she's alright. No harm'll come to her, provided everyone plays nice. But we're heavily guarded and armed and I love my little niece but these guys won't hesitate to use her to make you boys cooperate, y'hear me? Keep that in yer mind before you try to move in." He ended the call.

"How you turn this piece of shit off?"

"Just hit the button on the top quick," I lied. He did that and it made the click sound and the screen went dark so he seemed satisfied. He stuffed it in his pocket.

God, I hoped Deacon checked for my location. I also hoped he'd be careful if he had figured out where I was.

Uncle Willie stepped out and when he came back in what seemed like a long while later, there was a bottle of whiskey in his hand.

"God you grew up to be such a pretty little thing," he said, wiping booze off his chin.

"Can I use the bathroom?" I asked.

"Sure. But no fuckin' around, okay, girl? Your uncle here is keepin' you safe. The boys out there are rabid for another piece of Dom ass. I've told them you're off limits but if you don't be good, they won't listen. Y'hear?"

Bile rose in my throat. I nodded and followed him out of the room.

"Just takin' her to the can," he waved and took another swig from his bottle.

I glanced into the living area and there were a bunch of Jackal bikers sitting around, standing around. I could see out the big picture window that there were another half a dozen outside on the lawn.

A Jackal standing by the window looked at me, licked his lips, and grabbed his crotch and adjusted it. I felt sick. I averted my gaze and went into the washroom.

I was trembling with fear. I used the facilities in the filthy bathroom, splashed water on my face, looking at myself in the mirror. I looked afraid, too.

I took a deep breath and stepped back out and Uncle Willie led me back into that bedroom and shut the door with us in there. I sat back on the bed.

He leaned against the door and was staring at me, swigging from that bottle. He was hammered. He sucked on his teeth and eyed me and took a step toward the bed.

There was a knock on the door. "Fuck off!" he hollered and scowled at it.

"Dad. Open up!"

Chris. Holy shit. How would he factor into all of this?

Uncle Willie opened the door.

"Hey, Dad. What's up?" Chris glanced at me and shut the door.

"Just havin' a conversation," Uncle Willie replied, "How'd you know about this? Thought you were in Bismarck."

"We should take her somewhere else," Chris said, "Those fuckers are foamin' at the mouth."

"Naw, she's alright here." Uncle Willie took another swig of his drink and then adjusted himself at the crotch. Seriously gross. Chris looked down at his dad and then his face filled with disgust.

"Serious, Dad. These fuckers are talkin'. Don't like what I'm hearing. I think we gotta move her somewhere else. I was just talkin' to Mantis and if you back me up he'll agree. Me and Brute should take her to Locust's hideaway."

"That's a good spot," Uncle Willie agreed, takin' his eyes off me for a minute. I'm a comin', too."

Chris made a face, glanced at me, and then said. "Let's go run it all by Mantis and Gord. Back me up."

"I will," Uncle Willie said, teetering a bit as he walked out. Chris glanced over his shoulder at me and mouthed, "Just hang on."

I swallowed hard. Was he going to save me from this? He must be trying to do that. All that he'd done since this started ran through my head like it was on a movie reel. My heart was hammering rapidly and I was praying.

A few minutes later Chris was back with a dark pillowcase.

"Gotta hood ya, Lizzie."

I nodded.

"No backtalk? Whadaya know," he laughed.

I was shaking. He threw a pillowcase over my head but I caught a look in his eyes first like maybe he was trying to reassure me. He lifted me up and took me out of there.

I heard voices and was actually glad for the pillowcase.

We were on the move, inside a moving vehicle. I was on the floor of the vehicle, sitting with my knees up against my chest. The pillowcase still over my head.

"I get five minutes alone with her before you fuckers. I've been waitin' for my turn for near on 20 years."

Oh my god was that Uncle Willie? He'd been slurring. He was definitely more than hammered. He was completely shitfaced.

I was going to puke right inside this dark hood.

"Dad, fuck."

"No difference, son. Pussy's pussy. Got a rubber. It ain't like I'm gonna get her pregnant and have two headed nephew sons. They're not family anymore they fuck us over for Doms."

There was more laughter and I didn't know how many people were in the vehicle with us.

"You sure you don't want your shot? She's a sweet little thing." Another voice said.

"No, I'll just man the camera. Too dangerous. I got potent swimmers. So potent they'll rip their way through the rubber." Chris said. There was more laughter.

"You get rid of this little bitch's phone?" Someone asked, "in case they can trace where we're at with the cops?"

"Like they'll call the cops..."

"Shut it off. No worries." I heard a smashing sound of breaking glass.

"Fuck, that's littering, man."

"Bottle's empty. What good is it to me?" That was Uncle Willie.

All of a sudden, my body lurched forward as the vehicle came to a stop and I heard a grunt, then two gun shots in quick succession and then another one with the sound of a door opening and then a bunch of grunts and cussing.

"The fuck, boy?" and then another thud. I then had the sensation of us moving faster and there was wind hitting me, making the pillowcase flap.

"Take that hood off, Ella!" that was Chris.

I yanked it and saw that it was just he and I. I was in the back of a minivan with no seats in it and he was driving. The side door was wide open and it was windy out.

"Shut the door. Careful!"

I struggled with how fast we were going with not falling out but I got the sliding door shut.

"Call him. Three stars and then DVJ in my contact list."

He threw his phone at me.

I fumbled and then found Deacon's number and called.

"Fork! Where the fuck is she?" Deacon demanded, "She's on the move."

"Baby. It's me. Chris rescued me."

Chris called back over his shoulder, "Tell him to meet me where he and I met at last time. Fast. We're three minutes out. And on the road on the way, if Edge wants Mantis, Mantis is likely on the side of the road with my father and two dead Jackals. I left Mantis alive for Edge. He's been shot in the leg, should slow 'im down."

"I heard, Ella. Be right there, baby. We're not far behind you."

"Okay. He heard." I said and put Chris's phone down and climbed into the passenger seat and got the seatbelt buckled up and then I started to weep with relief.

Chris reached up into the visor and passed me a little package of Kleenex.

"You're not a douchebag," I informed him.

He let out a big barking laugh, "That might've been the nicest thing you've ever said to me, Lezzy-belle."

THREE MINUTES LATER, Chris and I were behind an abandoned warehouse. Three minutes after that, I was in Deacon's arms.

I found out that Bronto was in the hospital. Mantis and Uncle Willie? I wasn't sure what had happened to them but suspected that Edge, Deacon, and other Doms knew. Or Edge would know soon.

As a biker's girlfriend there were some things that I just didn't need to know.

But what I *did* know? I knew I was in Deacon's arms and I knew I was safe. Deacon and I went home, Chris disappeared, and a bunch of other

Doms and cops were apparently headed to the place all those other Jackals were sitting ducks at.

I also knew, through watching Deacon and the other Dom brothers who had rolled in and all took turns shaking Chris's hand before he took off, that my cousin Chris was not down with the mantra of the Wyld Jackals motorcycle club and hadn't been for a good long time. I had a feeling he wouldn't mind if the Dominion Brotherhood patched over his charter of the Wyld Jackals.

Epilogue
Seven years later

(Includes information about future books. Some have criticized this, but others have simply gotten excited about finding out how several couples found their way)

It was my thirtieth birthday and I was getting ready to close the dealership for the day. Business was booming and we now had three dealership / garage combos in South Dakota.

We were having a party at the clubhouse for my birthday and everyone was expected to be there. It'd start out as a family party and transition to a couples' party as a few people were taking the kids home or to sleepovers and grandparents' houses. And then after the couples' party, it'd be a Deacon & Ella party.

YUM.

Deke and Laura (who were now happily married, by the way. That was a long story [but a good one]) were taking our boys for the night so that I could tie one on, which I didn't do too often, but it was still highly entertaining, apparently, when I did.

I stared at the framed photo on my desk, at the sight of Deacon's big strong beautiful hand on my rounded belly, my wedding ring on his finger where the skull ring with the amber stones used to sit. It sent a surge of emotions through me.

That picture was five years ago, when we'd done a pregnancy photo shoot. I remembered that day well, two years to the day after we'd first met and a whole lot had happened since then. We'd gotten married in a lovely outdoor Fall wedding the year after we met and started working on our family not long after. We'd had three more babies after that first baby boy. All boys. My own little bevy of baby biker wannabes.

Deacon couldn't seem to stop getting me pregnant. Not that I'd complained. I never tried to stop it from happening. He was a phenomenal daddy. And my little brother Beau was an awesome uncle who spent a lot of time at our place hanging out with his nephews who adored him.

At least two and maybe even all four of our boys would undoubtedly be driving motorcycles if not helping run the family business. I had just stopped breastfeeding our youngest, hence the plan to tie one on, and wasn't sure if I'd go on the pill or maybe see if baby #5 was in the cards.

Maybe this time it would be a baby girl. I didn't know if I got blessed with a girl if she'd be a tomboy with four big brothers or just as sweet and girlie as her Auntie Jojo.

In the past seven years, we'd watched a lot of our friends fall in and out of love, saw too many deaths, were lucky enough to see plenty of births, and we also endured a whole lot of heartache. But there were many heartwarming moments, too.

And Jenna had lost in the bet with Rider and he kept his Harley. But then a few weeks later, she'd won it from him when he threw the keys to it in the kitty during one of the famous Forker Family and Friends Rummoli nights. Those two were happily married and madly in love. Jenna was my sister-in-law. I often called her my sister outlaw, though. She was still wild and crazy.

Deacon, his blood brothers, and several of his MC brothers had all taken their own journeys toward happily ever after in the past few years.

Some had truly found *it* and I had a tribe of great women in our chapter of The Dominion Brotherhood MC who Edge was now president of. He'd relocated here just after Jet died, after he got his revenge against Mantis. He wanted away from bad memories but did not want away from his MC, his brothers. He'd changed a lot, too. He was now happily married to our family doctor, Dr. Lola. That was another good story. Deacon wasn't even the VP. Rider was. Deacon loved the biker life and could've been president but he preferred instead to spend as much of his time as he could with me and our boys.

My cousin Chris was now President of the Doms in another South Dakota chapter. Yes, Doms. That was yep... yet another long story. And a pretty good one, too. He was happily married. To Joelle Valentine Forker.

We laughed about me being Ella Forker Valentine and her being Joelle Valentine Forker. I hated the Forker so stopped using it. Jojo loved it, though. She loved my cousin. They'd had two little girls together.

We, as a collective group of bikers and their babes, all laughed together, played together, and shared our lives with one another.

Life had been an amazingly beautiful ride so far and it was far from over. I didn't have any signs of a seven-year itch and I didn't think my beautiful biker hubby did, either. I still found myself watching him sometimes, still astounded he was actually mine. More than once he'd told me that he did the same thing when he looked at me. Little ole me. Cutesy Ella Forker, who was now Ella Valentine. And yep, sometimes I wrote it out with a heart over the letter i.

THE NIGHT WAS NO LONGER young. The night would soon be morning. We'd gotten dropped off at home by one of the cabs from my Dad's company. Dad took to running the cab business as a natural. Mom still did lots of her crafts and her hokey Namastwist classes, but she also helped Dad out in the office. We'd lost Gran two years ago. That had been hard. But she's with Grampa now, smiling down at us. I'm sure of this.

We'd had a great night at my party where I got fantastic presents, had way too much good food and a whole lot of Jell-O, orgasm, and pudding shooters. The good ole Dominion Sisterhood Holy Trinity Trifecta.

It was *the* trifecta in every single charter of the Dom Brotherhood. When The Sisterhood got together, we occasionally indulged. We danced. We did the Girls Just Wanna Have Fun train. And every time I did it, I thought about Jet. And I got a little bit sad afterwards. But at the end of my girlie dance train, the big red and black cake with Betty Boop on it with thirty birthday candles was presented and that's when I was also presented with my birthday present. Keys to a really really nice new Land Rover SUV.

"Pink fuzzy dice are hangin' up from the rearview already, Kitten," Deacon had said.

I'd put The Shitbox away a few years ago. It was still in Mint condition. It was tarped in our garage. I'd be gifting it to Beau when he turned 16 in a few years.

I never got my little Mini Cooper or my little VW bug. And now it wouldn't make sense since I had four boys to cart around with me. Oh well, I couldn't exactly complain. I had all sorts to be thankful for.

I giggled as we walked into our dark house in the country. Deacon had built us a huge and gorgeous Viceroy style home with all sorts of windows overlooking the creek on the property. It had a multi-tiered deck and six bedrooms. We'd lived in the Fifth Wheel for a year while he and his friends built it. I absolutely loved it. So did Tuvok, our Saint Bernard, and Borg, our fat Norwegian Forest Cat. Tuvok we'd gotten as a puppy but Borg came to us via the shelter, which I still volunteered at.

Deacon had gotten the puppy for me the day we moved into the house. He'd had my engagement ring tied with a ribbon around his neck. It was an amazing moment.

As soon as the door to our place was locked, I started divesting myself of my clothing and climbed the stairs to our room.

"You better get up here and service me, Buster," I called down to him as he put our coats and keys down and picked up my clothes behind me as he followed.

He was a pretty tidy husband. I was lucky in that department. I was lucky in many of the husbandly departments.

When we got into our room, he reached under the bed and pulled out a box.

"What'choo doing, beautiful biker?" I asked. I was seriously sloshed but I wasn't ready for bed. I was definitely ready to play.

"Getting out your other present. Though it's kind of a present for me, really."

"Lingerie?" I asked.

"Nope."

He opened the box and I lifted out a pile of straps.

I looked at them, confused in my drunken haze.

"Huh?" I asked.

"Under bed restraint system," He informed me and started undoing his button down shirt.

"Ooh. It looks complicated."

"I can manage," he smirked, his eyes a little glassy. He was drunk, too, but he was definitely someone who had his faculties when he was drunk. He also had serious stamina after drinking. I had a feeling I was gonna need all my energy.

I dropped the straps and got into bed and laid down on my back.

I'd given birth to four babies and my body wasn't quite as tiny and my ginormous boobs weren't near as perky as they had been when we met but he always made me feel beautiful.

He lifted up a silky black sleeping mask and slipped it over my head and covered my eyes.

I had a big smile on my face. But it felt like it took forever for him to fiddle with the straps until I was secured.

He'd complained when I'd had our bedroom suite upgraded a few months ago about the lack of playtime functionality in the headboard I'd chosen and I hadn't even realized at the time that I was interfering with 'play time' in that choice. He loved to restrain me and drive me to where I was pleading for his cock. We'd had a lot of very interesting 'play times' in the time we'd been together.

"This works well, the website has some interesting lookin' door-suspension kits," he said.

"Ooh," I purred.

I heard music start up.

It was Closer, by Nine Inch Nails. I'd recently told him about a fantasy about this song.

Oh my good good good god...

"Deacon," I whimpered.

How was he so perfect?

"I haven't even touched you yet." There was laughter in his voice. Sexy laughter.

"I know, right?" I was squirming. If there was any song intro that could make me cream myself without having visuals this was one. This was *the* one.

It felt like it took an eternity before his lips touched the arch of my foot when the singer began to sing.

"You let me violate you..."

Yowza.

I felt his hands slide up both legs and his lips followed up my left leg until his mouth was between my thighs and he hitched my legs up. And then he took me pretty darn close to heaven as his mouth tormented me down there until he was ready, just before I exploded, to move up to my lips and his beautiful monster cock drove hard into me and he fucked me.

He fucked me like an animal.

And we hadn't used any protection so chances were that right there, in our bed, on my thirtieth birthday, we'd get pregnant again.

Just to let you know, I didn't get my girl. It may or may not have been from that night but we got another boy.

It seemed I was destined to be the mother of five boys. We stopped there and I decided to just hope I'd get girl grandbabies in 20 something years. I had plenty of girlie nieces what with Rider and Jenna's girls and Jojo's girls, anyway. Spence and Pippa (Yep. Spence and Pippa) hadn't had kids yet but they were reportedly actively trying.

I'd found my special. I lived in Responsible-ville, for sure, and I was okay with that, it was who I was. But seven years ago I took a detour from Boring-ville and it hadn't always been easy, some of it had been really really hard, but it sure had been a beautiful beautiful ride.

And it was far from over.

About DD Prince & End of Book Notes

JOIN DD'S MAILING LIST at ddprince.com for news about upcoming books.

Joyride, Beautiful Biker 2; Rider and Jenna's love story is now available! So is Scenic Route, Beautiful Biker 3; Spencer and Pippa's story.

Check DD Prince's website in case more books are available. There is a lot more Beautiful Biker deliciousness to come!

Beautiful Biker Series page:

http://ddprince.com/dd-princes-books/series-the-beautiful-biker-series/

Facebook - http://facebook.com/ddprincebooks

Follow DD on Amazon: amazon.com/author/ddprince[1]

Visit her website at ddprince.com[2]

---

1. http://bit.ly/ddprinceonamazon
2. http://ddprince.com

Dear Reader,

Writing Detour, Beautiful Biker, book one, was a beautiful journey for me.

I really enjoyed getting to know these characters and feel like I've only just scratched the surface of the Valentine boys and the Dominion Brotherhood MC world. You can see plenty of foreshadowing as I have plans for several stories in this world. I hope you enjoyed this book.

Thank you so much to Divya, Pauline, Andrea, Joy, Marquitta, Tai, Lindsey, Jaime, Kass, Tai, and Shannon for offering to be beta or ARC readers. Thank you for your help, inspiration, enthusiasm, as well as the friendship and support for my work!

Want more?

I have written other books already out there that you might be interested in:

Aiden Carmichael: hot, bad boy. My boss. Oh, and a messy, selfish roomate. Worst roommate ever. In fact, I hate his alphahole guts. And I'm not usually a hater!

Carly Adler. Great rack. Cute AF sass. I get what I want. And I wanna tap that.

Alphahole, a contemporary, enemies-to-lovers, roommate, office romance. Aiden Carmichael is absolutely infuriating. You're going to effing love him!

Learn more: http://ddprince.com/alphahole-now-live/

Other DD Prince books:

The Dominator Series -—These are dark romances about a family with ties to organized crime, stories about arranged marriage, with dark themes.

The Nectar Trilogy -—Three book vampire romance trilogy. Dark and taboo vampire romance with kidnapping, bloodlust, sex, mystery, and true unrelenting symbiotic love.

Printed in Great Britain
by Amazon